I was hooked from the moment the house was descri... and terrible was going to happen, and Mickey Martin... edge throughout because everything seemed one way... was worse. The changing POV between Ariel, Jaxon, a... and depth to the story. I enjoyed how effortlessly and masterfully Martin weaved the past and present and the normal and paranormal. *A Chilling Summer in Inglewood* – another novel by Martin that is a truly gripping read.

Sonee Singh – Award-winning author of the Soul-Seeker Collection and *Lonely Dove*

A Chilling Summer in Inglewood ticks all the boxes if you're after a creepy paranormal thriller with a side of sexy romance.

I could not put this book down. Such a page turner. Ariel and her family have some seriously spooky activity going on in their house, and don't realise how closely they're tied to their poltergeists.

Mickey has a brilliant ability to weave interesting and endearing characters, intriguing back story and exciting suspense all together, while touching on important issues around mental health and familial bonds.

Another sensational book by a talented indie author.

Danielle Hughes – Author/Publisher

Wow! Mickey Martin never disappoints! Just when you think everything is resolved within her plot, there are always plenty of unexpected twists and turns that kept me hanging. I teetered on the edge of, 'this is too much' then she leaves me wanting more, and gives it! Martin's mind has always fascinated me, and once again, one of her creations has lived up to my expectations. *A Chilling Summer in Inglewood* is another novel I will re-read.

Sally Taylor – L2P Project Officer – Frankston City Council

Mickey Martin weaves her magic again, dipping her toe into the paranormal genre she has created a spine-chilling story that will raise the hairs on the back of your neck. For the readers who love her style of writing, she stays true to herself.

After the tragic loss of their mother, Ariel Harper adopted her young siblings, Hawk and Wren, 15-year-old twins and younger brother Timmy, 7 years. They moved back to the family home in the country town of Inglewood. She had many happy memories from her childhood staying with her Grandparents in their beautiful Victorian Mansion and thought this would be the perfect home in which to raise the children.

After settling in and adjusting to the noises a 200-year-old house makes they all enjoyed the new country lifestyle, but that was all about to change.

An unsettling disturbing presence started to interfere with their happy, settled lives. It was not just banging doors in the middle of the night but something more sinister, taking over and terrifying everyone. I loved every moment!

Sue Croft – Editor, Author and Historian

Mickey Martin has done it again! Her first attempt at paranormal horror is a page turner. Warning, if you start this book be prepared to be lured in by Mickey's prose until the very end. I abandoned all my other reading material for the 4 days it took me to finish the book.

It is a story set in the town of Inglewood, a house and the chilling secrets that it holds inside despite its beautiful welcoming facade.

The house seems inviting at first, a home we would all love to live, until we discover what lies within. As always Mickey, keeps her readers guessing about the mysterious things that are happening in this house. In the midst of the crazy that's happening in the book, there are beautiful scenes of family, friendship and community.

She paints beautiful scenes of beauty and comfort of the surroundings and of the people that I want to reach out and touch it all.

Even the paranormal scenes feel tangible. Her word pictures are very vivid and as a visually impaired reader I find myself engaged with them because they are also about sound, touch, taste and smell. I loved her development of each Character, as I got to see what was happening for each individual as the book flows on.

As in all of Mickey's books there are lots of twists and turns and in this one you feel some unexpected emotions about some of the characters.

It's full of romance, and spine-tingling moments. I wouldn't read this book at night. There are a few cliff hangers which left me at the edge of my seat. I find myself feeling sad to leave the world of Inglewood, and I want to hear more about Sebastian's story. I hope it will come back again in another book.

Nozi Phokhanda – Counsellor and avid reader

I thought I couldn't enjoy any of Martin's work more than *Soul Keepers of Glenormiston South*, or *Obsidian Souls* – but I was wrong. When I read *A Chilling Summer in Inglewood*, I was totally engrossed and absolutely loved the characters, story line and spine-tingling moments. I so look forward to getting my hands on a hard copy and read it again.

After living in a haunted house myself, I got chills and goosebumps from Martin's characters encounters with the paranormal.

A brilliant read that was very hard to put down… but… meh… housework can wait!

Kelly McDonald – Garden Babies Fine Fairy Art/Portraits and Photography

A CHILLING
SUMMER
—— IN ——
INGLEWOOD

A catalogue record for this
work is available from the
National Library of Australia

National Library of Australia Catalogue-in-Publication data:
A Chilling Summer in Inglewood/Mickey Martin

ISBN: 978- (Paperback)
ISBN: 978- (Ebook)

A CHILLING
SUMMER
— IN —
INGLEWOOD

MICKEY MARTIN

MMH PRESS

To those who believe in, and have experienced things that go bump-in-the-night.
It takes strength to protect yourself against a predator you can see.
And a golden heart of stone to protect yourself against the unseen.

Chapter One

The house stood silent and empty for months on end – the entities within waited impatiently, anticipating their next move as they drifted restlessly through the two-hundred-year-old estate. It wouldn't be long until they would eat again. The moving boxes haphazardly stacked in every room indicated that guests would soon follow. It was only a matter of time before their vicious fun would resume after months of boredom and insatiable hunger.

Present Day – Ariel

Ariel Harper stretched shapely arms above her head before rolling over, pushing her face into the arm of the sofa, not wanting the pleasant dream to end and willed herself back to sleep.

"Ariel." A quiet voice filtered through her foggy attempt to fall back into her dream before a hand shook her shoulder.

"Ariel, wake up. Timmy slept in the chook pen again."

"Time's it?" she asked groggily, not sure when she'd fallen asleep after coming out to her studio the night before.

"The school bell is about to go." Wren Harper replied.

Ariel's eyes flew open in panic. "Oh crap, he can't be late on his first day!" Lurching to her feet she kissed Wren's cheek before darting around her. Side-stepping the easel, she jumped over a pile of pillows on the ground where her loved-up clients had sat the day before for a portrait sitting and headed for the door.

"Um, Ariel." Wren called.

Ariel turned to look at her pretty fifteen-year-old sister, who was wearing a cropped white tee-shirt with denim shorts and sneakers. Her jet-black hair swept up in a messy bun; eyes crinkled in amusement.

"Yeah?"

Wren pointed to her own head, grinning. "You've got a little something in your hair."

Ariel touched her head and groaned when she discovered a paint brush stuck to her hair with dried paint. She must have been more tired last night than she'd realized. After working for hours on end, she'd sat down for a five-minute break to contemplate her upcoming art show; and had fallen asleep with the paint brush in hand.

She squealed as dried paint ripped strands of dark auburn hair out, before throwing it towards the easel and turned to slide the studio door open.

"Timothy," she called. "Please come out of there." She unsuccessfully pulled at the remaining dried paint in her hair as she raced across the lawn towards the chicken coop. A currant vine draped ornately over the top, gifting the chickens with some much-needed shade. Not even nine a.m. and the soaring Inglewood heat was already more than Ariel could handle. She missed Melbourne weather and its more forgiving summer heat.

Seven-year-old Timothy Harper pushed the chicken wire gate open and strolled out wearing a cheeky grin. Straw sticking to his hair and SpongeBob SquarePants pyjamas.

"I've made Timmy's lunch, and Hawk's made you a coffee." Wren winked at Timmy.

"Thanks," Ariel offered her a tired smile as she reached for Timmy's hand, who took hers reluctantly.

"Am I in trouble?" He asked, eyes squinting up at her as they followed Wren towards the house.

"Not one hundred percent, no."

"Fifty?" He asked, sounding hopeful.

"Sure, fifty." She couldn't help but grin back at him; his beautiful dark-blue eyes filled with mischief. But it was those grey shadows underneath his eyes that made her heart beat with worry.

Ever since they'd moved into their deceased Grandparents' house in Inglewood, Victoria three months ago, both she and Timmy had not slept well. Although it had been a decade since she'd spent any time at her Grandparents' house, she'd always slept decently.

Sighing, she looked up at the two-story weatherboard Victorian home that had been in her family for five generations. She was pleased with the work she and their Uncle Steven had done since late October. The bullnose veranda and surrounding timbers had been dressed in a fresh coat of Eucalyptus-green paint, which gleamed against the white window frames, balustrade and varnished decking. She had juggled the kids summer holiday with renovations and commissions amongst squeezing day trips in for them all to get accustomed to the area.

She'd been eighteen-years old on her last trip to Inglewood, when their mother had still been alive. The twins had been five, and Timmy had been a twinkle in their mother's eye.

The spring of the ornate wire screen door protested as Wren tugged it open, holding it ajar for them. It clattered shut behind them as they headed down the wide corridor and into an open kitchen adjoined to a large dining area. Potted plants and hanging baskets of greenery graced the space and relaxed her instantly. She'd brought every plant with her from her studio apartment in Carlton.

The smell of freshly ground coffee beans almost had her weeping in gratitude.

Hawk turned away from the counter and headed towards her.

"Here you go, sister dearest." He grinned giving her the once over. Silky, jet-black hair fell into eyes rimmed with eyeliner, wearing a smile that melted every heart. Twin to Wren, and a mere two minutes older, he stood close to six feet tall, compared to Ariel's and Wren's five foot five.

Ariel released Timmy's hand to take the steaming mug of coffee with a dollop of cream.

"You are a life saver, Hawk." She smiled before taking a tentative sip as she looked down at Timmy. "Three second shower for you, my friend. Let's go."

Timmy raced towards the stairs and Ariel followed at a slower pace to sip her coffee, glancing into each room as she passed by.

The main lounge was open, light and sparsely furnished with two chaise lounges sitting opposite each other, and a games table stacked with books in the middle. An open fireplace stood along the opposite wall. Floor to ceiling bookshelves were crammed with old, and new books, along with memorabilia from her Grandparents' era. The morning sun filtered through the large stained-glass windows, gifting the room with a kaleidoscope of colour.

She walked by her Grandfather's office that had not been touched since he had died several months prior. A waft of his aftershave drifted after her as she followed Timmy up the wide staircase, and into the renovated bathroom, respecting the heritage style of the home.

"Righto love, make it quick." She said, reaching over the claw foot tub to turn the shower on before wandering across to the window, keeping her back to him so he could get undressed.

Hearing the curtain close around him, she sighed on cue with the school bell, hoping whomever his new teacher was, they'd be understanding.

Draining her coffee, she put the mug on the windowsill and reached into the cupboard under the sink to grab her toothbrush, happy at least she had fallen asleep with her clothes on and wouldn't have to rush around to get dressed. Giving her teeth a quick brush, she grabbed her deodorant as Timmy turned the shower off.

"Towel," he called, hand sticking through the gap in the curtain.

She passed it to him as Wren called, "Clothes are on your bed Timmy, hurry up."

Timmy pulled the curtain back and climbed out of the tub heading towards his room, as Ariel mopped up the water drops.

Grabbing her empty cup she headed downstairs yelling, "See you in thirty seconds."

"We can do it in twenty," Timmy's voice was muffled through his school clothes.

Ariel ran downstairs, pausing outside her Grandmother's writing room that had doubled as her painting studio. She loved that she'd gotten her creative talent from her Grandmother, and had many fond memories painting in this room with her. Her Grandmother had also been well known for her poetry alongside her artwork and Ariel was proud to share the prestigious, 'Harper' name with her.

She had no idea who her father was, or who any of her sibling's fathers were. Her mother had always insisted that the only thing she had ever needed from a man was his help in creating her Angels. When their mother had died five years earlier, she had left a crater in all their hearts, and at the age of twenty-three, Ariel had become mother to two-year-old Timmy, and ten-year-old twins. Adoption was the only way to save them from the system and foster care. Their Grandparents had been too old to take on the responsibility of a toddler, and two pre-teens, and she refused to put that responsibility on their uncle.

She had never regretted a moment of it, not even when she had to make the decision to give up travelling overseas where clients had commissioned her to paint them in their lavish homes. At the age of eighteen, she had become well known for her incredible talent, and for five years she had travelled the globe wherever the commissions took her.

"Ready," Timmy yelled as he ran down the stairs with Wren on his heels.

Ariel was grateful her walk down memory-lane had been interrupted. "Let's go."

"See ya later," Hawk called from the kitchen, as Ariel led the way to the front door.

"Alligator," Timmy yelled back at the screen door slammed behind them.

"We're going to talk about you sleeping in the chook pen when you get home, okay?" Ariel said as they headed in the direction of the school.

"Okay," Timmy replied.

Although the primary school was only a three-minute walk from their house, they were fifteen minutes late by the time they walked through the front gate where the Principal was talking to another parent.

"Hello Ariel, Timmy." She smiled warmly.

"Hi Mrs Sommers," Timmy grinned.

"Excited for your first day with us, Timmy?" The blonde-haired, green-eyed lady asked.

"Yep," he nodded.

"Great. Your teacher is Mr Williams, and he'll be happy to see you." Mrs Sommers met Ariel's eyes before adding softly. "Room three, Ms Harper."

Ariel nodded, a little embarrassed—trying not to feel like a student herself who was being reprimanded for being late. She led Timmy in the direction of his classroom.

They passed the prep and grade one room and found room three where children's laughter spilled from within, before a deep, hypnotic voice began entertaining them with an amusing story about his Christmas holiday capers.

Ariel stood in the doorway as the students who were sitting around their teacher, stared up at him, quiet as mice and not moving a muscle, totally captivated as if he were the Pied Piper himself. Timmy peeked around Ariel, catching some of the students' eyes.

Noticing that his students were distracted, Mr Williams turned in his seat and followed the direction of their curious and excited gazes.

Ariel's breath caught in her throat as his molten-caramel eyes, with the longest lashes she'd ever seen on the opposite sex, met hers.

He wasn't just decent looking; he was sublimely beautiful. If a man could be called beautiful. As he stood to walk towards them, she added bewitching and alluring to that list. Chiselled cheekbones, made more prominent by his dark brooding eyes, framed with shapely brows that were forming a subtle frown as he quickly took in her appearance, before turning his attention to Timmy.

"Hello, you must be Timmy," he smiled at his late pupil.

"Yes, Sir."

"Why don't you hang your bag on that empty hook right there." He pointed a long finger towards the only empty bag space. "Today we are going to make name tags for our bag hooks."

Timmy nodded and headed across to hang his bag, as Mr Williams turned his full gaze to Ariel.

"I'm Mr Williams." He reached out to shake her hand.

"Ariel." She shook his hand, mesmerised by his luscious lips, tracing each generous line to her artists memory, before flushing in embarrassment as his gaze dropped to her mouth.

She noticed he was trying to hide a grin; a grin that seemed vaguely familiar.

"Ready!" Timmy said excitedly, cutting off Ariel's thought flow.

"Great," she tugged her hand free from Mr Williams' large, smooth clasp and smiled at Timmy. "I'll see you this afternoon." She bent to drop a kiss on top of his silky head.

"Let's see if we can get Timmy to class on time tomorrow morning shall we, Ariel?" His eyes roamed her hair for a moment.

She bit her tongue to halt the sharp retort and smiled brightly at Timmy.

"Bye Ariel," he chirped, before following Mr Williams into the classroom.

As Ariel headed down the corridor, she could hear 'Mr Yummy' announce to the class,

"Everyone, I'd like you to meet a new student to our school, Timothy Harper."

His smooth voice trailed off as Ariel walked past the office, flashing a smile to the receptionist as she bolted out the door.

"Great first day, could have been worse," she declared to herself as she headed home for a much-needed shower and five minutes quiet time. Her guests from Bendigo Community Health Services where due to arrive for a healing art therapy class in an hour's time. The day would surely improve.

Jaxon

Jaxon Williams strolled around the yard at lunchtime, appreciating the innocent schoolyard banter, content with how the first day was going so far. His class of grade two, and three was like a mixed bag of lollies, with personalities that promised both sweet and sour. It was sure to make it an interesting school year ahead to say the least. The one thing he had always loved about working with kids—there was never a dull moment.

As he tossed a wayward basketball back in the direction it had come, he noticed Ray Sommers heading his way.

"Thanks Mr Williams," Darren, a grade sixer yelled out.

He waved a hand as Ray smiled. "How's your day going, Jaxon?" She took a small sip from her water bottle.

He nodded, glancing across the yard. "So far so good, apart from one late student, nothing untoward."

"Yes, Timothy Harper. He comes from an eminent family." Ray capped her water bottle. "His mother passed away when he was two."

Jaxon met her gaze. "Yeah, I read his file, and am aware of his history. I should mention I went to school with his uncle and that we're good mates still."

"I see." Ray nodded.

"His parents were like my own for many years. It was devastating when they died."

"Yes, a great loss for the entire town I was told." Ray agreed. "I moved here shortly after they had passed."

"So, Ms Harper legally adopted the kids." He stated.

"Yes, she was working overseas at the time of their mother's death. She came home to look after the children."

Jaxon nodded, remembering Steven mentioning his niece was dealing with a lot at the time. His mind wandered to the pretty, although tired looking woman who had stood in front of him only four hours ago; hollow grooves beneath her eyes and emerald paint in her dark red hair. He wasn't comfortable with the fact that he'd felt an immediate attraction to her.

After seeing identical dark grooves beneath young Timothy's eyes, he'd wondered if it were in the kids best interest that he was in the sole custody of Ariel Harper? He didn't want to judge, but time would tell, and he'd be watching like a hawk in the meantime.

He'd always taken his role as a teacher, and his duty of care in his duties safeguarding those he was responsible for, extremely seriously.

After the tragedy of losing a student, and the heartache that followed he was even more diligent in that role.

A shadow of guilt stalked his every waking moment after the loss of that young life. Every night that he closed his eyes, a macabre nightmare of regret played on repeat. Of that, he was grateful for and vowed he'd never again lose a student to a neglectful, abusive parent, no matter the consequences.

Chapter Two
Ariel

A riel waved the bus off that was filled with counsellors and their clients, after a full morning of art therapy. Turning to her friend, Liv Collins, she shared the details of the embarrassing scene at school that morning.

"It can't have been all that bad," Liv chuckled as she rinsed the brushes out in the back room.

"You're right, it wasn't that bad, it was worse. Seriously Liv, I got home to shower, looked in the mirror and saw a dried-up, green birds nest jutting out the side of my head. Real classy."

"Yeah, okay maybe it wasn't the best first impression." Liv shrugged. "But it's not like you'll have anything to do with Timmy's teacher apart from parent-teacher interviews." Liv plonked the wet brushes into a bucket to dry and grabbed a towel to wipe her hands on.

"True," Ariel sighed.

"What's his name?"

"Mr Williams."

"*Jaxon* Williams, Steven's mate?"

"I think so… he did look kind of familiar." Ariel said as she stacked the wet canvases into slot-holds to dry without disturbing the paint, happy with the results of the students work.

"Oh, he is a honey all right. He left town a few years ago to teach in the city, and came home on the weekends to see Steven, and renovate his Grandfather's house. I heard he went to Scotland after an incident regarding a student."

"What incident?"

"I don't really know the details." Liv said as she headed out of the gallery and through to the front of the café.

Ariel finished tidying up and followed Liv, making sure the dainty table clothes sat straight around the quaint tables and that everything was in its place for the afternoon crowd.

"When do the twins start school?" Liv asked, checking that the coffee machine was filled and ready to go.

"Tomorrow. Thank goodness their bus stop is at the end of the street; I can at least get them to school on time."

"Hey, stop beating yourself up. They're all good kids and you're doing a great job, okay?"

Ariel turned and smiled gratefully. She'd had a firm friendship with Liv since they'd been toddlers, as their mothers had been close growing up in a small country town.

Christmas and Easter holidays at her Grandparents' house had been all the more enjoyable because of her friendship with Liv. When Ariel's mother Sparrow, had stopped the visits back home, Ariel and Liv had remained in contact through social media. Supporting each other's ups and downs as they had become young, successful entrepreneurs, and then women coming to terms with life after loss and living with grief. Ariel had lost her mother, Liv, her husband.

"Yeah, I am doing a great job, thanks." She grinned, pulling a yo-yo biscuit out of a decorative glass jar, and biting into it.

"Are we starting the night classes for the adults next week?" Liv asked.

Ariel nodded, her mouth full of yo-yo.

Liv raised an eyebrow as she placed her hands together in the prayer position. "Please tell me there will be wine involved?"

"Of course." Ariel grinned, checking her watch. "Shoot. I've gotta go, Uncle Steven is coming by the house."

"When did he get back in town?" Liv asked hurriedly. "I haven't seen him."

Ariel hid her smile, noticing Liv's face flush red at the mere mention of her uncle's name.

"Today."

"Great, well um, off you go. I hope Timmy has had a great first day of school." Liv waved dismissively.

"Thanks Liv, I'll see you tomorrow."

"See you."

Ariel dashed out the door and headed along main street where the traffic was sparse this time of afternoon. She smiled thinking of Liv crushing on her uncle, knowing that he too, thought Liv was something special. Ariel respected the fact that her uncle was treading carefully around her friend, who was still grieving the loss of her husband, John, who had died in a tragic accident three years prior.

After John's funeral, Liv had packed up her belongings in Castlemaine, and moved back home with her parents. She worked in the popular cosy café, which doubled as a book shop, and art gallery for Ariel's work.

Steven owned the building and lived upstairs. He ran a thriving landscaping business throughout Victoria, allowing him to come and go as he pleased. It had all worked out quite well really, and Ariel loved the fact that she could be here for her friend, and her uncle.

Finishing the yo-yo, she brushed the buttery crumbs off her fingertips and onto her jeans, thinking now all she needed to do was to get her siblings settled happily into school, and all would be well.

She returned a wave to Catherine and Barry Norman, the friendly couple who ran Fusspots. Like many stores in Inglewood, Fusspots was a popular antique shop that sold vintage and collectable old wares. Walking by the Appleby funeral home, she shivered; even as a child, before she knew what a funeral home was, she'd always felt uncomfortable in the building's shadow. Turning down Houston Street she walked towards Grant Street and turned towards her Grandparents' house.

"*Our* house." She whispered, pushing her grief aside. Opening the white picket gate and crossing under her Grandmother's arbour, adorned in yellow climbing roses, she jogged down the red bricked path lined with a rainbow of summertime lavender and agapanthus. A sprawling wisteria wrapped lovingly around the bullnose veranda. A large peppercorn tree sat to the side of the lawn; scented bulbs sprouted around a carpet of colour and a tyre swing dangled from a thick branch above.

She was grateful, not for the first time, that her uncle was such a passionate gardener. Opening the front door, she heard voices trailing from the sunroom and was happy to hear the twins chatting to their uncle.

He turned as she approached, and she loved seeing his blue eyes light up. Eyes so like their mothers.

"Hello, Uncle Steven." She stepped into his open arms and sighed as he wrapped them around her. Only six years older than she, his comforting presence still made her feel safe.

"Hello beautiful," he said softly. "How've you been?" He frowned as he looked down at her, holding her arm's length.

"What?" She asked the longer he stared at her, knowing he was seeing hollow eyes and a pale complexion.

"Have you been sleeping?"

"Of course."

Hawk coughed into his fist, masking the word, "*Bullshit.*"

"Hey," Ariel looked at her younger brother. "Easy now."

"Well, he's not wrong," Wren said, picking up the empty lemonade jug and turned towards the kitchen.

Steven dropped a kiss on top of Ariel's head as he followed Wren with their empty glasses. "Well," he called to Ariel over his shoulder. "I can always sleep over here in my old room if you like, help out a bit?"

"Uncle Steven, the twins are more help than you could possibly imagine, and apart from Timmy deciding to sleep in the oddest of places at times, he is an angel."

"Not to mention what you've been up to at night, Ariel." Hawk pointed out.

"What do you mean?" Steven asked as he rinsed the glasses in the kitchen sink beside Wren.

Wren wiped her hands on a tea towel. "The first night we moved in, I came down to get a glass of water. Ariel was standing in Grandpa's office in the corner. She did that every night for two months. Just stood in the corner, her nose an inch from the wall."

Steven looked at Ariel, who shrugged. "I don't remember any of it."

"Are you still doing it?" he asked.

Hawk answered, "We find her in there at least two, three times a week."

"Interesting," he raised an eyebrow towards her before quickly turning back to the sink to finish the dishes.

Ariel was convinced the colour had just drained from his face. She bit her lip. *What was that about?*

"Creepy too," Wren interrupted her thoughts.

"Then there's Timmy," Hawk continued. "He doesn't like sleeping in his room. He'll only sleep in the house if he is in one of our rooms, otherwise he goes out and sleeps with the chooks."

"Oh no," Steven laughed as he turned to grab the tea towel. "Really?"

Ariel watched her uncle for any more tell-tale signs, but his colour had returned.

"It's been a big change for you all," Steven said. "It shouldn't take too long for things to settle down and feel like normal."

"I hope so," Ariel sighed.

"Let's try some aromatherapy at night," he suggested.

She shrugged. "It can't hurt."

"I'll pick something up in Bendigo tomorrow. Now, let's go and collect the rug-rat then take him for a swim to cool down."

"Sounds great." Ariel nodded, stacking the glasses upside down on the glass tray, along with the empty lemonade jug, before following the others out the front door.

Squeals of excitement filled the hallway as parents collected their hot, sweaty children who were relieved that the first day of school was over.

Ariel watched Mr Williams bid each of his students goodbye as they filed by him as he stood beside the classroom doorway.

"Great effort today, Timothy," he said as Timmy walked by him. "I'll see you in the morning." He held his hand out for a high five.

"See you then, Mr Williams." Timmy slapped his small hand against Jaxon's large palm, before racing over to grab his school bag.

Wren ruffled his hair as Ariel bent to drop a kiss against his cheek. "How was your first day, love?" She asked, taking his bag.

"It was great. We made our bag tags and started our family tree, and I passed the maths test."

"What else did you learn today?" Hawk swooped him up onto his shoulders.

"I found out that the founder man of Ansett Airlines was born in Inglewood in 1909! Did you know that Hawk, did ya?" Timmy seemed quite proud of this fact.

"Sir Reginald Ansett, yes, I did. Nice one sport."

Timmy beamed, before yawning loudly.

Steven laughed as he looked at Jaxon. "Slave driver."

When Jaxon turned, a grin broke across his handsome features and his dark caramel eyes crinkled in delight. "When did you get back into town?"

Ariel watched as Mr Yummy pulled Steven against him for a manly hug. Firm, taunt muscles became defined with each movement.

Steven slapped Jaxon on the back, clearly happy to see his friend. "This afternoon. So, looks like my nephew got the best teacher in Victoria."

Jaxon grinned. "I'd like to think so."

"Ariel, do you remember Jaxon? He used to build go-carts with me, and we took you and Liv out yabbying with the twins when they were tiny."

As Steven mentioned the past, Ariel clearly recalled the handsome, active boy who had matched her uncle's vibrant personality and appreciation of the great outdoors.

"Yes, in a hazy kind of way," she nodded.

"I remember you," Jaxon tilted his head.

She forced herself not to squirm under his penetrating gaze.

"I'd like to add on behalf of the school if you require any extra support or assistance with Timothy in any way, we are here to help."

"Jesus." Steven clapped him on the back. "Don't get all official on me," he laughed.

Jaxon shrugged, "Well, whilst we're on school grounds…" He trailed off.

Ariel thought that was very responsible of him. "That won't be necessary, but thank you Mr…"

"Please," he interrupted. "Call me Jaxon."

She nodded. "Thank you, Jaxon."

"Pool time," Timmy called from the other end of the corridor where Wren, and Hawk were waiting.

"See you in the morning Timothy," Jaxon waved to Timmy.

"On time, Mr Williams." Timmy called.

Steven grinned as he put his arm around Ariel's shoulders and said, "Goodbye, *Mr Williams*."

As Steven turned her towards her siblings, Ariel heard Jaxon laugh quietly.

It was a dark, delicious sound that sent a warm shiver along her flesh.

Jaxon

Jaxon tidied up the classroom, preparing for the following days lessons when a memory from the past resurfaced. He chuckled as he recalled fourteen-year-old Steven going ballistic at an even younger Ariel. She and Liv would have been eight years old on this particular outing when the boys had taken them to the reservoir to catch yabbies. After Steven had discovered that Ariel and Liv had been releasing the yabbies back into the water just as soon as the boys had been catching them, he'd yelled and carried on as if she'd committed a serious offence. She'd remained silent as he'd yelled, standing in front of Liv, hands on hips, staring defiantly at her teenage uncle until he'd calmed down. Then, she'd said, "I hope you feel better now, Uncle Steven."

Then, taking Liv's hand, the girl's had walked towards the path that would take them home, completely unfazed by Steven's yelling. Ariel had been so damn proud that she and Liv had rescued the yabbies, according to Sparrow that night after he and Jaxon had complained to her about never taking the girls yabbying again.

He closed the classroom door and headed off towards the staff meeting, thinking how bright and kind she had been as a young girl.

Although she had looked refreshed this afternoon, compared to first thing that morning, he wondered about what had caused those dark shadows that hung under her tired green eyes.

Ariel

The grandfather clock chimed on the third hour of the morning; its reverberations swept through every room of the house like foul breath on unbrushed teeth.

A dark mass loomed above Ariel as she slept, casting cold fingers over her. Goosebumps formed across her flesh, despite the room holding a 23-degree night heat. She sighed, welcoming the cool relief those unknown fingers brought as the ceiling fan turned sluggishly above, blowing hot air around the room.

Rolling onto her back and placing her arm over her head, she sighed in pleasure. She became aware of the cool touch that swept over her bare midriff, before an overpowering rotten stench reached into in her slumber, waking her fully.

She froze, sensing that something was in the room with her. Her heart raced uncomfortably as a presence loomed close to her face. Almost like a sticky cobweb was trickling over her nose and mouth. Bolting upright she hit the touch lamp on, sending a dull glow around the room. Seeing nothing but her own reflection in her Grandmother's vanity mirror, her heartbeat steadied.

Running her hands over her face she rubbed that lingering 'cobweb-feeling' away and released a nervous laugh. Slipping out of bed she crossed towards the window and opened it wide, hoping that a cool night breeze would drift in and push the unpleasant feeling, and unwelcome stench away. Glancing down across the street, she noticed the dark figure of a man standing on the sidewalk, seeming to be staring straight at their house. Straight at her. A bright red glow lit his face for a moment, as he sucked on a cigarette.

"What are you doing?"

She jumped at the unexpected question from behind her and spun around to see Hawk in the doorway.

"Easy now," he chuckled, holding up his hands in surrender. "Just coming back from the loo and saw your light on. Everything okay?"

Ariel shook her head, looking back towards the man who had

disappeared. Sighing, she scooped her mass of damp hair off her neck and reached for a hair tie on the side table.

"Yeah, just thought I saw and heard something." Tying her hair up in a high ponytail she rubbed his shoulder as she walked by him before turning towards Timmy's room, flicking on the hallway light.

She quietly opened Timmy's door to check that he was asleep. "Bloody hell," she cursed, seeing his empty bed.

"He's not in the bathroom," Hawk said, before heading towards Wren's room. As Hawk pushed her door open Ariel peeked around his shoulder to see Wren curled up alone, sleeping peacefully. He looked at Ariel, shaking his head.

"Shit," she whispered, before heading downstairs. "Please don't let him be in the chook pen getting eaten alive by mosquitos!"

"If he is, we'll freshen him up and I'll bring him back to my room," Hawk said as he followed her downstairs and through the house, grabbing a torch on the shelf near the back door.

The moon was high, casting a beam across the yard as they ran towards the chicken coop. Pushing the gate open, Ariel ducked in and unlocked the night door to peek in at the chickens who clucked in alarm as Hawk shone the torch on them, disturbing their sleep.

"It's all right girls." Ariel cooed as she bent to scoop up a sleeping Timmy on a mound of hay.

"No Ariel," he murmured sleepily. "Sebastian says it's not safe inside."

"Well, unless you want a mosquito disease, sport, it's not that safe out here either." Hawk said as he led the way with the torch.

"Who's Sebastian?" Ariel asked, hefting his limp body up onto her knee as she locked the coop door.

"My friend." Timmy yawned, scratching at his hair, straw falling out of it.

"Great, well please tell your friend at school tomorrow that it is safer to sleep inside, than with mites, and mozzies would you?"

Hawk opened the back door as Ariel carried Timmy inside. "You're definitely having a shower if you're bunking in with me sport, you stink." Hawk reached out to lift his sleepy brother out of Ariel's arms.

"Make it quick Hawk, you both need sleep before school tomorrow." Ariel said, concerned that they'd both be exhausted.

"Don't worry sis, we'll be in and out, go back to bed." Hawk disappeared at the top of the stairs, taking Timmy into the bathroom for a clean-up.

Ariel headed to the kitchen, turning on the light at the same time as the train blasted its whistle making her jump a mile high.

"*Jesus* Christ," she whispered, rubbing a hand over her chest before switching the kettle on, hoping that a cup of chamomile would relax her and bring a welcoming, restful sleep for once.

"Ariel, can I please see you for a moment?" Ray Sommers called the following afternoon as they were heading out of the school gate.

Timmy looked up at Ariel. "Can I meet you at the gallery-cafe?"

Ariel took his school bag and slung it over her shoulder. "Sure, I'll be right behind you."

"Yeah!" He cried gleefully, fist pumping the air before taking off at a run.

"Careful crossing the road," she called, watching him for a moment, before turning to face the principal.

"Sorry, I won't keep you long." Ray apologised, tucking a flyaway strand of hair behind her ear.

"It's completely fine." Ariel tilted her head, waiting.

"I know how busy you are, but the school council was wondering if you'd be interested in painting a mural along the bricked tennis walls?"

"Absolutely, Mrs Sommers. I'd be thrilled to."

"Oh, that's wonderful! Please, call me Ray."

Ariel smiled. "Do you have a particular theme in mind, Ray?"

Ray beamed. "We were hoping you would create something entirely original that would brighten the yard. Maybe you could present some ideas to the school council for a vote?"

Ariel nodded. "When are you wanting it done by?"

"Within the month if that suits you."

"I have an art show this weekend at the gallery, but after that I can work on some designs to present to you all."

"That's perfect. I heard about your show."

"You and the staff are more than welcome to come. All proceeds from this event are going to the Bendigo centre for non-violence?"

"That sounds great. I'll let the staff know, and thanks so much for agreeing to the mural."

"No problem."

I'll let you catch up to Timmy."

"Sure."

"Have a good afternoon, Ariel."

"Thanks Ray, see you tomorrow." Ariel headed past a group of mothers whose conversation halted abruptly as she walked by. Their hushed voices resumed once she was out of their hearing range.

"Nice welcome, ladies." She whispered under her breath as she hurried down the street to catch up with Timmy. One thing she hadn't missed about any tiny town was some of the narrow-minded individuals who preferred gossip over fact.

Chapter Three
Wren

Wren tossed restlessly as the night train sounded its horn. Damn thing sounded like it was coming straight through her bedroom wall. She groaned when Timmy kneed her in the back, not for the first time that night. She snuggled into her pillow as the train chugged along its tracks before the commotion faded from her hearing. After several minutes of deep breathing, she felt sleep wrap it's comforting arms around her once more, pulling her into a blissful dream-world, before a small hand slapped her hard across the face.

"Ow! *Jesus* Timmy!" She cried, hitting her touch lamp on before turning towards her brother, only to see the bed was empty beside her. A prickle of unease ran along her flesh as she blinked and swallowed nervously. She *hadn't* dreamt about getting kneed in the back, and her cheek still stung from the slap mere seconds ago. She sat frozen in disbelief as she stared at the empty space, not knowing what to think.

"Wren?" Ariel knocked on the door making her jump.

"Come in," she called quickly.

"Are you okay? It's after three. Why is your light still on?" Ariel walked in.

Wren relaxed as soon as Ariel sat down on her bed, relieved not to be alone. "I was… missing mum." She lied guiltily, but knowing in that moment she could use that lie to her advantage.

Ariel ran a hand over Wren's hair. "Want to snuggle with me for the rest of the night, love?"

"Could I?" Wren grabbed her pillow before her sister said another word and headed out of her bedroom and towards Ariel's. Climbing up onto the king-sized bed, Wren snuggled down as Ariel walked into the room and across to her side.

Pulling the sheet up to her chin, she watched Ariel slip under the covers before touching the lamp off. As the room fell into darkness, Wren focused on her sister's breathing, not liking the possibilities the darkness brought with it.

"That train huh?" She said, hoping to engage Ariel in conversation.

Ariel laughed quietly. "I know. That, and the town hall clock chiming on the hour, make me feel at home."

"Really?"

"Mhm."

"All that noise?" Wren turned on her side to face Ariel.

"Yeah, weird huh?"

"Not if it brings happy memories with it."

"Very true. And it brings the happiest of memories." Ariel said quietly.

"Are you excited about your exhibition tomorrow night?" Wren whispered.

"You mean tonight. Yes, I am. Now sleep, little bird, or your eyes will start to match mine and Timmy's."

"Goodnight." Wren whispered, pulling the covers over her head. She couldn't explain why she hadn't told Ariel about what had happened in her room, only that speaking about it would make if feel more real. This way, she could delude herself into thinking it was a dream. Better that way. Squeezing her eyes shut, she focused on Ariel's breathing to help herself fall asleep.

Ariel

"Champagne and non-alcoholic beverages are set up, tasting table, check, and slug gun for gossiping mothers is loaded and under the we-won't-settle-for-bullshit-table, for easy access, and my work here, is done!" Liv cried theatrically; arms spread wide as she circled the gallery floor.

Ariel chuckled, shaking her head. "Maybe don't say that too loudly, considering this is a charity event for non-violence." She stood back after hanging a painting of the Loddon River, where red gum trees lined the riverbanks that were filled with waterlilies, and blue Iris'. The train track that had been built in 1876 sat above the wide river on its stately bridge in the background.

"I'll never get used to what you can do," Steven said quietly behind her.

Ariel turned to see her uncle staring at her with pride. Her cheeks grew warm with his praise. "Thanks Uncle Steven." She noticed Liv flush as she admired Steven in his casual suit. "You look handsome." She smiled at her uncle.

"Thought I'd get ready to meet and greet your distinguished guests whilst you run upstairs and get changed."

Ariel nodded, checking the time. "Thirty minutes is all I need."

Steven wandered over and began filling the champagne glasses for the guests. "You look lovely tonight, Liv," he said quietly.

Ariel watched heat flow up Liv's neck and fill her cheeks, and stopped a chuckle that wanted to escape.

"Thank you, Steven." Liv turned pleading eyes towards Ariel.

"The twins should be here soon. Liv, can you come upstairs with me? I need help with my zip. We won't be long Uncle Steven."

"No problem," he said.

"Here you go." Liv handed Ariel a glass of the bubbly nectar.

"Thank you," she sipped the sweet bubbles and sighed. "Perfect drop. Now let's get ready for a night of charming the pants off everyone in order to make as much money as possible for a worthy charity."

"Sounds good to me." Liv agreed.

"Press will be here soon." Steven called after them as they headed upstairs.

"We'll be down ASAP." Ariel threw over her shoulder, before disappearing into his guest bedroom to transform from jeans, t-shirt and sneakers to a strapless black one-piece dress that clung to every curve, matched with sexy, killer heels she hadn't worn since her last art show in Melbourne.

Three hours later, and despite her feet throbbing mercilessly, Ariel was pleased with how the night had gone. She had sold more than half of the exhibition paintings, and her interview with the Loddon Herald, Herald Sun, and the Bendigo Leader had gone exceptionally well. After a conversation with the chairman of the charity, he was certain that the news articles would reach an audience that would assist the charity further in the future.

After saying farewell to the eighty-odd art enthusiasts, leaving a far more relaxed crowd of locals who were enjoying a different Saturday night in their town, she enjoyed a quiet moment people-watching.

Ray approached her, a champagne twinkle in her eye.

Ariel smiled. "How have you enjoyed the night?"

"Oh, it's been fabulous!" Ray took a mouthful from her glass, before waving it around the gallery. "Your art is phenomenally phenomenal..." She ended on a hiccup. "Sorry, my last hurrah before I head home." She saluted her wine glass, swaying with the movement.

Ariel caught Ray's arm, steadying her as she looked about the room for someone who might be responsible for getting the principal home safely.

Her eyes collided with Jaxon Williams, who happened to be in a deep conversation with the chairman of the charity, who was gesturing towards her in that exact moment.

She watched Jaxon gauge her situation with Ray, then excuse himself before heading towards her. She tried not to think about how his casual grey summer suit with open collar, and the way he walked with quiet confidence and purpose that held such appeal, made her mouth water.

"Stop it," she whispered to herself. After all, he was Timmy's teacher, and her uncle's best mate.

"Stop what?" Ray asked.

Ariel shook her head as Jaxon reached them.

"Ariel, can I help?" He asked as Ray turned her attention towards him.

"Jaxon, isn't this artwork just boo-full." She slurred.

"It is, Ray," he answered, before turning his gaze to Ariel.

Ariel rubbed Ray's arm and said. "It would be good if we could get her home safe and sound."

"She lives around the corner, on Sullivan Street. I'll pull my car around the front, just give me a minute."

"Thank you." Ariel nodded, before Jaxon strode over to Steven and had a word with him before leaving via the front door.

Steven crossed towards Ariel. "Are you okay to help Jaxon?" He looked down at Ray, who was leaning against Ariel, smiling up at him with heavy eyes.

"I am."

"I'll get the twins and Timmy home. Liv said she'll lock up. Every-one's heading out now." He kissed the top of her head. "Great show sweetheart, I'm proud of you."

"Aw, thanks. And thanks for all your help setting up."

"Of course."

A car horn tooted out front, and Ariel led Ray towards the door. She halted for a second in awe at the gleaming black Hudson Greater Eight, that sat purring at the kerb.

"Here, let me." Jaxon reached out, taking Ray's arm and steered her towards the back of the car, tucking her gently into the back seat.

Ariel watched as he clicked the seatbelt across the inebriated woman before closing the door, careful to make sure her feet and hands were out of harm's way.

Turning towards Ariel, he asked, "Do you mind coming with me?"

"Of course. I feel partly responsible, being as she wiped herself out at my event."

He nodded, opening the car door for her before going around to the driver's side to get in.

"Gorgeous car," she stated, as he pulled out onto the road.

"Can't beat the classics," he patted the steering wheel. "This was my Grandfather's pride and joy."

"She's a beauty for sure." She watched his large hands caress the leather steering wheel in a loving gesture. His aftershave wrapped around her in an intoxicating way as she stole a quick look at his face, only to see him watching her out of the corner of his eye.

She quickly looked away, glad of the darkness that hid the tell-tale rush of blood which filled her cheeks. A gentle snore in the back seat broke the tension building between them, as his chuckle followed Ray's snore.

Turning the corner and down the next street, he pulled up in front of a small, charming weatherboard house. Shutting the engine off, he turned on the overhead light.

"Easier if we find her keys now so we're not doing a juggling act at her front door."

Ariel nodded and turned around, kneeling on the seat and reached over for Ray's fallen handbag. Retrieving it, she turned back around and opened it under the light, pulling the keys out.

"Got them," she smiled at Jaxon, only to see him staring at her with a slightly dazed expression before he quickly cleared his throat.

"Excellent," he said, voice slightly hoarse. He opened the door and headed around to Ray's side.

Ariel looked down at herself, confused for a moment at his expression before it dawned on her. Short dress, kneeling, reaching, bending over... Crap! Had he seen her next-to-nothing underwear?

She rolled her eyes and got out of the car as Jaxon hauled an unconscious Ray up into his arms and carried her to the front door. Ariel followed, and after two attempts to locate the correct key, finally had the door unlocked. Turning on the hallway light, Ariel went in search of Ray's bedroom, feeling slightly guilty that despite their good deed, they were invading Ray's privacy.

Finding a small bedroom with two empty single beds made up immaculately, she walked into the next.

"Here we go," she said quietly.

Jaxon walked in behind her to lay Ray on the double bed then stood back. "I'll wait in the lounge if you want to get her comfortable. I'll leave a note for her."

"No worries, it won't take me long."

He nodded, before heading out of the room.

Ariel turned to Ray and said softly. "That was very thoughtful of him." She tugged Ray's shoes off, before pulling the blankets from under her body, down and then up and over the sleeping lady.

"Sweet dreams, Ray," she whispered before heading out, and down the corridor looking for Jaxon. He stood by the front door, waiting for her.

"All good?" He asked.

"Well, she is safe and tucked in. I don't know how good she's going to feel in the morning though."

He grinned, locking the door before pulling it shut behind them.

"Not much anyone can do about that now."

"True," she chuckled. "Poor thing." She said kindly.

He looked down at her as they walked towards his car. "No judgment?"

"Why should there be? It's a Saturday night, it was a festive event." She shrugged.

"Not everyone around here is so compassionate." He opened the door for her, before heading over to open his.

"Thanks for your help getting her home safe," she said as he started the car and turned it in the direction of her house.

"It was my pleasure."

Within moments, he pulled up to her front door. Turning his dark, caramel gaze towards her, he said, "Congratulations on a great exhibition tonight."

"Thank you," she managed smoothly, despite the flutter of butterflies attacking her stomach.

"By the way, I've been assigned to your mural-crew, so any tips you can give me with a paintbrush will be greatly appreciated." He said.

"You'll be a great help prepping the surface and doing a few topcoats."

"Sounds easy enough," he smiled. "I've always appreciated the art of painting, but never taken the time to try my hand at it."

"I'm running sip and paint evenings at the café gallery on Thursday nights if you're interested?" She offered.

"That sounds great. Can I bring a friend?"

She didn't know why her heart dropped when he mentioned a friend, and forced another cheery smile as she opened the door. "Absolutely."

"Great well, goodnight then," he said.

"Goodnight. See you at school Monday," she called, before closing the door and hurrying down the path. Walking in the shadow of the house she felt a cold finger run down her spine, making her freeze momentarily, before she ran the rest of the way towards the front door and inside the sanctuary of her home.

Ariel sighed as she snuggled her face into her pillow, feeling like she could sleep forever and did not want her dream to end.

Her Grandmother sang to her as she painted. The sun filtered into the room spreading its rays across the crystals hung in front of the window, sending rainbow prisms to dance over every surface. Peace and utter happiness filled Ariel's soul, before a grey cloud covered the sun casting gloom about the room.

Her Grandmother suddenly stopped singing and met her gaze before she anxiously turned towards the doorway. Horror filled her sweet old face as she whispered in fright; "I'm so sorry dear. Sorry I couldn't protect you all."

"Grandma?" Ariel whispered in confusion, before her Grandmother suddenly evaporated into a thin white mist.

"Oh my Lord, *what* is happening?" she whispered, heart hammering as thudding footsteps sounded in the corridor. Running a trembling hand over her mouth, dread filled her as she waited to see what was coming, anticipating the worst after her grandmother's declaration.

A shadow loomed before her as a familiar, overpowering stench permeated her nostrils. She had nowhere to run, and no way to escape but the window. She spun around and ran towards it, hopeful she could escape whatever it was that had terrified her Grandmother. As she reached to open the latch, claws ripped along her back, breaking her skin. The scream jammed in her throat as she was flung into the air, and out of her Grandmother's painting room as if she were nothing but a tennis ball. The wind was knocked out of her as she hit the wall, then fell with a thump to the floor. She barely had a chance to pull in a shaken breath before her ankle was seized roughly and she was dragged along the corridor and into her Grandfather's office.

Every hair on her body stood to attention as an animalistic scream reached her ears. She was shocked to realise it was her making the gut-tural sounds before she was tossed with such force she flew over her Grandfather's desk and towards the wall. Raising her hands to protect her face from getting smashed to pieces, she squinted her eyes shut, wait-ing for more pain, when miraculously she jerked to a stop with her nose an inch from the corner of the wall. *What?*

She didn't have time to get her bearings or try to figure out what was going on, when an unnatural voice hissed in her ear.

"*Pay her penance.*"

Her body shook uncontrollably, and tears of fright flowed automati-cally. She had to get to the kids and make sure they were safe. But in all Gods honest truth she was too terrified to turn around as the 'thing' still had its unnatural body pressed against her back.

"Please," she whispered. "What do you want?" She didn't really expect an answer and jumped when the voice hissed again.

"*You'll find out soon enough.*" It ran dry hands along the flesh of her bare arms, and she released a frightened sob as she felt it push its face into the back of her neck, taking a deep breath.

"*Freeze,*" it hissed, and to her astonishment she found she could not move a muscle. But worse than that - she could not draw breath.

She wanted to scream, cry, anything, but was totally unable to do anything except feel fear creep into every corner of her mind as she strug-gled for air.

I'm going to die. I'm so sorry Mama… I can't protect the kids… Grandma, she silently begged.

Then, to her relief she escaped the terrifying situation as she blanked out, standing on the spot an inch from the corner wall.

Chapter Four
Wren

"What are you up to?" Wren asked Hawk, leaning against his doorway as she brushed her hair.

"I'm heading over to the bowls club to help out with the sausage sizzle fundraiser," he answered as he tied the shoelaces on his red Nikes.

"Oh yeah. Are you going with anyone?" She called over her shoulder as she went to throw her brush onto her bed.

"Lance Meek."

Wren flushed automatically, recalling the handsome blonde-haired, green-eyed student who'd been their school guide at East Loddon College. She'd noticed the way Lance hadn't been able to keep his eyes off her as he'd led them on a tour of the school.

Scooping her hair into a high ponytail, she wandered downstairs as Hawk called, "What about you?"

"I'm not sure."

"Wanna come?" he asked.

"Sure, why not," she tried to sound casual, but the idea of spending time with Lance had her heart racing. Walking by her Grandfather's office and heading towards the kitchen, she paused, not quite believing her eyes. Frowning, she walked backwards and turned into the office staring at the sight before her.

Ariel was standing in the corner, her nose an inch from the wall, her skin-tinged blue.

"Ariel?" She rushed towards her sister, grabbing her arm to turn her around. Her skin was as cold as ice.

"Hawk!" She screamed in panic and shook her sister's arm once more, getting no reaction. "*Hawk*, get down here!"

Hawk's footsteps thumped down the stairs as he ran in her direction.

"What's going on?" he asked rushing through the doorway.

Wren turned to her twin, seeing the worry in his eyes as his gaze fell on Ariel. "Something's wrong." Her voice shook.

"Is she sleepwalking?"

"I don't think so."

Hawk hesitantly reached a hand towards Ariel as Timmy walked into the room.

"What are you doing to Ariel?" Timmy asked.

The moment her name left Timmy's mouth, Ariel sucked in a lungful of air and fell back against the wall looking dazed.

Wren grabbed her arm, relieved to feel her skin was warm and returning to its natural colour.

"What were you doing in here, sis?" Hawk asked reaching for her.

"I…" Ariel looked around before meeting Hawk's gaze, blinking slowly in confusion. "I don't know," she whispered.

Timmy stepped between the twins and grabbed Ariel's hand. "I'm hungry," he half-shouted.

Ariel blinked down at him and nodded.

"Are you okay?" Wren asked.

"I think so."

"What happened?"

Ariel shook her head. "I don't remember, I think I've been sleepwalking again. It's okay." She shook her head and smiled at Timmy. "Let's put the kettle on then I'll make you a frog in the pond."

"Yeah, Sunday cooked breaky!" Timmy cried happily as he ran from the room.

"Come on," Ariel hugged the twins then followed him out.

Wren looked up at Hawk, who shrugged. "Sleepwalking huh?"

She sighed, "Apparently. But that was weird don't you think?"

"Weird, interesting, unusual. But all good."

She forced a smile for her twin. "If you say so."

"I do" he grinned, as they headed towards the kitchen.

Ariel

After the twins had left for the bowls club, Ariel finished cleaning up the breakfast dishes as Timmy raced downstairs.

"What would you like to do today?" she asked him as she ruffled his hair.

"Can we go to the park?"

"Good idea. Let's go now before it gets too hot."

"It's always hot here," Timmy grabbed his drink bottle out of the fridge and headed towards the front door.

"It will get cooler in Autumn, I promise," she said, looking forward to that day. Pulling the front door shut, they headed down Grant Street and towards the War memorial that commemorated soldiers from the town and surrounding district who served in the Boer War, World War One and World War Two. Ariel glanced up at the stone obelisk that was topped with a white marble statue of a World War One soldier, standing easy and holding a rifle as he appeared to look off into the distance.

She ran her finger over the name *Radnell* as Timmy yelled, "Come on Ariel!"

"I'm coming," she chuckled at his impatience before running across Verdon Street to grab his hand before they ran the rest of the way to the park.

The small park was filled with parents of toddlers and primary school aged kids. Teenage banter and laughter drifted across from the swimming pool which added to the relaxed Sunday morning vibe. Ariel pushed Timmy on a swing for several minutes, then sat under the shade of a gum tree as he joined in a game of tiggy.

Ariel flicked away another bull-ant that was heading towards her ankle and was relieved when Timmy had finally exhausted himself.

"Can we go to the Café and say hi to Liv?" he asked, wiping sweat off his brow.

"Great idea," she stood and dusted the dirt off her backside and took his hand.

They walked along Brooke Street that was busy with the usual Sunday crowds visiting the popular old wares shops. Inglewood Emporium, Fusspots, Loddon Larder and several others were especially a highlight for antique lovers. She waved to Alan and Leah, the proprietors of the popular and always busy Inglewood Take Away, before crossing the street towards Steven's café.

Sweat dripped down her back as she pushed the café door open, and Timmy raced inside, heading towards the counter to climb up onto a high stool to place his usual order, a smiley face cookie.

Ariel hadn't thought she was tense, until she felt herself relax as she wandered to the corner of the café where bookcases were filled with a wide range of books, scented candles, and black and white photographs of the towns history from days gone by. She ran a finger along the back of one of the three-seater, red leather couches before straightening a pile of books which sat in the middle of the coffee table.

"Want a latte?" Liv called.

"Sounds perfect," she replied. "Thanks." She watched Liv pass Timmy his cookie, noticing several customers wandering around the gallery.

Heading past the cosy dining tables, she straightened a starched white cloth and casually centred a glass jar filled with fresh cut flowers as she smiled at the customers on the opposite table.

"Busy morning?" She asked Liv, who poured her latte.

"Flat out actually. Things have only just started to quieten down." She passed Ariel the frothy drink and smiled. "Last night was great, wasn't it?"

Ariel grinned. "It was."

"So, had a late one did we?" A cheeky twinkle filled Liv's eyes.

Ariel took a mouthful as she sat beside Timmy, raising an eyebrow at Liv before pointedly looking down at her little brother.

"Timmy, wanna go upstairs and see what your uncle's doing?" Liv asked.

"Yeah. Can I take him a cookie?" He looked up at Ariel.

"Why not." She smoothed a hand over his hair as Liv passed him another cookie.

They watched him slide off the stool and run towards the gallery where the stairs would take him up to Steven.

"Okay now that small fry is gone, spill."

"Spill what?"

"Come on little minx. Is Jaxon Williams the reason for those dark shadows under your lovely eyes?" Liv grinned leaning forward, eager to catch the juicy gossip.

Ariel chuckled dryly, shaking her head. *If only.*

She sighed, recalling the way Jaxon had looked at her last night, after she'd knelt on the seat of his car as she'd reached for Ray's handbag. His expression was one of wanting to slowly peel every layer of clothing from her flesh, before devouring her, with a hungry look in his gorgeous eyes.

Flushing, she caught Liv's eye who in turn laughed gleefully. "Oh, I love it when romance blossoms."

"Calm down girlfriend." Ariel chuckled, looking over her shoulder to make sure they weren't being overheard as the café door opened.

And in walked the man himself.

"Speak of the mouth-watering Devil." Liv whispered for Ariel's ears only, who turned a bright red face back to her friend.

"Behave," Ariel hissed, before watching Jaxon stroll towards them wearing blue jeans and a green t-shirt that made his dark caramel eyes stand out more than usual.

"Hello, Jaxon," Liv sang out brightly.

"Hello, Liv." He smiled at Liv, as he sat on the stool beside Ariel; his knee and inch from hers.

She noticed his silky dark brown hair held caramel highlights and wondered if he did that deliberately to match his eyes.

"How are you, Ariel?" He asked in his smooth tone.

She shifted in her seat, clearing her throat. "Good thanks." Her cheeks grew warm under his intense appraisal. He was *entirely* too good looking. "How are you?"

He smiled knowingly. "Very well, thank you."

"What can I get you?" Liv asked as she waved a handful of customers off.

"I'll grab a turkey roll thanks Liv, and a latte to go."

"You want all the trimmings?" Liv asked as she walked to the coffee machine.

"Yes thanks." As Liv got busy, Jaxon turned in his seat to make Ariel his full focal point. "Are you coming to watch Timmy swim tomorrow?"

"Wouldn't miss it for the world." She watched his lips form a sexy smile and forced her gaze away.

Liv handed Jaxon his latte before going to make up his roll.

He removed the lid to blow on the frothy liquid, before placing his luscious lips over the rim taking a careful mouthful. His gaze swung around to hers, catching her staring. Heat flared in her cheeks and she quickly inspected her coffee as if it were the most interesting thing she'd seen all day.

His low chuckle had a flutter of butterflies dancing in her stomach. What was it with him?

Liv placed his wrapped roll on the counter, as Timmy raced into the room.

"Hi, Mr Williams."

"Hello, Timothy." Jaxon smiled warmly at his student as he ran up to tug on Ariel's shirt enthusiastically.

Ariel laughed, catching his hand, and pulling him towards her for a hug.

"What's got you all excited. Did you eat Uncle Steven's cookie as well?" Thinking that could be the answer to his hyperactive excitement.

"No, Uncle Steven is out the back, putting the boat trailer on the jeep. He told me to tell you, he's taking me fishing. Can I Ariel, can I?"

"Of course you can darling." She kissed the top of his head as he slid out of her arms, fist pumping the air before racing off once more.

Liv sighed. "Youthful energy. Now, if I could figure out how to bottle me some of that to sell, I'd be a millionaire."

Jaxon laughed as he pulled out his wallet and paid for his latte and roll.

"I think the same thing every day." He got off the stool as he collected his goods. "Thanks Liv."

"No worries." She put the money into the register.

"See you ladies."

"Um, Jaxon?" Ariel asked as he turned to go.

"Yes?"

"Can you point out Timmy's friend, Sebastian, at swimming tomorrow? I'd like to invite him over for a play date with Timmy."

Jaxon took a sip from his takeaway cup, peering at her over the rim. "Sebastian, you say?"

She nodded, trying not to get mesmerised by his perfectly shaped brows and smouldering eyes, which looked all the sexier through the latte steam.

She cleared her throat. "Yes, that's right. Timmy's been talking about him, and he mentioned him before school started. I was thinking he might've met him at the park, but then he keeps bringing him up so I figured he must be seeing him every day at school."

She tucked a mass of silky hair behind her ear, wishing his eyes would stop dropping to her lips as she spoke. It did weird things to her after another sleepless night.

He lowered his cup and shook his head slowly, a puzzled expression on his handsome face. "Nope, there's no Sebastian enrolled at the school."

Ariel frowned. "Really? Well, he must be from St Mary's then. Thanks."

He stood there for a movement, looking down at her before saying quietly. "No worries. I'm just going to pop out the back and see Steven. See you later."

"Bye." Liv and Ariel answered together as they watched him walk towards the gallery.

"What's with this Sebastian?" Liv asked, as the last lot of customers left.

"Just putting some interesting ideas into Timmy's head, about it not being safe to sleep in the house. Just kid stuff I'm sure, nothing to worry about." Ariel sighed. "I think I'll take another latte."

Liv laughed, shaking her head. "You need it, my friend. And now that we have no ears, I'm all yours. Spill the beans. What's between you and Mr Honey?" Liv turned to make the latte.

Ariel shook her head laughing quietly. "I don't know yet. But I feel something brewing and I like it."

"You'd be mad not too." Liv came around and sat beside her friend, passing her a latte, and sipping one herself.

"Cheers to possibilities." Ariel held her mug up to Liv, who clinked her mug against hers.

"Indeed, my friend."

They sat in comfortable silence as they watched the usual Sunday foot traffic of locals and tourists alike, venture up and down Brooke Street, exploring the possibilities the old gold mining town had to offer.

Chapter Five
Timothy

T immy swallowed another whimper that trembled against his lips. His skin, slick with sweat, his pyjamas clung to him, his sheet saturated beneath him. Despite the heat of the night he clung to his doona, wrapping it tightly around him. His night-light peeked through the feather clusters of the doona as he quivered beneath it, trying to remain as still as possible. The heavy footsteps continued dragging around his room in an unnerving waltz; around and around, nearing his bed before retreating towards the door then back again.

Silent tears mingled with sweat as the overpowering urge to scream out for Hawk threatened. But he didn't want the *thing* to know he was awake. When it knew Timmy was awake, it had the power to hurt him.

The footsteps stopped abruptly making Timmy freeze. Had it left? Was it safe for him to move? He waited, shoulders aching from holding them so stiffly. Inch by inch, he slowly lowered the doona until it sat just beneath his eyes. He released a sigh of relief seeing his room empty of the creepy *thing* and wiped his tears with a shaky hand. Pushing the doona off he slipped out of bed and went to reach for his Minkey Monkey that his mother had given him when he was two.

Heading towards the door he grabbed the handle as a rush of foul air flattened him against the door. The fear almost paralysed him but the sharp nails digging into his back had him screaming.

"*Mine.*" The entity whispered against his ear, sending another foul draft into his ear drum making him shiver in fear.

"No," Timmy whimpered and gripped the door handle, jiggling it desperately before being launched in the air and pressed against the ceiling.

How is this happening? He dropped Minkey Monkey and struggled uselessly against the force. His eyes bulged in fear as somehow, not quite believing what was happening, his face was pushed right through the plaster as if it were made of hot wax, and into a storm drain.

This isn't happening. This can't be real. He cried at the sight before him as blood flowed like a river through the drain, carrying disfigured and mutilated body parts along. The stench of warm blood and rotten corpses was unbearable and made his eyes water and his evening meal climbed up his throat. He squeezed his eyes shut and screamed repeatedly until his throat felt raw.

"Hawk, Hawk! Help me, *help me!*" He sobbed hysterically, trying to break free of the hold that pinned him in that godawful place.

Suddenly, he was being shaken by a different set of hands and his eyes burst open, widening in confusion as he found himself laying on his bed, the doona twisted around his shaking body, and Hawk staring down at him, concern etched in every line of his face.

"Hey sport, it's okay, you were having a bad dream."

Timmy lurched upright and into his big brother's arms, crying in relief that the incident was over.

"What's going on?" Ariel asked tiredly as she walked in, stopping to pick up Timmy's Monkey from the floor.

Hawk turned to Ariel. "Another bad dream."

Ariel handed Minkey to Timmy. "Are you alright love?"

Timmy wiped his eyes on Minkey's head. "Yeah, I think so."

"Do you want to jump in bed with Hawk?"

Timmy nodded slowly, trying to come to terms with what had just happened. Had it just been a dream? But if so, how had Minkey gotten into the middle of the floor?

"Come on sport, dry pj's first, then sleep." Hawk patted Timmy's wet back before releasing him and opening the top draw to grab fresh pyjamas.

Timmy tried not to flinch when Hawk had touched his back, and once Hawk turned around with the fresh pyjamas, he grabbed them off his brother and headed towards the bathroom.

"I've got to go to the loo," he called over his shoulder. "I'll be in yours in a minute."

"Sure thing." Hawk said. "Night Sis, I've got this." He said to Ariel.

"Thanks hun," Ariel said, before switching the light off and heading towards her room called, "Night Timmy."

He turned in the bathroom doorway, wanting to tell is sister everything, but a soft voice whispered, "*Not yet. She won't believe you.*"

"Night Ariel." He whispered instead, before closing the door behind him.

Ariel

After another restless night everyone seemed to be dragging their feet the following morning. Ariel was relieved the twins had a free period first thing, and that Steven was giving them a lift into school.

"Scrambled, fried, or poached?" She called, carrying in fresh eggs as the kettle screamed.

"No time," Wren opened the fridge to pull out a tub of yogurt and a protein drink. As Hawk ran down the stairs and along the corridor, he stuffed a towel into Timmy's school bag, then caught the protein drink Wren tossed in his direction.

"Ta," Hawk grinned before he turned to Timmy who walked into the kitchen, scratching at his head as he yawned loudly.

"Don't do that when you're in the race today sport, you'll drown." He chuckled.

"Will not." Timmy said.

"Oh the joys of primary school swimming sports." Wren grinned as she kissed Timmy's head and walked across to hug Ariel. "Have a good day."

"You too love," Ariel ran a hand over Wren's silky head before she walked off. "Hawk, are you on at the café this afternoon?"

"Yeah, I told Liv I'd help out." He grinned at Ariel, before turning to Timmy. "Have fun today." A car horn tooted from the front of the house.

"I will." Timmy climbed onto a kitchen stool and reached for his bowl of Vita Brits.

The twins headed out of the room and down the corridor. "See you." They called together as the front door slammed behind them.

Ariel smiled at Timmy before pouring a coffee, and leaning a hip against the bench asked, "You okay? Not too tired after last night?" Taking a mouthful of the rich blend, she watched his eyes darken as he stared into his bowl of cereal.

He shrugged slowly, breaking her heart. She hated seeing any of her siblings not be their usual, smiley selves.

"Do you want to skip swimming sports today? I've got some work to do here in the studio this morning. You can hang out with me before I have to go into the gallery."

Timmy quickly shook his head, scooping up another mouthful. "I want to go swimming. Sebastian says it's better to go to school than stay at home."

"Yeah, well, Sebastian's right. It's important not to skip a school day but, if you're not well love, I'd rather keep you at home."

"I'm fine." Timmy sang out convincingly, as he scraped the last soggy mouthful out of his bowl, then slid off the chair and took his bowl to the sink. After dropping it into the soapy water he turned, grabbing his glass of freshly squeezed orange, spinach, and apple juice, he sculled it in several mouthfuls.

"I'm impressed." Ariel smiled, putting her half-finished coffee cup down on the bench. "Have you got your hat?"

"Yeah, it's in here." Timmy grabbed his school bag and headed to the front door.

Ariel was about to remind him to brush his teeth, but thought she'd let it go this morning. They walked to school in comfortable silence, and as they neared the gate Timmy reached up to hug her, before running over to join his friend Paul Musgrove, whom Steven had introduced him to before Christmas.

"Good luck today," she called. "I'll be there for your first event."

He waved enthusiastically, indicating he'd heard her. At least being at school with Paul seemed to perk him up.

She turned to head back home, thinking about Sebastian's influence on Timmy. She liked the fact that he thought being at school was better than staying at home on a school day. Not so much the idea of sleeping in the chicken coop.

"Can't win 'em all I guess." She glanced up towards the bright sky wondering again about the intense Inglewood heat. This morning felt hot enough to fry an egg on a car bonnet, and she was glad that Timmy would spend most of his day in the water.

She was looking forward to starting the next project she'd been commissioned to do, by the Inglewood council. They wanted some of the historic buildings, and landmarks captured in a series of paintings of the town, including the drains that surrounded the town, all the churches, old hotels, and the golden triangle, which represented the glory of the gold mining days where the town had thrived in a different era.

Opening the front door, she smiled as golden silence greeted her.

"Absolute bliss," she sighed and headed down the cool hallway to grab her coffee to take out to the studio. She had a couple of hours before she'd have to head off to the swimming sports.

Stepping into the kitchen her relaxed vibe vanished in an instant at the sight before her.

Her coffee mug that she'd placed on the bench before leaving the house, now hung ten-feet mid-air with the remaining coffee frozen in its pour. She mirrored its frozen state automatically, her heart thumped uncomfortably against her rib cage.

"What is this…" She barely whispered and blinked rapidly.

Rubbing her hands quickly over her eyes, she hoped to remove this paranormal-activity-moment. Nothing. After several long nerve-wracking minutes of standing still and staring at the scene before her, too frightened to move, the grandfather clock bonged as if breaking a spell. The coffee poured onto the bench before splashing to the floor, the empty mug following to smash into pieces. Ariel jumped–a nervous scream escaped her lips as silence fell over the house once more.

Placing a hand over her heart she took a deep, steadying breath as she stared at the shattered contents for what felt like an hour.

Did that really just happen? Finally, she stepped over to the shattered mug for a closer inspection. Glancing over her shoulder to make sure no one was around, she swallowed, taking a moment to try to make sense of the situation. She couldn't. Not for a moment did any of this make sense. Shaking her head, she whispered.

"Not enough sleep, that's what it is." Although, not quite believing that excuse herself, she grabbed the dustpan and broom that nestled in the walk-in pantry and began to sweep up the mess. After dumping the pieces into the trash, she took the sponge from the sink and mopped up the liquid. After squeezing the sponge out, she rinsed shaking hands under the cold water before drying them on a tea towel. She turned the kettle on to make fresh coffee and looked over her shoulder again. Why did she get the feeling that something was watching her?

"Don't be silly," she scolded herself. "Tell me I'm imagining things, Grandma. I'm imagining things because I'm dead tired, that's why." She felt better somehow, having a conversation with her Grandmother. At least this way she felt as if she had back-up.

A knock at the front door had her jumping a mile, before Steven's, "Hello," rang out. Footsteps headed in her direction, and she forced a bright smile when he stepped into the kitchen, beyond grateful at the timing of his visit.

"You always know when I'm about to make a cuppa." She grinned, reaching for another mug.

"It's a skill, I won't lie." He smiled and dropped a kiss on her head.

She poured them a mug, wanting to get out of the kitchen. "Come on out to the studio, I was about to start work."

He nodded and followed her out the back door along the shiny deck and under the shade of the weeping peppercorn tree where her studio stood picturesquely against rows of purple, and white lavender he had planted. Their ancestor's grapevine trickled along the studios floor to ceiling windows, framing them like artwork itself.

Ariel slid the large barn door open for extra lighting and placed her mug on a table before turning her Tidal App on low. She grabbed a large sketch pad and pencil before sitting on a stool and balanced the pad on her lap. Grabbing her mug, she took a mouthful of coffee as Steven strolled around the spacious area that was lined with her creations.

"Timmy loved being on the boat yesterday."

"He loves doing anything with you." She replied, taking another scorching mouthful of coffee, hoping it would steady her nerves.

"Your show on Saturday was brilliant," he said quietly, turning to face her. "Do you miss it?"

"Miss what?"

"The lights, camera, action, fame?"

She laughed quietly, shaking her head. "Fame? No. Fame comes with a price and I'm grateful for the quiet fame of being your mother's grand-daughter, right here. And, we had lights, a few cameras and plenty of action Saturday night, so no, there's nothing to miss." She joked.

He tilted his head. "You know what I mean, love. Are you happy here?"

"You know I am."

"What about the kids?"

She sighed, putting her coffee down and picked up her pencil. "Those kids are the most resilient kids I've ever met. They're fine Uncle Steven, I promise."

"You all seem so tired; do you need a break?"

She laughed. "We've just had summer holidays. No, we're just getting used to the house, old noises and all that."

"You've been here nearly four months."

She sighed. "It's been a big move is all, but we're fine."

Steven nodded slowly, draining his cup. "I've got to leave town for a week, I've left a number with Liv if my mobile is out of range. If you need me for anything, call."

"Sure, thanks." She smiled at her uncle, who opened his arms for a hug. She leaned into his embrace and laughed when he kissed the tip of her nose.

"You do know I'm twenty-eight, right?"

"It's an uncle's rite of passage," he grinned. "I'm going to drop some dollars on the kid's pillows before I go."

"Uncle Steven, you don't have to…" She stopped as he held up a hand, walking backwards out of the barn door.

"Uncle's rite of passage." He repeated, before winking, and vanishing out of sight.

She laughed quietly before taking a deep breath and willed herself to forget about the disturbing mug incident, and everything else that gave her the shivers lately. She allowed the creative images to flow freely for the remaining time before her mobile alarm indicated it was time to head off to the pool for Timmy's first event.

Jaxon

Jaxon stood outside the boys changing room, assisting the kids with sunscreen and goggle adjustments. He enjoyed swimming sport days and the holiday atmosphere it produced. The majority of the kids were in high spirits knowing they would get to lounge about on the grass most of the day, in between cooling off in the water for races and activities.

Several kids shot past him, including Timmy who was wearing his school shirt tucked into his swimming trunks.

"No running," he called. "Timothy, come here please." He saw the boy's shoulders slump, before turning to face him.

Jaxon offered a kind smile. "Where's your rash vest, mate?"

Timmy looked up at him, "I'm just going to swim in my school shirt, Mr Williams."

Jaxon hid a grin. The kid was so damn cute, with his dark hair and big dark eyes who looked seriously intent on wearing his school shirt in the water.

"Do you have a rash vest?"

"No." he answered, too quickly.

Jaxon held in a sigh. The permission notes that went home at the start of last week, requested that all students who were participating in the sports, were to wear a rash vest.

"Where's your bag?"

Timmy hesitated, before pointing back into the change rooms.

"Come on then." Jaxon nodded, before heading into the change room to grab Timmy's bag. When Timmy dawdled in, Jaxon opened the bag for him to reach in and pull out his rash vest.

"Look at that." Jaxon grinned. "Pop it on, I'll be out here waiting."

Jaxon turned to walk out when Timmy groaned in pain. Jaxon turned and froze momentarily, shocked at what he saw.

Timmy had tugged his school shirt over his head and the reason for his groan was painstakingly evident. Long scratch marks covered his small shoulder blades and trailed down his back. His flesh bloody, torn, and bruised.

Jaxon cursed quietly under his breath as fury pumped in his veins, filling his vision with a red haze. He ran a shaky hand through his hair before saying gently, "Do you want a hand, mate?"

It broke his heart when the young boy turned around to look up at him with dark eyes, before nodding, as he passed Jaxon his rash vest.

Jaxon smiled as he pulled the vest over Timmy's head, and lowered it over his back, careful not to drag the material over his wounded flesh.

Timmy smiled up at him. "Thanks Mr Williams, now I can win my race." He headed towards the door with enthusiasm.

"That's the attitude, mate." Jaxon forced brightness in his tone, before adding, "Timothy, is there anything you'd like to tell me about how your back was hurt?"

Timmy turned slowly, meeting his gaze before shaking his head.

"Sebastian says I can't tell anyone."

"Oh, why is that?" Jaxon remained calm on the outside; his heart hammered uncomfortably.

"Because it's not safe."

"Timothy, I can help you if you just tell me who…" Jaxon held out a hand, wanting to reassure Timmy that he was here for him, when Ray called out.

"Jaxon, have you got Timothy Harper in there? He is being called for his race."

"Yes, he's on his way…" Jaxon replied.

Timmy bolted out of the change room and yelled happily. "Coming Mrs Sommers."

Jaxon followed Timmy out to see him dash past Ray, towards his lineup. Timmy waved to Ariel, who was standing just to the side of a group of mothers. Jaxon placed his hands on his hips and scowled when he saw Ariel waving encouragingly to Timmy. She looked fresh, and youthful wearing denim shorts and a white t-shirt that clung to shapely curves. Her silky auburn locks danced in the breeze, eyes shining brightly as she cheered Timmy on.

Was it even possible that she could have done that to the boy?

His lip automatically curled in disgust with the fact that right at this moment, he thought her breathtakingly beautiful. Abusers wore many masks; that he knew. He felt the urge to go over and shake her, to demand the answer as to why her brother, hell, her *adopted son*, had physical signs of abuse.

Ariel's eyes met his glaringly hostile ones from across the pool, and her bright smile slowly vanished, replaced with a puzzled frown.

"Jaxon?" Ray's questioning tone snapped him out of the fury, which was clearly evident upon his face. "What's going on?" She asked quietly, looking from him then across to where Ariel stood.

He had to admit watching Ariel now looking small, fragile, and alone, she didn't seem capable of hurting anyone. But he'd been in this situation before, and never again would he look past any sign where an innocent life could be in danger.

Jaxon tore his gaze from Ariel's alluring face and met Ray's curious gaze. Bending his head closer to the principal's ear he said quietly.

"I've just seen physical signs of abuse on Timothy."

Her head snapped up. "Oh no," she whispered, shocked. "Well, this will have to wait until after school. I'll make the appropriate calls after we have spoken to Timothy. For now, Jaxon let's focus on the day please. He is safe here with us."

He nodded, running a hand through his hair before his gaze flashed back towards Ariel, who was now watching Timothy. Frowning, he returned to his duties, glad that at least now, they were able to help the boy out of the unpleasant situation he was obviously in.

Ariel

Ariel was surprised to see so many parents turn up for the sports day. The lawn area around the pool was lined with colourful blankets and towels. Bodies sunbaking, others more sun-smart sitting under beach umbrellas with the stems burrowed into the grass. She noticed a tall man at the kiosk, wearing a baseball hat low over his face. He stood separate from everyone else, as if he didn't belong. His arms were folded, almost defensively and he was staring straight at her with his lip curled. He unhurriedly looked away when she raised an eyebrow in question.

Weird.

"Ariel!" Timmy yelled, breaking her focus on the intense man, as he scrambled out of the pool and ran up to her. "Did you see me, Ariel! Did you?"

She beamed at him, giving him a high five.

"Well done love, third place is wonderful!" She ruffled his wet hair as he grinned up at her.

"Yeah, I think I deserve a snake for that, and one for Paul too?" He asked hopefully.

Ariel laughed. "Of course. What about one for Sebastian?" She asked, pulling some change out of her pocket.

Timmy just laughed, holding out his hand.

She shook her head smiling as she placed the coins in his small palm.

"There you go, I'll see you after school."

"Thanks." Timmy waved before racing over to Paul. She grinned as she watched the boys run off across the grass before a stern voice interrupted her proud-mama moment.

"Miss Harper." Jaxon stood a few feet away, arms folded and wearing an angry frown.

Ariel slowly walked across to him, folding her own arms in defence at his unusual hostile demeanour.

"Yes, Mr Williams?" She replied, as equally formal wondering what this was all about, and why he had been shooting daggers at her since he had followed Timmy out of the change room earlier?

She looked up at him, tilting her head to the side, her hair slipping over her shoulder.

"I need you to come into the school this afternoon when you collect Timothy."

"Can I ask why?" She raised an eyebrow, not liking that he wore fury so well. Especially considering he seemed to be wearing it solely for her, as he glared down at her.

What's wrong with you? She snickered to herself. *Thinking he's scrumptious, while he looks like he wants to throttle you?*

"You can ask that question this afternoon." He looked at her silently, before turning away calling over his shoulder in a flat tone. "Ten to four. Don't be late."

She stood there for a moment, feeling the other mothers' gazes bore into her back, before she quickly headed out of the pool's gates. A sense of dread filled her, as tears of anger threatened.

"Don't be late," she whispered in fury as she headed home. "Who does he think he is?" She kicked at the gravel path before turning down her street and felt sorry for the canvas she knew that she was about to take her fury out on.

She had a little over three hours to kill, before she *had* to be at the school. She slammed the front door behind her before guiltily calling out, "Sorry Grandma."

Out of respect, she opened it and closed it gently behind her, before heading into the kitchen to make a relaxing herbal tea.

"Why does he want to see me anyway?" She shook her head and retrieved a cup and waited for the kettle to do its thing. Impatiently, she poured not quite boiling water into her cup and took it out into the garden and tugged a few lemon balm leaves off the bush, throwing them into her cup as she walked into her studio.

She turned Tidal onto her Twilight Instrumental station and turned it up to a respectable volume as in–her ear drums weren't quite bleeding.

Placing her cup on the table, she grabbed a large canvas and placed it on the easel, before selecting silver, white, black, and blue paint, then dispersed them onto her oversized pallet.

She stood there for several minutes staring at the blank canvas as the music swept around the studio, reverberating along the walls and high ceiling, before caressing her soul as she took some calming breaths. Closing her eyes for a moment, she willed the panic to recede, then, opening them, dipped her brush into the paint before stepping towards the canvas. She allowed every thought, every concern, every drop of anxiety to vanish into thin air and willed the music to take her and the paint on a journey of its own.

In two hours, she had transformed a blank canvas into a shimmering lake where a thunderous sky hung over the horizon, and silver tears fell onto the water's surface that looked like glass. She didn't realise she too, had tears pouring down her face until Liv's worried voice rang out.

"Ariel, honey, what's wrong?" A hand on her back had her snapping out of her daze.

She jumped, then quickly walked over to turn the music down.

"Why are you crying?" Liv asked, concerned.

"Oh," Ariel shook her head. "I guess I got lost in the painting." She shrugged and wiped her fingers over her face.

"It looks like it's more than that, my friend."

Ariel shrugged.

Liv folded her arms. "Out with it."

She sighed. "I have to go to the school for a meeting this afternoon."

"Why?"

"I have no idea. Only that your, *Mr honey*, has ordered me to, and he didn't have the decency to give me a reason as to why."

"Ordered? Sounds official."

"Yeah, you could say that. He was as cold as ice and appeared as angry as hell, at me."

"Well, shit this doesn't sound good."

"Truly."

"Okay, we've got this."

"Have we?" Ariel sounded defeated.

Liv squared her shoulder. "We do. And you most certainly do."

Ariel almost smiled at her friend's certainty.

"You can't go in like that though." Liv nodded to Ariel.

She glanced down and saw that she was covered in paint. She raised an eyebrow at Liv.

Liv smiled softly. "Come on my friend, let's get you cleaned up and adult looking."

"I'm not adult looking now?"

"Definitely not." Liv grabbed Ariel's arm and gently steered her into the house.

"Who's looking after the café till Hawk gets in?" Ariel asked as they walked upstairs.

"Nolan Radnell. The ladies flock in when the boys are on." Liv grinned, pointing towards the shower. "You, get in there, I'm choosing your outfit."

Ariel sighed as she ran the shower and stripped off before getting under the massaging spray. She could feel it relieve the tension in her muscles with a slight sting to her back.

"Liv?" she called.

"Yeah?"

"Do you believe in ghosts?" She waited, anxious that her friend would laugh at her.

"Ghosts?"

"Spirits."

"I used to," Liv replied quietly. "And then, after John died…"

Ariel felt bad for bringing it up, and peeked around the shower curtain at her friend who was leaning against the doorway.

"I'm sorry," Ariel said softly.

Liv shook her head. "Don't be. After John died, I waited for a sign, a message from him that he was okay. But I didn't get anything. I kinda stopped believing in the afterlife after that." She shrugged. "Why?"

Ariel turned the shower off and reached for her towel to wrap around herself, unsure of what to say. She stepped over the clawfoot tub and wandered past Liv, towards her bedroom to dry off and get dressed.

Liv stood against the hallway wall, to give Ariel privacy.

"It's just that, some weird things have been happening here. Things I can't explain." She rubbed herself dry, before putting on her underwear, and pulling the halter-neck, cotton dress up. Reaching into her cupboard, she grabbed a short sleeved white cardigan to cover her exposed back and pushed her feet into white pumps. Walking back into the bathroom she brushed her hair dry, which took minutes in the Inglewood heat. Pulling it up into a loose bun, she turned to Liv. "Adult enough for you?"

Liv smiled. "Very adult. Now to cover those dark circles, a spritz of perfume and your shield is set to go."

Ariel smiled and complied with Liv's instructions, feeling more confident once the pretty reflection looked back at her.

"What sort of weird things?" Liv asked as they headed downstairs.

"It's hard to explain." Ariel wasn't sure she wanted to explain anything. Even when she thought about her and Timmy's odd sleeping habits, along with the coffee mug incident, it sounded too bizarre to say out loud.

"I think you need a break," Liv said kindly.

"I don't need a break, *Uncle Steven*," Ariel chuckled as she opened the front door. "I'm fine." She insisted.

Liv smiled and patted Ariel's back, frowning when her friend flinched. "What's wrong?"

"Nothing, I slept on it funny, that's all."

"Do you want me to come to the school with you?"

Because she did, Ariel shook her head offering Liv a small smile.

"I'll be fine, hun. Honestly, what's the worst that could happen?"

"Yeah, exactly. Nothing for you to be nervous about."

"I wish I wasn't nervous."

"If things get too intense, imagine Mr Honey naked."

"Jesus, Liv." Ariel laughed.

Liv's eyes twinkled. "That's what I wanted to hear. Why don't I bring Pizza around for tea tonight?"

"That would be wonderful, the kids will love that. Thank you."

Liv hugged her friend gently, being careful she didn't touch her back.

"See you later and hold your head up when you walk in there. You've got nothing to worry about."

Ariel nodded as she headed towards the school. Liv was right, she had absolutely nothing to worry about, and Jaxon Williams had *no right* to speak to her as if she were a naughty schoolgirl who had been caught smoking behind the bike shed.

"You've got this," she whispered as she walked into the school yard and towards the office to wait for the meeting to start.

Chapter Six

Jaxon

J axon, Ray, and the school psychologist, Rick Jones had spent half an hour with Timothy. They had encouraged him to open up and share how he had acquired his injuries without applying too much pressure. He sat in front of them sullenly, arms folded wearing a disgruntled expression before he burst out.

"You're going to get us *hurt*! Sebastian says I *can't* tell you."

"Timothy," Jaxon tried in a gentle tone. "We can protect you if you just tell us who has hurt you."

"No. You. *Can't.*" Timmy cried blocking his ears and squeezing his eyes shut.

Jaxon sighed and said to Rick. "His sister will be here soon."

At the mention of Ariel's name, Timmy started crying.

"No, no, I don't want Ariel to get into trouble!" He was shaking his head from side to side, tears pouring down his face.

Rick exchanged a tell-tale look with Jaxon before saying to Ray. "I think it would be a good idea, Mrs Sommers, if you took Timothy into the mindful room for some afternoon tea before his Miss Harper arrives?"

"Yes, alright." Ray bent down to Timothy and said kindly. "Come on then, let's get some milk and fruit, okay?"

Timmy raised his tear-stained face to Ray, breaking Jaxon's heart for the second time that day, as he took Ray's hand. She led him out of the room.

Jaxon let out a pent-up breath. "What are your thoughts?"

"He became clearly distraught when you mentioned his sister, although we can't jump to conclusions just yet."

"It seems plain enough." Jaxon folded his arms.

Rick shook his head. "Yet, it rarely is. We'll contact DHS in the morning after our review. It doesn't look good for Miss Harper at this stage."

Jaxon ran his hands through his hair frustrated, and wondered how Steven may react to this mess.

"You know the family. Is she capable of this?"

Jaxon shook his head. "The family I know, Ariel personally, not so much. She has been through a lot recently. Gave up a high-flying carer after losing her mother, then having the responsibility of raising three kids." He shrugged "I don't know. I wouldn't like to think so, but I've been wrong before."

"Yes, Henry Lee. I read your history. You do know there was nothing you could have done differently, don't you?"

Jaxon scoffed, shaking his head. "Nothing legally different. That was my mistake."

Rick sighed, running a hand down his front straightening his tie. "And the difference being, the mother ended up in jail and not you."

"Yeah, but Henry still *died* Rick. And I could've done something about *that*. I could have changed the outcome if I'd acted sooner."

"That's debateable."

"Yeah, well what's not debateable is this; the kid would be alive today if I hadn't followed all the bloody *bureaucracy* bullshit." Jaxon spat in anger, still clearly affected.

"Do you want to start sessions again? I know they helped you when you were in Scotland."

Jaxon shook his head. "I'm fine, this just brings it all back to the surface."

Rick nodded. "I understand. But please remember Jaxon, that in this meeting, Miss Harper is *not* Jenny Lee. Okay?"

Jaxon met Rick's solemn expression. "Yeah, got it," he said, quietly resigned.

"Can you go and collect Miss Harper now?" Rick asked.

"Sure." Jaxon got up from the chair and walked out of the psychologist's office, and towards the reception area where he saw Ariel looking at the student's artwork that lined the walls.

She looked fresh as a daisy and the closer he got; her floral fragrance wrapped around him. *She's not Jenny Lee. Try not to judge.*

"Miss Harper." He kept his tone neutral and watched as her pretty expression become guarded as she turned to face him.

"Good afternoon, *Mr Williams*. I do hope I'm not late." She said, smiling sugar-sweet, yet he detected the sarcasm in her voice.

He forced a smile. "Right on time. This way please." He opened his palm for her to walk ahead of him and forced his eyes up from her perfectly round backside that swayed hypnotically beneath her thin summer dress.

Don't be a dick, he hissed inwardly.

Rick stood in the doorway and motioned for Ariel to come into the room. Reaching out a hand he smiled. "Nice to meet you Miss Harper, I'm Rick Jones, the school's psychologist. Please, come in."

Ariel looked over her shoulder at Jaxon, and he almost winced at the apprehension in her eyes. His gut tightened and he reminded himself he was here to protect Timothy, *not* Ariel.

Looking back at Rick, Ariel hesitantly shook his hand. "Nice to meet you," she replied politely, before sitting on a three-seater couch. Rick sat in the leather chair opposite her.

"Why am I having an appointment with you Rick? No offence, but I don't believe that Timmy needs to see a psychologist."

"None taken, Miss Harper,"

"Please," she held up a hand. "Call me Ariel."

Rick smiled as he sat back in his chair. "I'm afraid for this meeting it is best if we stick to formalities, Miss Harper."

Ariel raised an eyebrow but said nothing.

Jaxon sat on the other end of the couch and crossed an ankle over his knee, waiting for Rick to begin. He felt uneasy, as if his stomach were filled with restless eels seeking escape. He always hated the unpredictability of these formal meetings. He watched Ariel cross her legs; hands calmly placed in her lap. She certainly didn't look nervous, or like she had anything to hide.

"Unfortunately," Rick started. "We need to speak with you today because it has come to our attention that Timothy has been physically abused."

Jaxon kept his eyes on Ariel, watching for any rehearsed reaction. What he saw was legitimate concern as every ounce of blood drained from her face leaving her paler than last night's full moon.

"I *beg* your pardon?" She sat forward, hands gripping her knees. "Are you telling me that someone at *this* school is hurting Timmy?"

"No." Rick shook his head. "We believe he has acquired these injuries out of the school grounds, as the children are monitored at all times whilst they are in our care."

Ariel shook her head, clearly confused. "Well, it didn't happen on my watch. He is with our family at all times." She looked across at Jaxon.

He watched her eyes widen as the realisation of what this meeting was about, finally dawned on her. A pink flush crept up her neck, filling her cheeks with a rosy hue as her eyes flashed with anger and disbelief.

Looking away from Jaxon, she spoke to Rick in quiet fury. "Are you implying that someone in our home is hurting Timmy?"

"We aren't implying anything, Miss Harper. But we do need to get to the bottom of who has abused him. Agreed?"

Ariel stood, shaking with anger. "Where is Timmy now? I need to speak with him."

Jaxon stood, blocking her path as she went to walk by him.

"Ariel," he said quietly. "Until we get some answers, you won't be seeing Timothy. Please, sit down."

"Are you serious?" She glared up at him.

"I'm afraid so." He could have sworn he saw flames flicker in her eyes.

"Get out of my way, *Mr* Williams. Right now." She clipped and went to walk by him again, but he took her upper arm feeling her smooth skin beneath his fingers.

"Jaxon," Rick warned. "Let her go. Miss Harper please, sit down. This is in Timothy's best interest."

Jaxon absently ran his thumb along the flesh under her arm before releasing her, watching as she ran her hands over her face, taking a deep breath.

"If I could just see Timmy and talk to him, this would all be cleared up." She looked up at Jaxon. "I know you don't know me that well. But you *do* know Steven, and the family that we come from. Do you *really* think someone in my home could hurt Timmy, and me not know about it?" Her blue eyes implored him to believe her.

He shook his head slowly. "I'm sorry, but we've got a job to do." He stared down at her, unblinkingly.

"Oh my God," she whispered, a startled look swept across her pretty features, as if she'd only just realised the seriousness of the situation. She took a step back. "You don't think *I* could be hurting Timmy, do you?"

He folded his arms, "Look Ariel when Timothy heard you were coming in, he broke down. He was clearly terrified, saying he didn't want you to get into trouble."

"That makes no sense at all," she shook her head frowning, clearly confused.

"The only thing we got out of him prior to that was that his friend, Sebastian, has told him it's not safe for him to tell us, or they'll get hurt?" Jaxon dropped his arms, pushing his hands into his pockets.

"Sebastian, again." Ariel whispered, pushing a red lock behind her ear, which had slipped from her bun. She looked at Jaxon, waiting.

"We just need to ask you some questions before we call DHS tomorrow."

"*DHS!*" Ariel cried. "Are you kidding me?" She walked away from Jaxon, towards the window to look out onto the small courtyard garden.

Jaxon exchanged a look with Rick, before Ariel turned towards him and said calmly.

"Listen, I completely understand that a child's welfare is your number one priority. Hell, I'm grateful for it. But to base a decision to call DHS, before you allow Timmy and I to speak to you, in a group setting is grounds for defamation. So, I ask you, what are we going to do about this situation. Because right now, I can't give you any answer that is going to make you believe that myself, or Timmy's siblings, have *not*, nor would *ever* touch a hair on his head!"

Jaxon rubbed his jaw, perplexed at their predicament. "I guess if we bring Ray, and Timmy in it wouldn't do any harm?" He asked Rick.

Rick nodded slowly. "I'll go get them." He got up from his chair and quickly left the room, closing the door behind him leaving Jaxon and Ariel in a face off.

He crossed his arms, wishing they hadn't found themselves in this situation, and wasn't sure of what to say. "Do you want to call Steven?"

She let out a dry laugh as she looked away from him, shaking her head. "Why would I want to call my uncle?"

He shrugged as the door burst open and Timmy rushed into the room. Ariel knelt down as he launched himself into her arms, crying.

"Ariel, I'm sorry, I'm sorry. Sebastian said it's going to get really bad now because they know!" He pushed his face into her neck and sobbed in despair.

"Shh, it's okay love. Everything is going to be okay; I promise." She gathered him close, as the three stood watching.

Jaxon sighed internally, as he heard her voice break on the last word.

Ariel

Ariel tried to compose herself, but this entire situation was overwhelming. She didn't know how much longer she could manage staying in this room with those judging eyes watching her every move. She kissed Timmy's head, before running a hand over his silky hair, holding him at arm's length so she could look into his eyes. Taking a deep breath, to stop her voice from quivering, she asked calmly.

"Timmy love, do you know why we're here this afternoon?" She asked the question in a way that the teachers wouldn't think she was leading him to answer to benefit her.

Timmy wiped the back of his hand under his nose, before nodding slowly.

"Can you please tell me?" She waited, anxious for the words that were about to leave his lips.

"I can't, Ariel."

"You have to, baby."

"I don't want you to get hurt, Ariel."

"But you've been hurt, haven't you?"

He nodded.

"Show me," she whispered.

He turned his back to her. "On my back," he said quietly.

She paused for a second, then carefully took hold of the hem of his shirt and slowly lifted it up to expose his back. She gasped in horror when she saw his wounds. Angry, red scratches tore into the flesh across his little shoulder blades and back. She covered her mouth, halting the cry that wanted to escape.

"Thank you for showing me darling," she offered him a watery smile when he turned back to face her. "We need to know who did that to you?"

Timmy shook his head. "I can't say his name," he whispered.

"His name," she sighed in relief, at least the firing squad heard from Timmy's lips that it was a 'he.'

"Please darling, I promise everything will be okay. Just tell us who did this to you,"

Everyone in the room seemed to be holding their breath, waiting.

Finally, Timmy answered, barely above a whisper. "The butcher did this to me."

Aril's eyes filled with tears at the thought of anyone putting their hands on her baby brother.

"The *butcher*?" Jaxon stepped forward, placing his hands on his hips.

Timmy turned in Ariel's arms, to lean back against her as he looked up at his teacher, nodding.

"Where does the butcher live, Timothy?" Jaxon asked.

"In our house." Timmy answered quietly.

The air whooshed from Ariel's lungs, and every hair on her body reacted to his statement. "Our house, Timmy?" She whispered, fighting back tears of fright.

He turned around to face her, nodding. "And Sebastian can't protect us Ariel, he did try though."

Ariel looked past Timmy, towards Jaxon, who was wearing a worried frown.

"Timothy," Ray stepped forward. "Sebastian isn't a student at this school. Where did you meet him? Do you know where he lives?"

Timmy looked up at his principal. "He lives in our house too."

Ariel could feel herself leaning to the side as her hearing faded. The heat and the unexpected words coming from Timmy was startling. Black spots invaded her vision and as she tipped further, large hands grabbed her around her waist lifting her up and placing her on the couch.

"Can you get some water please Ray?" She vaguely heard Jaxon ask before he began removing her cardigan, presumably to help cool her off.

She winced in pain, as his fingers brushed against her back, and heard him gasp.

"What the *hell* is this?" He asked in disbelief.

Rick crossed towards them, looking down at what Jaxon was pointing to, and Ariel heard his breath exhale in a rush as he exclaimed. "What's going on here, the wounds look identical?"

"Ariel?" Jaxon knelt in front of her, cupping her chin as Ray returned with a glass of water. Taking it from her, he raised it to her lips.

Ariel wrapped her fingers around his wrist, and swallowed the cool liquid as her head spun, trying not to enjoy his touch so much. He was being so gentle, considering ten minutes ago he had basically *accused* her of child abuse. *Bastard!*

His gaze bore into hers, before he quietly asked. "Who did this to you?"

"Are you sure it wasn't *me*?" she whispered sarcastically.

"Come now," his breath caressed her face, and her gaze dropped to his lips a mere inch away before her gaze met his once more. His fingers still cupped her chin, as the black and white spots began to fade.

When she didn't answer, he frowned. "You okay?"

She didn't answer but moved away from him to give herself space. He released her chin, and she noticed Timmy talking to himself in the corner.

"Timmy, what are you doing?"

Timmy turned to his sister. "I'm talking to Sebastian."

"Sebastian?" She whispered, as a chill ran down her spine. "What is Sebastian saying?"

"That things are going to get worse now," his voice wobbled.

"Excuse me, please." Ariel looked pointedly at Jaxon who was still kneeling in front of her, blocking her path to Timmy.

He stood and held out a hand. She hesitated briefly, before placing her hand in his and allowed him to assist her to her feet.

"Again," he asked quietly. "Are you alright?"

She looked up at him. "Can we go?" She asked without answering his question, hating the fact that she sounded close to begging. She was exhausted to the bone, and frightened tears filled eyes. "Can we please just go home now?"

Jaxon looked across at Ray who nodded, but Rick stepped forward.

"I think we need to clear a few things up first, don't you?" He looked from Ray to Jaxon. "Clearly, they have both been abused no doubt by the same individual. Their home is not a safe environment for Timmy."

Ariel let out a humourless laugh, which ended on a sob. "Don't you get it? It's not an 'individual'," she made air quotes with her fingers as she looked at Rick, who in turn raised an eyebrow.

"It's a ghost, an entity or *whatever* you want to call it. There is no living thing of flesh and bone in our home that would hurt *anyone*. Now, we are going!" She spat, sounding stronger. "Timmy, come on!" She held her hand out towards her brother who quickly stepped forward and grabbed it.

"See you tomorrow, Mr Williams." Timmy said quietly to his teacher, as Ariel led him from the room.

"See you, mate." Jaxon replied equally as quiet.

Ariel led Timmy to his school hook and grabbed his school, and swimming bag before marching back down the corridor to see Jaxon standing in the doorway, hands in his pockets as he watched them leave.

Chapter Seven
Ariel

"What the hell, Ariel?" Liv cried, leaping up from Ariel's bed two hours later after they'd eaten pizza and left the kids downstairs with a movie.

Ariel pulled her cardigan back on, before Liv stopped her. "Let it breathe," she said softly, pulling the cardigan off and throwing it onto the rocking chair. "How can this be?" she asked, clearly confused.

Ariel shook her head, pulling the band out of her hair, to let it slide over her shoulders.

"Things started happening when we moved in but, I assumed the sleepwalking and bad dreams were attributed to settling in here after the move." She shrugged, noticing her friend looked slightly terrified.

"We have to get you out of this house." Liv whispered, looking over her shoulder as if someone might be listening.

Ariel sighed. "And go where Liv? This is our home, a house that has been in our family forever."

"Well shit, I'm not saying sell the house, or burn it to the ground–although."

Ariel chuckled quietly. "Liv."

"Yeah, kidding. Why don't you pack the kids up and go stay at Steven's while he's away?"

"No!" A shout came from the doorway making Ariel and Liv jump.

"Timmy, I thought you were watching the movie." Ariel got off the bed and walked over to him. "Why don't you want to stay at Uncle Steven's?"

"Because Sebastian won't be safe, and if *he's* not safe, neither will we be."

Ariel sighed and knelt on one knee." Sweetheart, you can tell Sebastian that he can come with us. Don't you think that would be fun? All of us having a sleepover?" She ran a hand over his hair.

He shook his head, his bottom lip trembling.

"Timmy." She implored softly. "We can't stay here. I can't allow this thing to hurt you anymore. Please? Just for a night or two, we need a break."

"Yeah, Timmy." Wren said from behind them. "Let's just go for a couple of nights, it will be fun. You can sneak downstairs and pinch Liv's cookies." She met Ariel's curious gaze.

"I think we need a family meeting." Ariel looked over her shoulder at Liv.

"I tell you what. I'll go to Steven's, get the lights on and the spare beds made up, and I'll be waiting with the kettle on."

Ariel stood and turned to give her friend a hug. "Thanks Liv, I appreciate that."

Liv nodded. "Just don't be too long." She said, looking out the window at the darkening sky, making Ariel nervous.

"Sure." Aril agreed.

As Liv walked by Timmy, she grinned down at him. "You know what, I may just make you your own fresh batch of cookies. How'd you like that?"

Timmy gave her a genuine smile. "Yes please."

"Actually Timmy, why don't you go with Liv, and Wren and I will pack your bag, okay?" Ariel felt a prickle of unease and wanted Timmy out of the house as soon as possible.

"Okay," he agreed easily.

Liv held out her hand, which Timmy grabbed. Sending Ariel and Wren a quick smile and led Timmy downstairs. Ariel heard her say. "Family meeting Hawk, I'll see you soon."

"Sure thing," Hawk replied before the front door closed.

Ariel took Wren's hands and squeezed them lightly. "Have you been hurt, baby girl?"

"No, just scared."

Ariel saw the fear in her sister's eyes and felt guilt with the fact that two of her siblings' and been scared and hurt yet hadn't come to her about it.

"What scared you, love?"

Wren sighed. "I don't really know. I thought Timmy was in bed with me. He kept kicking me in the back when he was sleeping, and then he slapped my face. When I turned on the light to move him, there was no one there. Nothing at all." She shook her head.

Ariel could feel the hairs on her arms rise as Wren spoke. She tucked a wayward, silky strand behind Wren's ear, and said quietly. "There was something, though."

"Yeah, I guess there was."

"I'm sorry if I've let you down."

Wren gasped in surprise and shook her head in denial. "Don't say that Ariel, you haven't let anyone down."

"Why didn't you feel you could come to me?"

"And what would I have said?"

"Exactly what you just did." Ariel sighed, as Hawk yelled from the bottom of the stairs.

"Why, and where is this family meeting occurring?"

"Come on." Ariel led Wren downstairs to find Hawk leaning against the wall.

"Let's make a cuppa." As Ariel walked by Hawk, she heard him gasp.

"What the F… *hell* happened to your back?" He shouted.

She turned, smiling softly and placed a calming hand on his arm. "I'm okay, let's just put the kettle on first, please."

He nodded, frowning and exchanged a look with Wren before they followed her into the kitchen. Putting the kettle on, and grabbing three mugs, Ariel turned to face the twins.

"Okay, where to start. Firstly, we all know that I've been sleepwalking since we've moved in."

"But in fact, it hasn't really been sleepwalking." Wren cut in.

"Maybe not." Ariel sighed, dumping coffee in the mugs for her and Hawk, and a tea bag for Wren.

"Can you please just hurry up and tell me about your back?" Hawk pulled out the milk and placed it on the counter.

Ariel nodded, took a breath and begun. "I remember going to bed and then, I was in Grandma's painting studio. She was singing to me as she painted, it was sunny. I was so happy to be with her again." Ariel smiled. "Then she sensed something was coming. She looked utterly terrified, then apologised for not being able to protect us all before vanishing into mist and fell through the cracks in the floorboards."

"Creepy as hell," Hawk said, reaching for the kettle as it sang out.

"That wasn't the worst part," Ariel whispered as the horror of the dream resurfaced.

As Hawk filled their mugs, Ariel shared what she could remember of her nightmare. The room fell into an uneasy silence once she'd finished.

"So, it wasn't really a dream then, was it?" Wren asked, gripping her cup for warmth as the temperature in the kitchen seemed to have dropped.

Ariel put her mug down, and ran her fingers through her hair, pulling her long strands over one shoulder. "It can't have been if it had the power to hurt me."

"So, this thing said you have to 'pay her penance.' What the hell does that mean?" Hawk paced the kitchen.

"I don't know. But it has hurt Timmy too. He has the same marks on his back."

Hawk slammed his mug into the sink making Ariel jump, and Wren squeal.

"Hawk," Ariel sighed.

"Sorry," he ran a hand though his hair. "We need to get the hell out of here. Now."

Ariel nodded. "We're going to stay at Uncle Steven's, just for a couple of nights."

"Right." Hawk walked across to Ariel and pulled her into a hug, careful not to touch her back. "I'm sorry, sis," he mumbled quietly into her neck.

"Hey, it's okay. Everything is going to be okay. We just need to have a couple of nights good sleep and then we'll figure this all out."

Hawk loosened his grip to look down at her. "I wish you'd told me sooner."

She laughed. "I... I didn't really know what was happening." She shrugged.

"Has anything weird happened to you, Hawk?" Wren asked.

Hawk looked at his twin, shaking his head. "Nothing at all."

"I'm glad," she offered him a small smile.

"Let's grab an overnight bag each and head out. Timmy has probably eaten way too many cookies by now." Ariel sighed.

"Well deserved, don't you think?" Hawk said as he led the way upstairs.

"Actually, yes." Ariel headed into Timmy's room and pulled out his

SpongeBob SquarePants backpack, and threw in his pj's, a puzzle, and reading books before going into the bathroom to get their toiletries.

"I'm done," Wren said, reaching for Timmy's backpack. "I'll meet you downstairs."

"Thanks love." Ariel went into her room as a loud knocking sounded at the front door, making her jump. "Jesus," she whispered, laughing at her own nerves.

"I'll get it." Hawk said, walking past her bedroom with his schoolbooks, and a small overnight bag.

"I won't be long," she called, grabbing her nighty and a handful of clothes, shoving them in her oversized Guess handbag, before heading out of her room. Hearing Jaxon's voice drift up the stairs, she froze.

"I just wanted to check in and make sure Ariel and Timothy are doing okay, and if there was anything I could do?"

"Oh, that's so sweet of you." She heard Wren's sincere reply. "We're just heading to Uncle Steven's for the night, would you like to join us for a hot drink and some of Liv's cookies?"

"Oh *Jesus* Wren," Ariel whispered to the hallway walls. She didn't know if she was ready to look Jaxon William's in the eye after all that had transpired that day.

"Come on, sis." Hawk called patiently. "We've got an escort, hurry up."

"It's alright," came Jaxon's smooth reassurance. "No rush."

The grandfather clock bonged on eight o'clock, its chimes sending a chill down Ariel's spine. She hurried down the remainder of the stairs as the clock chimed for the eighth time, when an unseen force slammed into the middle of her back, sending her flying forward.

A scream of fright escaped her lips, her eyes automatically squeezing shut waiting to connect with the hard floor before strong arms caught her in mid-flight.

"Ariel!" Wren cried, as Hawk whispered. "Bloody hell!"

Ariel's back was throbbing, and she could hear Jaxon breathing heavily, his breath blowing tendrils of hair on the top of her head; his arms still tightly wrapped around her.

There was silence for a handful of moments before Jaxon quietly asked. "What was that?"

"Well, I didn't *trip*, if that's what you're asking." Ariel looked up at him as she stepped out of his embrace, seeing the worry in his gorgeous dark eyes.

"Can we *please* get out of here, *now*?" Wren cried.

"Good idea." Hawk grabbed her arm and dragged her to the front door, calling to Ariel. "Come on!"

When Jaxon gently took her hand and led her to the front door, she didn't object. Her back ached, and tears of frustration and fright threatened. How *dare* this 'thing' make them run from their home.

Hawk locked the front door, as Jaxon pointed to the jeep parked out the front.

"Jump in," he nodded, and waited for everyone to climb in. The drive to Steven's was a silent one. Pulling up in the back lane, Jaxon cut off the engine and turned to Ariel as the twins got out.

"Has Steven got whiskey inside?"

"I'm sure he has." She replied, meeting his intense gaze.

He remained still for a moment, his gaze dropping to her lips before they roamed her face, returning to her eyes. "Good. We need it. Let's get you inside."

Watching him get out of the jeep, she wondered about her feelings towards him. After the rollercoaster events of late, she was emotionally drained. She got out of the jeep, surprised to see him waiting with his hand held out. She wanted to take it, so she did, saying. "I'm okay."

"Yeah well, maybe I'm not," he replied honestly.

She glanced at him as they walked through Steven's back door, which led into her gallery.

"Bloody hell Ariel, the twins just told me what happened?" Liv said in way of greeting as she rubbed Ariel's arm, then smiled up at Jaxon.

"Joining us for a hot chocolate?"

He slowly shook his head. "Nope, we're having whiskey."

Liv's eyes brightened. "Oh, wonderful." She winked at Ariel. "I'll lock up," she said heading towards the back door.

Ariel went to pull her hand free, but Jaxon tightened his grip. They stood, staring at each other before she quietly assured him.

"I'm just going to put my bag upstairs, and settle the kids in." She enjoyed the calming effect of his thumb as it brushed across the flesh of her pulse point.

Liv linked her arm through Jaxon's, grinning up at him. "Why don't you help me find the hard stuff, and we'll set up for a cosy chat. Does that sound good?"

Jaxon squeezed Ariel's fingers gently, before releasing her hand and nodded at Liv. "Sure."

Ariel ran upstairs, sliding her hand along the thickly varnished handrail, relieved to be here for now. The voices of the three people she loved most in this world greeted her on the landing. Throwing her bag onto the spare bed she wandered down the corridor towards Steven's room. The twins were snuggled in the king-sized bed with Timmy perched in the middle, an overloaded plate of cookies sat on his lap.

She leaned against the doorway, swallowing tears that wanted to rise. These precious babies. Her *mother's* babies were hers to keep safe.

"Hey," Hawk caught her gaze. "We're okay, aren't we?" He looked at Timmy, then at Wren.

"Of course we are," Wren nodded.

"Wren said we could watch a movie on Netflix. Can we Ariel, even though it's late, and a school night?" Timmy's little face looked hopeful.

"Do you know what?"

"What?" Timmy bit into a cookie.

"I think we'll skip school tomorrow. What do you think about that?" Her heart lifted, seeing his face brighten.

"Whoopee!" He cried gleefully, spitting choc chip cookie over Steven's crisp donna cover.

Ariel laughed. "Careful, we don't want you choking."

"What about us?" Wren asked, cleaning Timmy's chocolate spittle up with a tissue.

"That's completely up to you love."

"I'm happy to go into class in the morning, I've got a double free period in the afternoon, so I should be home by one." Wren looked at Hawk.

He shrugged. "I'm going to hang out with this little scraper, and help Liv run the café. What do you say, sport?"

Timmy nodded and climbed out of the covers, spilling the cookies off the plate as he jumped on Hawk's lap winding his arms around his neck.

Ariel quickly wiped a tear that fell as she walked over to hug Wren, dropping a kiss on her head before reaching to collect the cookies. Placing the plate at the end of the bed, she reached over to Hawk and Timmy, running a hand over their hair.

"I'm going to be downstairs with Liv, and Mr Williams. If you need me, just yell."

"We'll be fine, sis. Don't worry." Hawk nodded.

"I love you all, so much."

"And we love you. Thanks for making us feel safe." Wren said quietly.

"We're all going to be okay. As long as we're together." Hawk said firmly.

Ariel forced another reassuring smile. "I know." She closed the door behind her, their banter about movie selections trailed off as she headed downstairs.

Hearing Jaxon's quiet voice surprisingly calmed her, as she walked into the café where he and Liv were settled on a couch, a bottle of Fireball

Whiskey on the coffee table between them.

Liv had thrown together a small platter of cheese and biscuits and had lit the candles around the room. A fleece blanket was folded on both couches. It was a comforting setting and being surrounded by her artwork on the walls and the bookshelves lined with books, made her instantly relax for what seemed like the first time in days.

"All tucked in?" Liv asked, pouring her a shot.

Ariel nodded as Jaxon unfolded a blanket, placing it across his legs and lifted the corner for her to sit under with an eyebrow raised in question.

She hesitated briefly. Never one for games, she usually went after what she wanted. Despite their complicated *whatever-it-was*, and the fact that earlier today he had hauled her over the coals, she was interested in Jaxon Williams. For better or for worse.

"Thank you," she said, and sat beside him. He placed the blanket over her legs and Liv pushed a whiskey towards her. She nodded her thanks as she picked up the shot glass and drew it to her lips, enjoying the cinnamon scent before she swallowed it, choking on the heat as it spilled down her throat.

Liv poured her another, then topped up Jaxon's.

They sat quietly, candlelight flickering about the room before the front window lit up as a semi-trailer slowly headed down Brooke Street before leaving them in candlelight once more.

"So, what are we going to do about your situation?" Jaxon asked, leaning back as he put an arm over the couch behind her shoulders.

"We?" Ariel took a small sip as she met his caramel gaze. Sitting so close to him, his face shadowed by the candlelight with his scent lingering was doing complicated things to her insides.

"Yeah, *we*. You don't think we're going to leave you alone in all of this, do you?" He raised a perfectly shaped eyebrow.

"Are they natural?" She blurted.

He looked across at Liv, who burst out laughing, before returning his gaze to hers, pining her in place as his knee brushed hers underneath the blanket. "You can find out for yourself."

He remained as still as a statue as she traced a fingertip over his dark brow, watching his eyes darken as she moved closer.

"Happy?" He asked quietly.

She pressed her lips together as she moved back. "Mhm." Taking another shot of whiskey as her gaze met Liv's.

"Right, let's get down to business. You've got some sort of ghoul in your house, and we need to get rid of it. So, who are we going to call?"

"Please, no one say, *Ghost Busters*." Ariel groaned.

"Actually…" Jaxon started, as Liv and Ariel turned towards him. "I was going to say, Reverend Matthews."

"You mean Josh Matthews? Liv asked before she popped a piece of cheese on a cracker and handed it to Ariel, who shook her head and poured another shot, passing the cracker to Jaxon.

He took the cracker, his fingers brushing hers as he did so.

Ariel watched with interest as he nodded to Liv, placing the cracker into his gorgeous mouth, his sexy lips moving hypnotically as he chewed slowly.

Sexy lips?

She'd obviously had too much Fireball, but in that moment didn't care. "I've never been to yours." *Why would I? Sheesh.*

"It's the old double story on Verdon Street." He dropped his arm off the couch and gently placed it around her shoulders.

"Opposite the town hall?"

"That's the one," he replied as Liv passed him a plate of crackers and cheese, which he balanced on his knee.

"So, Josh Matthews?" Liv steered the conversation back on track. "He must be close to one hundred by now?"

Jaxon smiled, running a fingertip in a slow circle around the top of Ariel's bare shoulder, unaware of what he was doing to her.

"Not quite ninety but, he's had one hell of a life. As a boy, he travelled with his Grandfather who was known to perform blessings around old mining towns, and miner's cottages that were said to be haunted. It was even rumoured that he performed an exorcism or two." His gaze swung to Ariel who was staring unapologetically up at him.

"Do you think he could help me with our house?"

"If he can't, he may know someone in Bendigo who can. I think if we dive back into the history of the house that may help too."

"That house has been in my family for over one hundred years. There should not be anything evil in it."

"That may be so, but there is, isn't there? And it had the power to hurt you and Timothy, didn't it." It wasn't a question.

She nodded, before asking quietly, "Did you really think that I'd hurt Timmy?"

He sighed loudly, looking across at Liv.

"Do you want me to go?" She asked.

He shook his head. "No Liv, I need you to spend the night here with them, if that's okay?"

"Of course it is. I'm not going anywhere." Liv poured them all another shot of fireball, then saluted her glass before throwing the contents down.

"Tell me?" Ariel demanded.

"Right." Jaxon steadily met her gaze, his fingers stilled from their silky dance upon her bare shoulder.

"I didn't want to believe it. I try not to judge, but my duty of care first and foremost is to safeguard the children. Not worry about stepping on anyone's toes or hurting anyone's feelings."

She was silent for a moment, then said, "A sticky situation."

"Maybe, but statistics speak too loudly about children's physical and emotional abuse in this country, especially for Timothy's age group. Feelings cannot come into play when a child's safety and well-being is my number one priority."

She nodded slowly. "Have you experienced a situation like this before?"

He looked down at the plate of crackers, as if debating what to say before picking it up and setting it on the table.

"I'd been teaching at a private boy's school in Melbourne for about five years. Great school, terrific programs, bright kids. There was a young boy, Henry Lee, who was top of his class. He was confident, carefree and had a good group of friends. Then overnight, he became withdrawn, started isolating himself from his friends and stopped participating in his favourite activities." Jaxon paused and finished off his shot before smiling at Liv. "I'd love a tea."

"Then tea you shall have." Liv got up and headed behind the counter to flick the hot water on. "Ariel love?"

Ariel shook her head. The whiskey was numbing the pain in her back.

"Go on, Jaxon." Liv nodded.

"Right," he sighed, before continuing. "I made myself available, along with the school councillor for Henry to come to us whenever he needed. I made sure he knew I'd be there for him, that I'd be a safe space whenever he felt like talking, and that anything he told me would be confidential."

"That must have been a relief for him?" Liv said.

Jaxon shook his head. "Not enough. His mother, Jenny, was on the school's committee. Always overly generous with her time and donations. Running every fundraiser. She went above and beyond to support the school and its students." He swallowed, obviously stressed with having to retell this story.

Ariel placed her hand on his arm. "It's okay if you don't want to tell it."

He looked down at her hand, before slowly linking his fingers through hers. She smiled shyly at him as he squeezed her fingers.

"Long story short, ladies. Henry's mother had been physically and emotionally abusing him, and she got away with it for too long. She used her wealth and position at the school to hide behind. By the time Henry couldn't take it anymore, he opened up to me via an email and confessed everything his mother had done to him over the past several months. Unfortunately, it was too late. She killed him and made it look like a suicide."

"Made it look?" Ariel raised an eyebrow.

"Henry's mother had no idea that Henry was recording everything that went on in his room, and if he hadn't, she would have gotten away with murder." He smiled sadly. "Smart kid."

Ariel did not want the details of how the mother killed her own child. It made her nauseous.

"A video email. How did he send that to you after the fact that she killed him?" She asked instead.

"That is one thing the detective on the case could not figure out. It had us all bamboozled to say the least. It was sent an hour after Henry's time of death."

Liv placed his tea on the table in front of him and said softly. "That's spooky yet brilliant?"

Jaxon nodded. "It's something alright."

"How devastating for you all." Ariel said quietly.

"Yeah, it was." He dropped his gaze towards his fingers, entwined with Ariel's as she gently ran her thumb back and forward across his flesh in a soothing gesture.

She sniffed back tears thinking of the poor boy, alone and unprotected. "I hope she got what she deserved."

"Not nearly enough," he said, his voice dangerously low sending a chill to run down her spine.

They held each other's gaze for a few moments before Liv cut in. "I'm going to get some sleep. Ariel, I'll see you upstairs. Goodnight Jaxon, thanks for your help."

"I'll be right behind you." Ariel called as Liv headed up stairs.

Jaxon checked his watch and nodded. "It's late, I should be going. School in the morning and all that," he reached for the tea that Liv had gone to the effort to make and took a few mouthfuls.

"I'm keeping Timmy with me tomorrow."

He placed the mug down on the table before turning towards her.

"That's fine. I'll deal with Rick and the DHS situation in the morning."

"What are you going to say? That Casper the ghost had a temper tantrum?" She raised an eyebrow.

He released a short laugh at her attempt at humour, before leaning forward to cup her chin. "I'll say it was all a misunderstanding."

"You don't call DHS over a misunderstanding." She quipped quietly, mesmerised by the colour of his eyes.

"I'll say whatever I have to, to protect you and Timothy," he whispered. "Of course, there has to be an incident report." His breath caressed her face.

"Good luck with that," she returned equally as quiet.

They sat staring at each other for a few moments; the sexual tension building. The attraction between them and the Fireball whiskey became too much for Ariel. She pushed him back against the couch and sat on his lap before she could think about what she was doing. Her warm core pulsed directly over his groin, feeling him hard beneath her as she stared into his eyes.

Leaning forward slowly, perhaps to give him the opportunity to stop her, she slid her lips over his.

He didn't stop her; long fingers stroked up her thighs, before sliding around her hips. She sighed against his lips, and she slid her tongue into his mouth, tasting a pleasant mixture of whiskey and tea. Running her fingers through his hair she tilted his head to deepen their kiss. She rocked against him feeling her knickers become slick with desire.

His hands tightened around her waist as he gently pressed her down against him, tilting his hips towards her.

She moaned, wanting his growing erection inside of her, stroking her core. She cried out softly as he sucked on her tongue, feeling her bud pulse as her nipples stiffened.

Reaching between them she cupped him through his jeans, making him gasp before he sucked in a breath and pulled away from her.

Disappointment filled her, but she was satisfied to see him looking frustrated too; his dark gaze filled with desire, his lips glistening wet.

His gaze dropped to her hand that was still cupping him through his jeans, before returning to hers.

She ran her fingers over him once more, before trailing her fingers up his chest towards his chin and leaned forward to brush a sweet kiss against his lips.

"Goodnight, Mr Williams," she whispered, before dropping another soft, closed-mouth kiss against his mouth before getting off his lap.

Walking away from him, she was surprised when he caught her around the waist and drew her back against his chest to nuzzle the back of her neck. She pushed her backside against his groin, moaning softly, gasping when his hand caressed her waist, before dropping lower to cup her moist, throbbing bud that was crying for release.

She wantonly moved against his fingers, knowing she should stop but for the life of her could not. "Jaxon, if you are not going to take me right here, right now, please just stop."

And he did; Instantly. His fingers froze, then left her pulsing body; his lips withdrew from her neck.

She was simultaneously disappointed and relieved as she turned around to face him.

"Ariel, I want you. That goes without saying. But we should take things slow." He cupped her cheek, before brushing his lips across hers one final time. "If you need me, my number is on the counter."

"Thanks. Sorry about…" she shrugged.

He laughed dryly, "Don't you dare apologise for that. It was amazing, and you can count on the next time being better. But I'm not going to take advantage of you."

"You wouldn't be."

"Yes, I would be," he said, as he ran a hand down the length of her silky mane. "You've been through hell and back today, on top of our friend *Mr Fireball*." He smiled. "I'll see you tomorrow, okay?"

She nodded.

"Now, run upstairs. I'll turn the lights off and lock up."

Her heart thumped at his thoughtfulness and reached for one final kiss; heart melting when he met her halfway to drop a smouldering promise of what-was-to-come against her lips.

She smiled, before turning on her heel, and ran up the stairs, grateful not to be running up in the dark. She wasn't ashamed in the slightest that she slept with the light on all night, and a smile on her face.

Chapter Eight
Ariel

Ariel spent the following day straightening up the gallery, pleased to have sold two large canvases, and made a booking for one of the locals who wanted a generation portrait of the women in her family. Ranging from her ninety-three-year-old Grandmother, down to her two-year-old granddaughter, it was a project Ariel was excited to dive into and enjoyed the twenty-minute conversation with Mrs Roycroft.

Wandering into the café at lunch time, she was pleased to see Hawk getting stuck into some schoolwork, which he had spread out on the coffee table. Timmy was sitting on a stool at the front counter with Liv and was talking to Ena Musgrove, the towns eighty-seven-year-old darling and Paul's Nana. She delivered homemade Mulberry jam to her favourite people once a year and was telling Timmy how disappointed she was that his uncle wasn't in to personally accept her offering.

"Hello, Mrs Musgrove." Ariel smiled warmly.

"Hello dear, where is that uncle of yours off to now?"

Ariel loved seeing the twinkle in the elder lady's eyes, and hoped when she reached that age she'd have as much spark about her. "He'll be back in town by the weekend."

"He is such a good boy. Always was. Your Grandmother was so proud of him, not like that scoundrel Travis Lockwood and his traitorous father. They broke her heart into a million pieces they did." Ena reached for her teacup, rings glistening on every finger as the sunlight streamed through the window.

"Travis Lockwood?" Liv asked. "I don't recall him."

"Oh, it was before your time, love. Him and his father moved into the Harper's home. He was around the same age as Sparrow. Darling girl she was." She pushed gnarled fingers, twisted with rheumatism arthritis, through her silver curls, frowning in distaste. "I knew he was no good from the first moment I laid eyes on him but your Grandmother, bless her soul, had a heart that was too soft for this world, and a nature too forgiving."

Ariel exchanged a look with Liv, before asking, "How did they break my Grandmother's heart?"

The elderly lady put her teacup down and slowly swivelled around on the stool to look Ariel in the eye, blinking slowly, before saying quietly, "That my dear, is not for me to say."

Ariel's curiosity soared. Any story pertaining to her mother and family was important to her. She tried a gentle smile, "It's okay Mrs Musgrove, you can share anything about my Grandmother with me."

Mrs Musgrove reached out and gently stroked Ariel's cheek. "I'm sorry my dear. That, I cannot do."

Ariel could see the steely determination in Ena's watery blue eyes and smiled kindly. "I understand. Would you like Timmy and I to walk you home?"

"Why yes," she turned twinkling eyes towards Timmy. "That would be delightful. Ready young man?"

Timmy nodded and leapt off his stool to retrieve her wheely walker, and brought it close to her, as Ariel held her hand and helped her off the stool.

"Hawk, I'm just walking Mrs Musgrove home," she called.

"No worries," he said before turning back to his schoolwork.

"Bye Mrs Musgrove," Liv called, as they led Ena from the café.

The gentle breeze carried the scent of gum leaves, warmed by the sun as they began the short walk to Ena's house. Ariel was deep in thought about the men who had stayed with her Grandparents, and wanted to ask Ena more about them, but didn't have the heart to break up her and Timmy's conversation.

"Can I Ariel?" Timmy tugged on her hand, breaking her train of thoughts.

"What love?"

"Can I do some baking with Mrs Musgrove before Paul gets home from school?"

"Oh, I don't know…"

They came to a stop in front of Ena's double story, white bricked home, where a cottage garden crammed every inch of the front yard, leaving a tidy path towards the front door.

"It really isn't a problem dear. Paul will have missed Timmy at school today."

"Please Ariel?" Timmy jumped up and down, "we're going to make scones and gingerbread."

Ariel smiled. "If you're sure it won't be any trouble, that would be wonderful."

"No trouble at all dear, come on young man." Ena said, turning her wheely walker towards the path.

"Thank you. Timmy, make sure you and Paul help out with the cleaning up, okay?" she called to his retreating back as he helped Ena down the path.

"Of course!" He snorted.

Ariel chuckled as they disappeared behind a mauve Salvia bush, which hid the front door from her view. She was happy that Timmy would get to spend some time with his friend.

Crossing the road, she waved to a passing car and contemplated going home. She had commissions she wanted to finish and felt safe enough being in her studio. Nothing untoward had happened in there, and the chooks needed some TLC. She set off at a brisk pace, enjoying the peace and quiet and turned into her street. She paid attention to her physical response as she neared the house, relieved that there seemed to be no negative vibes. Jogging down the gravelled alleyway, heading through the back gate, she wandered between the lavender bushes towards the chook pen.

"Hello girls," she called as they clucked at the sight of her. She unlocked the gate and checked on the feed trays and water dishes. Still full, she lifted the hutch lid and pulled out several eggs, placing them in the little basket they kept handy by the door.

"Thank you, lovelies. Food scraps coming soon, I promise." She cooed, before locking the gate and headed towards her studio.

Stepping in, she sighed in pleasure. Being in her creative space was like stepping into a cathedral. Calming and nurturing for her soul. And, on top of a decent sleep in what felt like forever, she had a new burst of energy. Placing the egg basket onto the table, she sent Hawk a text message saying where she was, hoping he wouldn't be worried about her being home alone.

Hitting play on her Tidal, she tied her hair back and strolled across to select a canvas, before placing it on her easel. Grabbing her commission book, she checked her client list, and realised the next commission was a three-piece canvas for a five-star restaurant in Wilsons Prom. A pelican scene of her choosing.

"Fun times," she sang, dropping the book down to clap her hands before rubbing them together enthusiastically. She allowed the music to sweep her up in its instrumental melody as she lined three canvases up, the same height, but different widths.

Selecting several tubes of paint, she squeezed a cobalt blue onto her palette with a mix of white and black, and stood back for several minutes staring at the blank canvas, allowing it time to speak to her. And then it did, right on cue as the music peaked.

She dipped her brush, and swept it along the horizon, creating a sky so blue where a lone seagull would be carried by the breeze. The ocean melded with the horizon before gentle waves rolled to the foreshore holding two pelicans lovingly on gentle white caps. Those waves would fall softly against what would be, white sand scattered with seashells where three more pelicans would stroll along the shore; eyes filled with stories of an ocean before mankind made their imprint.

After a few hours, she sighed in satisfaction as it started to take shape. Dropping her paintbrush into a paint tin filled with turps, she grabbed an old apron to wipe her hands on. Leaning against the table she wished she had a coffee to make this moment complete.

Looking out the window she noticed the afternoon sun had lowered in the sky, and decided she'd earned that coffee after all. Dropping her apron on the table she headed out the door and jogged down the path before stepping up onto the decking. Reaching up into a hanging basket under the bullnose veranda, she grabbed the spare key and brushing the dirt off, pushed it into the keyhole.

"Honey, I'm home." She sang out joyfully to chase her own nerves away, as she walked into the kitchen to turn the kettle on. Grabbing a mug and a teaspoon, she dumped coffee in, singing along to the song that was spilling out from her studio. Glancing around the kitchen, she felt a peace settle over her and filled up the small watering can and watered her plants.

"There you go, loves." She stroked their leaves as the kettle boiled, and after they had all been watered, poured her coffee.

Taking that first mouthful after three hours of painting was like heaven. She headed out of the kitchen towards the back door and grabbed the door handle to pull it shut behind her, only to run into a solid wall of nothing.

"Jesus!" She cursed, gasping as hot coffee sloshed over the side of the mug, burning her hand. She shifted the mug into her other hand to blow on her scolded skin, before placing it on the hallway table.

Swallowing, she wiped her hands along her thighs, staring out towards the yard before raising her palm and pushed it towards the invisible barrier.

Her palm hit a solid wall and her heart thumped uncomfortably.

"This is not happening," she whispered, spinning around and heading down the hallway towards the front door. "Grandma, this *cannot* be happening." She called, as she unlocked the door and hesitantly took a step forward. Once again, she met with a solid wall of nothing.

"*No, no, no...*" The chant burst from her lips as she rushed towards the loungeroom and across to a window. She unlocked the latch and lifted the window, taking a deep breath and tried to push her hand outside; it too, met a solid invisible wall.

"*Shit.*" Shutting the window and turning the latch, she reached for her mobile in her back pocket, when her fingers met with nothing.

"Double shit," she hissed in frustration, realising she had left it in the studio playing her music. Biting her thumb nail she walked stiffly towards the back door, wanting her coffee. Rounding the corner her blood froze and every hair on her body rose to a stiff peak.

"Not again," she whispered, horrified.

The mug was upside down, the coffee frozen in its pour. She expected it to fall at any moment, but it remained frozen in mid-air.

She folded her arms anxiously, fingers digging into the flesh of her arms, waiting for a miracle to break the tension that was building around her. The air was ice cold, and her breath came out in little cloud puffs.

Turning, she ran upstairs to her room and reached for her winter coat, grateful for its fleecy interior to warm her icy skin. She didn't know what to do, how to get out, and the air seemed to be growing colder by the minute.

She dove towards her bed and pulled the doona back, sliding underneath it and tucked it tightly around her as she curled into a tight, shivering ball. She closed her eyes and hoped

it would all be over soon before she fell into an uncomfortable sleep. She didn't know how long she had slept when she heard Timmy cry out.

"Ariel? *Ariel.*"

She bolted up in the bed, throwing the doona off before she raced out of her room.

"Timmy?" The house was still freezing. She frowned when he didn't respond.

"Timmy, where are you?"

"Ariel," he called from his room.

Opening his door, she was relieved to see him sitting on his bed, pale-faced and shivering. She walked over to run a hand over his hair.

"How did you get in the house love?"

He didn't answer, just stared up at her with his big dark eyes filled with terror.

"What's wrong?" Her voice shook, resentful that they were both frightened in their own home. She sucked in her bottom lip when Timmy pointed down to under his bed.

She nodded to let him know she understood, and took a step back, before slowly kneeling to her hands and knees. Taking a deep breath and praying to her Grandmother and mother for safekeeping, she lowered herself to peek underneath the bed.

She frowned in confusion and slight terror at the sight before her.

Timmy was laying under the bed, flat on his tummy trying to make himself small. His eyes were squeezed shut.

"Timmy?" The air crackled as Ariel whispered his name.

His eyes shot open, and as his gaze met hers; a tear fell from his eye as he whispered in horror. "Ariel, there's something on my bed."

Her eyes widened in fear and for once, she wished she wasn't the adult in charge. She felt like crying and her body felt weak with her own terror that was building rapidly.

"Ariel?" He mouthed her name.

She nodded once and mouthed. "Stay there," before pulling in a quiet breath and slowly pushed herself to her feet. The scream that burst from her lungs, didn't sound human.

The small figure that had sat on Timmy's bed moments before, was now standing. Its head brushing against the ceiling, red eye's protruded from black eye sockets and hung like water balloons before they eerily began filling with liquid at an alarming rate. She stumbled back as Timmy whispered from under the bed.

"Ariel…"

"Timmy, come out… quickly." She knelt on one knee not taking her eyes off the *thing* as she motioned for Timmy to come out. As he did, she grabbed him under the arm and dragged him towards the door and went to step out. Once again, her exit was blocked by an invisible barrier.

"No." Ariel cried desperately. "*No, no, no…*" The *things* eyes were expanding rapidly and had surpassed the size of jumbo beanbags. Ariel could barely catch her breath as they continued expanding to all corners of the room, reaching closer to her and Timmy with every terrified breath that she took.

She felt bile rise in her throat as the engorged eyes appeared to have movement within them. Something was floating around behind the off milky-white surface.

"What the hell is this?" she whispered, more to herself as she gripped Timmy's hand for dear life, pushing him between her and the blocked doorway.

"Ariel?" Timmy cried sadly,

"It's okay, love," she whispered, hating the lie.

"Ariel, I'm sorry, but you have to see it to make it stop."

She didn't want to take her eyes off the abnormality that was about to press against them, but Timmy's statement confused her, and she quickly glanced down at him.

"What?" She whispered as her eyes met his. A whoosh of breath left her lungs.

She cried in fright and hurriedly stepped away from what was no longer Timmy.

The small figure before her stood dressed in dirty overalls and a torn shirt. A brown cap sat crookedly on his head, and boots with toes poking out of holes, encompassed small, dirty feet.

She looked between the boy and the swirling eyes that were about to pin her to the wall; her heartbeat out of control–like a cornered wild brumby. Surely, she'd drop dead of a heart attack at any moment.

"Who *are* you?" She managed to choke out.

"I'm Sebastian, and you have to see," he cried, pointing at the revolting eyes just as they pressed against them.

Ariel took a deep breath before she was encompassed by the jelly like nightmare, and to her absolute disgust was sucked into an avalanche of milky ice-water that swept her up in a current of filth. Eviscerated organs and body parts surrounded her as the milky water turned red. She couldn't cry out for fear of swallowing the filth she was submerged in and wondered briefly what had happened to Sebastian.

Her head emerged for a few moments, and relief filled her as she was able to pull in a lungful of air. She couldn't suppress the groan of disgust as the unbearable stench of death surrounded her, coating her tastebuds before she was dragged back under the bloody current of gore.

Her back scraped against jagged stones, which tore at her flesh. Terror filled her as a hand grabbed her ankle, holding her in place as objects slammed into her as they continued along the gushing current.

She pulled her leg with all her might, trying to escape the clutching hand that held her underneath the water as her lungs screamed for air. The fingers around her ankle were joined by another set, and slowly, she could feel them moving up her leg scrapping along the flesh of her belly, breasts, to then wrap around her throat.

Her eyes burst open, and her vision filled with red, before a black gaping hole opened up to swallow her, as crackling laughter filled her ears before a voice screamed in her face,

"*You must pay her penance!*" She struggled against those fingers and used whatever air was left in her lungs to scream, swallowing, and choking on the putrid water as her fingers clawed at her throat.

She thrashed desperately as the last tiny precious air bubble escaped her lungs. The last thing she saw as her head lolled back was the satisfied smile of a man who wore evil far too well.

Jaxon

Jaxon had walked Paul home to his Grandmothers, as requested by his mother who was working overtime in Bendigo, when he saw Hawk Harper racing down the street towards him, wearing a worried expression.

"Mr Williams, I can't get into our house, and I heard Ariel screaming!"

Jaxon paused for a split second before turning to bolt past Hawk, and towards the direction of their home. Tearing down the back laneway he threw open the gate and jogged up the tidy path before leaping up the stairs towards the back door. He could hear Ariel screaming, before silence ensued.

The wire screen door protested as loudly as Ariel's scream, and a prickle of unease crept up his spine. As he stepped through the back door a coffee cup flew at him from nowhere, and cold liquid dripped down his shirt.

"You got in!" Hawk cried as he raced past Jaxon, and up the stairs.

"Seems so," Jaxon said drily, wiping the coffee off his shirt as he ran up the stairs behind Hawk, hoping Ariel was simply having a nightmare.

Hawk bolted into Ariel's room, before turning towards Timmy's.

"*Jesus Christ*," he cried, his voice laced with terror.

Jaxon rushed in behind Hawk, and the air vanished from his lungs. Ariel was suspended in mid-air, back arched, fingers clawing at her throat, her face turning bluer by the second.

"Ariel!" Hawk yelled as he grabbed her ankle. She immediately fell limp, arms falling by her side when he made contact. Jaxon leapt forward and caught her around the waist.

The two men exchanged a look of uncertainty as Jaxon placed her down on Timmy's bed, wiping a hand over her brow. She looked peaceful, pretty even, despite the fact she was feverish and pale. Pressing a finger to her pulse point, he was relieved to find it steady. She appeared to be sleeping, which was disturbing as only a second ago she'd been thrashing about in mid-air, against a force he hadn't been able to see.

Placing a hand on her shoulder, he gently shook her. "Ariel, can you hear me?"

"It that a good idea?" Hawk asked in a shaky voice.

Jaxon looked over his shoulder at the handsome young man who was rubbing his chest. He turned, placing a reassuring hand on his shoulder.

"She seems fine, but maybe a cup of tea with sugar for when she wakes?" He thought a task would ease the young man's anxiety.

Hawk nodded stiffly. "Yeah, good idea," he said, before turning to head downstairs.

Jaxon let out a long breath as he turned to the sleeping beauty on the bed and was relieved when she started to stir.

"Ariel?" He wiped damp hair from her brow. "Are you okay?"

She began coughing violently before rolling onto her side and threw up an unthinkable amount of blood, whimpering as her body shook.

He cringed as he rubbed her back, horrified to see a mass of black worms wriggling about the vomit.

"Ariel?" He wasn't sure if she knew he was there.

She sat up, covering her face with her hands and started crying.

He looked away from the disturbing pile of vomit and put his arm around her shoulder.

"Ariel, what can I do?"

"Get me out of this room, please," she whispered through her fingers.

He swept her up in his arms, thinking she felt far too light, and carried her towards the bathroom. Sitting her gently on the edge of the bath, he waited in silence, giving her time to process what had happened. The minutes continued ticking by.

"What happened?" He asked finally, not wanting to push her but needing to know.

She shook her head, shaking.

He rubbed a hand slowly up and down her back to comfort her as her breathing steadied; her skin felt like ice.

"Do you think a warm shower would help?"

She nodded once but made no sign of moving.

"Hawk is making you a cup of tea."

She nodded again. He reached across and grabbed a face washer from the side of the tub, and taking her wrist, gently pried her hand away from her face and pressed it into her fingers. His heart stopped beating for a split second as she looked up at him, eyes filled with confusion and fear.

"I don't know what's happening here." She whispered, shaking her head as a tear fell.

"I know whatever happened must have been terrifying. But we will figure this out."

"Will we?"

"Yes."

"How?"

"Have some faith."

She shook her head and ran the face washer over her tear-stained face.

"How did you get inside the house?"

He shrugged. "I just opened the back door and walked right in."

"I couldn't get outside. Not through any door or window. Then I heard Timmy's voice, but it wasn't Timmy, and then–something else was there, something–unexplainable." Her voice broke.

"It's okay," he could feel her anxiety building and did what he did to his students when they became overwhelmed; he crouched down to her level.

"We will get to the bottom of this situation, but first things first. You've had a shock and a hot shower will help," he suggested.

She grabbed at his hands, shaking her head hurriedly. "Please, don't leave me."

"Hey," he soothed in what he hoped was a calm tone. "I won't, I promise. I will be right outside the door, okay?"

Her grip was tight on his hands as she stared at him before relaxing her hold slightly, sniffing once as she nodded.

"Good," he forced a smile.

Hawk walked in with a cup of tea. "Here you go sis," he said quietly, putting the tea down on the stool and crossed towards her. Folding her in his arms, he rocked her to and fro, before asking. "What happened?"

She shook her head against his chest.

Jaxon left the siblings to have a moment as he walked back into Timmy's room, to inspect the contents that Ariel had thrown up. He screwed up his nose at the stench, and the wriggling mass within it. *Rotten meat.*

Heading back into the bathroom he was happy to see Ariel take a mouthful of tea as Hawk left to get a fresh towel, before returning to place it on the towel rack.

"Hawk, can you bring me up a clean, empty container with a lid please?"

Hawk turned to Jaxon and nodded. "Sure," he looked at Ariel, before leaving the room.

"Okay," Jaxon said gently. "Shower time."

Ariel placed her tea down, and he watched a pink heat rise up her slender throat, to fill her cheeks.

That's better.

"You're going to be just out there?" she asked in a quiet voice.

"I am."

"Leave the door open, please."

"Ariel, I'm not going anywhere."

She nodded reluctantly, and he smiled before stepping out of the bathroom and into the hallway.

Sighing, he leaned against the wall folding his arms. What the hell was going on in this house?

Hawk jogged up the stairs, holding a glass jar. "This okay?"

"Perfect. Can you stay here for a second?"

"Of course."

Jaxon nodded before heading into Timmy's room. Scooping up the vile puddle, he screwed the lid on tight before ripping the pillowcase and doona off Timmy's bed. He headed back to Hawk, dropping the jar into the pillowcase.

Passing him the doona he said. "Toss that in the wash would you?"

"Sure thing," Hawk took the doona and headed towards the stairs, before turning to Jaxon. "How do we stop whatever's going on here?"

Jaxon saw the worry in the younger man's eyes, and wished he could comfort him as he had Ariel a few minutes ago.

"I don't know exactly mate, but I do know someone who might. If it's all right with you I'd like to ask him to come by and have a look around?"

Hawk nodded slowly. "That sounds good."

"I've no doubt that it will help."

Hawk pushed long fingers through his jet-black hair, moving it out of his eyes.

Handsome kid.

"We love this house and honestly being scared of whatever is in it, is starting to piss me off."

Jaxon released a low laugh at Hawk's honesty. "Fair enough. Well, I promise you this, I'll be right here with you while we figure it out."

Hawk bunched up the doona as he stared at Jaxon. "Thanks for that."

"You're welcome."

"No, really. Ariel has been holding us all together since our mum died, and yeah, Uncle Steven is a legend. But it's nice to know we can count on someone else to help Ariel."

Jaxon nodded as the water in the bathroom stopped running.

"Happy to help," he rubbed his jaw as Hawk headed downstairs, and turned as Ariel called his name.

"Jaxon?"

"I'm right here."

She stepped out of the bathroom, and he forced his eyes on hers; not the steam that radiated off her skin, which looked as smooth as porcelain. Green eyes still too round with fear for his liking, stared up at him trustingly.

"I just had an awful thought." She whispered, pushing wet tendrils off her face, her other hand holding the towel to her chest.

He tilted his head to the side, placing his hands on his hips. "Oh?" he asked softly.

"What if we can't leave the house? What if we are all locked in here?"

"One way to find out?" He turned around and was about to head down the stairs when she grabbed his arm.

"No, please."

He turned to face her.

"Don't leave me." She barely whispered.

"Sorry," he placed his hand on top of hers. "Why don't you get dressed and we'll test it out together?"

She nodded, looking down at his hand on top of hers.

He squeezed her hand lightly, before she drew hers away and took a step backwards towards her bedroom.

"You'll be right here?" She asked.

He leaned against the wall and folded his arms. "Sure will be."

"Okay, thanks."

Her vulnerability tore at his heart, and he smiled reassuringly before she turned and to go into her room. He tried not to imagine what her perfect, naked body looked like beneath her towel.

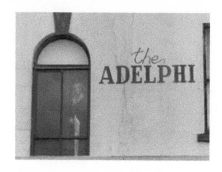

Chapter Nine
Ariel

A riel pulled the brush through her hair, before piling it over one shoulder to tie it back with a black ribbon. Spaying a spritz of perfume, she frowned, hating that her hand shook as she placed the perfume bottle down. She leaned closer to the mirror to inspect her pale features.

"Pull yourself together," she whispered to her reflection.

"You okay in there?" Jaxon's voice caressed her from the corridor, making her shiver.

"Yeah," she called, stepping over to push her feet into low heels.

She saw his eyes widen in approval as she stepped into the corridor, and was glad she chose the purple halter top, knowing it offset her skin and hair perfectly.

"Feel better?" He asked softly.

She nodded, looking away from his lips as a hum of electricity passed between them.

"Let's go and see if we can get out of here." He said taking her hand; a pillowcase clutched in his other.

"What's in there?" She asked as they headed downstairs.

"Something ominous," he shook his head before she could ask the next question. "You don't want to know."

She smiled tiredly, slightly amazed that she could. "How did you know what I was going to ask?"

"I work with curious minds, it's my job to pre-empt questions."

"Mhm." She mused as they reached the bottom step, enjoying the feel of her hand tucked safely in his.

The sound of the washing machine reached her ears before Hawk stepped out of the laundry. He looked relieved when he saw her.

"You look better sis. Ready to get out of here?"

"Yes, hopefully we can," she eyed the back door dubiously.

Jaxon squeezed her hand reassuringly. "Come on," he said, leading the way.

She sensed him hesitate briefly before stepping through the back door, taking her with him. She could have wept with relief that she was free of the house, and once again felt resentment at being made to feel this way by whatever it was that was tormenting them.

"I'm starving." Hawk said.

"Just let me grab my phone and we'll get tea sorted," she went to tug her hand free from Jaxon's, but he didn't release her. "I'm okay, nothing bad has happened outside of the house." She assured him.

He remained still for a moment as he stared down at her unblinking, before releasing her hand. "Let's make it quick then, shall we?"

She nodded and turned down the narrow path to her studio and raced inside to grab her phone before sliding the door shut behind her.

"Ready?" Jaxon asked, reaching for her hand again as he walked backwards towards the gate.

She smiled gratefully as she took his hand. "I am."

After tucking Timmy into bed with enough kisses and cuddles to last a lifetime, Ariel returned downstairs to sit between Wren and Hawk on the couch.

Silence was their companion as they sat sipping hot drinks, each deep in thought about what had been happening at the house. Liv had left after tea, and Jaxon had left earlier to locate Reverend Matthews and have a conversation.

Wren sighed loudly as she dropped her head back against the couch.

Ariel patted her knee. "We'll figure this out, love."

Wren turned a worried gaze towards her before saying. "I thought Sebastian was supposed to be a good guy?"

"Timmy seems to think so."

"Then why did he nearly drown you?"

Ariel shook her head. "I don't think he was trying to hurt me. He was trying to show me something, tell me something?"

"Poor kid," Hawk muttered around his cup.

"*What?*" Wren squeaked indignantly, leaning around Ariel to glare at her twin.

"What?" Hawk raised an eyebrow. "He is a little ghost-kid who's stuck in a nightmare," he shrugged. "He just wants someone to hear him out, to tell them what's going on."

"I wouldn't mind someone telling *me* what's going on." Ariel and Wren jumped at the quiet voice that startled them.

"Uncle Steven," Ariel placed her mug on the table, turning to look behind them. She laughed nervously, holding a hand against her chest.

"Jesus," Hawk chuckled.

"You scared us." Ariel got up to hug him hello but stopped short at the look on his face. His lips were drawn in a tight line; arms folded. He was clearly pissed off.

She tilted her head to the side and mirrored his stance. "Who rang you?"

"It *should* have been you," he replied. He obviously didn't want to betray his informer.

Hawk stood up. "Uncle Steven, if you knew what Ariel had been through, what we've all been through recently, you might want to cut us a little slack."

Steven looked across at Hawk, then Wren, before meeting Ariel's gaze. Letting out a long breath he dropped his arms and reached for Ariel.

"Sorry," he muttered as she stepped into his embrace.

She put her arms around him and was surprised to feel him trembling. "Uncle Steven?"

He shook his head, tightening his arms before reaching towards Wren, and Hawk. "Come here," he said gruffly.

Wren got up of the couch, followed by Hawk and Steven wrapped his arms around them all.

After a few moments he said quietly, "You all need to sit, there's something I need to discuss with you."

Hawk patted his uncle on the back before going over to the coffee machine. "I'll make you a coffee."

"No mate," Steven called. "I'll need a stiff drink for this one." He turned to Ariel. "Want to join me?"

She nodded. "Just one." She was grateful Liv had restocked his supply, but noticed he'd grabbed the Honey Whiskey.

Wren and Hawk sat on the couch opposite Steven, and Ariel sat beside her uncle tucking her feet up as she faced him, watching him pour two fingers into each glass, before passing her one.

"Thanks," she said quietly, worried about his solemn expression.

He took a mouthful before starting.

"Is Timmy asleep?" he asked.

"Yes," Wren answered.

Steven took a sip of whiskey before asking, "Have you ever wondered why your mother stopped bringing you here?"

Ariel nodded noticing the twins do the same. Steven nodded slowly too, before continuing.

"When I was a baby, mum and dad rented a couple of the rooms out to a widower, Mr Lockwood. His wife died in a car accident, or so my parents were told, and he came to us with his son, Travis." Steven rubbed the glass back and forth in his palms, watching the brown liquid swirl around. He remained silent for a few minutes.

Ariel exchanged a worried look with the twins. "Uncle Steven?"

Steven blew out a breath. "Right, sorry. I haven't spoken about all of this since your mother died." He shrugged, before continuing.

"Long story short, Mr Lockwood was a murdering psychopath, and raised his son to be the same, if not worse. Travis, Sparrow, and I, along with Jaxon, grew up together and were as close as any siblings could be. And for a long while we were all the best of friends who basically ran the neighbourhood. There's nothing like growing up in the country, especially in a tiny town. There's a type of freedom you have, unlike in the city." He swallowed the remainder of his whiskey then poured another two fingers.

"Sometimes too much freedom. Too much space to get away with things before people start noticing," he ended quietly.

Ariel's mouth grew dry, and she swallowed the whiskey, trying not to grimace as the spirit temporarily set her throat on fire.

"What happened?" Hawk asked, sounding impatient.

Steven sighed as he sat back, crossing an ankle over his knee as he ran his fingers through his hair, meeting Hawk's gaze.

"What happened was years of misery. Missing tourists, vanishing children around the Loddon Shire." He shook his head. "And our household was hiding the monsters who presented kind faces to the rest of the community." His tone held a bitter note as he looked at Ariel, then the twins. "I don't know if you two should hear the rest of what I have to say."

The twins looked from Steven to Ariel. "I think we can manage whatever you have to say just fine." Hawk answered for both of them.

"Wren?" Ariel asked her sister, knowing her gentle soul may not be able to stomach hearing what was to come.

Wren blinked slowly, clearly unsure if she wanted to hear the rest of the story or not.

"Go to bed love, if it's important I can tell you an edited version tomorrow." Ariel suggested.

Wren nodded, shooting to her feet and all but ran up the stairs.

Steven remained silent until they heard the bedroom door close above them. Placing his glass on the table, he placed his elbows onto his knees and lowered his head into his hands to rub his face.

"Uncle Steven, you can tell us. We're here for you." Ariel said quietly.

"Yeah, I'm sure the worst part is over. That poor Grandma had a couple of murdering *pricks* under her roof, and Grandpa didn't notice."

"Hawk," Ariel shot him a warning look, not wanting Steven to feel worse than he looked right at this moment.

Hawk shrugged sheepishly.

Steven raised his head and met Hawk's gaze, before turning to face Ariel.

"Your mother was a free spirit. She was never afraid of anything," he smiled sadly. "Even when she should have been," he whispered. "Being that much older than me, she was very protective. She'd often tell mum and dad that there was something off about Mr Lockwood. And as the years went by it was evident that there was something *very* off about his son too. Only by then, it was too late."

"What has this got to do with the house being haunted?" Ariel was getting a horrid feeling that this story was about to go somewhere she didn't want to hear about.

Steven got to his feet and paced beside the bookcase. "The house has always been haunted. But it was never a negative energy, not really. Not until the Lockwood's moved in and according to mum their presence stirred things up. Odd things started happening."

"Like what?" Hawk asked, folding his arms tight across his chest, one knee jiggling up and down.

Steven waved his hand in the air as he continued. "Unexplainable things, things moving about the house, shadows following you from room to room. Mum was locked in her painting studio a few times. Dad got pushed down the stairs, and I'd wake up some nights with my nose pressed against the ceiling."

"To the *ceiling?*" Hawk sounded horrified.

Steven nodded. "Of all places."

"What did the Lockwood's *do*, Uncle Steven?" Ariel wanted this story over.

He stopped pacing and looked down at her. "I promised your mother I would never tell you." He said, barely above a whisper.

She shook her head; fingers of fear ran down her spine. "Then don't."

Hawk shot to his feet. "Go to bed, Ariel."

Both Steven and Ariel turned to Hawk. He'd used a tone that he'd never used when speaking to her before. It was an order; and one she wanted to obey.

But how could she? Did she need to hear the full story to understand what was happening? Would it even make any difference?

"I don't know what to do?" She whispered in anguish, turning from her brother to her uncle, twisting her hands in her lap.

"Your story won't have any impact on what's already happened, will it?" Hawk asked.

"Correct."

"Then like I said, go to bed Ariel." Hawk repeated.

Ariel sat for a moment before getting to her feet.

"Please don't tell Hawk anything he doesn't need to hear, Uncle Steven." She looked at him meaningfully.

He nodded, reaching to give her a hug.

She held him tightly, before turning to Hawk. "Goodnight, love."

"Goodnight, sis." He returned her hug, before she headed upstairs, closing the door to the spare room behind her. It may have been her responsibility to listen to the history of the *why* things had been going so wrong in the house. But after the day she'd endured she just wanted to give herself some quiet time.

She tucked herself in bed beside Wren and forced herself to relax. It took her a while to feel sleepy, and she almost gave up on the idea of sleep when Jaxon's caramel eyes flashed before her, calming her. He'd been so steadfast the past forty-eight hours. Solid as a rock despite the unknown terror. He'd been there for them all. Apart from Steven and Liv, no one had been there for them since their mum had died. It sent a warm stirring deep within her, sending her into a comforting, deep sleep.

Chapter Ten
Hawk

Hawk turned dark blue eyes towards his uncle and folded his arms, waiting to hear the bedroom door upstairs close, anxious to hear what his uncle had to say.

Steven raised an eyebrow. "Maybe you should go to bed too?"

Hawk shook his head. "Nope. Mum might not have wanted Ariel to know whatever it was you promised not to tell, but she didn't say anything about me, did she?"

Steven sighed and sat down on the couch. "No actually, she didn't."

"Well, there's your guilt free loophole." Hawk sat opposite Steven, wondering if it was as bad as all that. He was glad Ariel and Wren were safely tucked upstairs with Timmy. He waited patiently.

Steven looked Hawk steadily in the eye.

"Mr Lockwood was the worst kind of deviant. Like I said, he was a psychopath. Kind to people in the community, helpful. Always the first to put his hand up for any volunteering around town. Of course, we didn't know about his hidden agenda to integrate himself so carefully within the community for the purpose of getting away with murder and God knows what else. He was good to my parents, but behind closed doors, when they weren't looking, he was a complete monster to his son."

"Didn't Grandma or Grandpa see him for what he was?"

Steven shook his head. "No one did. Not until it was too late."

"Why didn't you say anything?"

"We were terrified of him, of what he might do. We were kids," he shrugged. "He had that power over us."

"How bad was it?" Hawk asked.

"It wasn't good. Travis had festered in a life of abuse from the first day I met him, till his last. Living with the Lockwood's was like witnessing Armageddon every day. The mind games Mr Lockwood played with us. Travis, Jaxon, and I…we didn't know what was real, and what wasn't for a time."

"Real?"

"The threats of what he'd done to people, and what he'd do to us if we talked about the abuse he inflicted. He'd torment Travis in front of us, hit him, kick him, burn him with his coffee."

"Prick," Hawk whispered.

"Yeah. Sparrow saw things too, but he was cunning. Tried to act as nice as pie when she was around. But the times she did catch him out, she wasn't shy about telling mum and dad. When they confronted Mr Lockwood, he'd just laugh and say Sparrow had a fabulous imagination, that he'd never hurt his boy. But the things Jaxon and I saw…" Steven shuddered.

"Kids see everything."

"Kids see too much. As the years went by, Mr Lockwood would take us boys hunting. Taught us how to skin, and butcher everything he caught. Foxes, kangaroos, dingos. Jaxon and I were deciding to dob on him when we witnessed him trapping and killing the neighbourhood cats. Travis overheard our plan and told his dad." He shook his head. "He was a sick bastard. Told us if we ever told anyone what he was doing he'd skin us too."

"You were really that scared of him, you couldn't tell your parents?"

Steven met Hawk's gaze. "As I said, he was *that* terrifying, so no. We didn't tell a soul."

"How old were you at the time?"

"Almost nine."

"That's crazy."

"That's one word for it. It all fell apart one afternoon when Jaxon and I went bike riding deep in the bush and came across an old mine shaft. We found a boy around our age chained to a rusty pipe drilled in the ground. He begged us to free him. Told us his name was Stuart Kirkland."

"Jesus Christ," Hawk whispered.

"Well, he sure wasn't anywhere to be seen." Steven muttered.

"How long had he been down there?"

"Close to a year."

"Poor kid."

Steven nodded in agreement. "We tried to free him, but Mr Lockwood arrived. We thought he was going to kill us all." Steven whispered, a haunted look on his face.

"What happened?" Hawk asked quietly, feeling sick that all three boys had been in that situation.

"He let us go and said if we told a living soul Sparrow would be his next target.

Steven poured another finger of scotch. "We believed him."

"I'm so sorry that happened to you Uncle Steven…"

Steven quickly wiped the corners of his eyes and took a deep breath. "We went home, and I was sick all night. Mum rang Jaxon's Grandpa to see if Jaxon was feeling all right, only to discover Jaxon wasn't in his bed.

He was missing."

"Missing? You mean abducted?"

"That's what I thought when I heard mum on the phone to Jaxon's Grandpa. So, I panicked and told Sparrow about Stuart, and that I thought Mr Lockwood had taken Jaxon too."

Hawk swallowed, stuffing his fists under his arms pits, not sure if he wanted to hear any more of this story. Curiosity *did* in fact, kill the cat.

"What happened?"

"Sparrow told our parents. Mr Lockwood must have overheard the conversation, because when dad went to confront him, his and Travis's beds were empty. They were nowhere to be found in the house."

"What about Jaxon?"

"Jaxon left home after his Grandpa had gone to bed. He went back for Stuart with tools to break him out of the chains."

"Brave kid," Hawk said, imagining a kid a bit older than Timmy out in the middle of the Inglewood bush at night, with the intent of rescuing a kid from a murderer.

"Yeah, that's Jaxon through and through. After my parents told Jaxon's Grandpa everything, we rang the police. I was asked to escort them to the location. It took hours to find the mine shaft again. And there was Jaxon, trying everything to get Stuart out of those chains."

"Thank god the kid survived."

"Yeah, his parents were called. They were from Tasmania. Stuart had been taken from the Inglewood Hotel one night, when they were on a family holiday."

"Makes you want to stay at home." Hawk shivered.

"Yet, the predators lived in mine."

Hawk offered an understanding nod and Steven remained quiet for several moments.

"Is that all?" Hawk asked.

"I wish it were," Steven sighed. "There was a manhunt, but neither

Lockwood was found, and everything quietened down. Life eased back into a carefree rhythm."

Hawk was apprehensive for what was to come. It couldn't have been good from the look on his uncle's face.

"A month or so later, mum and dad took Jaxon and I to the Bendigo Festival. Sparrow was at home with Liv's mum, Beth. The Lockwood's broke in, knocked Beth out and raped your mother. Afterwards, they nearly beat her to death."

"No!" Hawk cried in denial.

Steven's face filled with regret. "I'm sorry mate, I shouldn't have told you."

Hawk shook his head. "No, it's alright, just… give me a second." He covered his face and took a few deep breaths. This was worse than he'd thought, and he was glad he'd asked Ariel to go upstairs. Ordered her. He looked across at his uncle who was wiping his eyes again.

"What happened next?" He asked resignedly.

Steven smiled sadly. "When Mr Lockwood went to get ropes from his car, Travis cornered Sparrow in dad's office and raped her again. Somehow, she managed to get a hold of dad's letter opener and jammed it into his throat." Steven sighed.

"Mum…" Hawk whispered, thinking of what a powerful force she'd always been.

"She was one of the strongest people I've ever met." Warmth filled Steven's voice.

Hawk nodded, as Steven continued.

"Beth had regained consciousness and rang the police, and Mr Lockwood escaped before they arrived, never to be heard of again. Travis bled out in the corner of dad's office before the ambulance arrived." Steven got up and wandered behind the counter to turn on the coffee machine. "Want one?"

Hawk shook his head. "I've got school tomorrow." He didn't know why he said that and felt younger than his fifteen-years. Older too, somehow. He was grateful Wren and Ariel had not heard this story.

"Don't tell Ariel about this. Ever." Hawk said.

Steven took a cup out of the cupboard as he met Hawk's gaze. "I don't intend to," he replied quietly.

Hawk sat silently for a moment, adding up the years. "Oh no, it can't be…" he whispered.

"What?" Steven asked, pouring a coffee, and walked over to Hawk.

Hawk raised his face to his uncle. "Is one of the Lockwood's Ariel's father?" He saw the regret on his uncle's face immediately.

Steven put his cup down and nodded slowly. "I'm sorry mate, truly I am."

Hawk fell back against the couch and closed his eyes, shaking his head. "She can *never* know."

Steven sat next to his nephew, pulling him into his arms. "She won't mate, not ever."

Hawk allowed his uncle to comfort him. He felt he'd earned it and hugged him back. His poor, sweet mother. What hell she must have endured.

"So, Mr Lockwood was never found?"

Steven was silent and looked like he was about to say something else but didn't.

"What else aren't you telling me, Uncle Steven?" Hawk frowned, feeling uneasy.

Steven sighed. "I think I've told you enough."

"And I think I'll be the judge of that."

"Sorry mate, that's all you're getting from me tonight."

"Can you at least tell me why mum stopped bringing us here?"

"Once Ariel turned eighteen, the same age your mother was when she was attacked, weird things started happening around the house. Weirder than normal. Frightening things. Sparrow left and never returned."

Hawk nodded; he guessed it made sense. "What are we going to do about the house?" He asked tiredly, feeling more exhausted than he could ever remember.

"Jaxon said he's got that covered. He has connections."

"Okay."

"Why don't you head up to bed. I'll sleep down here, and we'll figure out sleeping arrangements tomorrow."

"Sure, thanks Uncle Steven. I'm really sorry for all the crap you had to deal with as a kid."

"Don't be. I was lucky to have two incredible parents, a best friend and a sister who would do anything for anyone."

Hawk nodded. "Goodnight Uncle Steven."

"Goodnight mate. I'm here if you ever want to talk about any of this."

"Thanks, you too." Hawk headed upstairs, thinking the more he heard about Jaxon Williams, the more he sounded like a modern-day superhero. He didn't mind at all, that the man looked at Ariel like she was a damsel that needed his protection. He was glad for it.

Jaxon

Jaxon opened his front door an hour before the school bell was due to ring and saw a tired looking Steven leaning against the wall.

"Hey mate, you made it home in good time last night?"

"Yeah, thanks for the call." Steven said.

"No problem. Come in."

Jaxon led the way down a long, wide corridor and into an opulent kitchen and made them a coffee.

"What's up? You look like you didn't sleep a wink." He handed Steven a coffee then leaned back on his kitchen bench, waiting.

Steven nodded his thanks as he took a mouthful, sitting down on a chair. "I told Hawk about the Lockwood's."

Jaxon stilled for a moment, before asking, "How much did you tell him?"

"Enough."

"About Stuart? Sparrow?"

"Yeah, all of that."

"You didn't tell him that one of the Lockwood's is Ariel's father?"

"Unfortunately, he did the math, figured that part out himself."

"Well, shit." Jaxon placed his mug on the bench. "What about Sparrow's death?"

"*God no*! None of them can ever find out about that."

"Do you really think that's a good idea?"

Steven laughed dryly. "Some days I don't know. But I won't have them looking over their shoulder and living in fear. Not after losing their mother."

"What about the newspaper article and the evidence that was found on Sparrow?"

"It's locked up at my home office."

"I think Ariel could handle the information, don't you?" He asked his friend.

"That's my decision to make as her only uncle." Steven said, leaving no room for further argument.

"I'm not trying to tell you what to do, mate."

Steven closed his eyes briefly. "She doesn't have to handle it when we're here to protect them."

"Most days." Jaxon said quietly.

Steven sighed. "Yeah, most days."

"Are you okay?"

"I will be as long as they're safe. From the dead, and the living."

Jaxon nodded. "I've had a conversation with the Reverend. He'll settle things down at the house, you have my word."

Steven drained his cup. "Thanks, Jaxon. I can always count on you."

Jaxon grinned. "Yes, you can."

Chapter Eleven
Ariel

Ariel presented the school board with several mural options, hoping they'd appreciate the effort and back story behind each detailed sketch she'd poured hours into. From a selection of the town's historical buildings to the Loddon River and its flora and fauna, and a scene with the native birds which would no doubt be a hit with the kids.

Once she finished her presentation, she sat down and watched as the board members handed each sketch along, before reaching for the next. Ray's impressed 'oohs' and 'aahs' were the only complimentary comments.

Throughout the entire presentation she could feel Jaxon's gaze upon her but did not make eye-contact with him. The memory of the other night and how she had pressed herself against him, had her body pulsing with desire. She knew she'd blush like a schoolgirl if she looked at him. He was too damn sexy in *every* way. Yet, she couldn't help herself and risked a glance in his direction.

He was sitting back in his seat twirling a pen around his fingers, watching her with an intense expression. Her stomach automatically released a flutter of frenzied butterflies, and she could feel heat creep up her neck.

Damn it.

He looked as impatient as she felt for this meeting to be over. They had an appointment at the house with Reverend Matthews, and Steven and Liv had picked Timmy up from school and were taking him and the twins to Bendigo for dinner and a movie.

"Let's have a vote, shall we?" Ray interrupted her thoughts. "Birds, buildings, or the Loddon? How many for the birds?"

"I believe these are a little lacklustre. Is there nothing else?" A haughty blonde raised her eyebrow towards Ray in question, ignoring Ariel outright.

Ariel forced herself not to roll her eyes as another woman commented on Ariel's lack of creativity for the project.

"Lack of creativity you say?" Ray sounded furious. "I don't think you realise how lucky we are to have Miss Harper in our town, let alone agree to do this project for us free of charge."

"We're not implying her lack of… *talent*," a plump, dark-haired woman said.

"Just that her simple ideas could be a little more dynamic," another continued.

"We expected more from a *world-renowned* artist…" finished the haughty blonde who began the negative comments in the first place.

Valerie. Ariel recalled her name.

None of them addressed her outright, or even looked at her.

Like I need this bullshit right now. She stood abruptly, chair scrapping backwards noisily as she purposefully tossed her hair over her shoulder, placing a hand on her shapely hip. She knew she looked damn fine and was at least fifteen years younger than any of them, sitting looking at her as if she were beneath them all. *Screw them.*

"Thank you, Ray," she nodded politely, before turning her heated gaze on the vulture-like-mothers. "How about when ya'll decide this *life altering* decision, you just let me know." She snapped, before plastering a bright smile on her face then stormed from the room, slamming the door behind her.

She blew out a breath and relaxed her shoulders as she headed along the corridor. Hearing footsteps approach, she turned to see Jaxon strolling towards her, hands casually tucked in his pockets wearing a relaxed grin on his ever-gorgeous face.

What was he smirking at?

"Problem?" She raised an eyebrow.

"Oh no, Miss Harper, we love rude behaviour in our classrooms here at Inglewood primary school." He stopped a mere foot away as he gazed down at her.

She was about to reply snidely, but her lips that had been set to snarl, returned his playful grin. She couldn't help herself.

His dark caramel eyes searched every inch of her face. She wanted to run her fingers in his silken, tawny locks. Her gaze dropped to his full, beautiful lips and she must have forgotten to breathe for a moment as a dizzy wave, combined with the heat, and lack of any decent sleep—had her swaying.

"Take a breath," he said softly, reaching to steady her. His fingers wrapped around her upper arm, creating a sweet current to flow along her flesh.

She didn't think; she acted. Standing on tiptoe, she leaned against his chest, needing to kiss him as if her life depended on it.

In a fluent movement his arm slid around her waist, and he turned them into the room behind them, closing the door. As soon as the door shut behind him, she pushed him against it, and herself flush against him; her hands drifting up his muscular chest.

She sighed as their gazes collided. She bit her lip, running her fingers along his jaw then reached to slide them through his hair. She almost purred as he stroked her back through her thin cotton dress, and moved against him, pressing her breasts against his chest. His broody eyes darkened as he stared at her, allowing her a moment to explore what it meant being in his arms.

"Kiss me," she whispered, running her tongue across her bottom lip in anticipation.

"My pleasure," he replied and bent his head slowly before his lips swept her up in a tsunami of pleasure. Every pulse point was on fire as his hands ran down her back. Gripping her hips, he ran a finger down between her buttocks to brush gently up and down.

She lifted her knee around his hip, rocking against him as his lips swept across hers; their tongues meeting in a delicious swirl of fire and lust had her breathless and panting for more. A sweet, pulsing heat flowed between her legs as his fingers gently manipulated pleasure with each stroke.

She literally felt weak at the knees and didn't know how much longer she could stand. As if reading her mind, he lifted her and turned to press her back against the door wrapping her legs around his hips. She sucked on his tongue, feeling carefree in that moment and forced down a laugh as she felt his engorged shaft press against her throbbing desire through her silk knickers.

"Something funny?" He whispered against her lips.

She hadn't realised the chuckle had slipped out, and ignored his question, deepening the kiss.

He ran his hands upwards, thumbs caressing the sides of her breasts making her moan with longing against his mouth which was assaulting hers with pleasure. She wriggled against him wanting to be closer. Hell, wanting him *inside* her.

"Jaxon, are you in there?" Ray's voice called from the other side of the door.

They froze, lips locked but not moving, eyes wide in shock at first, but

Ariel could feel a bubble of laughter begin to erupt.

"Don't you dare," he whispered at her, a sexy smile spread across his lips, melting her heart.

"Jaxon, hello?" Ray called.

She bit her lip as she looked into his molten eyes before he closed his, and started whispering the primary colours, gently removing her off his hips.

"What are you doing," she whispered.

"Stop talking, minx," he replied, before whispering colours again.

She felt the overwhelming urge to giggle, as he gently held her away from him, then turned his back to her. She put her hand over her mouth, as Ray tried again.

"Jaxon, I really need you to sign a few things before I go."

He cleared his throat, before calling. "Hang on Ray, just grabbing some... stuff. I'll be there in a sec."

"See you at reception," Ray called before footsteps trailed off.

Ariel laughed quietly, shaking her head. "Stuff hey? Very descriptive, Mr Williams."

He slowly turned to face her, and her laugh disappeared. He ran a hand through his hair, tidying it up before running a hand down his front cupping himself, checking he wasn't too obvious.

"Keep reciting colours," she whispered.

He cupped her chin and bent down. "Red, white, and blue," he said, before dropping a sweeping kiss across her swollen lips.

She sighed, melting into him, before he pulled away.

"I'll meet you out front in five," he said, running a finger down the slope of her nose and tapping the end of it, making her smile again.

She nodded before he turned and exited the room.

"Mr Honey, indeed," she whispered to the room, and waited a handful of minutes before heading out towards the back door and out of the school building.

He was waiting for her, leaning against his car watching her like an apex predator.

"Did you deal with all your… stuff?" She grinned.

"Smarty pants huh? Yeah, I did, thanks." He opened the car door for her.

She smiled up at him as one of the opinionated mothers walked by.

"See you on Monday, Mr Williams," the haughty blonde smiled at him, before turning a judging eye towards Ariel.

Ariel beamed at her. "Why have a great weekend, Vanessa." She slammed the car door before the woman could respond.

Jaxon got in beside her, closing his door, chuckling. "I assume you know her name is Valeria?" He started the engine.

She continued to beam at him and said. "I couldn't care less."

He shook his head laughing, and drove to her house.

Her smile faded as they pulled up at the front, behind a black Volkswagen. An elderly man, who Ariel presumed was Reverend Matthews, was waiting on the footpath. He was wearing a serious expression along with a tidy black suit and a bowler hat that sat on a thick mop of grey hair.

"It's going to be okay." Jaxon said, turning the engine off and looking her in the eye. "I'm going to be with you every step of the way."

She took her gaze off the serious looking man at the front of her house and met Jaxon's eyes as he patted her knee. Placing her hand on top of his, she nodded once, squeezing his fingers before getting out of the car.

"Reverend, it's so good of you to meet us." Jaxon called as he closed his door and walked around to shake the older man's hand.

"Please Jaxon, call me Josh." He smiled, showing Ariel a softer face filled with kindness as she approached them.

"You know I can't do that Reverend; my Grandfather would be most disappointed. Reverend, this is Ariel Harper, Ariel, Reverend Matthews."

Ariel shook the man's smooth hand, dotted with aged spots. "Nice to meet you Reverend." She offered a small smile.

He placed his other hand on top of hers and patted it gently. "Nice to meet you child.

"Thank you for coming," she said.

"Of course. Let's take a look at this house of yours, shall we?"

She nodded, shoulders relaxing at his calm tone. He went to the back seat of his car to pull out a small briefcase. Glancing at the house, which sat prettily under the summer sky, she thought it looked picturesque and calm, as if it were waiting patiently for her to return.

She jumped when Jaxon placed his arm around her waist, and chuckled nervously as she looked up at him. Her breath caught in her throat as he was looking at her with such tenderness. How had they become so comfortable with one another so quickly?

"Ready?" He asked quietly, linking his fingers through hers.

"As I'll ever be," she replied, and led the way towards the house. Opening the front door, she hesitated for a second before stepping inside, grateful for Jaxon's warm hand around hers.

Reverend Matthews stepped through the door behind them, closing it as the grandfather clock began chiming out of time.

"Let's have a nice cup of tea, shall we?" He beamed, ignoring the bonging.

Ariel nodded heading down the corridor and into the kitchen to put the kettle on. Jaxon leaned against the aged, butchers block, and she had to admit to herself that she liked seeing him here in her kitchen, relaxed, looking like he belonged.

Glancing over his shoulder as she reached for the teapot and tea leaves, she saw the Reverend slowly walking from one room to another, before approaching her Grandfather's office. The instant he stepped through the doorway, the grandfather clock's chiming stopped.

"Hey," Jaxon reached across and rubbed her arm.

She forced a smile, spooning up tealeaves. "I'm okay," she lied.

His eyes followed her shaking hand as she missed the teapot and scattered tealeaves along the bench.

"Here," he offered. "Let me." Taking the spoon off her he scooped tea and cleaned the bench. Ariel reached for the boiled kettle and felt Jaxon step behind her, his breath blew tendrils of her hair along her neck. She leaned back against him, taking comfort in his presence.

He dropped a sweet kiss against her neck, making her laugh quietly before he reached around her and picked the kettle up.

She looked over her shoulder at him, before turning around to cup his jaw. "You're distracting me."

He grinned, leaning down to brush the sweetest kiss across her lips that immediately had her pulse racing. "Then my work here is done."

"Not quite I'm afraid." Reverend Matthews called from the doorway, making them both jump, which had the three sharing a laugh. "Let's go into the main lounge to discuss my findings thus far."

Jaxon nodded as he filled the tea pot and carried the tray into the lounge where Reverend Matthews was already seated.

"Just black, thank you," he said.

Jaxon poured, and Ariel passed the cup to the polite man, anxious to hear what he had discovered in the short amount of time he'd been here.

Once they each sat with their tea, he began. "I knew your Grandparents quite well. Your mother too, of course."

Ariel took a mouthful of tea, moving her legs close to Jaxon's. "Uncle Steven still lives here."

"Yes, I see him about town," he smiled. "I was sorry to hear about your mother." His voice laced with sympathy, before a door began opening and slamming shut repeatedly down the corridor.

Ariel jumped in fright, sloshing tea over the rim of her cup before she placed it on the table. Jaxon stood quickly, as Reverend Matthews held up his hand, stilling him.

The door continued slamming open and shut for another minute before silence fell over the house.

Ariel stood, wrapping her arms around herself, glancing from Reverend Matthews to Jaxon, waiting for what, she didn't know.

Jaxon stepped close, placing an arm around her shoulders before asking, "What have you found Reverend?"

Reverend Matthews took a mouthful of tea, before placing it onto the tray. Reaching for his briefcase he opened it and pulled out an old leatherbound bible.

"There is both shadow and light within these walls and have been for some time." He looked pointedly at Ariel. "Your Grandfather once had me perform a blessing on this house. Like many houses in old towns across Australia, Inglewood has seen some heart rendering days."

Ariel swallowed and leaned against Jaxon's side for warmth. The temperature in the room had dropped several degrees the moment the door had started slamming.

"This house has stood for well over a century and was lucky to have escaped one of the most destructive fires recorded in the colony in 1862."

"Lucky?" Jaxon tilted his head. "According to my Grandfather the fire was contained to the business area of town?"

"Yes, that is correct. Lucky is the wrong word, but I use it because two tons of gunpowder had been stored in a shop within two doors down from that fire."

"I can only imagine the catastrophe that would have created for the entire town if it had of gone off." Jaxon said, holding Ariel against him.

"Indeed, and regardless of that saving grace the damage to the town business sector that day was irreparable."

"My Grandfather said that looters attributed to the devastation?"

"True. Looters not only hit the stores but took advantage of the absence when people fled their homes to assist with the fire. Many were robbed and left destitute. It was an era when the simplest action could devastate someone's life."

"That could be said for every era." Ariel said quietly.

"True my dear. Although if you lost everything today, you'd have a community, friends or family to offer you help, because they could. Quite often back then, it was a choice of survival. Not everyone had the means to open their homes to help someone in need, without starving themselves."

Ariel nodded as Jaxon sat, gently pulling her down beside him before topping up her tea. Passing it to her, they waited for Reverend Matthews to continue with the town's history lesson.

"Once the gold production in the town began to diminish at the turn of the twentieth century, the towns folk despaired and times grew ugly. As times do when humans despair, faced with hunger and desperation." He paused for a moment, taking a mouthful of tea before continuing in a lighter tone.

"Then the town had cause for celebration when it discovered that the Blue Mallee trees that grow in abundance around Inglewood, produced some of the highest quality eucalyptus in the world. The eucalyptus oil industry boomed and offered new opportunities for the town, as many new forms of employment were formed."

"Sounds like good timing," Jaxon nodded.

"Indeed. The town flourished, the population increased, and it was in many ways, the beginning of this house's journey. It became a boarding house, then an orphanage for many years. As you can imagine these walls have witnessed a great deal."

"If only walls could talk," Ariel said as she glanced around the room.

"Yes, what stories they could tell." Reverend Matthews smiled knowingly.

"Did the blessing you performed for my Grandfather help?"

"For a time, yes." He titled his head towards Jaxon, before meeting Ariel's curious gaze. "Jaxon has filled me in on your activity. Young Timothy has names for these entities?"

"Yes, he calls the friendly one, Sebastian. The other one is called the Butch…"

Before Ariel could finish, the teapot flew in the air above their heads, spinning around like a spinning top shooting tea from the spout, casting a wide circle around them. As soon as the teapot emptied it clattered down on the table, shattering into pieces. The spilt tea on the rug burst into white flames, reaching the ceiling, scorching it black before disappearing altogether. The rug smouldered, yet the scorch marks on the ceiling had vanished.

Reverend Matthews nodded slowly. "A warning, yet harmless enough," he whispered, rubbing his throat.

"For now." Ariel ran her hands over her face before meeting Jaxon's worried gaze.

"Interesting." he whispered; eyebrows raised.

"To say the least." Reverend Matthews agreed.

"Was that the good guy or the bad guy?" Ariel asked Reverend Matthews, who stood, clutching his Bible as he walked towards the door.

"We are about to find out." He stood in the corridor taking a deep breath, before calling in a calm tone. "If there is a presence here, please make yourself known."

Jaxon ran a hand over Ariel's hair, before getting up to walk closer to the door. She steadied her nerves by taking in his broad shoulders and narrow hips.

Mr Yummy indeed.

She appreciated his male form, grateful to have him here.

He turned then, catching her staring and grinned as he folded his arms, then turned back to Reverend Matthews, who had begun talking softly in what Ariel knew to be Latin, after spending a year in Italy.

The hairs on the back of her neck rose as a door upstairs began opening and slamming; the temperature dropped another few degrees. Jaxon was briskly rubbing his arms, feeling it too.

"Reveal yourself." The Reverend demanded.

Ariel stepped over the rug scorched by the flames and felt large hands circle about her waist. A cry of fear slipped from her lips as she felt herself being lifted in the air.

"*Jaxon!*" She cried before the entity threw her clear across the room. Screaming, she covered her head before smashing into the bookcase, gasping in pain as her spine thumped into the wooden shelves.

"*Ariel.*" Jaxon raced to her side, pulling her to her feet, holding her close as he ran his hands gently down her back. "Are you alright?" His voice shook.

"I think…" Her voice broke and she cleared her throat. "I think so," she finished quietly, as her gaze darted around the room trying to see whatever it was that had flung her.

"You are *not welcome here!*" Reverend Matthews cried, making a sign of the cross with his right hand as he held his bible in front of him.

"I demand you leave this place, it is no longer yours, by the grace that is gifted to me by our Lord and Saviour, Jesus Christ, I *command* that you depart." Once again, he began speaking in Latin for several minutes as the house rumbled and shook around them.

Ariel closed her eyes, pushing her face into Jaxon's chest; her back throbbed. She needed it all to be over and prayed that her Grandparents' beloved stained-glass windows would not shatter. Throughout the chaos she could distinctly hear the unpleasant sound of fingernails running along glass in a slow, methodical way. She opened her eyes to peer at the photographs that adorned the shelves and walls around the room. To her horror, she noticed that the glass was shattered across the throats of every female in the photographs.

"Jaxon," she whispered, pointing to a picture where her mother had her arms around Wren, Hawk and herself. The glass was cracked across their throats, and a red liquid oozed from each slit, accompanied by tiny black wriggling worms.

"Just like the sample," Jaxon sounded shocked as he addressed the Reverend. "The black worms I sent you, that Ariel had thrown up after the incident."

"Yes," Reverend Matthews nodded. "The evidence from the lab indicated they were from deep within the earth that line the towns drains."

"That's disgusting," Ariel whispered, noticing that Hawk was the only one in the photograph who was unmarked. "It doesn't make sense. How could I throw up worms?"

"Wicked has a way of getting inside us all." The reverend said quietly.

"For God sakes," Ariel moaned in anguish. "What the hell…"

"It's okay," Jaxon soothed as he held her close, his chin nestled on top of her head.

Reverend Matthews fell silent, along with the house. The door upstairs ceased its slamming and silence ensued. Ariel sighed in relief, dropping her forehead against Jaxon's chest.

"What do you think, Reverend?" Jaxon asked.

They stood silently, exchanging watchful glances as they waited for anything untoward to follow. Finally, the Reverend said. "I do believe it has departed."

"How can you be sure?" Ariel noted that the air *was* warmer, and wanted to believe it was as easy as that. Prayed that it was.

"I can feel the energy within the house. There is only light here right at this moment."

"Will that darkness stay away, Reverend?" Jaxon asked.

"I will place protective wards around the house before I leave." Reverend Matthews nodded as he bent to retrieve his briefcase. He opened it and removed a bottle of water, a bag of salt, and a white candle. He smiled, seeing her curious expression. "Holly water, salt and a purifying candle."

She nodded. "I've got plenty of white candles."

"That's good, I suggest you burn them when you are home."

"Anything else that may help?"

"Ignore anything that goes bump in the night."

"Ignore it?" She asked bewildered.

"If you can, yes. Fear feeds the dark side of things."

"Seriously, give it the cold shoulder? Will that really work?" Jaxon asked.

"It has been known to in certain circumstances." Reverend Matthews smiled, opening his bible. "I will begin by blessing each room of the house. Excuse me." He said quietly, focusing on the task at hand.

Making the sign of the cross in one corner of the room, he began praying quietly before walking to the other three corners and then exited the room.

Ariel could feel herself relax as the Reverend walked from one room to the next.

Jaxon dropped a kiss against her forehead before picking up the pieces of the smashed teapot, whilst she wandered to the photograph that oozed the red liquid, and leaned towards it, taking an apprehensive sniff. "Ew," she muttered.

"What is it?" Jaxon asked.

"It smells like rotten meat."

He joined her and leaned down to take a closer look. "It's super off, for sure." He removed it from the shelf, juggling it with the smashed teapot pieces. "We'll clean it up." He said, heading towards the kitchen.

Collecting the teacups she followed him into the kitchen, as Reverend Matthews' quiet prayer sounded throughout the house.

"How are you doing?" He asked, dumping the broken pieces into the bin, and tore off a piece of paper towel to wipe the red ooze from the glass.

She turned to run some water into the sink, adding detergent. "I'm not quite sure how to answer that."

He placed the ooze-free photograph on the bench, dropping the bloody towel into the bin before placing his hands on her shoulders and gently moved her from the sink, so he could plunge his hands into the soapy water and wash the cups.

She sighed. "I'm not made of glass, Jaxon."

He met her gaze steadily. "Clearly. But my Grandpa raised me with manners." He finished washing the cups before drying his hands on a tea towel.

She ran her hands through her hair and grimaced at the ache in her back.

"Let me see," he said softly, turning her around to pull her dress away at the neckline to peek at her back. "Ouch," he said sounding unimpressed.

"That bad?"

"The skin isn't broken, but it's bruising up a nice shade of purple already."

He dropped a kiss on her neck, before heading over to the fridge and opened the top freezer compartment to pull out a pack of frozen peas.

Thoughtful. Sexy. Solid.

He stopped in front of her, as she stared up at him. "You alright?"

"I will be," she replied, stepping against him and lifted her mouth towards his; hopeful.

He didn't disappoint her. She watched a lazy smile spread across his lips as he bent his head slowly to hers.

She sighed the second before his mouth swept over hers, taking her on a sensual ride of pure bliss. He cupped the back of her neck to angle her head and deepen the kiss.

It sent a delicious jolt of heat straight to her belly, then spread to her loins, flooding her with instant warmth. She moaned against his mouth, wrapping her arms around his neck as she pressed herself against him.

His low chuckle had her pulling back. "If you don't behave yourself, I'm going to take you right here with the Reverend right under our noses." His voice was husky, filling her with female satisfaction.

She was about to say something smart, when she gasped suddenly as he held the icy bag of peas against her back; the aching temporarily forgotten due to his thoroughly delightful kisses.

"Not fair," she whispered.

"I hear that every day in the playground, Miss Harper." He grinned.

"I bet you do, Mr Williams." She ran her tongue over her bottom lip, loving that his grin disappeared, and lust filled his eyes.

He bent his head towards her when Reverend Matthews delicately coughed behind them.

Jaxon stepped beside her so he could still hold the bag of peas against her back.

"How'd you go Reverend?"

Reverend Matthews nodded, closing the clasp on his briefcase. "I have cleansed the entire house, and placed salt at both entrances to keep harmful spirits at bay. Miss Harper, please let Jaxon know if you need me for anything, won't you?"

Ariel smiled; her heart warmed with gratitude. She crossed towards the kind man and shook his hand. "I really can't thank you enough. It means the world to be able to bring my kids back under our Grandparent's roof again."

He returned her warm smile, patting her hand. "You are welcome," he nodded to Jaxon. "I'll see you around Jaxon."

"Here," Jaxon said kindly. "Let me walk you out."

"Thank you. Goodbye Miss Harper."

"Bye Reverend."

Jaxon placed the bag of peas into her hands, running his fingers over hers, before he walked Reverend Matthews out the front door.

She stood in the kitchen, gauging the feeling of the house now that she stood here, alone. It did feel different. Peaceful. As it had done when she was a child. She sighed.

"That's better," she whispered. "Please stay this way."

Chapter Twelve
Ariel

"Well done everyone," Ariel laughed, clapping her hands. "Absolute masterpieces."

The group of painters, and wine partakers applauded themselves for a job well done, before thanking Ariel for the night class.

The two-hour self-portrait class had been filled with a high energy vibe from the get-go and continued for the duration of the evening as conversations flowed effortlessly, along with harmless town gossip filtered with laughter.

Ray had participated in her classes for three weeks now, and Ariel could see her potential if she continued with classes. "You know Ray, you really should add some of your flair to the school mural."

"Oh no. I enjoy this small scale, but I'll leave the big projects to the professional. It really is coming along nicely."

"Thank you, I'm pretty pleased with it so far. It should be finished soon." Ariel smiled as she waved to the others as they headed out.

"This was another fun class." Ray said, helping Ariel wash out the paint brushes as they began tidying up.

"I'm glad you're enjoying it." She smiled, plonking the brushes in a bucket to dry off.

"Creating art is so cathartic. I tried journaling once, after my ex took the kids …" Ray froze, her startled gaze meeting Ariels, as heat filled her cheeks.

Poor woman. "Hey," Ariel reached across and took her hand, squeezing it lightly. She'd heard the rumours about town that Ray's ex-husband had taken the children and left her, after her drinking got out of control. Ariel had always despised small minded, tiny-town gossips.

"This is a safe space. What's said in the studio, stays in the studio." She was relieved to see Ray return her smile.

"That's very kind of you," she said gratefully.

"Not at all. We all have a past and shouldn't be persecuted for it." Ariel collected the wine glasses and coffee mugs and carried them into the Café's sink to let them soak in the soapy water Liv had run before leaving.

"I've been dry for six weeks now," Ray started quietly. "It hasn't been easy."

"I can only imagine," Ariel turned off the café light as Ray took her bag off the back of a chair.

"Keeping busy is the key," Ray smiled as she pulled out her car keys. "Especially at night."

Turning the gallery lights off, they walked out into the back entrance where Ray's car was parked.

"Do you want to come to mine for a coffee?" Ariel asked.

"Oh, no, thank you. After the day I've had, I am more than happy to crawl into bed with a good book."

"That actually sounds wonderful." Ariel agreed, as Ray opened her car door.

"Want a lift?" Ray asked.

"No thanks, it takes me two minutes to walk home."

"Well, goodnight then. I'll see you tomorrow."

"Night." Ariel waved and headed down the alley and onto Verdon Street before crossing onto Grant Street.

The refreshing scent of eucalyptus filled the night air, and a cool breeze chased the mugginess from her skin. She hadn't felt this relaxed in so long, she'd forgotten what it felt like to feel carefree. She'd been able to catch up on months of disrupted sleep and was starting to feel human again. With zero paranormal activity in the house, even Timmy had been sleeping in his own bed for the first time since they had moved in.

Pushing the gate open and heading towards the front door, she smiled as she heard Steven's laughter boom from inside the house. Closing the door behind her she recognised the laughter that followed.

Jaxon's dry chuckle sent butterflies scattering inside her stomach and she paused, before strolling down towards the loungeroom, and leaned against the door jam, watching her loved ones play a game of Pictionary.

"That is *so not* a couch potato," Liv cried, holding her sides laughing at Steven's attempt at a potato that looked like a pile of horse dung, sitting on a couch in the shape of a square.

"Hey, you wanted to partner with me, this is what you get." He looked across the room at Liv, hands on hips.

"Remind me in future to opt for a different partner," Liv replied, tucking a strand of hair behind her ear.

"I don't know Uncle Steven, I'm impressed." Hawk grinned, getting to his feet to take his turn.

Steven high-fived Hawk as he walked by him to sit beside Liv, throwing his arm casually behind her shoulders, to rest along the back of the settee.

"I thought you knew how to read my mind?" His voice purred quietly, filled with inuendo as he tilted his head towards her.

Colour filled Liv's cheeks. "Not quite yet." She avoided his eye contact as she reached for her glass of wine.

Poor Liv doesn't stand a chance. Ariel thought as she watched Steven and Jaxon exchange a meaningful look. She found it fascinating, watching the two men share a moment, before Timmy cried out.

"You're home! Can I have a sleepover at Paul's tomorrow night, please Ariel?"

All eyes turned towards her, and as she met Jaxon's gaze, heat flooded her cheeks as she recalled his kisses. A knowing grin flashed across his face.

"Sure, why not," she replied to Timmy, grateful her voice came out smoothly.

Timmy got up and raced towards her, wrapping his arms around her legs. Smiling down at him, she ran a hand over his sweet face as he peered up at her.

"How was paint class?" Wren asked, giving Hawk the time out signal.

"It was good, everyone left happy, and a few have promised to come back next month with a friend."

"Who doesn't like art, and wine." Liv smiled across at her friend. "How'd the clean-up go?"

"Good. Ray stayed behind to help." Ariel looked down at Timmy. "If you're wanting a sleep over tomorrow night, I think you best get to bed now, love."

"But Ariel, it's not a school night." Timmy cried.

Hawk scooped him up from behind, lifting him in the air. "Yeah, we know sport, but let's face it, it's not like you and Paul are going to get much sleep tomorrow night, so like sis says, bedtime."

"I've got homework too." Wren stood.

"You've got all weekend, honey." Steven said.

"Actually, Wren and I are having a sleepover too." Hawk said to Steven, as he put Timmy down.

"Oh?" Ariel pointed upstairs and said to Timmy. "Go brush your teeth, love, I'll be up soon."

"Night everyone." Timmy waved, as everyone called out 'goodnight' before he bolted upstairs.

Hawk pushed his hands in his pockets as he looked down at Ariel.

He's such a sweetheart. She thought of their mother, and of how proud she would have been of him, and Wren.

"What exciting plans have you got?" she asked.

"We've been invited over to Lance's to go camping." Hawk said.

"Where does he live?"

"Bridgewater. His dad is taking us night fishing."

"Night fishing?" Ariel raised an eyebrow in Steven's direction.

"It's safe enough, love." He assured her.

She nodded, before asking Wren. "Who else is going to be there?"

"My friend from school, Carly Stante."

"Okay, that sounds nice. As long as you both have your phones on you at all times, and I'll need Lance's, and his dad's numbers too."

"No worries, thanks sis." Hawk hugged her with one arm as he said to Steven, Jaxon and Liv. "Have a great weekend guys, I'm off to pack and hit the books."

"Night mate," Jaxon, and Steve called together.

"Goodnight." Wren dropped a kiss on Steven's, and Liv's cheeks, and smiled down at Jaxon. "Night Jaxon."

"Goodnight," he replied, smiling.

Ariel's heart melted a little, watching him smile at her sister. He caught her eye and she quickly looked away, pointing behind her towards the kitchen.

"Anyone want a quick hot drink before you depart?"

"Are you kicking us out, niece of mine?" Steven called to her retreating back.

"Yes actually, I'm exhausted."

Walking into the kitchen, she flicked the kettle on as she heard glasses and cups being collected in the lounge, along with quiet chatter. As she reached up to grab a mug from the top cupboard, large hands slid around her waist, pulling her back against a firm chest as lips nuzzled her neck.

She sighed, leaning against him as she dropped her head onto his shoulder.

"Hello," she whispered.

"Hello," Jaxon replied, turning her in his arms, and carefully slid his hands along her back, gazing into her eyes. "How about I cook tea for you tomorrow night, seeing that you'll be child free?"

"Can you cook?"

"I can, and very well I might add."

She shifted her gaze from his eyes to his lips and nodded. "That would be lovely, I'll do dessert."

He lowered his head slowly, his lips stopping a breath away from hers as he whispered. "You'll be dessert."

Her breath caught as his lips slid over hers. She sighed against his mouth, wrapping her arms around his neck as she moulded herself to him, returning his penetrating kisses. Her tongue swirled with his, enjoying the sweet flavour of red wine.

A clattering of dishes in the sink had them both jolting apart.

Steven's wicked laughter followed. "Sorry kids, was I interrupting?"

Jaxon turned to glare at him making Steven laugh harder.

Ariel chuckled. "Okay boys, time to call it a night."

Liv walked in the kitchen. "I gave the girls the scraps from the café earlier and they repaid me with a basket of eggs, which I will grab now before I head off."

"I've got a three-hour session with a client in the morning, but I'll pop in after the lunch crowd."

"That'll be great," Liv nodded. "Night then." She called before heading out the back door to retrieve her eggs.

The grandfather clock bonged on ten o'clock, as a door slammed.

Ariel jumped and met Jaxon's concerned look before Hawk yelled downstairs.

"Sorry, that was me."

Ariel laughed quietly. "Things have been so lovely and quiet on that front."

"I'm glad the Reverend helped." Steven pulled his keys out of his back pocket. "Call me if you need me." He dropped a kiss on Ariel's cheek.

"I will, thanks Uncle Steven." She smiled.

Steven gave Jaxon a meaningful glance. "Goodnight." He said simply.

Jaxon smiled. "Goodnight my friend."

That statement seemed to relax Steven, and he winked at Ariel.

"Goodnight love."

"Goodnight." She watched as he headed out the back door after Liv, before turning to Jaxon, eyebrow raised in question. "What was that about?"

He shook his head slowly. "Some other time. But in the meantime, I look forward to picking up where we left off," he said, reaching for her.

She looked up at him wistfully, nodding slowly. "Me too."

He slipped an arm around her waist, and she gladly allowed him to pull her back against him. Running her hands up his chest, she could feel every defined muscle sing beneath her fingertips as his scent wrapped around her in heady delight.

Footsteps headed in their direction.

She stepped back regretfully, fascinated to watch his dark caramel eyes turn broody, which immediately made her want to haul him up to her bedroom.

Jaxon pushed his hands deep into his pockets, and turned as Wren walked into the kitchen, tying her hair into a long plait. "Oh, I thought everyone had gone. Sorry."

"Don't be silly love, Jaxon was just saying goodnight."

"I was," he nodded to Wren. "Have fun camping, be safe."

"Thanks."

He turned to Ariel, "Is there anything you don't like to eat?"

"Nope, I am the most non-fussy person you'll ever encounter."

"Great. What time would you like me."

She stared at him and grinned slowly. "I'd like you anytime."

Hearing Wren snicker, she looked across at her sister who had pulled the fridge open and was hiding her face behind the door.

Jaxon returned Ariel's grin. "I'll need a few hours cooking time. Say, three p.m.?"

"Sounds good."

"I'll see myself out. Goodnight." He headed down the corridor towards the front door.

Wren turned to Ariel as the front door closed. "So, you and Mr Williams, huh?"

Ariel grabbed a mug, and a herbal tea. "Does that bother you?" She poured water over the teabag, before glancing over her shoulder at Wren.

"Of course not. He is kinda cute, for an old guy."

Ariel laughed, shaking her head. "Thanks, I think."

"You're welcome." Wren bit into a crispy apple. "So, tomorrow night, you, him, no kids around." She stated around a juicy mouthful.

"Yes, I'm looking forward to it." Ariel took a sip of tea, watching Wren closely over the rim of her mug.

"What?"

"My sister-radar is picking up some feels from you, whenever this *Lance* is mentioned."

Wren shrugged, and Ariel watched in amusement as heat flooded her little sister's cheeks.

"I haven't told Hawk yet, that I'm crushing on his best mate."

"Sweety, I don't think Hawk would mind. In fact, with your *twin-thing*, I'm guessing he already knows."

Wren sighed. "Yeah, probably. He is good like that."

"Just be careful, okay?"

"Yes, Mum." Wren snickered playfully, rolling her eyes. "You too."

Ariel tilted her head. "I don't think Jaxon has a mean bone in his body."

"I hope not, or he'll have to answer to three of your younger siblings."

Ariel chuckled. "And for that, I'm grateful."

"Good. Well, I'm going to do an hour of legal studies before I hit the sack."

"Sounds good," Ariel followed Wren out of the kitchen, turning off the light before heading down the corridor, past the grandfather clock just outside of her Grandfather's office.

Pausing, she looked into the darkened room, thinking she saw movement in the corner. Frowning, she turned the light on, relieved to see nothing untoward. The smell of her Grandfather's old leather-bound books greeted her, and she was swamped with a lifetime of happy memories. How she missed them all, her loved ones, gone forever from this world.

"Goodnight Grandpa." She whispered, before turning the light off. She headed upstairs, pushing Timmy's door open a crack, her heart filled with joy as she saw her little brother fast asleep, clutching his Minkey Monkey close wearing a peaceful look upon his face.

"Night my love," she whispered, closing the door and heading into her room.

Pulling the covers back she looked forward to falling into a deep sleep and hoped to dream of a handsome man with smouldering dark eyes.

Ariel handed the bubble-wrapped painting to a tourist who had enjoyed an expresso in the café before he'd taken a stroll around the gallery.

"I'll make sure to tell my friends what a gem of a store this is." He said, tucking the canvas under his arm as he popped his wallet into his back pocket.

"You'll find most of the stores along Brooke Street a real treasure trove. Loddon Larder is full of surprises," she smiled at him.

"I look forward to exploring more next time I'm in town. Thank you." He nodded before leaving.

Ariel didn't think the day could get any better. All the kids had been excited when they left for their weekend filled with activities. Her morning session with her clients for the generation portrait had been entertaining and productive. It had been delightful being surrounded by the lively women, along with their intriguing conversations and family gossip that ended in fits of laughter. The bond between them, their love and respect for each other had overwhelmed Ariel in the best possible way. It made her grateful for the relationships she shared with each of her siblings, and Steven. She vowed to always maintain those relationships with clear communication and open love.

"I'll take two pink donuts and two cream buns, please," Ray beamed at Liv as Ariel headed towards the counter.

"Sure thing," Liv efficiently bagged up the sweet order. "There you go, Ray."

Ariel noticed Ray was dressed up nicely for a Saturday and had a particular glow about her.

"Thanks so much," Ray smiled, catching Ariel's eye as she turned. She leaned closer, dropping her voice so the other customers wouldn't hear. "My ex is bringing our kids down for a visit. They always loved sweet treats."

Ariel's heart melted and she reached out, taking Ray's hand and smiled warmly. "Have the most wonderful time, won't you?"

Ray nodded. "I intend to. I just hope my ex hasn't poisoned them too much against me."

The nervous edge to her voice had Ariel's protective side flare. "You just shine and be the beautiful person that you are. Show them that and nothing else will matter. They'll work it out for themselves."

"Yes," Liv nodded, leaning against the counter. "Kids are smart like that."

Ray took a deep breath, squaring her shoulders. "Yes, you're both right, thanks for that. Have a great afternoon." She called as she headed out the door.

Ariel exchanged a look with Liv, who was grinning like a Cheshire cat.

"I do love it when the world rights itself," Liv sighed as she waved to the last of the late afternoon customers, before turning the 'closed' sign over and locking the door.

Steven walked in from the gallery dressed in black jeans and a snug fitting tee-shirt with a loose jacket thrown over his shoulder, hooked by a finger. "

"Afternoon," he smiled at them both. "Are you ready Liv?"

Ariel looked at her friend, hiding her grin as she watched Liv nervously run her fingers through her shiny blonde locks. "Yes, I just have to finish cleaning up a bit."

Thinking she'd do her uncle a kindness, Ariel said. "No, I've got this, you go."

"Are you sure?" Liv sounded hopeful.

Ariel couldn't help her grin. "Totally. I need to do a couple of things in the gallery before I go anyway."

"Great," Steven reached for Liv's hand, not giving her an option. "Let's go. Bye sweets," he smiled at Ariel as Liv placed her hand in his.

"Have fun," she waited till they left the room, before releasing a dry laugh.

It seemed like love was in the air. She turned the café's radio up, and sang along to Justin Bieber's *Die for you*, as she collected cups and plates and took them to the sink, rinsing them all before popping them into the dishwasher.

Straightening the table clothes, she centred the jars of flowers and made sure all the souvenir spoons from around the world were clean. The books on the coffee table in the lounge area were all in neat piles.

"Café, check." She sang out as she headed into the gallery to finalize some paperwork. It wasn't long before she was turning the radio off and heading out the backdoor. She enjoyed her walk in the sun that was brushing the tops of the Mallee trees, as the Corellas called to their noisy competitors, the Galahs.

The thought of seeing Jaxon, being alone with him, ignited excited nerves in her belly.

"*Jesus,* stop it," she whispered as heat pooled between her thighs with each step and every thought of the man himself. "I know it's been a while, but this is ridiculous." She shook her head and jogged the rest of the way home, looking forward to a cold shower to tidy up all her girly-bits; hoping to have his mouth on every inch of her when the time was right.

Chapter Thirteen
Jaxon

J axon arrived on time like the punctual man he'd been raised to be. Pleasure spread in his belly when Ariel opened the door, standing there dressed in an off the shoulder, knee length black dress that clung to every lush curve; her fiery red locks caressing her creamy shoulders, her feet bare.

"Hello," he said, grateful that his greeting didn't sound like an aroused teenager.

She grinned up at him. "Hi there. Please, come in."

As she stood back holding the door open for him, he walked by making sure not to knock his basket into her as he bent to drop a sweeping kiss across her cheek.

"Mm," he said quietly. "You smell divine."

She closed the door and smiled. "Thank you, it's my mother's favourite scent."

"Channel?"

She led the way along the corridor and threw an impressed look over her shoulder as he followed. "Yes."

Following her into the kitchen, he sat the basket on the butchers block and began pulling items out, lining them up on the bench as she opened the fridge and grabbed a craft beer.

"I'll join you in a wine, if you don't mind." He nodded towards the open bottle she had breathing on the counter.

"Perfect." She put the beer back and took out an extra glass, filling them before passing him one. "What shall we cheers to?"

He looked down at her as she swirled the liquid about her glass. She was looking up at him with large, bright green eyes with what he could only assume was excitement, and anticipation for what this afternoon might hold. He was feeling it too. Wanting to pin her beneath him and have his wicked way with her.

But he wasn't going to rush this moment. He wanted to saviour the build-up, her taste and their climax, as one would relish a good meal.

"How about to blossoming friendships?" He tilted his head as he watched her pretty lips part. Her gaze dropped to his mouth and a ball of lust slammed straight into his gut. Surely one kiss wouldn't hurt. He gently clicked his glass against hers before they both took a mouthful.

Sitting his glass down carefully he moved against her, placing his hands either side of her hips on the butchers block, caging her in. He bent his head; grateful she was still holding her glass between them which would slow things down.

"Is this an hors d'oeuvre?" She whispered as he held his lips a fraction above hers.

"Sure, why not," his male pride backflipped as he watched her eyes cloud over, before sweeping his lips slowly along hers, not deepening the kiss, but letting her know nothing about this union would be rushed.

The giggle she released surprised him, and he drew back raising an eyebrow.

"Feel free to share?"

He reached around her and picked up his wine, taking a mouthful, enjoying the red flush that filled her pretty face.

"Oh, I couldn't possibly. I'd embarrass my Grandmother." She reached on tiptoes, and he held still as her gaze locked on his, before she ran her tongue over his bottom lip, making him grow hard instantly.

"Mm," she smiled sheepishly, stepping away. "Best hors d'oeuvre I've had in a very long time."

"Have to agree with you there," he forced his mind out of the gutter as she turned away and bent to turn the oven on.

"What temperature do you want?"

"Hot," he murmured. "Very hot."

She turned, grinning at him. "Exactly how hot?"

He cleared his throat before taking a cool swallow of wine. "Two-eighty degrees, to start."

She closed the oven door and walked over to peek at the items he had removed from the basket. Picking up a bag of rolls, she asked. "And what are we having?"

He removed the last item from the basket which was wrapped in a tea-towel, and smiled easily at her. "Pulled pork rolls, with coleslaw and gravy."

"Are you a mind reader?"

He chuckled as she turned to pull an iron pot with a lid from the cupboard. "I kind of have to be to some extent with my job. But no. Why?"

"Pork rolls were my go-to for lunch when I lived in the city. There was a food van just around the corner from my gallery. Best rolls ever. I haven't had one since we moved here." She took a mouthful of wine, leaning against the bench.

"Inglewood has some decent places to eat, like the Inglewood Take Away, Cousin Jack's and Liv's café, but there's nothing really around here that makes your tastebuds want to party."

"The Bridgewater pub does a nice meal." She said.

"True, but we are going to do better than, *just nice.*" He pulled the cling wrap off a small bowl and grabbed a handful of the contents.

"What have you got there?" She asked.

"Brown sugar, salt, paprika, cumin, onion and garlic powder, and a bit of cracked black pepper." He watched her, watching him as he began to rub the pork tenderly and thoroughly, massaging the rub mix in.

As her eyes raised to his, he grinned. "I can do a pretty decent massage too."

She laughed. "I don't doubt it."

He loved the way her eyes brightened and wondered if she knew how beautiful she was? Did she know what affect she had on the opposite sex? Some women did, and used it to their advantage, which was never attractive. He didn't think she was one of them. Plopping the pork into the dish he asked. "Can you grab me that beer now?"

She raised an eyebrow before pulling the beer out of the fridge and passed it to him.

"Thanks." Twisting the cap off, he poured the beer into the dish.

"Perfect," he said as he popped the lid on, scooped up the dish and headed across to the oven as Ariel opened it for him. Placing it on the rack, he shut the door before heading across to the sink to wash the rub from his hands.

"Well, that should only take about three or so hours." He turned to her as he wiped his hands on a tea towel, before dropping it onto the bench. "What would you like to do while we wait?"

Ariel

Does he really need to ask? She took another mouthful of her wine, feeling a relaxed buzz sweep through her, almost blurting out what she wanted to do with him; to him. But said instead. "Would you like to take a look at my studio?"

He picked up his wine, his gaze holding hers as he took a swallow. "I'd love to."

Ariel grabbed the bottle and topped up their glasses before clinking hers against his, and said "Follow me."

She led the way along the smooth floorboards and out the back door, heading down the bricked pathway, before sliding the barn door open.

"I've always loved this space." Jaxon said following her into the spacious studio. "Steven and I practically grew up in this barn," he chuckled as he walked by her and further into the studio. "The things we thought we got away with in here."

Ariel laughed. "I can only imagine."

"Your Grandmother was one hell of a lady," he said fondly.

"She certainly was." Ariel quietly agreed, watching him walk around her space taking in her many creations.

"So was your mother," he stated.

"Yes, she was," Ariel sighed.

He walked like a man who had all the time in the world, yet not one movement was wasted as he weaved between the rows of displayed canvases.

"They'd be so proud of you. You really are extraordinary," he called, vanishing behind a canvas wall. She rested her hip against the table feeling a rush of pride.

"Thank you, Mr Williams." She always got a thrill when anyone appreciated her work. Although, their compliments didn't usually make heat pool between her thighs.

"All these completed ones, who are they for?"

She quickly swallowed some wine hoping her voice wouldn't sound breathless when she answered. "Galleries, hotels, cafes, and restaurants. A hospital too, along with a mental health, and disability organisation. All sorts really."

He walked around another canvas so he could see her. "How do you get them to the clients when they are so large?"

"Sometimes Steven delivers them for me, as he's always travelling around Victoria. But, for overseas or interstate, I make crates designed for each canvas's specifications, and when they are all safe and sound, pop them in the post."

"That sounds expensive."

"For some. For those who prefer it, I cut them off the canvas and post them in a protective cardboard tube."

He nodded as he walked towards her. "I'd like you to do one of my Great Grandparents' house and gardens whenever you have the time."

"It's such a beautiful home, it would be my pleasure." She felt her heart race out of control the closer he came to her, and hoped her cheeks weren't going red. She could feel heat sweep up her neck. "Are you enjoying the wine?"

He stopped a foot away from her, taking another mouthful before nodding slowly. "Mhm."

She stared into his caramel pools of honey as he stared unblinkingly down at her.

She swallowed. "It was a high school in Melbourne that you taught at, wasn't it?"

"It was."

She nodded. "You must have driven those teenage girls insane with those brooding eyes of yours."

He smiled, shaking his head. "It was an all-boy's school."

"Oh, well… their mothers then." She whispered as he closed the gap between them, taking her glass from her and setting both glasses down on the table.

He moved against her and his scent wrapped around her, making her head spin. His hands swept up her throat, caressing her flesh before cupping her face gently. "You are so incredibly beautiful."

"Is that how you see me?" She asked, titling her head back so she could look into his eyes, taking in every handsome detail.

"Mhm."

A pleasant sensation built within her, and her body hummed in anticipation. She traced her fingertip along his dark brow, whispering, "Beautiful," watching in fascination as he frowned.

She couldn't help the quiet laugh that slipped from her lips.

He smiled, shaking his head. "What now?"

"You, dammit. You're entirely too good looking."

"I'll take *that*, over beautiful." His gaze dropped to her lips.

She cupped his jaw, running her palm along his flesh that was soft with just a hint of stubble, before slipping her fingers behind his neck and drawing him to her. If she didn't have him soon, she'd have to slip into the bathroom and take care of her burning desire herself. And she did not want to waste an orgasm when she had Mr Yummy right here, right now.

As his lips lowered, she stood on tiptoe to meet him halfway. His arms tightened around her waist and held her close as his tongue mated sensually with hers, before gently sucking it into his mouth, lapping at her like she was his favourite ice-cream. She moaned as her knickers grew slick, her bud throbbed, and she rubbed against his bulging crotch seeking release.

He gripped her hips tighter, holding her still as she moved against him and his tongue circled hers before kissing her solidly.

Running her hands over his shoulders, she tried to rub herself against him once more, but his fingers were like a steel vice. She pulled back, looking into his eyes as he closed his and took a deep breath.

"Is something wrong?" She prayed not, her thighs were wet, and if she pressed her legs together and rubbed for a second, she'd explode.

He opened his eyes slowly, shaking his head as he ran a finger across her swollen lips. Back and forward before bending to sweep his tongue along them, then between her lips in a rhythmic dance as he ran a hand down her chest and over her belly, towards the hem of her dress.

She almost cried in pleasure when he cupped her moist knickers with purposeful, knowing fingers. She couldn't help her wanton-self and moved against him, relishing every touch before he moved the silky material aside, and stroked her flesh.

His sigh of pleasure against her mouth had her melting.

She spread her legs wider, rocking against his hand as she sucked his tongue into her mouth. Heat spread into the pit of her belly, building between her thighs as his thumb stroked her throbbing bud. Up and down his fingers glided over her slick, wet heat. He massaged and manipulated her in the most delicious way, creating tension that was building and on the brink of exploding.

She gasped against his lips, disappointed when he removed his hand, before pulling away.

He chuckled and kissed her between arched brows, as he ran his hands down her back, before cupping her bottom and lifting her effortlessly on the table, mindful of their glasses.

She smiled; glad the game wasn't over just yet. "You had me worried for a second," she whispered, delighted.

"Oh, we're just getting started," he returned smoothly. "We've got all afternoon." His fingers made circle motions across her hips, before moving to her thighs, opening them wide to step between them. Hooking his hands under her knees, he slid her against his bulging crotch, causing her to cry out.

"If you don't take me soon, I'm going to slide right off this table, you know that don't you?"

He grinned slyly. "I do," he whispered before kissing her deeply. He cleverly demonstrated with his tongue what he wanted to do to the rest of her.

Holding her close he slid his lips over her neck, trailing sweet kisses along her flesh, creating goosebumps and slowly pulled her dress down under her breasts. She saw the look of surprise on his face when he saw she wasn't wearing a bra.

She was going to mention something about the perks of not having breast fed just yet when he lowered his mouth to her breast. Any smartarse comment she was about to make disappeared as he drew her plump nipple into his mouth, making her throb desperately. She wrapped her legs around him and arched her back so he could take more of her; silently begging him to do so.

He leaned her down onto the table as his mouth left her breast to glide down her belly. She closed her eyes, sighing as his lips tickled the inside of her thigh, kissing her flesh gently before pushing her legs wider apart.

Yes, yes, yes! She nearly laughed in delight.

"Like a kitten," he whispered.

She couldn't respond if her life depended on it, and stretched her arms above her head, tilting her hips up in anticipation as he pulled her knickers aside.

Now, now, now. She chanted silently as his nose rubbed along the inside of her thigh before kissing a damp trail along her silken flesh, inching closer and closer to her core. She spread her legs wider as his fingers swept over her bottom split. She cried out as his tongue swept along her throbbing lips, parting her, tasting her, before he pushed his mouth closer, kissing her deeply as he had done to her mouth moments before.

"Oh, my Lordy," she moaned as she felt her climax build, rocking wantonly against the heat of his mouth and greedily relished every sensation as he ravished her. His fingers gently slipped into her, pushing deeply to stroke her G-spot, as his tongue swirled around her throbbing bud before sucking on it repeatedly. His long, clever fingers manipulated the most divine orgasm she'd ever had.

She screamed in pleasure, swept away in sheer delight as her body tingled all over, riding on the rainbow of sensations. She lay there, panting and satisfied, yet wanting more. She raised herself on her elbows as he raised his head to stare into her eyes.

He slowly ran his tongue over his glistening lips as he stood, reaching into his back pocket to pull out a foil wrapped condom.

She raised an eyebrow, "I appreciate a man who comes prepared."

"I thought you might," he said, before raising the packet to his mouth and cautiously ripping it open with his teeth as he popped his jeans button open and drew the zipper down.

Her belly clenched. She'd just had the most satisfying orgasm of her life, and yet could not wait to have this scrumptious man inside of her. Her gaze dropped, then widened at the sheer size of his swollen shaft, watching as he slid the condom over the head of his manhood, a clear pearl-drop trapped inside.

Saliva pooled in her mouth, and she raised her gaze to his.

Rich laughter burst from Jaxon as he wrapped his arms around her waist, drawing her close, kissing her neck. "I'll be gentle, I promise."

"Please, don't be," she said, reaching around his broad shoulders, pulling him closer and spreading her legs wide, pushing her moist core against him.

"I'm not going to last long with you doing things like that." He groaned, nuzzling her neck as his fingers danced over the flesh of her back.

"I don't want you to last long, I want you hard, and fast." She ran her tongue over his jaw, along his neck, and lapped at his ear, flicking the tip inside his lobe, feeling him shiver before he lifted his head.

"Whatever you say," he said, and cupped her bottom, his gaze not leaving hers as he nestled the tip of his erection against her still throbbing core. He waited one heart stopping second, before slowly sliding inside her, filling her completely.

"Mm," he moaned, holding still for a moment. She wondered if her eyes had clouded over as much as his had.

Sighing, she slid her fingers into his thick hair, gently bringing his head down towards hers. She parted her lips, wanting to feast on him as she opened her legs wider, needing all of him.

He moved then, pulling out of her as his lips sank over hers before sliding back into her moist centre, penetrating deeply as his tongue slipped into her mouth. She moaned then, and moved against him, before he lifted her bottom off the table and turned them around. He leaned back against the table, her legs wrapping around him as he pumped faster, pushing himself inside her in a rhythmic beat that was sending her over the edge once again.

She sucked on his tongue as her climax began to peak, and rocked against him, moving in harmony to build a powerful orgasm for them both. He spun them around again, setting her on the table before pumping furiously inside her, gripping her hips and slamming her centre against him, making her scream as another orgasm exploded, shooting pulsating fireworks throughout every nerve ending in her body.

She fell limp against him, thoroughly spent as he buried himself inside her, shooting his desire into the condom. He held her close, burying his face into her neck as he moaned in satisfaction.

Silence surrounded them as they caught their breath.

"I think you've earned your nickname," she sounded husky, breaking the silence. She cleared her throat.

He raised his face from her neck, gently tucking a strand of hair behind her ear. "I have a nickname?"

"Mhm, although, it's not very original for someone like yourself." She felt embarrassed for a moment that she'd mentioned it.

He dropped a kiss on the tip of her nose. "Can't wait to hear it," he dropped another kiss on her cheek as she sighed.

"Mr Yummy," she murmured as he kissed her other cheek.

"Mr... Yummy?" He raised an eyebrow.

"Like I said, not very original." She sighed as he kissed her gently before she felt him slip out of her.

"I don't know. It has a nice ring to it." He grinned stepping back, pulling the condom off, and his jeans up.

She tugged her dress down, enjoying seeing him slightly dishevelled. "Over there," she pointed to the bin, pulling the top of her dress up to cover her breasts.

"Thanks," he turned towards the bin.

She appreciated his strong back as he strolled over and dropped the evidence of their lustful union into the bin.

She slid off the table, feeling extremely relaxed and reached for her wine, passing him his as he drew near.

"I'm impressed we didn't knock them over." He smiled, taking the glass and dropping a sweet kiss across her lips.

"Me too," she raised her glass and said, "To friendships that blossom."

"And to their continued growth," he clinked his glass against hers before putting an arm around her shoulders.

"Oh, I like that." She took a deep swallow, slipping her arm around his waist and led him out of the studio. The backyard was a symphony of crickets, and cicadas popping and snapping their wings as the afternoon sun lowered in a pink shaded sky.

"Red sky at night…" Ariel began.

"Is a sailor's delight." Jaxon finished.

She smiled up at him. "Thank god we're on the same page."

"Pardon?"

"I had a client who commissioned a sunset scene. Flew me to New Zealand to capture the essence of his childhood view overlooking the Pacific Ocean. He insisted on it being titled, 'A shepherd's delight.' Didn't sit well with me." She mock shuddered.

He laughed. "That concept first appears in the Bible."

"Yeah, so he said. Still, it went against what my Mother, and Grandmother said, so…" She shrugged.

"We are creatures of our culture and habit."

The scent of the roasting pork greeted them as they crossed the porch and through the back door. "That smells delectable," she sighed, her stomach rumbling.

"It will be, I promise you that. Want to help me make the sauce?"

"Sure," she smiled, before grabbing the wine to top up their glasses.

They worked together in harmony, moving around her kitchen, grabbing bowls and whisks, adding spices, and liquids. Aromas filled the entire house and had Ariel's mouth watering. And it wasn't just the food. Watching Jaxon throw ingredients into a bowl and whisk away till it thickened, his muscles bunching like a large cat that needed stroking. His handsome features relaxed as he concentrated on getting the balance of flavours just right.

His gaze met hers across the butchers block as she sipped her wine, and he smiled knowingly.

"Taste this," he dipped a finger into the thick sauce and offered it to her.

She took his wrist, before wrapping her lips around his finger and delicately sucked it clean, all the while her gaze was pinned to his. She tried to stop her satisfied grin as she watched his eyes widen, after she ran her tongue over the tip of his finger, before releasing his wrist.

"Mm, it's good." She wiped a finger over her lips, as his eyes traced its journey.

He passed her the bowl. "That can sit in the fridge, thanks."

She took it and popped it in the fridge before turning to ask. "You want to look at some of Grandma's albums?"

His eyes brightened as he nodded. "Actually, yes. There is a picture I've been wanting to see for a while, when Steven and I helped put in the stained-glass windows."

Ariel nodded as she led the way into the lounge and across to the bookcase as Jaxon strolled over to the stained-glass window.

She pulled out a stack of her Grandmother's albums from the bottom shelf and turned to see Jaxon run a finger gently over the ornate pattern.

"It really is beautiful, isn't it?" She said, sitting the albums on the coffee table.

"It is. Most of the stained glass in this house came from old buildings around the town that were neglected over time. Your Grandfather wanted to preserve as much of the town's history within this house. It has been renovated painstakingly over the years, with the skeletons of many homes, churches, and buildings."

"Yes, Mum was always proud of this house. We all are really."

He joined her as she sat on the settee and picked up an album, running his hand over the front before opening it.

Ariel sat closer so she could look at the black and white photographs with him, of an era when her Grandmother was a girl, standing with her siblings and parents. The front of the house looked quaint and elegant as they stood beside the peppercorn tree that was no higher than her Grandmother's waist.

Ariel ran her finger over her Grandmother's face. "So young," she whispered. "The things she must have seen as the decades rolled by."

"What a privilege." Jaxon said, looping his arm over her shoulder. They turned the pages, taking in the changes of the house and the town of Inglewood. Seeing the images as her Grandmother's family faced death, and the loss of her parents, placing her siblings in her care. As the years turned and they left home, happy photographs filled the album as she had married Ariel's Grandfather. Then the house receiving renovations to preserve its grandeur old style with the respect it deserved, with the historical society's approval.

Finally, the next album showed her Grandmother pregnant with her mother, then many years later, baby Steven.

"Butter wouldn't melt." Jaxon laughed, turning the next page to see Steven in a sandpit flinging a shovel of sand at a light-haired little boy.

"Is that you?"

"It is, and he copped a hiding after delivering that spadeful of sand to my face." He sighed reaching for his wine. "Squawked like a newborn baby he did."

Ariel laughed as she turned the page. "Parenting was so different back then."

"Simpler, you could say."

"Yeah, in some ways." She saw her teenage mother holding the hands of the two little boys all smiling happily into the camera, wearing bathers and standing knee deep in the reservoir's brown waters.

She leaned back against Jaxon's arm, stroking a finger over her mother's face. Her throat restricted as grief tiptoed into her soul. "I miss her so much," she whispered.

Jaxon dropped a sweet kiss onto her shoulder. "Of course you do love."

She blinked away tears that threatened and offered him a smile.

"It's hard not to. She was so special, the best mum a kid could ask for."

"As mothers are meant to be." There was a hard edge to his voice, and Ariel reached for his hand.

"I don't really know anything about your mother." She wished she hadn't said a thing, as his eyes became distant.

He rubbed her arm again before pulling away and reached for another album. "There's nothing to tell. My Grandfather raised me and when he couldn't, your Grandparents did. They were always there for me."

Ariel sat silently for a moment as he turned another page.

"Jaxon, whatever happened to you, you can share it with me. I'm sure you'd be the first to tell your students, it's always better to discuss the things that hurt us, and not hold onto the pain?"

He sighed, before his dark gaze met hers.

"I'm sorry, I don't want to upset you." She bit her lip, unsure if she was making him mad.

He must have noticed her uncertainty. "You haven't, love. I'm okay," he assured her, before turning back to the album.

She *loved* it when he called her love and tried not to read anything into it. *Early, early days…* She caught a smile that fleetingly swept across his face and followed his gaze to what had lifted his spirits. He and Steven were in tattered overalls helping her Grandfather insert the stained-glass window with the most intricate patterns of a goldmining scene set on the Loddon River.

"Stunning craftsmanship, and you were both so adorable."

He nodded, remaining silent.

"Of course, my Grandparents would have loved you like you were theirs, how could they not?"

It felt like a lifetime before he finally spoke. "My mother had a vicious temper. She was raised from hard stock in an abusive home. She was always angry. From my very first memory of her to the last before she disappeared."

"Disappeared? How old were you?"

"I was seven."

"Oh Jaxon." *Timmy's age now.* She placed her hand on his knee and squeezed gently.

"My father was a gentle spoken man, very much like my Grandfather had been. My Grandfather told me that my mother blamed my dad when they couldn't have more children. She would belittle him, physically assault him and degraded him on a regular basis, and not just behind closed doors."

"Your poor father." Ariel interjected softly. "That's disgusting behaviour."

He nodded, before continuing. "After she disappeared my father fell into a black hole. One he struggled to get out of, but no matter how hard he tried he couldn't. Unfortunately, he lost his battle with depression and committed suicide.

"How old were you?" She whispered.

"It was just before my eighth birthday." He ran his fingers through his hair. "After he died my Grandfather, and your Grandparents gave me the stability I needed to have a fairly happy childhood. I hit more troubled waters with my own mental health when I was a teenager, but those younger years with your family meant everything to me."

Ariel shook her head. "Still, it would have been so difficult for you."

He shrugged. "I've been luckier than most."

"No one avoids heartache in this world, do they?"

He smiled, shaking his head. "Nope."

"Ah, to be human."

"Opposed to?"

"Let me think on that." She laughed, before asking. "When did you decide you wanted to become a teacher?"

"When I was fourteen, I started school refusal because of my anxiety. My Grandfather was confused as to why a kid who loved school suddenly couldn't get out of bed in the morning and go to class. It confused him more when I didn't even have the desire to attend footy practise with my mates."

"A very revealing sign to parents and carers now days.

He nodded. "Yes, when people distance themselves from their usual activities that they'd normally thrive in, it says it all."

"So, what happened?"

"Thankfully, I had a very observant teacher who really gave a damn. Essentially, he was the reason I wanted to become a teacher. Along with your family and a wonderful counsellor, they turned my life around."

"Inspiring humans truly deserve more than medals." She mused, curling a fiery strand around her finger as her eyes drifted back to the next page that he turned.

"I think inspiring people who improve others' lives are reward enough," he said, before leaning closer to a photograph. "What is that?" He whispered.

Ariel reached for the album, and peeling the clear protective layer back, gently pulled the photo off the album's page. Frowning, she held the photo up so they could both take a better look at it.

Teenage Steven and Jaxon stood on either side of the stained-glass window in the lounge, that the darkening sky now peered through. The boys were smiling and pointing towards the window with one hand and giving the thumbs-up sign to the photographer. Looming over Jaxon was a distinctive dark figure.

"That looks like a shadow of a woman," Jaxon said quietly.

"And if that's not disturbing enough…" Ariel pointed to a small figure standing in front of Steven. "That looks like a child?"

"One shadow is black, and the other has a white orb around it?"

"That's weird," Ariel said.

Jaxon opened his mouth to respond but before he could utter a word, the photo album flew off his lap and floated five feet above their heads before slamming shut, making the windows rattle. It dropped to the rug at their feet with an explosive thump making them jump.

Ariel's heart was racing as her mouth went dry. Jaxon reached for her hand and stood, stepping slightly in front of her as if to protect her.

Ariel rose on shaking legs as she peered around Jaxon's shoulder.

He looked down at her. "You alright?"

"I'm a little pissed off if you want the truth," she frowned.

He raised an eyebrow but remained silent.

She shrugged. "It's been so lovely and quiet around here I just don't want anything to start up again." She glanced at the album that lay at their feet, before pulling her fingers from his and bent to pick it up.

"I know I'm not an expert, but the energy doesn't feel negative?" Jaxon remarked, as Ariel opened the album back to the page that they had pulled the photo from, before sliding it back into its space.

She nodded, placing the album on top of the others, then scooped them all up and carried them across to the bookcase.

"I agree with you, it doesn't feel sinister." She said, placing them back onto the lower shelf, before turning to face him. "But I need this house to be peaceful and safe for my kids." She folded her arms, feeling a slight chill in the air.

"Hey," he crossed towards her, placing his arm around her waist. "Why don't we go for a walk and by the time we get back that pork will be mouth-watering, and then I can either get out of your hair, or..."

"*No*, please stay!" She blurted, not allowing him to finish. She felt heat fill her cheeks, and watched as his lips formed a gorgeous smile.

He cupped her chin and brushed a kiss across her lips. "I'd love to."

She smiled, releasing a breath. "Thank you."

"Please, don't thank me. I couldn't think of a more pleasant way to spend a Saturday night, than with a beautiful woman and her tantalising conversation."

She tilted her head, smiling cheekily. "*Just* the tantalising conversation?"

He grinned. "Hell no. But it certainly is as delicious as the rest of the menu. Let's go."

She nodded and was grateful when he took her hand and led her out of the room. Glancing towards the window a fleeting cold touch gripped her bare shoulder before vanishing completely.

Stepping out into the warm night air, the scent of heated eucalyptus leaves and peppercorn pods reached her. Taking a calming breath she felt herself relax enough to focus on the intriguing man beside her.

Chapter Fourteen
Ariel

"Wow, this is fabulous, Ariel." Ray beamed Thursday afternoon as she stood back looking at the old tennis wall. The handmade red bricks were now covered in vibrant botanicals and native animals and birds. It was detailed, bright and cheerful.

"Thank you, I can't take all the credit though. I did have some good help." She smiled, nodding towards Jaxon and a few of the mums. When the mothers had found out Jaxon was staying behind after school to finish the mural project, they readily volunteered their time. It had been a long week with clients, the kids and the gallery, on top of dealing with the opinionated women to discuss and finalise the mural.

"I bet you did." Ray waved to Jaxon, who was washing brushes out in the drinking trough with Valeria.

"How was last weekend with your kids?" Ariel asked. "Were the donuts a hit?"

"They were." Ray said quietly, the cheer dissipating from her tone.

"What happened?" Ariel asked, placing a hand on Ray's arm.

Ray forced a smile, patting the top of Ariel's arm. "Nothing that can't be sorted in time."

"If you ever want to stop by the gallery or come by the house for a cuppa and a chat, you're always welcome." Ariel said softly.

Ray smiled genuinely this time. "Thank you, I may just do that."

"Ariel, Ariel." Timmy yelled racing over, sweat dripping down his face. "Can Paul and Aaron come over for a sleepover tonight?"

"Oh, I don't know, it's a school night…" Ariel trailed off as Valeria, Aaron's mother, headed towards her.

"Ariel, I've said Aaron is more than welcome to sleep over at yours tonight, with your permission of course." The tall, impeccably dressed woman said, tucking a perfect blonde strand behind her ear, not a drop of sweat or paint in sight.

"Oh, okay then. Um, I…" Why was this woman suddenly wanting to be civil to her, when she'd made no previous attempt in the month and a half that they'd been at the school?

"It's no problem, is it? I can drop a casserole off for your dinner." She said, sounding condescending.

"That won't be necessary Valeria." Jaxon said as he approached them. "We're doing a BBQ for tea tonight."

Ariel felt a warm glow spread throughout her body as her heart fluttered when he stepped closer towards her and gently placed a hand on her shoulder. She didn't need a knight in shining armour… but he'd do nicely.

"Isn't that right?" He asked.

"Can they Ariel, can they *please*," Timmy cried, jumping up and down.

Ariel laughed, placing her hand on top of Timmy's head. "Yes okay, as long as it's alright with Mrs Musgrove."

"I've already asked her, Paul's gone home to pack his bag." Timmy beamed looking proud of himself.

"How thoughtful of you." She grinned at him before meeting Valeria's cool gaze. "That should be fine then."

"Wonderful. Aaron likes a bedtime story at seven thirty, and a back rub as he goes to sleep." Valeria stated, before looking at Jaxon. "I'm sure if you're still there, he'd love you to read to him?"

Jaxon nodded. "Shouldn't be a problem."

Ariel forced a smile. "Anything else you'd like us to do for Aaron?" *Like, chew his food, wipe his backside...*

"No, that's fine. As long as he gets to school on time."

Ariel bit her tongue as Jaxon replied. "Too easy."

Valeria beamed at him. "Well, you've always been reliable Mr Williams. Thank you. I'll drop Aaron off at five." She nodded, before turning on her heel and joining the group of women.

"Can we go Ariel? I need to set my room up!" Timmy cried, running towards the front gate.

"Looks like Timmy is all set for a good night," Ray chuckled.

"Would you like to join us?" Ariel asked.

"Oh no. But thank you." Ray nodded. "See you tomorrow Jaxon, Have a good night Ariel."

"You too." Ariel replied.

"See you tomorrow." Jaxon called, as Ray headed into the school building.

When they were alone, Jaxon slid his arm around her waist and nodded towards the mural. "That went well."

"I think it went well because of your help with the women." Ariel tipped her head back to meet his gaze. "They'd still be bickering about my colour choices if it weren't for you."

"You're welcome," he said, massaging her through her tee shirt that was damp with perspiration.

"I need a shower before Lord Aaron arrives."

Jaxon raised an eyebrow, "Lord Aaron?"

"Sure. Back rub, foot massage, let me tell you a story and peel a grape for you."

He chuckled darkly as he bent his head towards her. "You're too damn cute for your own good Miss Harper."

She had a witty reply, but watching his beautiful lips part, and his caramel eyes darken, all banter disappeared as his lips captured hers in the sweetest kiss that promised more.

"Ariel!" Timmy yelled. "Hurry up!"

Jaxon chuckled against her lips as she released a sigh.

"How about you get home and have that shower. I'll go pick up Paul." Jaxon dropped another quick kiss against her lips.

She stared up at him, feeling a rush of love for a man who'd been entwined in her family for many years, and who was slowly and steadily stealing her heart.

"What?" He asked quietly, cupping her chin.

She took a breath to reply when Timmy yelled again, "*Ariel.*"

Jaxon smiled. "Keep that thought."

"Oh, it's not going anywhere."

He smiled as he stepped back. "See you soon."

She nodded as she headed towards the school gate. "Coming Timmy." She called.

Jaxon

Jaxon turned the BBQ off as Wren carried the plate of sausages and hamburgers.

"Dinners ready," she called, as he followed her into the kitchen where Ariel was tossing a green salad and Hawk was buttering bread.

"Just pop it on the dining table hun," Ariel called, carrying the salad to the table where the three hungry school-boys sat.

"Where's the chops and ribs?" Aaron asked, nose screwed up at the simple presentation of sausages and hamburgers.

Paul yelled in delight. "Oh yeah, nothing better than a snag," he reached across and grabbed a slice of bread and held it open for Wren to drop a sausage into it.

"Thanks," he chirped happily.

"Sauce, mate?" Hawk asked the easy to please boy.

"Yes please."

Jaxon sat beside Wren, as he shared a smile with Ariel, watching as she dolloped potato salad onto the boys' plates, followed by coleslaw and a green salad.

How could her doing something as simple as dishing out salad make her that much more appealing to him? Because she was doing it with love and kindness, even to snarly, spoilt Aaron.

"Thank you, Ariel." Paul gushed, scooping up some potatoes and taking a bite of his sausage.

"You're welcome, Paul. Aaron, would you like a hamburger?" She asked kindly.

Jaxon watched the entitled boy frown before replying, "I suppose so."

Wren scoffed, and Jaxon saw Hawk gently brush a hand over her shoulder, as he deposited a serving of meat on Timmy, and Aaron's plates.

Wren whispered to Hawk, "I can't stand bad manners."

Hawk grinned, dropping a hamburger onto her plate. "You're welcome."

"Hah," She smiled sweetly. "Thank you." She reached for the chutney jar and smeared a sticky layer over her hamburger.

"So, boys, are you looking forward to the excursion next week with the historical society?" Jaxon asked.

"Yeah, it's going to be awesome!" Paul mumbled around a mouthful of food.

Jaxon shared another grin with Ariel. They were both obviously enjoying Paul's zest for life.

"We're going to visit the courthouse and get locked in the jail. How cool's that?" Timmy slapped his hamburger in between two slices of bread, smeared with tomato sauce.

"Very cool," Wren smiled. "Because it's pretend."

"Boring," Aaron used his fork to push his green salad around on his plate. "Can I have some lemonade?"

"We have lemon cordial," Ariel said, reaching for the jug that jingled with ice blocks as she lifted it.

"That'll do I guess," he said, sounding sulky.

"How about some manners, Aaron." Jaxon clipped.

Aaron met his teacher's gaze. "Sure. Thanks."

"Wow Aaron, Sebastian says your manners are up your bum!" Timmy laughed.

"Timmy…" Ariel said.

"Who's Sebastian?" Paul yelled out.

"Timmy's a baby, he's got a make-believe friend," Aaron snickered.

"Shut up! He's not make-believe, he's as real as you and me." Timmy cried.

"You're an idiot!" Aaron yelled.

"You are!" Timmy threw back.

"That's enough, boys, please." Ariel said calmly, pouring them all a glass of cordial. "Let's just get through the meal, then you can have a play outside before it's time to settle down for the night."

"I am *not* having kids," Wren muttered around a mouthful of green beans.

Jaxon chuckled as he speared a slice of cucumber, adding it to his hamburger sandwich.

"I enjoy the calming conversation a dinner table provides a family," he smiled sweetly at Ariel before taking a mouthful, watching her as he chewed.

"Oh yeah, you're welcome to come back and be entertained anytime,

Mr Williams." She grinned.

"Thank you," he reached for his cordial.

"Do you want a beer Mr Williams?" Hawk asked, heading towards the fridge.

"No thanks, mate."

Hawk returned with a ginger beer, and twisting the top poured a glass for himself and Wren.

Timmy and Aaron sat opposite each other, exchanging sullen looks, whilst Paul watched them both with bright eyes as he cleared his plate.

Jaxon noticed Timmy turn his head to the side, as if listening to someone then all but threw his knife under the table and disappeared to retrieve it. He remained under the table for a few moments longer, then returned to his seat. Timmy met his curious gaze, before asking Ariel.

"Can we play hide and seek after tea?"

"Of course you can." She scooped up some potato salad and Jaxon watched her pretty lips part, before placing the creamy salad into her mouth. He was looking forward to kissing those sweet lips of hers very soon.

Timmy

"One, two, three, four, five..." Timmy leaned against the side of the house with his hands covering his face, counting off for his friends to go hide. When he'd dropped his knife under the table, Sebastian had been waiting underneath for him and had suggested the hide and seek game. Timmy thought it was a great idea, especially that Sebastian wanted to join in.

"Ten! Coming, ready or not!" He yelled; a few seconds too early. "Come on Sebastian,

let's go," he laughed, and with his friend on his heels they ran to find the others.

Racing towards the chook pen first, he thought that was one of the coolest places to hide. It would have been his first choice, and knowing that Paul loved the chickens too, thought it was a no-brainer.

Giggling to himself he pushed the door open and rushed through the coops small hatch; disappointed to find only the chickens settling in for the night. They clucked unhappily at being disturbed.

"Drats," he said, turning to Sebastian, only to find himself alone. "Where'd ya go, Sebastian?" He whispered. Nothing. Oh well, sometimes Sebastian did that. Took clear off without warning.

"I guess I'm on my own then," he said, before running around the side of the house, under the peppercorn tree and glanced upwards, making sure no one was hiding in its branches. He jumped over the row of lavender before crouching down to look under the front porch steps. No one. Maybe they were hiding in the garage? He ran off, filled with glee at the prospect of finding them so quickly and quietened his footsteps, hoping to frighten them. He stopped a giggle that wanted to burst out and snuck towards the garage door, delighted to see it slightly ajar.

"*Got 'cha.*" he whispered, slipping in between the opening and ducking low. He crept inside the musty garage, tiptoeing over the concrete covered in dry leaves that crackled as he stepped on them. He held his breath as he dropped to his hands and knees, peeking under his Grandfather's mint-green Kingston, and towards the back of the garage where aged-worn suitcase-trunks, and boxes were stacked against the corrugated-tin wall. Most of their Grandparent's things were stored in here. Things Ariel had told them she didn't have the heart to throw out.

Creeping along the side of the car he heard a whispered voice hushing someone, and nearly laughed. How could they *both* hide in the same place? *Dummies.*

A shuffling of boxes, then a thump as one of the trunks hit the ground. He jumped up from behind the car and yelled, "Found ya!"

He lunged behind the stacked trunks and boxes laughing, and reached between a gap that would have been a perfect hiding place, only to find emptiness.

His laughter quietened when he realised neither boy was hiding behind the storage trunks. But he *had* heard them. At least… he'd heard *something*.

He swallowed the tiny ball of unease that crept up his throat.

"Sebastian…?" he called quietly. It wasn't the heat of the night that had sweat trickling down his back.

An eerie silence filled the garage, and he knew without a doubt that he had to get out of there, and fast. Spinning on his heel he turned around before the click of the trunks latch opened, halting him in his tracks. He froze before hesitantly turning around to watch the lid pop open.

"*Sebastian?*" He whispered again, watching the dust mites flutter in the stream of light filtering in from the doorway. Taking a small step forward he peered inside the trunk and blinked, trying to comprehend what he was seeing. His eyes filled with unshed tears of terror, and every hair on his body stood stiff to attention.

Paul lay inside, arms and legs twisted in unnatural angles. The expression on his ever-happy face, was now one that would give Timmy nightmares for the rest of his life. His skin was grey and taunt, his jaw broken leaving his mouth hanging open at an odd angle. Eyes wide, pupilless, and yellow looking. A rotten stench omitted, wrapping itself around Timmy.

He sobbed, stumbling away from the terrifying sight, feeling as if he were about to vomit. He spun around to bolt out of the garage when he ran straight into Aaron, knocking the boy over and falling down with him.

The back of Aaron's skull cracked against the concrete, before he screamed, "God, get *off* me you *cry* baby!" He shoved Timmy off him.

Timmy couldn't stop the flood of tears. Tears of fright turned to tears of relief that he was no longer alone with poor, broken Paul.

Aaron got off the dusty ground and sneered down at him. "What are you crying about? You were supposed to be looking for me and Paul."

"I… I found Paul." He whimpered, wiping the back of his hand under his dripping nose, pointing towards the trunk."

"Don't be stupid, Paul's inside eating ice-cream with Mr Williams. You've been gone for half an hour."

Half an hour?

Aaron kicked the empty trunk. "Man, you and this place are lame." As the last word left Aaron's mouth, Timmy watched in fascination as a head popped through the concrete floor.

Sebastian floated up, straightening his cap as he pushed his tattered, dirty sleeves up and grinned at Timmy.

Still in shock by what he'd seen, Timmy didn't have a moment to think about what Sebastian might be up to. He watched, mesmerised as Sebastian's small fists became the size of a large mans. He raised them and slammed then into Aaron's back like a battering ram, sending the boy flying through the air to then land face-first into the deep trunk.

"*OW!* What'd you do that for, ya *maggot?*" Aaron roared, rubbing his back as he untangled himself.

"It wasn't me," Timmy shook his head.

"Liar! There's no one else here. Wait till my mum hears about this!"

Aaron leapt up and ran around Timmy, and out of the garage.

Timmy sighed, wiping tears off his face, turning to Sebastian. "Why did you have to do that?"

Sebastian stuffed his hands in his pockets. His fingers poking out through the holes as he shrugged. "*He deserved it.*"

"Yeah, thanks. But now I'm going to get into trouble."

"*Sorry.*"

"*Timothy Harper*, come here right now." Ariel called in a tone that didn't bode well for him.

He sighed again. "Here we go."

Sebastian grinned. "*I'll be right there with you and if anyone upsets you,*

I'll deal with them."

"Please don't." Timmy muttered, before heading out of the garage and towards a frustrated looking Ariel.

Chapter Fifteen
Ariel

After seeing the bruisy-red punch marks on Aaron's back, anxiety clawed its way around Ariel's chest.

How am I going to explain this to his mother?

Wren was holding frozen peas against Aaron's back as he sucked on an icy-pole, as Jaxon made the call to Valeria. Having all the parents numbers on his mobile was a bonus and having him make the call relieved a tiny bit of Ariel's nerves. Valeria seemed to have a soft spot for the entirely-too-good-looking teacher, and Ariel hoped it would make the bad news coming from his lips, easier to swallow.

Hawk was giving Paul a piggy-back ride over to the tyre swing that hung from the gumtree near the chicken pen and the young boy's laughter filled the yard with cheer, despite the circumstances.

Jaxon hung up his phone. "Valeria is on her way," he informed her quietly.

"Great," she sighed, folding her arms as she waited on the back porch for Timmy.

"It's going to be okay," he placed a hand on the small of her back, his thumb stroking in a soothing manner.

"Is it?" Ariel met his concerned look.

"Kids, boys especially, scrapple at times," he shrugged. "It's normal."

"If Timmy had been hurt whilst staying at someone's home, I'd be upset."

"Let's just wait to hear what Timmy has to say." Jaxon said calmly, sounding very much like the teacher he was.

Ariel held his gaze for a few moments longer, as a million thoughts pounded in her head.

He brushed a stray curl behind her ear as he asked quietly. "What else is going on in that beautiful mind of yours?"

"I know Timmy didn't do this," she whispered.

"And?"

"Then what worries me is, who did? *What*, did this?" She shook her head once.

He nodded, opening his mouth to reply when Timmy dragged his feet up the porch steps, stopping in front of them.

"What?" Timmy asked defensively.

Jaxon's hand stilled on her back, before he removed it and shoved it in his jeans pocket.

"Let's go inside, Timmy." Ariel said firmly.

Timmy nodded.

"Do you want to go on the swing too, Aaron?" Wren asked, passing the thawing peas to Ariel.

"Sure," he said, giving Timmy a foul look before heading down towards Hawk and Paul.

"Thanks hun," Ariel said to Wren, before following Timmy inside. Placing the peas back in the freezer, she turned to watch Timmy climb up on a kitchen stool before facing her.

Jaxon remained in the doorway. "Do you want me to go?"

"No, please stay," she said.

He nodded, and they both looked at Timmy who sat nervously pulling at a thread on his cut off shorts.

"What happened in the garage Timmy?" Ariel asked after a few moments silence.

"You won't believe me."

"Try me."

"You won't like it," he whispered.

Ariel sighed and sat on the stool beside him. "It doesn't matter what I will or won't like. I need you to tell me the truth."

He raised his eyes, and she was saddened to see his fill with unshed tears.

"Oh Timmy, it's going to be okay darling, I promise." She pulled him into her arms, and kissed the top of his silky hair, feeling him shake against her.

"It was Sebastian," he mumbled against her chest. "He didn't like that Aaron was rude."

"What did Sebastian do?" She met Jaxon's gaze across the top of Timmy's head.

"Not much, he just shoved Aaron into a big old empty trunk."

"Timmy, I've told you not to play in the garage for safety reasons. Did you, or Aaron tip Grandpa, and Grandma's things out?"

"No. It was… empty." A strange look crossed his face.

"There are no empty trunks in the garage. I hope when I go in there, I won't find a mess."

Timmy looked up at her, a frown on his face, as he rubbed tears out of his eyes.

"What is it?" The worried look on his little face tugged at her heartstrings. "What else happened?"

"Nothing."

Impatient knocking sounded at the front door.

"Shall I get that?" Jaxon asked.

"Please." Ariel nodded, dropping a kiss on Timmy's head before getting off the stool, to open a drawer. Pulling out a cloth, she rinsed it under cold water before turning to wipe Timmy's face free of dirt and sweat.

Hearing Jaxon's quiet voice explain that the boys had had a harmless scrap, followed by Valeria's shrill protest, had her cringing internally.

"A harmless scrap is when no-one gets hurt. This, is not that."

Jaxon led Valeria into the kitchen, and Ariel felt Timmy stiffen instantly. She placed a comforting hand on his shoulder.

"Hi Valeria, sorry about this," she said.

Valeria simply raised an eyebrow at Ariel, before looking down her nose at Timmy, as she addressed Jaxon. "Where is my son, Mr Williams?"

"He's out on the swing with Paul. I'll get him," he said, before quickly leaving the room. Seconds later, he returned with Aaron, followed by Hawk, Wren and Paul.

"*Mum*," Aaron cried when he saw his mother and ran across to her. "Timmy hit me hard."

"Did not!" Timmy cried.

"Did too, cry-baby-liar," Aaron retorted.

"Stop calling me that!"

"Nothing but a cry-baby-liar who hits like a weakling."

"Boys, that's enough," Jaxon said sternly.

"I'll say," Wren scoffed, folding her arms.

"I cannot believe my son has been hurt whilst under *your* care." Valeria hissed at Ariel.

"Let's be reasonable, Valeria." Ariel shook her head.

"Reasonable? Are you serious? Where were you when this happened?" Valeria raised a cool eyebrow.

"They were playing hide and seek when the incident occurred. I'm sorry Aaron was hurt, but...."

"You're sorry? Is this how you supervise all your play dates?"

Ariel released an exasperated sigh. "I wasn't shadowing their every move if that's what you're asking."

"You call *that* supervising? I call it *lazy* parenting…"

"I *beg* your pardon," Ariel cried ramming her hands on hips. "How *dare* you suggest my parenting is lazy! If you *stalk* your son's friends during a playdate, then I could call *that* suffocating parenting."

"Oh, that's just *charming*, your Grandmother would be rolling in her…"

"Don't you *dare* mention my Grandmother…" Ariel cried, halting Valeria's rant.

"Ladies, please, this isn't helping." Jaxon cut in, in a calm, stern tone without sounding condescending. He stepped closer to Ariel, as if to offer her support. His action immediately calmed her. She pulled in a deep breath.

"Regardless of your opinion of my parenting. I'm sorry Aaron was hurt."

"Boys will be boys, after all," Hawk defended his sister.

"Do you think that excuses this kind of barbaric behaviour?" Valeria raised an eyebrow towards Hawk.

"Hardly barbaric," Wren scoffed.

Valeria snorted, turning to Ariel. "Well, I can see that your siblings have no respect or manners in how to address an adult."

"I wouldn't say that." Ariel could feel any sympathy she had for the mother whose child was hurt under her care, vanish completely.

"It's getting late," Jaxon intervened again. "How about we call it a night?"

"Right. Well, don't think Aaron will be coming back here to play." Valeria snatched up her son's hand and marched towards the front door. "Mr Williams, if you could bring Aaron's night bag to school tomorrow, I'd appreciate it."

"Sure," he replied simply.

"Good. Goodnight," she clipped before slamming the front door behind her.

"Thanks for coming good riddance." Hawk called cheerfully after them.

"*Hawk.*" Ariel reprimanded, but with no heat to her voice.

"Yes?" he grinned as he walked backwards.

She shook her head, sighing. "Nothing."

"I'll go grab Aaron's bag for you," he said to Jaxon.

"Thanks," Jaxon said as Hawk ran upstairs. "Are you alright?" He asked Ariel, stroking his fingers down her arm.

She shrugged, liking the way his touch sent a distracting tingle of fire along her flesh. She watched as his caramel eyes darkened, taking in her every movement, her every breath. She was falling under his spell. *Had* fallen, so quickly.

"I should get going too," he said, breaking her out of her trance.

"Oh?"

"I've got an early start before the kids arrive to class tomorrow." He nodded. "Unless you need me to stay?"

"No, it'll be fine."

"You sure?"

"Of course. Thanks for your help with tea tonight and the... incident." She offered him a strained smile.

He returned a relaxed smile and ran a finger along her cheek. "No problem, pretty girl."

She blushed, feeling like a teenager.

"I'm going to run the boys a bath." Wren interrupted.

"Thanks love." Ariel nodded. "Boys, put your dirty clothes in the wash basket and Paul, I'll have them dried and returned to your Grandma tomorrow."

"Thanks Ariel." Paul said as he started to follow Wren upstairs.

"Goodnight Mr Williams." He chortled.

"Goodnight Paul." Jaxon called, before turning to Timmy. "I'll see you tomorrow Timothy."

"Yes Mr Williams." Timmy slid off the stool. "Thanks for not telling Aaron's mum about Sebastian," he said quietly.

"I don't think she would have believed us if we had," Jaxon said. "Do you?"

Timmy paused for a few moments. "No, I don't think she's smart enough."

Ariel bit her lip to stop the inappropriate laugh.

"Mm." Jaxon pondered. "Perhaps not, but we won't tell her that, will we?"

"No sir," Timmy grinned before he raced out of the room and flew up the stairs behind his friend.

Jaxon turned, giving her his full attention.

"Well, tonight didn't go according to plan, did it?" She sighed.

"Just like a typical school day." He slid his hands around her waist, pulling her flush against him. "Expect everything and anything, then appreciate the most mundane day."

She felt nurtured being held so tenderly in his arms. Resting her cheek against his firm chest she took a deep breath; his scent calmed her. She closed her eyes wishing he didn't have to go.

"Are you *sure* you're okay?" he asked softly.

She smiled up at him and cupped his jaw. "I will be, if you kiss me goodnight."

He grinned, bending his head towards her. "Now that I can happily do, Miss Harper."

She thrilled as his eyes darkened and his beautiful lips parted before sweeping across hers.

"Thank you, Mr Williams," she whispered against his lips, before the kiss deepened and stole her breath and any further witty comment, away.

"Um, here's Aaron's bag." Hawk interrupted.

Jaxon stepped back, offering her a smile as he headed across to Hawk, taking the bag from him. "Thanks. Well, goodnight." He said, before offering them both a smile and headed out the front door.

Ariel caught Hawk's cheeky grin and raised an eyebrow. "Don't say anything."

"I won't."

"Thanks," she sighed. "It's been a big day. I'll finish up these dishes. Do you want to play a quick game of monopoly with the boys after their bath?"

"Yep. You doing good, sis?"

She smiled. "Yes. I love you."

"Love you too," Hawk said before heading upstairs.

She turned to the sink and pushed her hands into the cooling water, praying that Sebastian was the only entity that had returned to their home.

After Hawk played monopoly with the boys, Ariel read them a few pages of *Little People Big Emotions,* by Kylie Mort, before giving them a soothing back massage with Lavender aromatherapy. Timmy's night light sent a spaceship flying round the room, and once their breathing regulated she pulled the door shut. Sighing, she headed downstairs.

"Ariel?"

She turned looking up at Hawk. "Yeah."

"That Valarie's a piece of work, huh?"

She laughed quietly, "That's an understatement."

He nodded. "Things have been quiet around here on the paranormal front."

"So far so good."

"But does that mean we're safe here?"

Her heart thudded heavily, wishing she could lie to him–needing to protect him, to protect them all. "I'm going to do everything in my power to make it safe."

"And I'll do everything in my power to keep you all safe too. I promise."

Ariel sighed. "That's my job sweetheart, not yours."

He shook his head. "No, as the eldest boy, it *is* my job."

She smiled up at him. "Just like your Grandpa and Uncle."

He nodded, running a hand through his hair. "I don't want to leave here. Being here, in this town, it's the first time I've felt at home, even happy since mum died."

"I know," she nodded, swallowing the lump in her throat. They all missed their mother. "Whatever, *whoever* these entities are, we'll get the right help to get rid of them and cleanse the house for good."

He opened his mouth, as if to say something, but stopped himself.

"What?" She asked.

He shook his head. "I can't."

"Hawk, tell me."

"I promised Uncle Steven I wouldn't. He promised mum, so...." Hawk rubbed the back of his neck.

"The Lockwoods?"

The instant the Lockwood name left Ariel's lips, a blast of fowl wind struck her, whipping her hair across her face with such ferocity she had to squeeze her eyes shut. She clung to the balustrade; afraid the force would send her down the stairs.

"Ariel?" Hawk started down the stairs towards her when an unseen hand slapped her face.

She cried out, raising shaky fingers to where her cheek burned, coating her fingertips in sticky blood.

"*Ariel!*" Hawk yelled, reaching to steady her when the blast of wind changed direction and slammed directly into him, propelling him backwards into the air like a puppet on an unseen string before he fell down hard.

Ariel heard ribs crack as he hit the wooden steps and rushed towards him.

"Hawk?" Her voice wobbled, hand trembling as she rested it gently on his chest. Thankfully, the wind had vanished along with the putrid stench.

"Ow," he groaned. "It hurts."

"I'll ring the ambulance."

"No," he shook his head.

"Yes," she insisted.

"What's happened?" Wren stood above them in her pj's, empty water bottle in hand. "Ariel, your face!" She cried.

Hawk and Ariel exchanged a worried look, as Hawk pushed himself up, groaning as he clutched his side.

Ariel gently cupped her bleeding cheek, cringing as she felt raised flesh. "I'm okay," she whispered.

"No, you're not." Wren knelt beside Hawk. "You both need to go to the hospital."

Ariel nodded.

"You do know I've had broken ribs playing footy before. I'm all right." Hawk assured them both.

"What happened?" Wren asked again.

Ariel shook her head in disbelief. "A gust of foul wind… attacked us."

"Wind?" Wren shook her head. "Things have been so good. Why now?" she cried.

"It'll be okay, baby-girl." Ariel whispered, hoping to God that would be the case.

Hawk grunted as he got to his feet, one arm tucked across his ribs as he held a hand out to Ariel. She took it, grateful that despite their injuries they were okay.

"Let's clean up your face," he said softly.

She nodded "It's all right, I'll have a shower and pop some Bepanthen on it." Squeezing his hand she asked, "Are you sure you don't want me to run you to the hospital?"

"No, I'll strap it. I've got some old bandages."

"We'll get new ones tomorrow." Ariel said.

He nodded. "Wren, can you help me."

"Of course."

"Ariel, if anything weird happens just yell for us, okay?" Hawk said.

"Likewise," she hugged him gently, before hugging Wren. "Good-night, loves."

She watched them head upstairs and into Hawk's room and waited for the door to close before she sagged against the balustrade.

"I wish I could ask you a million questions, Grandma… Mama." She wiped at an escaped tear, and shook her head. Heading towards the bathroom she prayed her cheek wouldn't look as bad as it felt.

Hawk

Every movement he made, no matter how slight, was sheer torture. Excruciating pain stole his every breath, as every breath in turn played havoc with his broken ribs. He tossed and turned throughout the night as an unusual fever gripped him, tormented him… consumed him. He threw the soggy blankets off in frustration, hissing in pain as his ribs protested.

"Crap," he cursed, and slid out of bed making his way carefully out of his bedroom and towards the bathroom.

He spotted a small figure at the end of the hallway, standing as still as a statue as if he'd been waiting for Hawk to step out of his room.

"Hey sport, you okay?"

The figure didn't move.

"Timmy, what are you doing? Can't sleep either, huh?" As Hawk inched closer to the silent boy, reaching him after several painful steps; it was his turn to freeze. It wasn't Timmy, but a boy dressed in tattered clothing and holey shoes. A miner's cap sat crookedly on his head... a head that was transparent, as was the rest of him.

"Jesus Christ..." he whispered.

"*Don't be afraid. I'm here to help.*"

"Help?" Hawk shook his head, amazed that he could hear him so clearly. He looked about to see if Timmy was lurking nearby. "Why would I need your help, little guy? I'm presuming you're Sebastian, my brother's friend?"

The grubby ghost nodded.

"You know," Hawk whispered. "You're welcome to take a bath here. Can you do that?"

Sebastian shrugged. "*You need to get outside of this house and stay out till he's gone.*"

"Until who is gone?"

"*Lockwood,*" Sebastian looked about as if he didn't want to be overheard, moving closer, he whispered again. "*Travis Lockwood.*"

Hawk frowned, feeling his cooling flesh tingle. "Travis Lockwood?"

Sebastian nodded.

"Here, in this house?"

Again, Sebastian nodded.

"You're talking about his spirit?"

"*Yes.*"

"Why would *I* need to get out of the house, for Travis Lockwood's spirit to go?"

Sebastian slowly raised a finger and pointed it straight towards Hawk's chest.

Hawk raised an eyebrow. "What does that mean?"

The little ghost-boy walked forward, and Hawk was shocked when

Sebastian's icy fingertip tapped against his chest. *"He's in you... the only way to get him out is for you to get outside."*

"Not possible... I think I'd know if a serial-killing-raping-psychopath was inside of me, sport."

"Hawk, who are you talking to?" Wren asked.

He spun around, cringing as his ribs protested with the quick movement. He thumbed in the direction behind him. "Sebastian."

Wren raised an eyebrow as she walked around him. "Hi Sebastian, nice of you to keep my brother company in the middle of the night."

Hawk turned to see Sebastian was nowhere to be found, and Wren's sarcastic smile said it all as she feigned to shake Sebastian's hand.

"Yeah, funny." Hawk snapped, feeling uneasy. "He was there a second ago, I'm not bullshitting."

Wren's grin disappeared. "I'm sorry, I was just having some fun."

He ran his hands through his hair, wincing as the movement caused pain.

Wren placed her hand on his arm. "Are you okay? Want me to get you some Panadol?"

He nodded, "Please."

She headed towards the bathroom, before turning in the doorway. "Did Sebastian really talk to you?"

"Yeah, it was kinda freaky."

"What did he say?"

It was his turn to pause as he looked at his sibling. He didn't want Wren worrying any more than she already was, and he sure as hell didn't want her knowing anything about Travis Lockwood, or why Sebastian was pointing towards him before she'd interrupted.

"Nothing important, just ghosty-kid stuff."

"Oh?"

"Panadol, please." He knew by the way his twin was looking at him, she was about to interrogate him further, so played on her soft side by leaning against the wall, holding his ribs.

When she disappeared into the bathroom, he sighed, slowly heading in after her to pop the pills he was hoping would do more than chase the pain of his broken ribs, away.

Chapter Sixteen
Travis Lockwood

T he morning sun filtered in through the bathroom window. He stood, looking at himself for a good half an hour. Turning his face this way and that as he appreciated the angles of the youthful reflection. *Any* reflection would have been a gift, but this face. *Dang* he was fine looking!

"Have you finished perving at yourself yet? I need a shower; we're going to be late."

He turned slowly, locking eyes with the pretty girl who was leaning against the doorway; a towel flung over one shoulder, arms folded with a raised eyebrow as she regarded him.

What a tasty piece.

He grinned slowly. "Sure."

"How are your ribs?" She asked as she walked in dropping the towel on the bathroom stool and kicked off her ballet slippers.

"Fine and dandy," he said, mesmerised by her movements, as she reached to pull her oversized tee shirt over her head, before realising he was still standing there.

"What are you still doing here? Go, like I said, we're going to be late." She frowned at him.

He saluted as he walked by her, taking a deep breath of her youthful scent which tempted him in the most alluring way. He pulled the door closed, keeping it open a crack to watch her as she pulled the shirt over her head. The flesh around her slim waist had his mouth watering.

"What are ya doin?" The young boy surprised him, making him jump as he clicked the bathroom door shut.

"Nothing. What are you doing?" He reached down and tickled the cute little mite; his delightful laughter making him feel carefree. Alive.

"Boys, hurry up." *She* called. His *sister*. Or was it his *daughter*? That, they'll never know.

"Can you give me a piggy-back ride downstairs?" The little fella asked, peering up at him with the darkest eyes.

He smiled and knelt. "Climb on board, bud."

Timmy ran behind him and climbed up on his back, wrapping his little arms around Hawk's neck.

"Yippee!" He yelled, laughing.

Travis took off down the stairs at a fast past, before lifting a leg and sat on the balustrade, sliding the rest of the way down. The little kid's laughter made him feel invincible.

"Careful," *She* called as he landed with cat like grace and headed towards her. Her glossy hair was pulled high in a sweeping ponytail, revealing a biteable neck. A bright orange dress scattered with daises clung to a curvy body he imagined would fit so nicely beneath his. When she turned her bright green eyes in his direction, his gut tightened immediately. But not with lust; with anger. She looked just like her mother. He felt a rush of pleasure at seeing his handy work mark her soft flesh. Three long grazes ran from her left eye towards her jaw line.

"Ariel," Timmy cried, climbing off Hawk's back and towards her sister. "What happened?"

"A tiger crept into her dreams and kissed her," The other young boy said around a mouthful of pancakes, stuffing more into his mouth before he'd swallowed what he'd been chewing on. He was sitting at the breakfast bench swinging his legs to and fro.

Travis chuckled, heading across to Paul and ruffled his hair. "Careful you don't choke on that, bud."

"Your ribs don't seem to be causing you too much grief, Hawk. How are you feeling? She reached for two oranges in a large glass bowl, before slicing them in half and popped them into a citrus squeezer.

"Good as gold," he replied, watching her every move.

She filled a tall glass with juice for Timmy, then served up two plump pancakes topped with fruit and maple syrup. "Eat up." She kissed the top of Timmy's head, before turning towards him.

"Juice?" She asked.

He nodded, "Thanks."

"Paul," she said, reaching for more oranges and a fresh glass. "Do you want an egg and lettuce sandwich for lunch?"

"Is that what Timmy's having?"

"It is."

"Then, yes please." Paul grinned at Timmy.

"I'll make them fresh and bring them to school at lunchtime." She placed the glass of juice on the bench in front of him.

"There you go," she smiled, before turning to tidy up the bench.

"Thanks," Travis took the glass, before taking a tentative sip. Closing his eyes in ecstasy as the pure sweetness hit his tongue, greeting his tastebuds like a long-lost lover opening her legs wide for the first time in eternity. He swallowed it down in three greedy gulps.

"Thirsty?" Ariel laughed.

The musical lilt of her laughter had his gut tightening again. "You could say that." He wiped the back of his hand across his mouth.

"Pancakes, yum," the other delightful female of the house wandered in, backpack over her shoulder, and scooped up a pancake. "Hello boys." She sang to the little ones. "Want me to walk you to school?"

"Yeah," they answered.

"Five minutes and we'll go." Wren said, before pouring oat milk into a glass.

"Want me to come with you?" He asked, watching her lips part as she raised her glass. She took a few mouthfuls, nodding.

"Wren, can you watch Timmy tonight for a couple of hours? I've got an art class."

"Sure. What time?"

"Six thirty. By the time Liv and I clean up it shouldn't be much past nine?"

"How are you going to explain that?" Wren indicated towards Ariel's cheek.

Travis watched her gently cup Ariel's chin as she inspected the scratch marks.

"Thanks to full coverage make-up, I won't need to."

"Even full coverage won't hide that."

"It will have to do," Ariel sighed.

"How could this happen?" Wren whispered.

Ariel shrugged, nodding her head to the little boys as she said in a cheerful tone. "Come on boys, finish up." Before meeting her sister's gaze and saying quietly. "Not now."

Wren nodded, then turned to him. "Hawk, are you going to be here tonight?"

"Where else would I be?" He replied, wishing he had more of the boys memories than what went on in this house.

"I wasn't sure if you were going out with Lance."

Her cheeks filled with a very becoming pink when she mentioned the Lance characters name.

"No."

"Oh." She nodded, adjusting her backpack. "Come on boys, let's go."

"Have a great day everyone." Ariel called. "Lasagne will in the fridge to heat up for tea."

"Bye Ariel, thanks for having me," Paul called as he ran to the door with Timmy, followed by Wren.

"Anytime," she said, before she started gathering the dishes and taking them to the sink.

"Come on, Hawk." Wren yelled from the front door.

Ariel turned then, noticing him standing there watching her.

"What's wrong?" She asked, concern replaced her carefree smile. "Are your ribs hurting?"

"No, it's nothing. See you later." *Play it cool.*

He turned and headed towards the front door where the pretty little thing was waiting. The two boys had already run halfway down the street, despite the stifling, dry heat of the morning. An Inglewood summer. There wasn't anything like it and he couldn't wait to step out into it and have the sun warm this strong, capable body which he planned to use to its fullest capacity.

He flashed her a charming smile. "Come on, gorgeous."

"Gorgeous?" She raised an eyebrow. "Aren't you full of compliments this morning."

He stepped around her and over the threshold, about to make a witty comment when pain exploded in his head. Heat pushed behind his eyes, making them stream with tears. His legs were heavy, as if he was wearing jeans made of concrete and he was incapable of taking another step forward.

"Argh!" He screamed, dropping to his knees. *What is this?* He was losing his grip on the boy, could feel himself slipping out, squeezing through the tear ducts, which was utter torture.

"Ariel!" Wren cried, dropping beside him, placing a warm hand on his back. "Hawk, what's wrong?"

He shook his head, hearing footsteps running towards them, but couldn't open his eyes; squeezing them tighter, trying to prevent himself from falling out.

"What's happened?" Ariel asked.

"I don't know, he was fine one second and then he just collapsed." Fear filled her voice. "We should have taken you both to the hospital last night."

"It's okay love. Hawk, can you stand? Let's get you inside."

He couldn't stand for anything, but with great effort, forced himself to crawl back inside. As soon as he crossed the threshold, every ounce of pain dissipated as he fell in a heap. He could literally feel the tears trail back up along the flesh of the boy's cheekbones, and feel himself slip back through the tear ducts, fully returning inside the boy's body. He kept his head hung so the women wouldn't notice the oddity and took a few deep breathes, relieved he was still inside the boy.

"Hawk?" Ariel swept his fringe out of his eyes. "Are you all right, love?"

"I think I just need to go lay down," he replied in a quiet tone.

"Good idea," she helped him to his feet, running a hand along his back.

"Are you sure you don't want to see a doctor?" Wren asked, sounding worried.

"I'm fine."

"Last night's incident has obviously had a delayed impact. It might be a good idea to get checked out." Ariel suggested as she led him into the lounge room.

"I said, I'm *fine*." He snapped, not intending to sound so harsh, and quickly softened his tone as he added. "Sorry, I'm in a bit of pain, but I promise it's nothing to worry about." He watched the women exchange a concerned look, before Ariel nodded.

"I'll make you a jug of lemon water and ring the school."

"Gastro was going around last week." Wren said. "You could use that excuse."

"Thanks, love. I will." Ariel rubbed Wren's shoulder. "Can you run by the school on your way to the bus? Make sure the boys got in?"

"Of course." Wren nodded.

"I'll see you tonight." Ariel said.

"Have a good class later."

"Thanks."

Travis watched Ariel disappear through the doorway, as he lay back on the couch, kicking his shoes off and pulled a pillow behind his head.

Wren headed towards the door. "I'll see you later," she called over her shoulder.

"I'll be here," he joked. "Say hi to Lucas for me."

She turned, frowning. "Lucas? How hard did you hit your head last night? You mean, Lance, right?"

Dammit. "Of course, I meant Lance, I was just seeing if you were paying attention." He forced a smile.

She paused for a moment, staring at him before nodding and left the room.

Ariel returned carrying a jug jingling with ice blocks and lemon slices and placed it in front of him on the coffee table, along with a glass.

"I've got a client coming to the studio for a sitting. I shouldn't be more than a couple of hours.

"I'll be fine."

"If you need me, buzz my mobile."

He nodded. "Thanks."

She dropped a kiss on the top of his head, before heading out of the room.

He sighed, rubbing his hands over his face, grateful to be alone for a moment. As fun as it was feeling 'alive' again, he'd better be careful. He didn't want any of them catching on just yet. There was too much fun to be had.

Hawk

Hawk woke, yet felt as though he were still dreaming. The morning passed in a sluggish dream that was rapidly becoming a nightmare. He had no control over his movements. Words formed yet he could not utter a single one. He felt as though he'd been shoved into a small box and pushed into a dark corner with only a keyhole to peek out of. He didn't understand why he couldn't speak for himself. He didn't understand how his sisters or Timmy, could not tell that it wasn't him speaking. But he could *feel* everything Travis Lockwood was feeling. And it was dangerous and *foul*. Lust for his sisters. Hatred too. He could *hear* every perverted, filthy thought Travis Lockwood had, and it filled him with an uncontrollable rage which he could do nothing about.

Ariel

"My god, Ariel you need to get Reverend Matthews back in that house," Liv cried, inspecting Ariel's scratch mark, shaking her head.

"Yes, I'll ask Jaxon to reach out to him tomorrow." Ariel sighed, before applying a thin layer of concealer, then giving it a spray with setting mist before dropping the products in her bag.

"That's better," Liv nodded. "What will Steven say?" She asked, as Ariel reached for her favourite painting apron.

"Liv, I don't want him to know."

"Ariel…" Liv began to protest.

"Please Liv, not yet."

"Is that really a good decision?"

"For the moment, yes. Promise me you won't say anything?" She begged her friend.

Liv sighed, "I may be getting something really sweet on with your uncle, but you're my best friend. I'm loyal to you, despite the fact that I don't agree with you keeping something as serious as this from him."

Ariel nodded. "Thanks Liv, I owe you."

"Yeah well, whatta friends for."

Ariel smiled, feeling lighter in that moment. Thank goodness for Liv and the busy day she'd had, which had kept her mind off Hawk and last night's incident. Checking around the studio, everything looked to be in place for the budding artists who were due to arrive any second. Easels were set up with comfy high stools and on every artist's table, a selection of paints and brushes, along with a small plate of biscuits, cheese and antipasto. Liv had coffees and teas, along with chocolates and wine ready to serve.

A knock sounded at the front door.

"Show time," she headed over to answer it and saw Jaxon with his arm linked through Mrs Musgrove's, arm, and a group of chatty clients behind him.

"Hello, and welcome," she beamed at them as she held the door open.

"Hello dear," Mrs Musgrove patted her arm as Jaxon led her inside.

"Please help yourselves to a beverage and sit where you're most comfortable." She smiled at her eight guests as they followed Jaxon and Mrs Musgrove into the gallery.

Locking the door, she followed them inside, grateful for Liv's lively conversation as she poured to each guests drinking preference.

She watched Jaxon help Mrs Musgrove onto the one plush armchair in the front row, with an easel sitting on a table in front of it. There was no way she'd risk the older lady falling off a high stool.

Liv wandered over with a glass of red that she knew Mrs Musgrove liked and handed it to her. As she was making sure the older lady was comfortable, Jaxon turned and caught Ariel's gaze. He smiled slowly, but the longer he stared at her his smile froze on his lips before disappearing altogether.

She swallowed, wanting to take comfort in his warm, strong arms but shook her head, halting him as he made a move towards her. She forced a bright smile.

"Hello everyone, it's so good to see you." She clapped her hands together as she walked down the aisle of easels, towards her own and stood at the front of the class.

"It's nice to see a few familiar faces return, and welcome to our newcomers. I'm Ariel Harper, and this is my associate Liv Collins, and this class is designed for all painting enthusiasts from beginners to the more experienced. Today's class is about capturing the heart of Inglewood in any way that calls to you."

"Can we please paint a scene of the Loddon River?" Gayle, a cheerful local called out.

"You certainly can," Ariel nodded.

"I'd like to capture a mine shaft at midnight under the moonlight." An elegant man mused.

"That would make a haunting image," She agreed.

"How are you going to depict that it's midnight?" His equally handsome partner asked, laughing.

"I'll paint a grandfather clock in the trunk of a eucalyptus tree, of course," he replied.

"Now that, I look forward to seeing." Ariel hid her shiver and rubbed her hands together. "Let's get started and remember, we've got next week as well, so don't panic if you don't finish tonight."

"Excuse me," a newcomer with 'Naomi' on her name tag held up a hand. "Can you help me get started with some ideas?"

"Of course," she smiled at the rest of the class. "Liv and I will be right here so just yell if you need us. Feel free to refill your beverages and the toilets are through the back to your right. Enjoy."

She headed towards Naomi, but her path became blocked when Jaxon stepped in front of her. She kept a sigh at bay, refusing to look at him.

His finger under her chin forced her gaze upwards, and she finally met his brooding eyes as they swept across her face.

"Are you okay?"

She nodded.

"We'll talk later," he whispered.

It sounded like a threat. "Sure. Excuse me."

He stepped aside and she headed across to help Naomi, grateful the lady needed a bit of assistance throughout the duration of the class, along with the other newcomers. They were a vibrant bunch and inappropriate laughter flowed throughout the night along with diverse conversations. Mrs Musgrove seemed to be thoroughly enjoying herself as she sat with a twinkle in her eye, holding her wine glass more often than her paintbrush.

"How did you enjoy your first class, Mrs Musgrove?" Ariel asked as she was going around the room collecting brushes.

"Good dear, I was hoping to see that uncle of yours."

Ariel hid her smile. "He's in Melbourne this weekend for a landscaping convention."

"Lovely. Well, it was very thoughtful of Mr Williams to bring me along tonight. Paul is with Timmy; I hope you don't mind?"

"Not at all. Timmy says having a friend like Paul is like having a cousin. It's wonderful for him."

"For them both, dear." Mrs Musgrove reached out and patted her hand. "Mr Williams, I'm ready to go home," she stated.

"Of course," he offered his arm, and gently helped her up from her chair.

"Shall we pick up Paul?" She asked looking up at him.

"Oh no, leave him." Ariel said, glancing at the clock. "Wren's probably got them both in bed by now."

"She's a good girl that Wren." Mrs Musgrove said. "Well, considering it is Saturday tomorrow, I'm sure the boys will be happy with this arrangement."

"I'll bring Paul home after lunch if that's fine with you?"

"More than fine, dear, thank you. Goodnight then."

"I'll come by after I've got her home." Jaxon said quietly as he walked by her.

She nodded again, before turning her attention to the others as they were saying their goodbyes.

Locking the door after their last guest had left, Ariel got busy cleaning brushes and storing paintings, as Liv cleaned up the dishes.

"Nice group," Liv called from the kitchen.

"They were," Ariel agreed, wiping her hands on a towel.

"Jaxon looked intense there for a hot minute."

Ariel laughed dryly, dropping the towel onto a rail, and hanging her apron onto a hook. "He sure did."

"I'm nervous for you."

"Don't be. He's a kitten."

"Ha," Liv chuckled. "Well, you'll want to make sure you've got kitty an extra bowl of cream to sweeten him up, because after seeing the look he gave you, gave me the indication that kitty wants to claw at something."

Ariel shook her head, turning off the gallery light. "You want to come over for a slab of lasagne?"

"As much as I'd like to see you tiptoe around Mr Williams, I've got an appointment bright and early in Bendigo."

"Okay, well enjoy that, and thanks for tonight."

"Thank you. And, if you need me for anything, call me." Liv turned and headed upstairs.

"I will. Hey Liv?"

Liv paused on the stairs and turned to face Ariel. "Yeah."

"I really like this thing you've got going on with Uncle Steven."

Liv smiled, sighing. "Me too. Thanks for saying that."

"No worries, *Aunty* Liv."

Liv laughed, and Ariel joined in.

"Funny girl." Liv said shaking her head.

Goodnight."

"Night."

Ariel opened the front door, before pulling it shut behind her and locking it. The walk home was peaceful, interrupted only by a lone dog barking as she passed by Brooke's Lane. Walking under the arbour of her Grandmother's roses, she headed towards the front door. Taking a deep breath, she hoped the kids night had gone smoothly without incident and opened the door calling, "I'm home."

She headed down the corridor past her Grandmother's writing studio, then her Grandfather's office, noticing the house was quiet. The aroma of coffee and lasagne drifted from the kitchen and walking by the empty lounge room, headed towards the aromas. Dropping her bag on the back door hall stand, she leaned against the kitchen doorway to watch Jaxon serve up salad beside two slices of lasagne; coffee and wine were poured.

"You must be hungry," was his way of greeting, his back to her as he dropped the serving utensils in the sink.

"I am." She crossed towards the food, and sat on a stool, reaching for a wine glass and took three large swallows.

"Like that, is it?" He sat beside her, turning on his seat to watch her.

"I'm afraid so." Placing her wine glass down, she pivoted on her stool to meet his gaze. They sat, knees touching, staring at each other in the comfortably quiet kitchen. She placed her hand over his, which rested on his knee.

"Thank you for this," she nodded to the food.

"You cooked it, I just wanted to make sure you ate something." He picked up her fork, handing it to her.

She smiled. "Thanks."

"You're welcome. I rang Reverend Matthews after I dropped Ena home."

"Oh?"

"He's coming by tomorrow."

"Thank you. I was actually going to ask you if you'd call him for me."

"Great minds think alike," he said.

She nodded and scooped up a piece of lasagne dripping in white sauce that oozed with melted cheese. Grabbing a slice of lemon she squeezed it over her salad, before stabbing into it, loving the combination of citrus salad and warm lasagne.

She noticed him watching her eat a few mouthfuls, not moving towards his food and raised an eyebrow. "What's the matter?"

"Why didn't you call me last night?"

She swallowed and reached for her wine, finishing it off before answering him. "I don't know."

"Don't you trust me?"

"It's not about trust."

"Then what's it about?"

"I guess maybe I didn't want to bother you?" she shrugged.

He released a heavy sigh, shaking his head. "Ariel Harper, you could never bother me. Especially with this."

"It all happened so suddenly, and I handled it. I've handled problems on my own before you came into my life, Jaxon." She was quiet for a few moments, pushing her salad around on her plate before placing her fork down.

"This is a little more serious than a simple 'problem' I think, don't you agree?"

She shrugged again, unable to meet his gaze.

"And, I know you're a capable, strong young woman, Ariel. But you don't have to deal with things on your own anymore. You have Steven, and you have me."

She blinked exhausted tears away.

"Ariel?" His voice was low, soothing.

She finally raised her eyes to meet his, brooding and dark. Her heart skipped a beat. He was too beautiful, inside and out.

"You're not alone. I care about you and the kids."

She groaned, knowing she couldn't hold the tears back with that statement and dropped her face into her hands. The citrus juice stung her scratches, and she cried in pain. "Ow!"

"Hey," he gently took her wrists, pulling them towards his chest as he bent his head close to hers. "How about we finish tea, and I'll wash up whilst you have a shower? Then we can pop some soothing balm on those scratches, okay?"

She sniffed back tears, nodding, meeting his gaze. "I'm sorry."

He looked stunned. "For what?"

"For being such a drag."

"I beg your pardon?"

"Well, as far as new relationships go, this one's been pretty dark don't you think?"

She raised an eyebrow, not understanding why he was smiling. "What?"

"So, we *are* in a relationship. Good. I was thinking it was just me who wanted to spend every single spare second I had with you."

Her heart was going to slide right out of the souls of her feet if it melted any further. She bit her lip as she slid off the stool and tugged her wrists free from his hands before sliding them around his neck.

"No, it's not just you, and yes," she whispered, stepping in between his thighs as he parted them for her. "I do believe we are in a relationship."

"Happy to hear it, Miss Harper." He bent his head as he wrapped his arms around her waist, bringing her closer before his lips slid over hers in an all-consuming kiss.

In that moment, she forgot about her scratches, her hunger pains, or any entity that could be lurking in her ancestral home. She forgot about everything other than the pleasure of being in Jaxon's arms.

Chapter Seventeen
Travis Lockwood

He kicked the wall and cursed again before slamming the window shut. Even putting his head outside caused severe pain to split his skull. It wasn't worth the effort in trying to leave. Would he forever be a prisoner in this house? Maybe burning it down was the answer.

"Hawk?" The girl's sweet voice called through the closed doorway.

He sighed and thumped his head against the wall once before taking a deep breath, then called out, "Come in." He turned, folding his arms as he leaned against the wall watching her walk in.

"You okay?" Wren asked.

He tilted his head, "Why wouldn't I be?" How he longed to throw her down on the bed and have his way with her. Man, it would feel so good to pump in and out of her young body. He felt himself growing hard at the mere thought of her writhing and screaming beneath him. Sure, being able to wrap his hand around the boy's shaft in the shower earlier had been sheer bliss, but having a warm, resistant body beneath his, to do with it as he saw fit? He nearly groaned aloud at the thought. But he guessed that wouldn't work out so well in his favour.

"I heard a bang, I wasn't sure if it was you or... the entities." She shrugged.

"Entities," he laughed. "They can kiss my arse."

"Careful, Ariel said we shouldn't threaten them or engage them in any way, or they could become more dangerous." She looked so cute, standing there being all serious about something she truly had no idea about. None of them did.

He smiled slowly. "I'm not afraid of them."

She frowned. "Even after what happened the other night?"

He shook his head.

"Okay."

"Are you scared?"

"A little."

"You want to sleep in here tonight?" *Please say yes.* At least he could jerk off whilst he watched her sleep.

Wren raised an eyebrow. "No."

"You sure?"

She nodded. "I heard Jaxon tell Ariel that Reverend Matthews is coming back."

He frowned.

"What's wrong?"

He shook his head. "I just don't know what good it will do."

"Well, we have to try something."

"Yeah, I guess."

"Well, goodnight." She turned and headed towards the door.

"What, no hug goodnight for your dear brother?" He had to try.

She paused, turning around and went to step towards him when she staggered backwards as if she'd been shoved.

He frowned when she spun around and opened the door calling, "Goodnight," before slamming it shut behind her.

What the hell was that? He sighed, before going to stand in the front of the mirror and dropped his jeans, then tugged his tee shirt over his head to stare at the strong, defined naked body in front of him. He smiled at the impressive cock which stood to attention as he thought about the girl. Even looking at the boy's sculptured body had him aroused. He fisted the pulsing cock, grunting at how good it felt to massage it, and took his time pleasuring himself throughout the night.

Wren

Wren ran to her bedroom and closed the door with a bang, heart thumping uncomfortably. She paused, before doing something she'd never done before. She locked it. Her body felt like ice, despite the heat of the night. She wrapped shaking arms around herself as she walked slowly to her bed and sat on the edge, staring at nothing. Something was off with Hawk. That much was clear. How hard had he hit his head? And what was the thing that had pushed her away from him when she went to hug him goodnight? It felt like some kind of warning.

She fell backwards, pulling the doona around her body, cocooning herself in safety as she rolled over and pushed her face into her pillow. This house wasn't the problem. It was what occupied it that she hoped they could sort out. She left the light on and willed herself to fall asleep before she heard any 'bump-in-the-night' noises, which would no doubt keep her awake for the entirety of it.

Ariel

Ariel smiled to herself as she pulled the garage door open. Spending last night with Jaxon had beaten the hell out of reading any Harlequin romance, and this morning topped last night. She shook her head. She'd certainly gotten lucky with Mr Williams. He hadn't just worshipped her body as if she were the only woman on the planet but had tended to her scratches as if she were made of the finest crystal.

She could hear the boys laughter float through the kitchen window where they were making pancakes with Jaxon and Wren. She frowned momentarily, worried about how exhausted her sister looked this morning. Wren had blamed her exhaustion on 'that-time-of-the-month' issues, but Ariel knew that was a lie. Their monthly cycle had been the same since she'd adopted the kids and they had all lived together.

She was grateful nevertheless that Jaxon had organised for Reverend Matthews to pop in later. Surely another cleansing would help out with this 'entity' situation?

Not having time to sort out the trunk incident since Aaron was 'attacked' she thought she'd make sure their Grandparents' things hadn't been disturbed or ruined. Walking around the back of her Grandfather's car, she was dismayed to see several trunks had toppled off their ordered stack. Three of them had popped open and the contents lay scattered across the garage's dusty floor. Clothes, old keepsakes, newspapers, and dusty picture frames were strewn haphazardly about.

"Damn," she muttered, kneeling to tackle the clothes first, shaking the dust off them before stuffing them back into a trunk. Closing the lid and lifting it back onto the pile, she turned and noticed the glass of several picture frames had shattered. She wandered across to the rickety wooden shelves which housed clear jars filled with rusty nails and screws.

"Making a mental note to make this space a little more kid friendly, Grandpa," she whispered, careful not to catch her hand on a rusty hook hanging above the old metal dustpan and shovel. Dragging the rubbish bin across to the pile, she carefully lifted the broken frames, shaking any residual glass off them before stacking the frames back into the trunk then swept up the glass before dumping it in the bin.

"Ariel," Wren called from behind her.

"Yeah," she turned around, wiping her brow with the back of her hand.

"Jaxon asked me to tell you that Reverend Matthews will be here in twenty minutes."

"Okay love. Can you please ask Hawk to come give me a hand with the newspaper trunk? It will be too heavy for me to lift on my own."

"Sure," Wren nodded before heading back inside the house.

Dragging the bin back to the corner where splintered-handled brooms and rakes stood, she placed the dustpan and shovel back on the shelf before stacking the newspapers. She handled them carefully, knowing they were old, and paused after several minutes, mesmerised by the face of a man on the front cover. She knew that face, but where had she seen it? His dark eyes seemed to be staring right into her soul. A crooked smile on his angled face might not have seemed appealing on another, yet it gave him a charming quality. A 'butter-wouldn't-melt' quality. There was something off about him, yet she couldn't put her finger on it.

"Who are you?" She unfolded the newspaper, and the headline had her breath catching.

'MURDERS UNDER ESTEEMED FAMILY'S ROOF'

"Oh no," she whispered. "Lockwood." She quickly scanned the article, reading about how Travis Lockwood had been lovingly raised under the same roof as Steven and Sparrow Harper, son and daughter of Inglewood's 'high-society' couple–Victor and Elizabeth Harper. *'Where did they go wrong?'* It asked.

"Bullshit," She spat, opening to the suggested page which was a double page spread. Travis Lockwood's face enlarged on the front page revealed him here, standing in her family kitchen, arms around the smiling faces of her uncle and mother.

"Oh Mama," she whispered, running her finger over her mother's sweet face, before hurriedly glancing over the rest of the article. She bit her lip as she read about how her Grandparent's had been Inglewood's most gracious hosts to any in need. That Travis Lockwood and his father, Phillip, had lived for over a decade with the Harper's, and had gruesomely kidnapped, tortured, raped and murdered too many victims to count. Including the barbaric rape and attempted murder of the Harper's own daughter, eighteen-year-old Sparrow Harper. *'How could they not have known what was occurring under their own roof'*– *'Did justice prevail when Sparrow Harper killed Travis Lockwood in her father's study?'* Ariel stopped reading, feeling numb as she stared at her mother's face. Another tear fell, joining the first that she was unaware had spilled. Her mother's face become a blotch under her damp assault.

"Ariel," Wren called.

Sniffing quickly, she dropped the newspaper to wipe her eyes, before stacking other papers on top of it, then dumping them randomly back into the trunk.

"Still here," she cursed when her voice wobbled.

"Ariel?" Wren stepped into the garage. "What's wrong?"

"Nothing love. Just going through Grandma and Grandpa's things have made me sentimental is all."

She turned to her sister and forced a smile.

Wren studied her, then looked towards the pile behind her.

She had to distract her younger sibling, and quickly wiping her eyes said, "This is thirsty work, let's get a cold drink."

"Oh no," Wren smiled, before laughing.

"What is it?" Ariel dropped another pile of newspapers into the trunk, then brushed dirt off her knees.

"You look like a panda bear."

Ariel crossed to check out her face in the cars side mirror and grimaced. Dirt had amended itself to tears and sweat. She chuckled. "Nothing a face washer won't fix. Where's Hawk?"

"He said his ribs are too sore to lift anything heavy," Wren shrugged.

"Oh, of course. Silly me."

"Did Hawk hit his head on the stairs?"

"Um, I don't think so, but he could have. Why?"

"Nothing, it's just…"

"Ariel, Ariel!" Timmy's yelling could no doubt be heard down the end of the street.

Wren laughed. "Can I please extract some of his energy?"

"When you figure out how to do that, tell me. We'll make a fortune." Ariel chuckled as she headed out of the garage and to where Timmy was standing on the back porch.

She pushed her concern regarding the Lockwood's, and her mother aside for now, and focused on her youngest brother. Her heart skipped a beat when she saw Jaxon, leaning against the porch railing, nursing a cup of coffee smiling down at Paul who seemed to be telling him an entertaining story, by his exaggerated hand movements.

He looked up in that moment as he took a mouthful of coffee and his gaze met hers. She couldn't stop the smile if she'd wanted to.

"Ariel, I wanted Hawk to come and play with me and Paul, but he told me to piss off!"

Ariel's smile was replaced with a frown as she headed towards Timmy. She knelt in front of him, putting her hands on his hips. "I'm sorry he said that to you, darling. I don't think Hawk is feeling very much like himself at the moment."

"Well, he didn't need to be so *rude*. Sebastian says Hawk *stinks* and I agree with him!"

"I wanna see Sebastian," Paul joined in.

"You will." Timmy said. "He's standing right behind you!"

Paul spun around, laughing. "He must've run away," he joked, running along the porch.

"Let's find him." Timmy hugged Ariel quickly, before racing down the stairs after Paul, as they ran towards the lavender hedge and disappeared around the side of the house.

"Stay out of the garage, boys!" She called after them. Laughter was her only answer.

The front door chimed. "That will be the Reverend." Jaxon said.

"I'll let him in," Wren said as she headed through the back door and into the house.

Jaxon reached for her, and slipped his arm around her waist as he studied her face. "Have you been crying?" He asked softly.

"Why do you have to be so observant?" She shook her head, wrapping her arms around his waist.

"It's part of the job," he grinned as he bent his head. "You okay?" His breath was sweet across her face.

She nodded, and tipped her head back, lips parting softly before his ascended and swept across hers. She sighed in pleasure as his scent wrapped around her, the warmth of his strong body grounded her. His arms around her made her feel safe, like she *was* home.

"Ariel, Jaxon, Reverend Matthews is here," Wren called as she opened the back door, smiling sweetly.

Ariel smiled at Wren, before looking at Jaxon. "I'm just going to have a quick chat to my moody brother, and wash up, then I'll join you."

He dropped another quick kiss across her lips.

"Sure," he ran a hand along the length of her long ponytail. "Take your time, Wren and I will make sure the Reverend has everything he needs."

"Thank you," she whispered, before cupping his chin. "For everything." She kissed his stubbled jaw.

"You're welcome, beautiful." He smiled, taking her hand and leading her inside.

"Jaxon, Ariel, it's good to see you again." The Reverend smiled warmly as he extended his hand.

Jaxon stepped forward, clasping the older man's hand and shook it. "It's so good of you to come."

"Of course, it's my pleasure." He nodded, before turning to Ariel. "How have you been?"

She wasn't sure how to answer that question. "Good." She thought that should cover it for now.

The Reverend studied Ariel.

"Would you like to come into the sitting room Reverend and have some tea?" Wren asked.

His gaze remained on Ariel for a moment longer, before turning to smile at Wren. "That would be lovely, thank you child."

Ariel sighed as the Reverend followed Wren into the sunny sitting room.

"Hey," Jaxon rubbed her arm. "It's going to be fine. Go check on Hawk, wash your face."

She nodded, as he turned and headed into the sitting room. She ran upstairs as the grandfather clock bonged on eleven a.m. and knocked on Hawk's door. No answer.

"Hawk?"

Nothing.

"Hawk, have you gone back to sleep?"

"How could I with all the constant interruptions around here?" He snapped.

She frowned. Hawk was *not* a rude person. "Tone it down a bit thank you. Why were you rude to Timmy?"

A loud sigh was accompanied by footsteps that thumped towards the bedroom door before it was flung open. Hawk glared at her; his dark hair dishevelled. He was wearing black boxer shorts and behind him, his usually immaculate room looked like a bomb had gone off.

"I was *what?*" He snapped.

"Rude to your brother."

"He was annoying me. So?"

"What's gotten into you?"

He laughed. "You don't want to know."

"I *beg* your pardon?" She folded her arms.

"Really, you don't want to know what's gotten into me." He stepped closer, as if to intimidate her.

She raised her head and stepped forward so they were nose to nose. "Hawk Harper, you might want to watch your attitude, as of right this minute."

"Oh yeah… what are you going to do about it?" He challenged.

"Hawk!" She cried. What on earth was his problem?

"Ariel," Wren called for downstairs. "Reverend Matthews says that you and Hawk should come downstairs now so he can talk to us all."

"All right, love." Ariel called, noting that Hawk had gone pale. He stepped back, head hung and wrapped his arms around his waist; suddenly losing his bad-boy attitude.

"What's wrong?" She asked impatiently, not ready to forgive his filthy attitude.

He shook his head. "I don't feel well. I don't want to go downstairs."

"It won't be for long, and if Reverend Matthews has asked us to join him it must be important."

"No Ariel, please." He begged in his usual sweet tone. "My ribs are actually killing me. I'm sorry for being an arsehole, I think it's the pain."

Ariel sighed and reached to rub his arm. His skin was like ice. "Listen, you're freezing, put something warm on. I'll get Jaxon to come and feel your ribs."

"No," He said hurriedly. "I'm okay."

"No, obviously, you are not. He did triage oversees; he'll be able to ascertain if your ribs are broken or bruised."

He shook his head.

"It's Jaxon, or the hospital," she stated firmly.

"Sure. Jaxon." He agreed quietly. "Just give me five minutes. I want to go to the loo and get dressed."

"Okay," she agreed. "And Hawk, please lose the attitude. Especially when it comes to Timmy, understood?"

"Yeah, I'm sorry."

She nodded and headed to the bathroom to quickly wash her face before going downstairs, hoping that was the end of that.

Travis Lockwood

He stood there, panicking. If Jaxon put his hands on him, he'd know the boy's ribs were no longer broken and he needed an excuse to stay up here. If the Reverend got close to him, he might suspect he was in the boy. He needed to act, and fast. He searched the room and found a cricket bat. "Have to do," he mumbled.

He held the tip end against his lower rib cage, facing the handle towards the door. "Here goes," he whispered, taking a deep breath then lunged forward, slamming the end of the bat against the hardwood, holding the other end firmly against his ribs. The impact was immediate, and he heard the snap of bone. Despite the pain that radiated through his body, he grinned, dropping the bat and running a hand over his chest. There was some kind of pleasure in hurting the boy's beautiful body.

He bent to snatch up a black hoodie off the floor, grunting slightly as the broken rib protested. Pulling it over his head, he slipped back into bed, pulling the covers up. Hoping that when Jaxon put his hands on him, he wouldn't feel like a corpse.

"Hey Hawk, can I come in?" Jaxon called from the other side of the door.

"Sure, come in," he called. *Just play nice...*

Jaxon

"Ariel said you're in a bit of pain?" Jaxon said, leaving the bedroom door open behind him.

"Yeah, a little."

"That's no good. You've had broken ribs before?"

"Yeah," he shrugged, grimacing at the movement.

"Can you take a deep breath?"

Hawk nodded, pulling in a lungful of air, wincing in pain.

"Do you mind if I have a look, mate?"

"Sure."

Jaxon leaned over and pulled the covers back to Hawk's waist, thinking the boy looked paler than his usual self. As he tugged the waistband of Hawk's hoodie up, his fingers brushed his flesh. He was cold. Ice cold. Wearing a hoodie on an Inglewood summers day, which currently the temperature was sitting at 38 degrees. The house was cool, but in no way did it feel like an ice box. "Cold mate?"

"Sorta."

Jaxon straightened to compare Hawk's left and right rib cage. "Left side's sunken."

"Yeah, that's the one." Hawk tugged his jumper down.

"Ariel mentioned you gave Timmy a piggyback ride the morning after you hit the stairs?"

Hawk shrugged. "Weird, huh."

"Mhm." Jaxon watched him carefully for a moment. "I'll help you strap them if you like?"

"Later?"

"The sooner the better.

"Yeah, I know, but I really need some sleep."

Jaxon nodded.

"Can you tell Ariel, I'm sorry, about before," he looked sheepish.

"Of course. I take it you don't want Reverend Matthews coming in here?"

"Nah, there's never been any activity in this room anyway." Hawk said, pulling the covers up to his chest.

"Okay." Jaxon nodded. "Well, get some sleep. Maybe you can play a board game with Timmy later, to make up for your..." he hesitated, not wanting to overstep. "Anyway, get some sleep."

"Thanks."

Jaxon closed the bedroom door running a hand over the back of his neck. Okay, so maybe Hawk wasn't acting one hundred percent like himself, but pain did that to a person. On top of the added trauma of living in a house where paranormal activity occurred.

He headed downstairs hearing Ariel's musical laughter and grinned. Despite the responsibility of raising three kids in a house oozing paranormal activity whilst maintaining her success as a highly respected artist, she remained a bright light for her family. Her resilience and strength was one of the things he loved about her.

He paused on the bottom stair. *Loved?* Where had that come from?

Her laughter spilled out of the room once more, joined by Wren. His smile would have matched that of a Cheshire cat, he was sure of it. Hell yes! *Loved.* Well, be damned.

The back door slammed, and his thought flow regarding his feelings for Ariel were halted as Timmy and Paul raced inside laughing their heads off.

His grin widened. These were the kind of kids that fuelled his passion as a teacher. Good kids at heart with an innocent enthusiasm for life.

"Mr Williams?"

"Yes Timmy."

"Sebastian says you're a good guy."

Jaxon raised an eyebrow. "Really?"

"Oh yeah, he knows who the scumbags are. You're not one of them."

"Well, that's nice of Sebastian. Tell him, thanks from me."

Timmy's grin widened. "Tell him yourself he's right behind you." He laughed.

Jaxon immediately felt a chill to his left side, and goosebumps spread along every inch of exposed flesh.

"Why can't I talk to Sebastian?" Paul whined. "I've been wait'n all darned week!"

Cold little fingers wrapped around Jaxon's wrist, halting the dry chuckle that almost slipped out at Paul's comment. He swallowed. *It's just a little ghost, calm down.*

"Well, thank you Sebastian," he said calmly, feeling anything but.

"Let's go play with your train set Timmy, it's getting too hot outside." Paul suggested.

"Timmy, Paul." Ariel stepped into the wide corridor, offering Jaxon a sweet smile.

"Would you like to take some frozen fruit upstairs?"

"And an icy pole?" Timmy ran across and wrapped his arms around Ariel, beaming up at her like she was his everything.

She cupped his chin, bending to drop a kiss on his nose. "Yes, baby. Whatever you like. Run upstairs, I'll bring it up in a moment."

"Thanks Ariel." Timmy raced passed Jaxon. "Come on Paul."

"Boys, just keep the noise level down a bit outside Hawk's room. He's needing a bit more sleep." Jaxon said.

"Okay." They yelled.

"Shh." Ariel begged.

Jaxon chuckled as Reverend Matthews joined them. "That tea hit the spot Ariel. What was it?"

"It's one that Liv serves at the café. Lavender Grey maybe?"

"It was," Wren confirmed from the kitchen.

"I'll have to check it out." He nodded, wooden cross and bible held loosely in his long, gnarled fingers. "I might just go for a wander around, if that's all right with you?"

"Of course Reverend, thank you." She touched Jaxon's arm, frowning. "You feel cold."

"Yeah, there's a story there." He answered quietly, looking over his shoulder to see the Reverend wander down the corridor before slipping into Mrs Harper's writing studio. "But it will keep. You want some help with the fruit."

"Sure." She led the way to the kitchen where Wren was rinsing the tea pot.

"How was Hawk?" Ariel asked, reaching to pull a container of frozen fruit from the freezer.

Wren glanced at him, waiting.

"He's in a bit of pain. Left ribs broken, I don't know how many."

"Shall I go to the chemist and get new bandages to strap him?" Wren asked.

"Yes please, thanks love, grab my purse from the hallway stand."

"I'll visit the café on my way back." Wren said as she grabbed the purse before heading to the front door. "Bye Reverend," she called before they heard the front door shut.

Jaxon watched as Ariel selected fruit, placing it onto a plate forming a smiley face with the grapes, pineapple, watermelon and blueberries. A frown marred her exquisite features.

"What is it?"

"I should have booked him in for an X-ray." She sounded guilty, before adding. "He was running around with the boys yesterday morning, so I assumed they were bruised, not broken. It doesn't make sense."

"Kids are durable," he soothed. "He'll be okay, there's nothing to be done but to strap them."

She nodded, biting her lip.

"Is there something else troubling you?" He asked. She seemed distracted.

She shrugged. "I'm just processing some information."

"Want to share?"

Her gaze lifted, meeting his before she shook her head. Seeing her defeated look crushed him. He reached for her hand, bringing it to his lips, nibbling on the pineapple pinched between her fingers. He watched her eyes darken as they traced his lips, his tongue swept the juices from her fingertips before tugging her against him.

Her arms immediately wound around his neck, and she pressed herself against him offering him her lips which he happily devoured in a long, deep kiss.

"Mmm," she sighed, closing her eyes. "Can I stay here for the rest of the day?"

He chuckled, running his hands down her sides to rest on her hips. "The Reverend may have something to say about that."

"Ariel! We're hungry!" Timmy whisper shouted.

"Or, perhaps Timmy," he added, before sweeping another kiss against her lips. "Delicious," he whispered.

She laughed, patting his chest, then crossed to grab two icy-poles from the freezer. Picking up the plate of fruit she headed towards the stairs to find Reverend Matthews about to head up.

"Frozen fruit?" She offered him as they walked up together.

"Why, thank you."

Jaxon noticed the old man's hand shook as he selected a blueberry. The house was cooler inside than outside, but he was conscious of the elderly during this time of year.

"Reverend, I'll bring up a glass of ice-water for you, it's always hotter upstairs despite the ceiling fans."

"I'd appreciate that, thank you Jaxon." Reverend Matthews said as he followed Ariel up the stairs to where the boys quiet laughter trickled in stops and starts.

Ariel

"Oh, Reverend, that's Hawk's room. He's sleeping." Ariel said quietly as the Reverend placed his hand on the doorknob.

"Oh," his hand stilled for a few moments longer.

"Is everything okay?"

"I may need to come back another time to bless the room is all," he smiled.

"You are welcome anytime and I'd love to cook you a meal to say thank you."

"There's no need to do that, dear."

"I know but I'd like to, and I know my grandmother would appreciate me cooking for you too." She smiled, before heading off to Timmy's room.

Opening the door, her heart warmed seeing the boys laying on their stomachs, pushing toy trains along the tracks. She placed the fruit in the middle of a plastic forest, careful not to knock the village over, and handed them an icy-pole each.

"Thank you, Ariel." Paul said politely. She smiled, falling in love with the little blonde boy every time he spoke.

"You're welcome."

"Ariel?" Timmy looked up at her, seeming small as he lay amongst his toys scattered far and wide.

"Yes love."

"Sebastian says we had better keep our eyes wide open or bad things are gonna happen."

She squatted down, keeping her voice calm. "Oh, did he? What does he mean?"

"He says the core is starting to rot, and soon the outside will too." Timmy sat up, sucking on his icy-pole as he stared at her with round eyes.

"What does that even mean?" Paul asked around a mouthful of fruit. "There's no apple's around here?"

Timmy shrugged. "That's all he said before he ran off."

Ariel nodded. "Well, that was thoughtful of Sebastian to warn us." She wondered if it was the right thing to even want to thank him.

Getting up off the floor, she wandered out of the room and down the corridor, hearing the Reverend bless Wren's room. She waited outside the door, not wanting to interrupt. A few minutes later he emerged.

"Reverend, can I ask you a few questions?"

"Of course. I was about to bless your room."

"Let's talk in there shall we?" She led the way towards the large bedroom and wandered across to sit at the window seat as the Reverend stood by the bed. "I don't know where to start."

"It doesn't matter really; just whatever question comes to you first."

"I'm wondering if it's dangerous for Timmy to continue talking with this Sebastian?"

"So far, from what you've said, Sebastian seems to be a protective soul."

She nodded. "I'm scared he's starting out nice in order to get something from Timmy?" As the words left her lips, the bedroom door slammed shut and a child's wailing filled the room; the temperature dropped rapidly.

"Sorry Sebastian," she whispered, guessing she'd offended him. The door flew open, and the wailing ceased as quickly as it had begun. Ariel shook her head. "Well, he does seem harmless."

"Indeed."

"Maybe I'll stop doing my own research." She muttered to herself.

"Oh?"

She laughed, embarrassed to admit that she'd been watching the 'Conjuring' movies and episodes of 'Hauntings' on Netflix. She shook her head. "Never mind. Can I ask you about my mother, and the Lockwoods?"

He stiffened, looking slightly uncomfortable. "I'm not sure I can do that, I'm sorry. Perhaps if your uncle were here?"

"Reverend, please," she sighed. "I don't need protecting."

"That may be so, but I made a promise to keep certain information to myself for the sake of your mental health and reputation."

"I appreciate your good intentions, but trust me when I say, my mental health is just fine. As far as my reputation, I am who I am regardless of any information you share."

He opened his mouth, closed it again as he frowned and remained silent.

"I found a newspaper article in the garage, a full spread about the Lockwoods and their despicable crimes, including raping and attempting to murder my mother."

His eyes darkened at her statement.

"I've done the math, and I'm aware of my mother's timely relationships." She took a deep breath, hating that her voice trembled. Not really wanting anyone to confirm what she thought may be true. That a Lockwood was her father. Men who had killed, tortured and were the vilest of individuals. She swallowed, folding her arms as if that could protect her from feeling tainted.

The Reverend cleared his throat looking uncomfortable.

"Is it true? That one of the Lockwood's is my father?"

Silence filled the room that was heating up once more, before the Reverend finally said, "Ariel, your mother and Grandparent's never wanted you to know."

"I understand that, but I've got nothing to be ashamed about."

"Of course not, dear. But as a parental figure yourself wouldn't you do everything in your power to protect Timmy, Wren or Hawk from anything distasteful if you could, if it were to affect them?"

She thought about it, knowing she would. But something as important as to who their father was? She shrugged. "Maybe you're right."

"The only thing that changes with you knowing this information, is how you see yourself. How it will impact you moving forward."

"I'll be fine," she whispered. "As long as this house settles down and the kids are safe. How can we get rid of the entity that's trying to hurt us?"

"Blessings will only work so far. I may need help performing an exorcism."

"Do you think that if we found out who the entities are, it would help?"

"Possibly. But not if they are soulless."

"Soulless… like, a demon?" *Please no.*

"Possibly. Earlier you mentioned that the wind had a foul stench to it?"

"Yes, like rotting meat."

"That's usually a tell-tale sign that the entity is demonic."

She shivered, suddenly wanting to check on all the kids, grateful that Wren was out of the house. "Will an exorcism on the house expel the good spirits?" She was thinking of her grandmother, and Sebastian.

"Only if they are ready to step into the light. "They may be content here, or something may be holding them here against their will. An exorcism can be helpful to those seeking the light but are trapped due to demonic or dark forces."

She nodded. "All this talk is making me want to sleep with every light on."

"Have you been burning your white candles?"

"I know it sounds silly, but it's been too hot to burn candles. I will start though, tonight."

"Very good. Well, let me finish up here and when I get home, I'll make a few phone calls. I've a colleague in Bendigo and Melbourne who can help me with some research."

"Thank you Reverend. I truly appreciate it."

He nodded before turning towards a corner, opening his arms open wide and began whispering in Latin holding his cross and bible outwards.

Ariel quietly left the room and checked on the boys before heading downstairs to find Jaxon.

Chapter Eighteen
Ariel

Mrs Roycroft beamed as Ariel unveiled the finished painting of the five-generation family portrait. It looked stunning sitting above the grand fireplace in their country estate home in Maldon.

Ariel reached into her bag and pulled out a travel pack of Kleenex tissues, holding them out as she watched another tear escape her client's eye.

"Oh, Ariel," she laughed as more tears flowed. "I'm just overjoyed is all. This is so wonderful, a simple thank you, although extremely heartfelt just doesn't seem enough." She plucked a tissue out of the pack and wiped her eyes.

Three-thousand dollars was thanks enough. Ariel smiled. "It was my pleasure. Knowing that it will hang in your gorgeous home for your family to enjoy for years to come, is thanks enough."

"It's not just a portrait, the way you've captured light, colour, texture in every brush stroke… it's just sublime."

"I wouldn't be very good as an artist if I couldn't do all those things."

Mrs Roycroft shook her head. "You're being too modest."

"No, just realistic." Ariel smiled.

"You know, I'm hosting a charity ball here at the end of next month. You'll have to come. With the crowd attending there is no doubt you'll have a hundred more clients after they see this."

"That would be lovely. What charity is it?"

"Homeless Victoria. We intend to raise funds to provide adequate support and more accessible services for those who have found themselves in difficult situations. Along with several building projects we hope to provide more shelters. Safe shelters."

"That sounds incredible. I'd love to donate a few paintings for you to auction off."

"Would you? How generous! That would be incredible. We have some of Victoria's most influential people attending who would be sure to dig deep."

"You know, I've a friend who lives down Warrnambool way, Glenormiston South. *Jess Fowler Art* – her paintings are remarkable. She paints native flora and fauna, coupled with native birds, and wildlife. I'll ask if she'd like to donate a couple of pieces too."

"Well by all means, please extend an invitation for Jess to join us. It would be an honour to have such exceptional Victorian artists attend."

"Thank you." Ariel smiled.

"Have you heard of Lorena Carrington?" Mrs Roycroft asked.

"Yes, she's an incredible illustrator and photographer." Ariel had her, *Wiser than Evening* book that she read to Timmy.

"Well, she's just down the road in Castlemaine and will be attending too."

"Sounds like a fabulous line-up."

"It's going to be a wonderful event."

"I look forward to it."

"Fantastic, and please feel free to bring a plus one."

"Thank you, well I'd better be going, I've got to pick Timmy up from school."

"Thank you so much for delivering the painting Ariel. I can't wait to show the rest of the family." Mrs Roycroft walked her out of the room and down the hallway towards the front door.

Ariel grinned. "You'll have to tell me about their reactions."

Ariel pulled out her car keys and headed towards her SUV.

"Goodbye." Mrs Roycroft waved her off as she drove by a sea of Agapanthus planted under the Mallee trees that lined the opulent driveway.

Heading back to Inglewood and into town, she parked across the street from the school and sighed, not wanting to get out of the airconditioned vehicle. The three-thirty school bell had her stepping out into the afternoon heat and she wandered to the school gate to wait. She noticed that Valeria and her flock of 'pigeon-mothers' were sending her their usual sidelong glances. She'd hoped by now, several weeks into the school year, that she wouldn't be such an item for them to talk about. She did not want to think of them as 'bored housewives' but they were pushing her to feel small-minded towards them. She was grateful to several other mums who offered her a kind smile, or returned her hello's.

As the kids poured out of the building, she noticed that Timmy wasn't his usual smiley self and was dragging his feet as he approached her.

"Hey darling, how was your day?" She asked, bending to drop a kiss against his sweaty forehead before taking his hand to cross the road.

"Fine," he mumbled, dragging his school bag along the asphalt.

She reached down to pick it up. Opening his door, she made sure he was safely strapped in, before walking to the driver's side, noticing that the flock of mother's were surrounded by excited kids who were jumping up and down around Aaron. Paul was amongst them, looking less enthusiastic as he watched their car pull out.

"Do you want to go to the pool for a swim, love?" Checking in the review mirror, she was sad to see he'd rested his face against the window staring out of it with a lacklustre expression.

"What's wrong?"

He shrugged, not answering.

Pulling into the driveway, she held in her sigh as she got out and opened his door. He clicked open his seat belt and walked inside, dragging his bag on the ground. Following him inside she dropped the car keys on the hallstand as Timmy threw his bag with all his seven-year-old might.

"I hate those kids!" He yelled, letting it out.

"Come in the kitchen," she offered, turning on the ceiling fan before heading over to the freezer to grab him an icy-pole.

He climbed up onto a stool, kicking his shoes off, wearing an angry frown as he took the icy-pole from her. "Thanks," he mumbled before jamming it into his mouth and sucking furiously.

She poured herself a drink and leaned against the bench, waiting. She knew he'd get it out of his system when he was ready.

Hawk strolled into the room. "Hello family members," he said, reaching for an apple in the crisper.

He hadn't left the house in well over a week and was looking pale and a little gaunt. Once again, Ariel held in a sigh. *Just another sibling to worry about.* She forced a smile, before focusing on Timmy. He finished sucking all the juice and placed the wrapper on the bench before meeting Ariel's gaze.

"Aaron's best mate, Dave, is having a birthday party and I wasn't invited. Aaron told me that his mum warned Dave's mum that I was rude and undisciplined, and now I'm the only kid in my entire class that didn't get an invite to Dave's pool party." He finished in one breath, tears building in his eyes.

Ariel shook her head, biting her tongue on the choice swear words that wanted to come out with her opinion on what absolute arseholes Valeria, and Dave's mother were. Instead, she took a calming breath as she leaned down to meet Timmy's eyes.

"That was extremely rude of them all, and I'm so sorry you've been left out, darling."

"Invite that kid over here so I can beat his arse." Hawk said around a mouthful of apple.

"Hawk, not helpful." Ariel frowned. *And once again, so unlike him.*

He shrugged.

"You taught me to care about other people's feelings Ariel. Why didn't Aaron and Dave care about mine?" A fat tear spilled from his dark blue eyes, followed by a stream as he cried.

She quickly reached for him, pulling him into a comforting hug and gave him time to cry out his pain. She met Hawk's gaze over the top of Timmy's head. He was shaking his head slowly, running a finger along his throat, mouthing *Pricks,* before turning to leave the room. She heard him go upstairs, a door closing soon after.

She rolled her eyes as she ran a hand up and down Timmy's back as his crying ceased, followed by small hiccups.

"I've got an idea."

"Yeah?" He looked up at her with a tear-stained face.

She brushed his tears away, nodding. "How about we go to the café, and ask Liv to make you her super delicious Sundae with all the toppings?"

His eyes brightened. "All the toppings?"

"Every single one of them."

"Really?"

"Absolutely. Go wash your face love and we'll go. I'll text Wren to meet us there when she gets off the bus."

"Will Hawk come too?"

"We can ask him. Maybe we'll have tea at Uncle Steven's tonight. Would that be fun?"

He jumped off the stool and ran towards the stairs. "I'm going to wear something awesome."

She laughed, relieved he was happy once more. Running up the stairs behind him, she knocked on Hawk's door.

"Yep," he called.

"Do you want to come to the café? We'll have tea with Uncle Steven."

"No thanks. Wren bought home heaps of schoolwork that I need to catch up on."

"Are you sure?" He hadn't joined them for any meals, or family conversations since Reverend Matthews had left the house last Saturday.

"Yeah, sorry," he sounded remorseful.

"It's okay."

Timmy raced out of his room wearing a Captain America tee shirt and shorts. She grinned at him, ruffling his hair as he ran past her. "I'll bring you some food back with us."

"Thanks," Hawk replied through the closed door. "Have fun."

"See you." She turned, following Timmy downstairs, trying not to worry about Hawk's lack of family engagement. She knew he was at that age of needing space to figure things out. She sent a text to Wren, and Jaxon, inviting them along.

"Are we walking or driving?" Timmy yelled from the back porch.

"Driving and aircon," she called, snatching up the car keys looking forward to being with her tribe.

"Those little shits!" Liv whispered to Ariel as Timmy explained to Steven, why Captain America was cooler than Antman, as they were setting the table.

They'd closed the café just after five-thirty when the last customer had left and had cooked barbeque steak that Steven had marinated.

"I was so angry, I still am. The look on his sweet face." She shook her head.

"What are you going to do?"

"I'll be having a word with Valeria and the pigeon squad tomorrow."

"Pigeon squad?" Liv laughed. "I like it."

"I want to come with you," Wren said, placing a tomato salad on the table.

"No, you'll be getting yourself to school, young lady." Steven said, sitting at the table. "I'll be going along as a silent support person."

Ariel laughed. "You will not."

"Try and stop me."

She met his serious gaze. "Let's just eat shall we." She decided to discuss it further when Timmy wasn't around.

As everyone took a seat around the table, Ariel spotted Jaxon at the shop-front door carrying a tray covered in aluminium foil. She unlocked the door smiling at him; her heartbeat quickened as he stepped close to her.

"Good evening, Miss Harper," he grinned, before leaning down to drop a kiss across her cheek.

"Good evening, Mr Williams." She returned, moving aside so he could enter. She locked the door behind him as he went to greet the others, placing the tray on the table.

Steven got up to shake his hand, before they man hugged. "How's it been going?"

"Oh, you know, kids, their parents and school stuff in general." He clapped Steven on the back. "How was the landscaping convention?"

"Fantastic. I'll be putting another team together soon. Business is booming." Steven sat.

"Glad to hear it. How've you been Liv?"

Ariel watched her friend get that 'Mr-Honey-is-talking-to-me' look on her face and bit the inside of her cheek so she wouldn't laugh.

"I'm good, thank you Jaxon. Would you like some steak?" She offered.

"Yes please."

"What's in there?" Wren asked, pointing to his tray.

"That there, is my Grandpa's family recipe for Bread-and-Butter pudding."

"Yum." Wren grinned.

"It certainly is." Jaxon pulled out a chair and reached across to high-five Timmy. "How was your day?"

Timmy stabbed his fork into a cube of cheese, shrugging. "It was good when I came here. Liv made me the best Sundae ever." He shoved the cube into his mouth.

"Liv does that." Jaxon agreed.

"Oh please," Liv said, flushing pink. "It's not hard combining ice-cream, cream and a bunch of fruit, syrup and sprinkles."

Steven reached across and took Liv's hand, waiting for her to meet his gaze. When she did, Ariel's heart melted with the look they exchanged.

"What is hard," Steven began. "Is keeping a welcoming, pretty smile on your face as you serve people all day, day in - day out, and run this business successfully. Part of that success is making the best sundaes in town and is something to be proud of."

Liv's flush deepened and she leaned across to kiss Steven soundly.

"Yuck," Timmy closed his eyes, making Ariel and Wren chuckle.

"Nice words, Dr Phil." Jaxon added, making everyone laugh louder.

"Thanks." Steven nodded, kissing Liv once more.

Ariel sat beside Jaxon and served salad, as Wren placed steak onto their plates. "Thanks love."

"Now for the serious part of tonight's entertainment. What's your school policy on ostracizing and bullying?" Steven asked as he sliced his steak.

"We have a framework in place, policies to follow and in most cases it works well. Unfortunately, there's always going to be some actions that slip through the cracks and impact students in a negative way. Why?"

"Ariel can tell you," Steven looked pointedly at his niece.

"I really don't want to talk about it right now." She raised her eyebrow and angled her head towards Timmy.

Jaxon nodded, taking her hand in his under the table and squeezed it lightly, letting her know he wouldn't push it.

She squeezed his hand back, leaving hers in his as they started eating one handed.

"No Hawk tonight?" Jaxon asked.

"No, he's catching up on schoolwork," she said. His aftershave, mingling with his scent and the steak, was making her mouth water double time.

She caught Liv's eye and grinned, noticing Liv was leaning against Steven's side with a satisfied look on her face.

"He hasn't left the house in over a week," Wren said.

"Why?" Steven asked.

Ariel sent Wren a look, and Wren shifted in her seat as soon as she met Ariel's gaze. Ariel had mentioned to Wren that she didn't want to bother Steven with what had happened at the house whilst he'd been away. Not yet. Not till he had time to settle back in.

"He had an incident on the stairs, broke a rib. But he's coming good." She explained.

Steven nodded. "Well, I'll pop in tomorrow morning, see how he's doing."

"That would be great." They finished the meal with light conversation, then served Jaxon's Bread and Butter pudding with coffee.

"Wren, do you want to take Timmy upstairs?" Steven asked.

"Sure Uncle Steven," she said.

"Can we play your Play Station?" Timmy jumped up and down.

"Whatever makes you happy, sport."

As Wren and Timmy disappeared upstairs, Jaxon turned to Ariel. "What happened today."

She sighed, taking her coffee across to the couches and sat. The others joined her.

"Valeria has spread rumours that Timmy is an unsavoury character. He was the only child excluded from Dave - whoever's party today."

Jaxon nodded; eyes gleaming darkly. "Dave Taylor."

"Right," she whispered, shrugging.

"Well, that's very unfortunate to hear," he clipped.

"I'd say," Steven agreed. "What are you going to do about it?"

"I'll need to discuss this with Ray. Then, no doubt both Ariel and Valeria will need to come in for a meeting."

Ariel sighed. "Great."

He put his arm around her shoulder. "It'll be all right. I'll be there."

She met his gaze, and nodded, desperate to be alone with him. To *be* with him. She'd told Liv earlier that with everything going on in the house, Hawk not feeling inclined to leave his room, and the responsibility of all the kids happiness, she could feel herself fading away.

"You know Jaxon." Liv piped up. "Steven and I were planning to have a pizza and games night with the kids tomorrow night. I was wondering what you were up to?"

Jaxon smiled. "Are you inviting me over, Liv?"

"No. I'm hoping you'll invite Ariel over to yours and keep her there with you all night for some TLC."

Jaxon nodded as he met Liv's gaze. "I was planning on having you all over for a BBQ, but this suits me just fine." He turned to Ariel, wearing a sexy smile. "Would you like to come over for a sleepover?"

She tried to keep her reply steady in front of her uncle. "I'd love to. Do I need to bring my pillow?"

He shook his head.

"Lovely." She said, feeling excited at the thought of having him all to herself, without any interruptions.

"So that's settled," Liv beamed. "Shall we say, six pm?"

Ariel nodded. "Sure."

"And how about Saturday lunch, we head down to the river? Take the kids for a swim and do some paddle boarding?" Steven suggested.

"Lunch at Bridgewater pub?" Jaxon asked.

"Yes!" Liv jumped in, then chuckled. "Sorry, it's nice to be served, and not serving all the time. As much as I love it." She shrugged.

"That sounds really good." Ariel checked the time. "Well, we better be off. School night and all."

Jaxon agreed as he stood, offering his hand to pull her to her feet.

"Thank you."

"You're welcome." He smiled.

Liv had made up a plate for Hawk, along with a bowl of pudding. "Tell Hawk we missed him," she said.

"Thanks Liv, I will." Ariel said taking the packed food she headed across to the bottom of the stairs. "Wren, Timmy, it's time to go." She called.

"Oh no, Ariel! Can't we stay a bit longer?" Timmy whined.

"No love, it's nearly ten o'clock, way past your bedtime."

"Aw!"

"Come on Timmy," Wren soothed as she took his hand and led him downstairs.

"And guess what sport," Steven bent and scooped him up for a hug.

"What?"

"Liv and I are coming to yours tomorrow night for a pizza and games."

"Yippee!" Timmy cried.

"And," Steven continued. "On Saturday, we'll go to the river and hang out. Sound good?"

"Double yippee!" Timmy wrapped his arm around his uncle's neck.

"I've got Carly coming for a sleepover tomorrow night." Wren said.

"That's fine sweets, we won't get in your way." Steven dropped a kiss on her head.

As they all said their goodnights and headed out, Wren grabbed the food off Ariel, before climbing in the car after Timmy.

Ariel turned to Jaxon. "Well, Mr Williams, no doubt I'll see you at school tomorrow?"

He ran his hand along Ariel's arm, stepping close. "You will Miss Harper. And I cannot wait for the school day to be done, so I can have you all to myself."

His voice was low and smooth, and she imagined him naked and pleasing her as she hoped to please him. Heat immediately pooled between her thighs.

"Me too," was all she could manage.

He kissed her sweetly, as her two siblings waited in the car.

"Ariel," Timmy knocked against the window.

She smiled against his lips and mumbled, "Gotta go."

He nodded, eyes dark as he stepped back. She headed around to the driver's door,

and getting in started the engine. Waving a hand, she pulled away from the kerb, then released a steady breath.

Wren laughed.

"What was that for?" Ariel looked at her briefly, before turning down their street.

"Oh, you know, young love and all that." Wren said.

"I need to pee," Timmy started bouncing up and down on his seat.

"Hold on love, we're here." Ariel pulled the car into the back driveway, parking behind the art studio.

Timmy flew out of the back door and towards the house, as Wren got out she closed Timmy's door.

"He could have peed on the lemon tree," Ariel sighed, locking the car and following Wren into the house.

"I'm totally beat," Wren said over her shoulder, putting the food on the hallway stand as she headed towards the stairs.

"Go to bed love, sleep well."

"Goodnight."

Ariel watched Wren run upstairs and dropped her keys and bag on the hall stand as she collected the containers. Heading into the kitchen she grabbed some cutlery and went upstairs to knock on Hawk's door.

"Yeah," he called.

"I've got your tea, and pudding from Jaxon."

Silence.

"Hawk?"

The door opened, and she was shocked to see darker grooves than earlier, beneath his lovely eyes.

"Darling, are you okay?" She reached for his face.

He jerked his head away, avoiding her touch and snatched the food and cutlery from her hands, before slamming the door in her face.

She stood, mouth gaping, hardly believing his behaviour. Taking a deep breath, she grabbed the doorknob twisting it, only to find it locked. She raised her hand to thump against it.

"Sebastian says you shouldn't do that."

Ariel turned to her little brother, seeing he'd put his pyjamas on and was clutching Minkey Monkey to his chest.

She didn't like seeing the worried look on his sweet face. She dropped her hand and knelt in front of him.

"Why does Sebastian say that?"

"Coz, the apple is really starting to rot now. Soon, the skin will decay too and then we'll be in big trouble." Timmy said.

Ariel nodded, not really understanding. "Okay, well. Let's get you, Minkey and Sebastian into bed, shall we?"

Timmy whispered under his breath as she took his hand and led him into his bedroom.

"What's that, love?"

"Oh, just that Sebastian likes the idea of being able to go and hop into a real, soft bed. He bounces on mine sometimes."

"Does he?" Ariel had wondered why, after making Timmy's bed of a morning, it got so messy when Timmy was at school.

"Up you get, love."

Timmy climbed into bed, and she tucked the covers around him, trying to focus solely on him and not Hawk's disturbingly rude behaviour. Or his physical demise. "Did you enjoy tonight?"

"Yeah," Timmy nodded. "I don't feel so sad about being left out of Dave's party."

"I'm glad you feel better."

"I hope Paul had a good time though," he said around a yawn.

She smiled, loving his kind heart.

"I'm sure he did, although no doubt he would have missed you very much." She dropped a kiss on his forehead. "Goodnight, Timmy."

"Night Ariel."

Stepping out into the corridor, she stood, and listened to the house as it creaked and groaned as the summer wind outside increased. Feeling exhausted, she leaned against the wall dropping her head back, closing her eyes.

"Are you okay?" Wren asked quietly.

Ariel jumped, covering her mouth to stop the nervous laugh as Wren rubbed her shoulder, fighting her own laughter.

"Sorry," she whispered around a giggle.

Ariel shook her head. "I'll admit, I could have fallen asleep standing up."

"Go to bed."

Ariel nodded, and hugged Wren. "Goodnight."

"Sleep tight." Wren headed into her room and closed her door.

Ariel sighed, shaking her head at herself as she searched for her nighty. Getting undressed and slipping it over her head, she went and brushed her teeth, before falling face first into bed, and into a restless slumber.

Chapter Nineteen
Wren

W ren rolled onto her back, tossing the sheet off her as she felt another trickle of sweat roll down her face.

"Agh!" She groaned, reaching to tap on her touch lamp. Her sheets beneath her were saturated and her room felt like a furnace. Her desk fan had stopped working.

"Dammit," she pressed the top button. Nothing. She sat up pressing all three buttons, hoping to jar it into action. *Nada.* Getting out of bed she crossed to her dressing table and grabbed a hair band. Scooping her hair into a high ponytail, another trail of sweat made its way down her back as she picked up her mobile to check the time; three a.m. Her mouth was dry, and reaching for her water bottle, found it empty.

"Didn't I fill this up before bed?" She whispered, frowning before she slowly placed it back down on the bedside table. Her eyes adjusted to the light, and she noticed how wet her sheets were. Pressing her palm against them she was startled to feel them not just wet but drenched. No wonder she was thirsty. It was like every ounce of liquid in her body had leaked out. Sighing, she decided to have a cold shower and wash the clamminess from her skin.

Yanking the sheet off the bed, followed by the mattress protector she headed to the door and twisted the knob. It didn't budge.

I didn't lock it, did I? She reached for the key and found it missing from the keyhole. Frowning, she rattled the doorknob back and forth to no avail and cursed under her breath.

Giving up, she dumped the bedding on the ground and crossed towards the wall that adjoined her bedroom to Hawk's, and knocked quietly.

"Hawk?" She knocked against the wall three times. "Hawk, can you hear me?" She waited, giving him time to wake up.

She licked her lips as a dizzy wave hit her; she was dehydrated. Leaning her palm against the wall she frowned, certain the temperature had risen ten degrees. Her room was a hot box. Knocking again, she used the side of her fist.

"*Hawk.*" *Bang-bang-bang.* "Hawk, my bedroom door's stuck and I can't get out."

She waited, banging her fist against the wall again before crossing to the window. Pushing the lace curtain aside, stained yellow with age and sunlight, she swivelled the latch and tried to slide the windowpane up, but like the door, it wouldn't budge.

"Damn it!" she cried and stormed back to the wall, banging as hard as she could.

"Hawk, are you bloody deaf?"

Silence ensued.

The sound of a key sliding into a metal lock, and a latch clicking open behind her sounded like a shotgun in the quiet room.

"Well, you took your sweet time answering me," she whispered turning around.

The door slammed open hitting the wall with a bang, making her jump.

"Real funny!" She marched towards the door stepping out into the corridor ready to give him a blasting, and froze. No one was there. Hairs stood along her damp flesh, and she hurried to turn the corridor light on, hoping that by chasing the darkness away it would make this moment less terrifying. Seeing the empty corridor only made it worse. She stepped back in her room and shut the door quickly.

"What is happening," she whispered, hating how scared she sounded, and turning towards her bed squealed when she saw Hawk standing there.

"Jesus *Christ*, Hawk, are you trying to scare me to damn death!" She hissed, rubbing a hand over her chest. "How the hell did you get in here?"

He was looking about the room, a frown marring his handsome features as he held his arms out in front of him, looking as confused as she felt. His gaze met hers, eyes wide. It was then that she realised something was off. Something was *very* off. She could see *through* him.

"Hawk?" She whispered as tears of fright clogged her throat. She stepped forward reaching for him.

Wren, he mouthed. But no sound came out. *Wren*.

His look of utter confusion, grief even–broke her heart.

"It's okay, it's okay," she chanted, trying to calm them both. Silent tears poured from her eyes, and she hastily wiped them away as he became a watery vision.

"Tell me what happened... I can read your lips."

He shook his head, rubbing his face then shrugged as he dropped his hand and mouthed, *be careful... don't trust me... don't trust him.*

"*Him*? I don't understand, who are you talking about."

Travis Lockwood.

As soon as Hawk mouthed the name Wren felt herself tipping. She didn't know the ins-and-outs of what the Lockwoods were about. She just knew they'd been dangerous.

Get him out of the house. Get him outside.

"Why?"

Because that's the only way I can come back.

"Where are you Hawk, and better still… where is he?" She had a sick feeling she already knew.

He jabbed a finger towards his chest. *In me. You have to get him outside.* He pointed towards the window.

She nodded, wiping more tears away. "Okay Hawk, okay." She sniffed back tears.

His lip curled in disgust. *"He wants you, badly. Play nice. Don't let him know that you know it's not me…"*

"I will," she nodded. "I can do this." She was grateful that his hand signals and their twin connection made it easier to understand him.

He looked relieved.

You can't tell Ariel. You can't tell anyone.

"Why?"

He'll kill me, I don't know how I know this, but I can hear his thoughts. If he can't have my body, he'll kill it! His eyes were wide, begging.

"Oh my god… Hawk." She covered her mouth with shaking hands.

Will you be okay?

"I will, I promise. I'll do everything I can," she soothed, wanting to chase the worried look away. "How are you here now?"

He shook his head. *He's in a deep sleep and I heard you call out to me. Suddenly I was here.* He shrugged, reaching for her hand. *You have to be careful. He's deranged, dangerous.*

"I'll be careful, he won't suspect a thing." As she placed her hand in his, he evaporated before her very eyes. "Hawk, *no!*" She cried in despair, allowing the tears to flow then.

It was all too much to process in her exhausted state; the information he'd shared and then seeing him fade into nothingness. The room spun, and she grabbed for the bed, missing it completely and collapsed on the floor.

"Wren." Timmy tapped her shoulder before shaking her arm. "Wren, wake up."

"Aw, hi Timmy," she whispered, mouth dry, throat sore. She rubbed a hand over her face, wincing as her temples throbbed. She needed water.

"What're ya sleeping on the floor for?"

She shrugged, not knowing what answer to give her little brother.

"Well, it's time to get up. Ariel says you and me are gonna make fruit smoothies."

"Okay, okay Timmy, just please stop shouting," she whispered, pushing herself up, hoping that the sunlight streaming in through the window wouldn't increase the pain in her head. It did; she stumbled to her feet towards the window and reached through the lace curtains for the cord to pull the blind down.

"There we go," she sighed. "Just give me a few minutes to wake up, would you? I need a quick shower."

"Okay," he stood there looking at her with a funny expression on his face.

"What?" She asked as she grabbed her towel off the hook on her closet door.

He tilted his head on the side. "Sebastian says you'd better be careful Wren, he says you being smart is only gonna get you into big trouble."

"Well geez, tell your friend to keep his thoughts to himself would you, Timmy."

He opened his mouth to say something else when she walked by him towards the bathroom.

"Sorry," she whispered, as he followed her out, before shutting the door. She tugged her allocated bathroom drawer open and pulled out her Panadol. Popping two, she turned on the cold tap and guzzled straight from the faucet, hearing mumbled voices in the corridor.

"Wren, are you okay? Timmy says you were asleep on the floor, and your sheets are saturated." Ariel called through the door.

She sighed, turning off the tap and reached to turn on the shower as she tugged her nighty over her head and flung it towards the laundry basket.

"I've got a migraine and my fan stopped working throughout the night," she called, stepping under the soothing spray of water.

"Oh hun," Ariel sympathised. "Can I do anything for you?"

"I've just taken Panadol."

"Do you need something stronger?"

"Maybe."

"I think we're out of Imigran, but we'll get something from the pharmacy.

"Thanks. I don't think I'll go into school today."

"That's okay, love. I'll cancel Jaxon and stay home."

Wren thought about games night with Carly, Liv and Steven. "No, don't do that, I'll be fine by tonight. Once the Panadol kicks in and I sleep it off."

"Are you sure?"

"Yeah."

"I'll pop a smoothie in the fridge for you."

"Thanks," she called, placing her hands against the white tiles and leaned her head forward against them. Closing her eyes, she relaxed as the water massaged the back of her neck, soothing her anxiety. *Why am I feeling so anxious?*

Her eyes flew open as everything came rushing back to her. The apparition or whatever it was, of Hawk visiting her and telling her *Travis Lockwood* was in *his* body, and the possible danger he was in. And where *exactly* was Hawk? *Oh, my Lord… what is going on?* She groaned, rubbing her hands over her face, forcing back overwhelmed tears.

Shutting the shower off she wrung the excess water from her hair and stepped out of the claw foot tub. Grabbing her towel she wrapped it around herself and headed towards her room.

Don't trust me, don't trust him… Hawk had said. So, Hawk was no longer Hawk? Travis Lockwood was inside of him, possessing him? Controlling him?

"Shit," she whispered, opening her door and ran straight into Hawk.

No. Straight into *Travis Lockwood*. She hated the cold, calculated look on her twin's face that did not belong there. She wanted to punch *him* in her handsome brother's face!

"What are you doing in here?" She asked, hating that her voice wobbled.

He tilted his head, as his gaze swept her from head to toe. "Oh, you know, just seeing if you're okay. Heard you had a rough night."

"I'm fine, I've just got a migraine. Can you get out so I can get changed."

"Oh, little sister you don't have to hide from me, I've seen it all before," he stepped forward, running his finger along the top of her towel where it was wrapped below her collarbone, before flicking his finger up under her nose. It stung.

"You're an arsehole. Get out." She snapped and stepped aside waving her hand towards the door.

"Excuse me? An *arsehole*? Who do you think you are talking to me like that?" He took another step toward her.

She hastily stepped back, "Ariel!"

Footsteps approached and Wren frowned as he scuttled away from her like the cockroach he was, invading her twin's body.

"What is it, love?" Ariel stepped in the room. "Hawk, aren't you getting ready for school?"

"Nah, I'm still not feeling well."

"You don't look well at all." Ariel grabbed his chin. "We need to get you to the doctor."

"I'm fine."

Ariel frowned, releasing his chin. "I hate to say it Hawk but you're looking green."

He grinned. "Yeah, like the incredible Hulk, huh?"

Wren snickered.

Travis turned to her; eyebrow raised. "Problem?"

"Wren has a migraine." Ariel saved Wren from making a smart arsed response.

"Oh no, poor baby-girl." his lips dropped at the corners. "Want me to kiss your temples better?"

"Hawk?" Ariel shook her head. "Why are you being so antagonistic lately?"

Wren was about to tell him to piss off, but had never spoken to Hawk that way, even on the odd occasion when he had annoyed her. They just didn't roll that way. Then she remembered what Hawk had said. *Be careful... he's dangerous. Don't let him know, that you know it's not me...*

"Can you go to the pharmacy and get me some Imigran?" She asked him, interrupting his and Ariel's exchange.

"Yeah sure, after I shower." He sounded doubtful.

I will get you outside, and out of my twin if it's the last thing I do.

"I've got a client coming in twenty minutes." Ariel checked her watch. "It would be helpful if you dashed out to grab a handful of things if you're not going to school. I'll leave a list on the kitchen bench."

"Okay," *Travis* nodded.

"And I want that room of yours cleaned up today. Grandma would have a heart attack at the state of it."

"Yeah," he shrugged.

"And can you please feed the girls?" Ariel continued. "The scrap bucket is starting to reek."

Wren felt hopeful. *This could be easier than I thought, getting him outside.*

"Sure, anything else?" He sounded sarcastic.

"Can you hang out the washing?"

He was watching Ariel with a glint in his eye before replying. "Sure, *sis.*"

"Thanks," she smiled sugar sweet.

"Ariel, I'm hungry." Timmy yelled from downstairs breaking the weird tension that was building between them.

"Coming," Ariel turned to the twins. "How about we leave Wren in peace."

"Sure thing," *Travis* looked at Wren through Hawk's narrowed eyes.

Ariel waited for Hawk to leave before saying, "Hop back into bed," she headed across and turned the desk fan on, facing it towards the freshly made bed.

Weird, it works now?

"Thanks for changing my sheets," she said gratefully.

"Of course."

Wren grabbed a fresh oversized tee shirt and slipped it over her head. The heat of the morning had dried her almost instantly, and she rubbed the towel through her hair before sitting on the bed grateful to have cool, dry sheets.

"When my client leaves, I'll come check on you before I head to the gallery. If you need me before then just buzz my mobile." Ariel ran a hand softly over her hair.

Wren nodded.

"I'll make sure Hawk get your meds."

"Thank you," she said quietly, wishing she could tell Ariel everything, but remembered what Hawk had said.

Don't tell Ariel, don't tell anyone. He'll kill me.

But how? She desperately needed her sisters help. And wouldn't it be better if they could work together to get Travis outside? And surely, she could help protect Ariel from Travis?

"Get some rest," Ariel interrupted her internal conversation.

"Ariel, I love you so much," Wren whispered.

"Oh sweet girl. I love you too." Ariel brushed a kiss on the top of her head. "Now sleep."

Wren nodded and lay back amongst the sheets and nestled her head on her pillow, closing her eyes. She was grateful when Ariel left, closing the door to leave her alone to construct a plan to save her brother. To save them all.

Jaxon

Jaxon arrived home from school in record time and put the air-conditioner on before racing around in his boxer shorts and a tee shirt making sure every room in the three story, thirteen roomed estate was in order.

"I guess when you're hardly home, things are always going to look this good," he said, impressed with himself, before diving into the kitchen to start the prep for his Grandfather's famous corned beef and cabbage, plus sides.

He set the table in the parlour and uncorked a sweet red that he knew Ariel liked. Once everything was done, he sprinted up his ornate staircase, stripped his bed and made it up with fresh linen. After dumping the used sheets into the wash, he dove into a refreshing shower where he stood for longer than he'd intended. Afterwards he dressed in a pair of cut-off jeans and a tee shirt, shoving his feet into a comfortable pair of Nikes and headed back downstairs to pour an ice-cold beer. He took it into the parlour and lit the scented candles he'd purchased last week from the café.

Checking his watch, it was almost time for Ariel to arrive. He put on some chillout beats and sat back to enjoy his beer, thinking about having her all to himself for an entire night.

To be able to watch her every move, the way her gorgeous face lit up and her eyes twinkled when they dove into varied conversations, whether deep and meaningful or about life in general, her art or her siblings. To be able to hold her, touch her, kiss her. Have her in every sense that a man could have a woman. He grew hard instantly, thinking about the last time he was between her legs.

"Christ." He jumped up to water the garden. He *did not* want her arriving on his doorstep and him looking like a horny teenager.

"Decorum, Williams," he muttered, downing the remainder of his beer before going to water the plants that his grandfather had tended to many years before.

Chapter Twenty
Ariel

A riel was furious that Hawk had not only neglected to get anything on the list, let alone the pain relief for Wren, but that he hadn't done a single chore she'd asked him to do. It was so unlike him.

"What has gotten into you Hawk?" She cried as she raced out of the bathroom and into her room to get changed.

"I wasn't feeling well," he snapped from his bedroom.

"Well you could have texted me when I was at the cafe! Now I'm going to have to run down the street to get everything, which will make me late getting to Jaxon's."

"I think your wet pussy will survive."

She froze, staring at herself in her bedroom mirror.

He did not just say that! *Surely*, she'd misheard him. She tugged her dress over her head and stormed towards his bedroom where his door was open. She could feel an unfamiliar haze of fury sweep through her.

Hawk was laying on his back, hands behind his head looking like he didn't have one single care in the world. His bedroom was still a disaster.

She balled her fists by her side as he casually looked across at her, raising an eyebrow. She swore she could feel steam blowing out of her ears.

"What the *hell* did you just say to me?" She hissed quietly, trying to remain calm with the knowledge that Timmy was just two doors down the hallway.

He slowly sat up, hands dangling between his thighs that were spread wide, resting his elbows on his knees he replied calmly, "I *said*, I think your wet pussy will survive ten minutes until you can get Jaxon William's pretty face between your legs to lick you out." He stared at her unblinking, as if he'd recited nothing more innocent than the alphabet.

She gasped, unable to comprehend what her younger brother had just said to her. *Never* in all these years had he *ever* spoken to her with such disregard or disrespect.

He ran his tongue along his bottom lip as his gaze dropped to her crotch. It was then that she snapped, and crossed over to him in three strides and slapped his face as hard as she could.

"How *dare* you speak to me, and *act* this way, Hawk Harper! What the *hell* has gotten into you?"

He stood then, her angry red handprint emerging against his pale, greyish skin as he stared down at her. "Try that again," he whispered.

She opened her mouth not even sure she had a response. Who *was* this person? She was partially grateful when Liv interrupted.

"Hello, the party people have arrived bearing goodies." She called cheerfully from downstairs.

Ariel stared silently at Hawk; her fury almost made her lost for words.

"We are not done here, Hawk, not by a longshot. And you can stay in this room until it is spotless. Do you hear me?"

He bent towards her. "I'm not deaf," he whispered.

She shook her head in disbelief. "To say I'm disappointed in you right now is an understatement."

"Well prepare yourself, *sister*… I'm only just getting warmed up." He leered in her face.

"What does that even mean?"

"You'll see soon enough."

"You'll want to pull your head in real quick smart, Hawk."

"Or what?" He raised an eyebrow.

Conflicting emotions swamped her, and she stepped away from him, tempted to do more than slap him. Shaking in anger she turned to find Wren standing in the doorway with a strange look on her face.

"Wren, I'm sorry love, I'll run down the street and get your meds."

"You can't, look at the time." Wren held up her mobile phone.

"Oh no," Ariel noted that the pharmacy would have been closed for at least forty minutes by now. "I'm sorry darling."

"Don't be, I'm feeling much better. The Panadol, plus sleep really helped. Just have a good night with Jaxon."

Ariel frowned, looking over her shoulder at Hawk, not really feeling in the mood now. She wasn't sure if it was a good idea to leave Liv and Steven alone to deal with his filthy attitude.

"Go," Wren took her hand and dragged her out of Hawk's room, shutting the door in his face before she turned to Ariel. "You deserve a break, I'll keep my eye on Hawk."

"I don't want him downstairs; I don't even know what Uncle Steven will do if he hears him speaking this way. He can stay up here and clean his room."

Wren nodded as Timmy raced by them heading downstairs. His laughter trickled up a few moments later as they heard Steven start his usual tickling game.

"Love, do me a favour?" Ariel asked Wren, who nodded. "Please cancel Carly. I don't want her under this roof around Hawk when I'm not here."

Wren bit her lip, looking thoughtful before nodding. "Okay, I'll ring her now."

Ariel sighed. "Thanks. Are you sure you're feeling better?"

"I really am, and I'm starving for pizza."

"Well, that's a good sign," she said quietly, distracted by Hawk's odd behaviour and foul manners. She couldn't shake the uncomfortable feeling that something was really off.

"Anyone else home?" Steven called upstairs.

"Coming," Wren yelled over the banister.

"I'm just going to finish getting ready." Ariel said to Wren, heading back into her room. "I'll be down soon."

"Do you want me to send Liv up?" Wren asked heading towards the stairs.

"Sure."

Within three minutes, as Ariel was applying an apricot-shimmer eyeshadow, Liv walked in, holding two glasses.

"Hello stranger," she joked. They'd only just seen each other an hour ago at the cafe.

Ariel chuckled reaching for the glass, and taking a sip, sighed in pleasure. "Pineapple juice and Midori. Yum."

"Yeah, I thought it was a good way to start the weekend."

Ariel took another mouthful, before finishing her basic, yet flattering makeup.

"Are you excited to spend the night with Mr Yummy?" Liv sat at the end of the bed.

"I am, it's just…" Ariel didn't want to put a damper on Liv's cheerful mood.

"What?"

"Hawk." Ariel closed her bedroom door, lowering her voice as she picked up her glass and sat near her friend. "He's acting strange, and his attitude has me stumped."

"He is a teenage boy." Liv reasoned.

"I slapped his face just before you arrived."

"You what?" Liv was clearly shocked.

Ariel nodded, feeling guilty enough, and swallowed the tears that tried to climb up her throat. She shook her head as Liv placed a comforting hand on her knee.

"What happened?"

"I can't even repeat what he said to me, it's that foul."

"Shit, really?" Liv took a sip of her drink.

Ariel nodded.

"Try me." Liv said.

Ariel repeated the revolting comment.

"This *is* Hawk we're talking about?" Liv gasped.

Ariel met her gaze. "I can't believe it myself."

"*Our* Hawk Harper."

Ariel sighed. "The one and only. I've never slapped him a day in his life, yet he barely flinched."

Liv frowned. "Ariel, I would have slapped him too." She shook her head, puzzled. "Has he broken up with a boyfriend? A girlfriend?"

"Not as far as I know."

"There has to be some explanation for him acting out."

"I wish I knew what is was." Ariel took a sip of the cold, sweet beverage, then finished it in four large gulps.

"I think you need another."

"I do, but I don't think it's a good idea. In fact, I don't think it's a good idea that I go to Jaxon's while Hawk is acting this way."

"Nonsense, you'll have a great time. Steven and I will be here for *all* three kids, no matter their attitude." Liv took the empty glass from her hand. "Now finish getting ready and get out of here."

Ariel smiled, hugging her friend as they stood. "Thanks Liv."

"Steven can drop you off."

Ariel nodded. "That's a good idea." Walking in the Inglewood heat with a strong Midori rolling around her belly, wasn't. "I'll be down in a minute."

"Hurry up, you don't want to keep Mr Honey waiting." Liv grinned as she closed the bedroom door behind her.

Ariel chuckled, shaking her head as she found her sandals and grabbed her perfume. Spritzing herself with Channel, she checked her reflection in the mirror.

"What would you do with Hawk, Mama?" She whispered, then paused, half expecting an answer before releasing a long sigh. "I'll figure it out. Promise." Grabbing her summer shawl, she headed downstairs towards the sounds of her loved ones.

Jaxon

Jaxon's heartbeat accelerated when he heard the toot of a horn, followed closely by a rap at his front door. His gut clenched as he pulled the door open. She was dressed in a cute little number that displayed her body to perfection, pearl-pink nail polished fingers and toes gleamed in the afternoon sun, and her dark red highlights glistened as the gentlest breeze swept its fingers through her hair. Her scent wrapped around him as her glossy pink lips smiled up at him. Yet, his all-seeing teacher's eye noticed that her smile did not reach her eyes.

"Hello," she said.

"Hello beautiful," he brushed a soft kiss against her smooth cheek and took her hand. "Come in out of the heat," he rubbed his thumb over her flesh in a soothing manner as he pulled her inside. Closing the door behind her he raised her hand, kissing the back of it gently, watching her eyes light up. *That's better.*

"I need your cooling system," she sighed, wiping a droplet of sweat from her brow.

"You do," he agreed and led her into the kitchen and took two glasses out of the freezer that had been chilling. "Is a bubbly red okay?"

"Perfect," she said, looking around his space.

She is, in every way.

"I'm in love with your home, Jaxon, It's gorgeous. I feel like Early Settler and Provincial had a baby, and Grand Design and Better Homes and Gardens are its parents."

He laughed. "Interesting compliment. Steven and a good friend of ours, Alex worked on every aspect of the renovation. Funnily enough, Alex is a part of the Grand Design team."

"That's incredible."

"Yeah, I was lucky."

"Sublime, opulent and beautiful doesn't describe the perfection of everything I'm seeing, yet it's so homey too."

He followed her gaze, imagining seeing it for the first time through her eyes. How could she not be impressed? It was everything she said and more. One day he hoped to fill it with a stunning redhead, three children and one of their own.

Slow down.

"Can I have a tour?"

He loved the way her eyes had returned to their sparkling green. The sadness he'd seen moments ago had been chased away by her enthusiasm of his home.

"Of course," he poured wine, handing her a glass enjoying the way her neck elongated as she looked up at him offering him a breathtaking smile.

"What shall we cheers to?" She asked.

He stepped closer, tapping his glass against hers and said, "For a start, lets cheers to you relaxing and unwinding for a few hours and allowing me the pleasure of seeing you do so."

She raised an eyebrow, tapping her glass against his. "I think that can easily be achieved. Thank you."

They took a sip of the sweet red, before Jaxon slid his arm around her waist and gently pulled her against him. Lowering his head, his male ego chuckled as she sighed in pleasure just before their lips collided in a sweet, open-mouthed kiss that built into something desperately hungry in seconds.

He poured every bit of love and affection that he felt for her into the kiss, before pulling back, pleased when she smiled up at him looking dazed and relaxed.

Much, much better.

"Let the tour begin, Miss Harper."

"By all means, lead the way."

Ariel

Impressive didn't encapsulate everything she was feeling as they walked around Jaxon's lavish three-story home and grand gardens. It may have been polished and immaculate, yet it was homey and comfortable. A large black and white photograph hung above a mahogany desk in Jaxon's large, airy office. A weathered looking, white bearded man stood with his hand on the shoulder of a sandy-haired teenager who stared into the camera with soulful eyes that were narrowed slightly.

Jaxon saluted the photo. "Pops," he said, his voice filled with pride. "This is Ariel, Ariel, Pops."

She laughed. "Hello Pops. He looks like a very kind man."

"The kindest," he replied.

"How old were you?"

"Fifteen."

Same age as Hawk now.

"So handsome," she said softly, thinking of everything that he'd endured to that point in his fifteen-year-old life. His mother abusing his father. His mother goes missing. His father falls into a depressed state, then kills himself. He finds an abducted child and then rescues him. Battles with mental health issues. So much trauma, yet it hadn't defined the amazing human he was today. What was she going to do about Hawk? How could she support him whilst he was going through whatever the hell he seemed to be going through?

"Hey," he said, tapping a finger gently under her chin, turning her face towards him.

Her breath caught seeing his concerned expression as his gaze penetrated hers.

"What is it?"

She shook her head. "I don't want to talk about it, even think about it, just for one night." She watched him process the fact that she wasn't up for sharing before he nodded.

"Okay. Well, if that's the case, and I can still see that beautiful mind of yours ticking over regarding unsaid situation, then I may have a short-term solution."

"Oh?"

"How about unwinding in the spa?"

"That sounds lovely, only I didn't bring my togs."

"Oh, I'll make sure we have enough bubbles to make you comfortable," he smiled.

She grinned, holding up her empty glass. "Bubbles all round then, huh?"

"Oh yes. Are you opposed to nibbling on a cheese platter whilst you soak?"

"Absolutely not," he was being so damn considerate.

"Good." He took her empty glass, then her hand and led her up the cedar staircase to the ornate bathroom she'd seen earlier. A four-person claw-foot tub sat under a window overlooking his gardens. Despite the Inglewood heat, vibrant blooms burst between layers of green foliage that stood underneath a canopy of fruit trees.

Dragonflies soared and swooped above the waterlily pond. During their tour of the grounds, he'd explained that as much as he enjoyed gardening, he had Steven to thank for his stunning yards year-round.

Maybe that could help Hawk? Getting him out in the fresh air and sunshine along with some physical labour. Surely that would snap him out of his current surly, unpredictable mood? In fact, the energy of Jaxon's entire house and grounds would no doubt benefit all the kids. She could imagine the twins and Timmy sprawled out in the second family room where the eight-seater lounge wrapped around the spacious room in front of floor to ceiling windows. A sliding door led out to the patio, where a pool table and a lap pool were neatly nestled into the landscaped yard.

Any one of the spacious rooms with their fourteen-foot-high ceilings and all the glorious light pouring in from those ornate, bay windows, would make a perfect art studio.

She wondered if Jaxon would mind having them all over for tea so she could see if the kids would like it here.

Hang on... *like it here? We have our own home... what are you thinking?*

"Ariel, are you okay?" Jaxon gently shook her arm.

She drew her gaze away from the serenity of his yard and blinked up at him. "Sorry?" She noticed that the tub was full of steam rising from the bubbling water.

"Where did you go?" He asked softly, concern etched in his caramel gaze.

She shook her head and ran her hand along his shadowed jawline, before reaching up to kiss where her fingers had traced. "I'm right here, maybe enjoying the peace a little too much."

That seemed to please him. He pulled her against him and leaned down to kiss her softly. "I'll go pop a platter together and bring up more wine. Enjoy the water."

"Thank you." She enjoyed the view as he left the bathroom. Dropping her dress and kicking off her sandals, she placed them on the lid of a wicker basket that sat in the corner. Sinking into the water she sighed in pleasure as the jets forced cool bubbles against her tense muscles.

When Jaxon returned wearing tight boxer shorts that displayed strong, firm thighs, carrying a tray loaded with cheese, biscuits, dips, olives and cold cuts of meat, along with their wine–she felt as if she were in heaven.

As he joined her in the soothing water, handing her a glass of wine, she pushed all worried thoughts regarding her family away. She promised herself for the next several hours at least, she was going to do nothing but focus on living in the moment, with the devilishly good-looking Mr Jaxon Williams. They both deserved that much.

Chapter Twenty-One
Travis Lockwood

Travis slammed the bathroom door, locking it behind him as he sauntered across to Hawk's draw. Jerking it open he rummaged through the contents before grabbing the safety razor. He twisted the bottom knob releasing the razor from its safety door and pinched the blade between his fingers. Dropping the handle back into the draw he grinned at himself in the mirror as he lowered his pants. Watching his reflection, he slowly ran the blade across the top of his thigh slicing the flesh open. Blood glistened along the cut before it trailed down his thigh.

"Ah," he sighed in pleasure. There was something about hurting the boy's body that satisfied him to no end. "That's better." He stood there for a moment longer, running his finger through the blood before he threw the bloody blade into the sink. Pulling his pants up, he unlocked the door and nearly knocked the little boy over as he stepped out.

"Whoa there, bud," he chuckled as he grabbed Timmy's shoulders, steadying him before he fell backwards.

Timmy was jiggling from one foot to the other holding his hands to his crotch, clearly desperate for the toilet. He frowned up at him as he jerked away from Travis's touch.

"Don't touch me, Sebastian says you're a rotten egg."

Travis grabbed Timmy by the arm and swung him inside the bathroom. Banging the door closed, he lifted him against it.

"What did you say to me, little maggot?" He got a kick out of seeing the boy's eyes widen in fear as he struggled to get down.

"Put me down!"

"Oh I can't do that, didn't you needed to take a piss, *baby?*"

"Yeah, that's why I came in here, stupid!"

Travis laughed. "Stupid, huh?" His comment ended with a vicious snarl.

Timmy stopped struggling. "That's what Sebastian said," his reply was quieter.

"Can't talk for yourself huh, kid? You need Sebastian to talk for you? Why don't you ask Sebastian what I do to dumb kids who talk too much?" He watched Timmy turn his head, as if listening to someone else in the room. The blood drained from the boy's face before he turned eyes filled with terrified tears towards him.

"Yeah," Travis sneered. "That's what I thought. Now you came in here to piss, so do it."

"But" Timmy whispered. "You have to put me down first." A fat tear rolled down his cheek.

"Not gonna happen," Travis tightened his fingers around Timmy's skinny arms where he held him against the door. "Piss in your pants like the stupid little kid that you are."

"Please..." Timmy whimpered.

Travis sneered. "Do it or I'll stick your head in the dunny and piss on you."

Timmy squeezed his eyes shut before the smell of urine filled the air. Drips fell through his soaked shorts, forming a puddle on the tiles. Travis watched in fascination as Timmy started to cry.

Dropping him in the urine, he snickered. "Calm down."

"I'm telling Ariel." Timmy cried.

"Pay attention, kid." Travis leaned down bringing his snarling face closer to the cringing boy on the floor. "If you tell Ariel, I'll piss on you every night when you're sleeping. Would you like that?"

Timmy shook his head.

"So, you'll keep your mouth shut then, won't you?" He tilted his head, watching Timmy wipe at his tears, nodding, not looking up as he hiccupped in fright.

"Good, now have a shower. You stink." He opened the bathroom door, clicking it shut behind him before he sauntered back to Hawk's room, whistling a merry tune.

Hawk

Jesus Christ in hell... this cannot be happening! Hawk crouched low in the tiny, dark corner of his mind in which he'd been trapped. Wrapping his arms around his head, he rocked back and forth in disbelief and anger. How could he stop Travis from hurting his family? Scaring poor Timmy, and treating his sisters like they were nothing?

The look on Ariel's face as Travis had said that disgusting crap to her, had him seeing red. And how dare that *bastard* bully Timmy that way! Yet no matter what he did, no matter how hard he tried to take back control of his own body; he was powerless. He could feel himself growing smaller every time Travis hurt someone with his vicious words, and every time he hurt *his* body. His only hope was that Wren knew what was going on. That she would help him expel Travis somehow. He had faith in his twin. It was the one thing that was stopping his tears of fury. Knowing that Wren would do everything she could to help him return.

Timmy

Timmy locked the door as soon as, *not Hawk* closed it, and stared down at the puddle of pee, trying to comprehend what Sebastian had told him. Some guy called Travis Lockwood used to live here with his uncle and mum. That his Grandparents had cared for them, not knowing they were evil scum. That Travis and his dad used to skin animals when they were alive. That they did it to a kid once – and a woman. Timmy wiped a shaking hand under his nose and walked across to the toilet and grabbed a bunch of toilet paper. Dropping down to his hands and knees, he soaked up his puddle of pee.

He was worried about Hawk. Where was he? Was he in his body? Was he still here, in this house? Sebastian didn't have all the answers, and that scared him. Not knowing where Hawk was.

Dropping the soggy paper into the loo he flushed it, then tugged off his sodden shorts, and reached into the shower. A knock at the door had him jumping out of his skin and he froze, waiting to see who it was.

"Timmy, are you in there?" Wren called.

He sighed in relief. "Yeah."

"What are you doing mate? You've been gone for ages."

He made a non-committal grunt.

"Ice-creams ready."

He remained silent.

"Timmy, are you okay?"

"I was hot, I'm having a cold shower."

"Okay mate, I'll see you downstairs."

"*No!*" He shouted, hand trembling on the tap. He did not want to walk past *not Hawk's* room; in case he came out when he walked by.

"Timmy, what is it?" She called softly through the door.

"I… can you just wait for me?"

There was a pause, followed by, "Of course."

In a quieter voice he asked. "Can you get my SpongeBob pj's?"

"Yes, mate."

"Thanks," he turned the tap on and got under the spray. He grabbed his banana-bubble gum scented body wash and scrubbed himself clean. As long as he stayed close to Wren, surely *not Hawk* would stay away from him.

Wren

Wren waited outside the bathroom after Timmy had shoved his hand through the crack in the door, snatching his pj's from her.

"Ta," he mumbled.

She frowned thinking something was definitely up. No doubt about it. After a minute, Timmy opened the door and stepped out smelling of banana-bubble-gum shower gel. It upset her to see his puffy, red-rimmed eyes. Why had he been crying? She ruffled her fingers through his mop of wet, dark hair as he blinked up at her.

"It's okay, love. Whatever it is, it's going to be okay."

"You sound just like your sister." Steven said from behind them.

Wren and Timmy jumped, making Steven laugh softly. "Sorry. Liv and I were just wondering where you were."

"Timmy needed to cool off." Wren said as Timmy ran around her and straight into their uncle's arms.

"Yeah, it's sticky heat all right. We have to get a new cooling unit installed. Although, it's cold up here."

Wren agreed. It was freezing upstairs; yet there were only the ceiling and desk fans in their rooms. There was nothing, and no reason why the corridor should be feeling this cold.

"Come on," Steven said, turning to head downstairs. "Liv made her special sundae boats for you."

"Yummo!" Timmy yelled in Steven's ear; his eyes brightened instantly at the mention of Liv's ice-cream sundaes. His reaction lightened Wren's mood.

"I'll be down in a second," she said, grabbing her phone and blue-tooth speaker before going into the bathroom. It stank of urine. Walking over to Timmy's shorts and singlet, she hesitantly picked up the wet clothing, not needing to smell his shorts to know he'd peed in them. She frowned, dumping them in the laundry basket and headed towards the stairs. Getting that uncomfortable feeling of being watched, she glanced towards Hawk's door and saw it was open a crack.

You catch more flies with honey…

She forced a smile. "Want to join us for ice-cream?"

The crack widened an inch. "Nah."

She needed to get him outside. Out of this house. What would tempt a sick, demented psycho to follow her outside? *Hang on, that could actually work…*

"Hey," she leaned against the balustrade, resting the washing basket on her hip and gave him her sexiest grin that she'd been practising in the mirror for Lance. "Why don't we take off to the Quarry and go skinny-dipping?"

He opened the door and stepped through, leaning against the wall and folded his arms as he stared at her with a flat gaze. She forced the smile to remain on her face, as fear and worry gripped her. The flesh across Hawk's face was gaunt and grey. His cheekbones protruded at sharp angles, making his eyes appear sunken in their sockets. Her smile slipped away the longer she returned his stare.

"What's wrong, little sister?" He dropped his head against the wall.

"You need some sunshine and fresh air," she returned.

"My windows open. I've got all the fresh air I need."

"Wouldn't it be nice to go swimming though? Let's wash this insistent heat off."

The tip of his tongue slipped through his lips as his narrowed gaze dropped towards her chest, then her groin. "Me and you, naked, huh?"

She bit her tongue, stopping the sarcastic retort that would only jeopardise what she was trying to achieve. "Well, that *is* what skinny-dipping means, Hawk," she lowered her voice, hoping it would entice him. "But you can keep your shorts on if you're shy. But I'll be taking everything off."

"Will you now? Why don't you come here, and I'll apply some insect repellent so you won't get bitten on all your precious parts?" He raised an eyebrow. "That's if you're being serious about skinny-dipping of course."

She sensed he was playing a game with her. A game she knew she wouldn't win. She didn't have the skillset to manipulate someone as dangerous as Travis Lockwood.

"I've got to put this washing on, but if you want to come swimming, come. If not." She shrugged, flipping a cascade of hair over her shoulder as she headed downstairs, happy to be out of his line of vision, and shuddered with relief once she was. Plan one, failed. She wasn't great at deception.

Pausing outside the loungeroom door she watched Timmy leaning against Steven's legs as he gobbled up his ice-cream. She turned, almost bumping into Liv.

"What are you up to Wren?" Liv asked, balancing a tray with a milo and two cups of tea.

"Timmy had an accident. I'm just going to pop the laundry on."

"You're a good girl," Liv said. "Want to join us for a quick game of monopoly before Timmy goes to bed?"

"No, I'm going to tidy up some things in the garage."

"Do you want a hand?"

"No, it's okay. I'm going to play some music and chill."

"Sounds perfect." Liv smiled as she headed into the lounge.

Wren turned into the laundry and dumped the clothes into the machine. Pouring in a scoop of detergent she dropped the lid and spun the dial to economy. Heading into the kitchen she opened the fridge and pulled out a bottle of filtered water before going out into the garage.

Selecting an album by Halsey, she turned the speaker to a medium volume and propped her phone and speaker on her Grandfather's work bench. Cracking the lid open on her water bottle, she took a few mouthfuls as she walked towards the trunks where she had seen Ariel upset the day after she and Hawk had been attacked on the stairs.

The trunk lay open with piles of newspapers haphazardly thrown inside. Squatting beside the trunk, she placed her water bottle on the cement floor and reached to pull out the newspapers and began stacking them in neat piles, straightening them and folding them as she went.

Her hand stilled landing on a paper where the headline screamed, *'MURDERERS UNDER ESTEEMED FAMILY'S ROOF'* – and beneath the caption was the face of a man whose dark eyes penetrated her to her core in the worst kind of way.

Scooping up the newspaper, she read every word pertaining to the despicable people her Grandparents had supported. As she read about her mother's rape and attempted murder, she cried out in anger, "Travis Lockwood, you bastard!"

She sobbed, wiping her eyes, filled with regret for what her mother and the other victims had endured. Along with a sense of pride that her mother had gained some form of justice by killing him. She wondered what her legal studies teacher would think about her controversy thoughts regarding her mother's act in taking another persons life.

She turned back to the front page to stare into Travis Lockwood's eyes. Once a man who took pleasure in killing and torturing the innocent, now an entity who inhabited Hawk's body like a parasite. She *had* to get him out. But how? He'd have to be physically forced, and she couldn't do that alone. She'd hoped that the idea of her flesh would entice him enough. Hawk had told her that Travis wanted her. But obviously him wanting to remain in Hawk's body overrode any desire to have her.

She needed the strength of her uncle or Jaxon to get him out of the house. At least now she had the plan, and she needed to let them all know; immediately. Despite Hawk telling her not to tell Ariel–not to tell anyone.

Dropping the newspaper back inside the trunk, she stacked her straightened piles on top before closing the lid and shutting down her music. Heading out, she turned the light off and pulling the door shut, turned as a tall man stepped out of the shadows.

Her breath caught in surprise as he loomed five feet in front of her. Her heartbeat quickened the longer he stood there, staring at her silently. He didn't feel... *safe.*

"Hell... Hello?" she stammered when he remained as frozen as she was.

He took a step forward, and she one back, finding herself pressed up against the garage door.

"What do you want?" she whispered, fear making her voice wobble.

"I'll take one of hers," he replied in a gravelly voice.

The back door opened, and the porch light flashed across the yard, lighting up a section of the driveway where the man stood.

He walked backwards, disappearing into the shadows and out of sight.

Wren's heart was thumping in fright as she stared after him.

"Wren," Steven called, making her squeal. "What is it love?"

"There was a man here when I came out of the garage. He was standing right there." She pointed in front of her.

"Are you okay?"

She shrugged. "He ran that way when the light came on," she pointed towards the street that lay in darkness.

"Get in the house and lock the door," he said, jogging in the direction she had pointed to.

"Uncle Steven?"

"Now, baby," he yelled, disappearing into the darkness.

She ran inside, trembling as she pulled the back door shut, locking it.

Running towards the front door she did the same.

"What's happened?" Liv asked, tea towel in hand as she walked out of the kitchen.

Wren wrapped shaking arms around herself, tears of fright, fatigue and frustration leaked from her eyes as she shook her head. Why couldn't things be normal and boring?

"Hey, come here." Liv pulled her into her arms, rubbing her back.

She sniffed back a sob, fighting the onslaught of tears that wanted to fall.

"What is it?"

"There was a man outside," she whispered, returning Liv's hug.

"What?" Liv tightened her arms around her.

"Steven's gone after him."

"I should help him," Liv rubbed her arm before turning to go.

"Please don't leave me," Wren grabbed Liv's hand.

Liv turned, "Of course not, silly me. Let's get you a cup of chamomile." Liv turned the kettle on and pulled a mug out of the cupboard as Wren sat on the kitchen stool.

"That must have given you such a fright," Liv said quietly as she dropped a teabag into the mug along with a squirt of honey.

Wren nodded. "It did," she said as the already hot kettle boiled quickly. Liv filled the mug and placed it in front of Wren as a quiet knock sounded at the front door.

"That will be Uncle Steven."

"I'll get it," Liv started towards the front door as Wren wrapped her hands around the steaming mug. Moments later, Steven walked in and sat on the stool beside her.

"You all right love?" He tucked a long strand behind her ear.

She nodded.

"Did he say anything to you?"

She nodded again, sipping the warm tea sweetened with honey. "He said, I'll take one of hers." She frowned up at him and watched the blood drain from her uncle's face.

"Steven… what is it?" Liv asked, as Steven stood abruptly, snatching his mobile out of his back pocket.

"I need you both to stay here. I'm sorry, but I don't have time to explain. I need you to lock the door behind me." He said, marching towards the front door.

"Steven?" Liv cried quietly.

He spun around, reaching for her and cupped her chin. "Baby, I *don't* have time to explain, but I need you to stay here with the kids. Can you do that for me?"

She nodded. "Of course."

He dropped a chaste kiss across her lips before nodding to Wren. "Everything is going to be all right. Just stay here. I'll be back soon." With that, he stormed down the corridor and out the front door, shutting it firmly behind him. Liv followed to make sure it was locked.

Wren stared into her tea before heading to the sink, tipping it out.

"Do you want sit in the lounge?" Liv asked.

"Yeah, sure."

"Things just keep getting stranger around here, don't they?"

Wren nodded as she followed Liv into the lounge, wondering what uncle Steven was going to do. She was grateful Timmy was upstairs in his room, and that Ariel was having a much-needed break from all the crazy. She sat next to Liv who flicked Netflix on to distract them as they waited.

Chapter Twenty-Two
Jaxon

J axon's body clock woke him at six a.m. sharp, and he was pleased to find his arms still wrapped around Ariel's soft body. Her head nestled against his chest as hers rose and fell in a peaceful rhythm. He'd be happy to hold her close for the rest of their lives. He'd never felt this way about a woman before. Not that he'd ever had a little black book filled with names, but he'd had his fair share of relationships.

She was entirely unlike anyone he'd ever been with. Even last night, when she was in a safe place and clearly had a burden to share, she'd focused on their one-on-one time together. He respected her and her resilience, greatly. He couldn't imagine some of the other school mum's handling everything she had on her place, so efficiently. So selflessly.

A quiet, yet frantic knocking sounded below at the front door.

He gently slid his arms from around her, cradling her head on the pillow as she moaned softly.

"Shh baby, go back to sleep," he kissed her cheek before reaching for a pair of shorts. Pulling them on, he snagged a tee shirt from the floor and tugged it over his head, stuffing his feet into sneakers before jogging downstairs.

Opening the door, he was surprised to see Steven. "Hey mate, come in."

"Thanks." Steven walked by him, clapping him on the shoulder before heading into the kitchen. "Coffee?" He called.

Jaxon grinned. "Sure, if you're making it, why not." He was curious as to why his friend had decided to pop over at a quarter to seven Saturday morning. He pulled a chair out and sat as Steven busied shaking hands, as he got the coffee machine on and pulled out two mugs.

Jaxon waited patiently, knowing his friend would speak in good time.

Steven leaned his hip against the kitchen bench as the coffee percolated, folding his arms he said quietly. "I think Phillip Lockwood is in town."

Jaxon's light mood dissipated in a flash. "Come again?"

Steven sighed, running his hand through his hair. "Last night, Wren was in the garage. When she came out there was a man waiting for her."

Jaxon stood, folding his arms. "Did he hurt her?"

"No, no," Steven held up a hand, shaking his head to reassure him. "No, she's fine."

"Well, what did he want? Did he say anything to her?"

"Right before he ran off, he said, I'll take one of hers."

Jaxon stilled, meeting his friend's eyes. An unspoken secret passed between them.

"Yeah," Steven nodded.

"Jesus," Jaxon rubbed a hand over his jaw before resting his hand around the back of his neck. "This is bad."

"Yeah, it is."

"Have you been to the police?"

Steven nodded. "I went down to the station last night to make a report. Then I stayed with Liv and the kids. I couldn't sleep much, so I went home to go over Sparrow's case notes at some odd hour. I got the sergeant out of bed before I came here, filling him in on everything we know to date." He turned and filled the mugs with the richly scented brew, placing one in front of Jaxon.

"You told him about the note they found on Sparrow's body?"

Steven nodded before taking a mouthful, then replied, "Yes, he's contacting the cold case unit as we speak."

"Shit," Jaxon sipped his coffee. "You'll have to tell Ariel everything."

"Yeah, I know."

"She'll be fine. She can handle it."

"She can handle what?" Ariel asked as she walked into the kitchen, wearing an oversized tee shirt, looking refreshed and too damn pretty considering the conversation that was about to take place.

Her walk slowed when she noticed the expression on both of their faces as she looked between them.

"What's happened? Tell me right now."

"Come sit down love, I'll make you a coffee." Steven said.

She met Jaxon's gaze, and his heart pinched seeing her shoulders stiffen. All the good work he'd done getting her to relax throughout the night vanished instantly.

"It's okay," he soothed, patting the seat beside him.

She hesitated briefly, before crossing towards him and taking a seat. He took her hand in his as Steven placed a coffee in front of her.

"The kids are fine, safe with Liv," Steven began, running a hand over her hair before he picked up his own coffee and sat opposite her.

She seemed to relax; marginally.

"This is going to be hard to hear sweetheart, but please let me get through in the telling of it."

Ariel nodded, her fingers tightening around Jaxon's. He gently squeezed her hand, letting her know he was here for her.

"I've told you about the Lockwoods."

"Not all of it, but yes."

Steven nodded. "There's more that I haven't told you, to protect you."

"Like the fact that the Lockwoods' raped and attempted to murder my mother, and that one of them is my father?"

Steven froze, eyes widening as he looked from Jaxon to Ariel.

"Yeah," she said softly. "I found the newspaper article in Grandma's storage trunks. I did the math, and Revered Matthews confirmed the rest."

Jaxon watched her closely as she stared at her uncle. "I had a right to know."

"I'm sorry baby, I made a promise to your mother," he held her disappointed gaze.

Ariel shook her head. "I'm not a little girl anymore Uncle Steven! I'm responsible for three kids now!"

"I know that, and you are doing a phenomenal job. But you knowing that your father was a murdering psychopath, doesn't help, or change anything."

She groaned, tugging her hand from Jaxon's to fold her arms as she leaned back in the chair.

"You know I'm right," he said calmly.

She sighed, shaking her head. "What else haven't you told me?"

His gaze dropped to the table, before slowly lifting back to hers.

"That bad," she whispered.

He shook his head. "No, but I'm regretful about it." He looked at Jaxon, who offered him a supportive nod.

"Uncle Steven, please just tell me."

He sighed. "Your mother wasn't killed in a car accident as I led you to believe. She was murdered."

Silence filled the room, before Ariel's chair scraped back and she shot to her feet. "Excuse me? You told me she died in a car accident, that she died instantly on impact?"

Steven nodded. "I know I did baby. I lied to you."

"But why?" She shook her head.

"Losing your mother, packing up your career and becoming a mother yourself at such a young age was enough for you to handle. I made the decision to keep it from you. I was wrong, I'm sorry. I've only ever acted in yours, and the kids best interest."

Ariel wrapped her arms around her waist as a tear ran down her cheek. She met Jaxon's gaze. "You knew?" she whispered.

He unblinkingly returned her gaze, not answering, before Steven cut in. "Yes, he knew, and I swore him to secrecy."

Ariel frowned, asking Steven. "Did they catch the killer?"

Steven shook his head. "And up until last night the lead's been cold."

"What do you mean, up until last night?"

"Last night, Wren was startled by a man in the yard."

Jaxon watched the colour drain from Ariel's face and quickly stood, catching her around the waist and gently forced her to sit, standing behind her with his hands on her shoulders.

"She's fine love, when I turned the porch light on he took off."

She frowned, nodding. "Does she know him?"

"No, but he said something to her, that led me to believe that I know who he is."

"Then hurry up and tell me, please."

"I believe it was Phillip Lockwood."

"Phillip Lockwood?" She whispered. "But how has this anything to do with mum's murder?"

"When your mother's body was discovered, there was a note placed in her womb. It read; I'll take one of hers – an eye for an eye."

"I'll take one of hers…" Ariel trailed off. "But why do you think it was Phillip Lockwood last night?"

"The man said the same thing to Wren. Your mother only ever took one life. One son. Travis Lockwood."

The air whooshed from her lungs and Jaxon felt her tipping. He quickly scooped her up into his arms and headed into the lounge to lay her on the couch.

"Shit," he heard Steven curse as he followed them. "I've made a mess of this."

"It's okay mate. Don't beat yourself up, it is what it is. Can't change it now."

"Guess so," he mumbled, reaching for his mobile as it began ringing. "Hey Wren, how are…" he trailed off.

Jaxon turned his head at Steven's abrupt change of mood from regretful, to alert as he straightened his shoulders.

"You've called the police? An ambulance?" He closed his eyes briefly. "Okay love don't touch a thing. We're on our way." He hung up, staring at Jaxon. "We need to wake her, now." He nodded down to Ariel, who was already coming to.

Steven knelt in front of her cupping her face, holding her firmly so she could look at him. "Ariel, baby, I'm sorry. I know you've had a shock, but I need you to be strong right now. Can you do that?"

Jaxon watched the fog lift from her eyes as she nodded.

"There's been a break-in. Liv's been injured and Timmy has been taken. Wren has called the police and they're on their way. We need to…"

Ariel sprang from the couch before he could finish and ran towards the front door. Jaxon exchanged a worried look with Steven before he ran after her.

"I'll get the car," Steven yelled as Jaxon hit the road, grateful he had sneakers on.

He watched her legs pump as she turned onto Brooke Street and ran by the Fat Butcher. Her feet would be torn up by the bitumen if she wasn't careful. He reached her just as Steven tooted the car horn. Grabbing her hand, he pulled her towards the car.

"Come on, it will be quicker."

Ariel nodded as they leapt in the backseat, and Steven took off, tyres screeching.

Jaxon held Ariel's shaking body against his, and prayed with everything he had, for the safe return of Timmy.

Ariel

Ariel wiped at another tear, grateful for Jaxon's arms around her, fearing that if they weren't she'd fall apart. Police lights silently flashed on the cruiser parked beside the ambulance. As soon as the car stopped, she leapt out and ran towards the front door, ignoring a police officer who was speaking to their neighbour.

"Wren, Liv!" she yelled as she ran down the corridor.

"Ariel," Wren cried, running from the dining room and into her open arms. "Someone took Timmy, and I didn't hear them. I'm so sorry... I couldn't stop them, and Liv got hurt... and I didn't stop them..." she sobbed, pushing her face into Ariel's shoulder.

"Hey, hey," she soothed. "It wasn't your fault. None of it." She watched the paramedics lift Liv onto a stretcher, laying limp, blood dripping down her forehead.

"Liv," she whispered.

Wren cried harder.

"Is she going to be okay?" she asked, rubbing Wren's back.

One of the paramedic's met her gaze. "We believe so. We'll know more when we get to the hospital." He nodded before they carried her outside to the waiting ambulance.

"Liv," she heard Steven's worried cry. Footsteps approached and she turned as Jaxon reached her, putting his arm around her shoulders as he gently rubbed Wren's back.

The sergeant stepped out of the lounge, notepad in hand. Ariel saw Hawk sitting on the couch, arms folded across his chest wearing a frown. He met her gaze, and she was about to ask him if he was okay when the sergeant stepped forward, blocking her view from Hawk.

"Miss Ariel Harper?"

She nodded.

"I'm Sergeant Cox, I'll be running the investigation concerning the abduction of Timothy. I want to assure you we are going to do everything in our power to get him home to you safe and sound."

She nodded, grateful that Wren's sobs had quietened.

Steven joined them in the corridor. "Liv's on her way to the hospital," he said to Wren. "She's going to be okay sweety."

Wren turned and stepped into Steven's arms as he said, "I suggest we talk in the dining room, Sergeant."

"Can I get you something?" Jaxon asked Ariel.

"Timmy," she whispered. "I just need Timmy."

He nodded, dropping a kiss on the top of her head. "I know love. We'll get him back."

"Hawk," she whispered, nodding towards her brother who remained still as a statue on the couch.

"Join the others, I'll make sure he's okay," Jaxon said.

"Thank you," she said, and headed towards the conversation she hoped would help bring her little brother home.

"There was no sign of a break in. All the locks were intact. Either a door was unlocked, or someone let the perpetrator in?" The sergeant said.

"No one would do that," Wren whispered.

"Apart from the incident last night with the stranger, have you noticed anyone watching the house? Watching Timothy?" The sergeant didn't waste any time asking Ariel questions. She'd barely pulled the chair out before the first question was fired.

That's a good thing. "I saw someone watching the house one night." She remembered the man smoking, who seemed to be looking up at her bedroom window. She frowned as another thought came to her. "There was a man at the swimming sports a few weeks ago… he seemed separate from the other parents; I think he could be the same man?"

"We'll have the sketch artist sit with you and see if we can make an identification." The sergeant said as Steven got up and headed into another room, returning moments later with a sketch pad and a pencil.

Handing it to Ariel, he said, "I don't know if you know this Sergeant, but my niece is an artist."

The sergeant nodded, before adding quietly. "That may be so, Mr Harper, but our artists are trained to capture the identifying details of the individual described."

Steven simply raised an eyebrow and folded his arms. Ariel looked away from her uncle, and paused over the pad for a moment, closing her eyes, trying to recall the man's features that day at the pool. Taking a breath, she opened her eyes and began sketching. Once she was done, she turned the page over before anyone could see the sketch and turned to Wren.

"Describe who you saw baby, as best as you can."

Wren nodded and slowly gave Ariel as many details she could recall. Ariel sketched quickly, considering every minute detail Wren described.

"Sergeant, there's something else." Steven said.

"Yes?"

Steven looked from Wren to Ariel, before telling the sergeant everything he'd told Ariel earlier, about the evidence on his sister's body. The sergeant took notes, nodding here and there asking relevant questions, as the constable who'd been interviewing the neighbours, joined them.

Ariel finished her sketch, ripped both sketches from the pad and laid them side by side on the table. Both drawings revealed the same face.

The sergeant made an impressed sound. "Well, this is a good start. We'll run this through the database."

"There's no need," Steven said darkly. "That is Phillip Lockwood."

"Are you saying that *Phillip Lockwood* has Timmy?" Wren cried.

"It certainly appears that way," the constable said.

Phillip Lockwood. Ariel bit her tongue to stop the anguished sound that climbed up her throat. The voices around her became white noise as she ticked off everything she knew about Phillip Lockwood. Murderer. Child abductor. Killer. Torturer. Rapist. Psychopath.

The room swam as tears filled her eyes, and she felt the overwhelming urge to vomit. She shot to her feet, rushing from the room, noticing Jaxon exit the lounge, ending a call on his mobile. She made it into the guest toilet before throwing up, then dry retched as her stomach had nothing substantial in it bar the mouthful of coffee she'd had earlier.

Finally, her stomach settled, and she allowed the floodgates of tears to fall. She sobbed, sitting on the cold tiles of the toilet before the door opened and strong arms scooped her up.

"I'm okay," she said quietly as Jaxon walked towards the stairs.

"Is that so, love?" he continued upstairs and into the bathroom.

"I need to help find Timmy," she insisted.

"And we will. But first, you're going to take a hot shower and eat something."

Her head jerked back, and she frowned up at him. "Eat something? How on God's green earth do you expect me to eat at a time like this?" She pointed towards the door that he'd shut behind them. "I need to get out there and start looking for Timmy right *now!*" Her voice broke as she went to march past him.

His strong hands held her by the shoulders, and he bent his head so their eyes were level.

"Ariel, sweetheart, please listen to me."

She struggled to get free when he whispered, "Ariel."

She stopped, before finally meeting his warm gaze, filled with worry. "What?"

"When you were speaking to the sergeant, I made a call to an old contact of mine. Someone who knows the Lockwoods better than anyone else. He is the lead investigator in the National Missing Persons Unit. He and his team are exceptional at what they do, and they'll be here within the hour."

She stood silently, gazing at him. He was worried about Timmy too. She could see that clearly, yet he was doing everything in his power to calm her and get them as much help as possible. She threw her arms around his neck and hugged him, swallowing tears.

"Thank you, Jaxon, really. Thank you," she choked out.

He kissed her cheek, his hands massaging her through her tee shirt. "You know how you can thank me?"

She leaned back so she could see his face.

"You can start by having a shower and eating something, and maybe not walking around in an oversized tee shirt for all to see your beautiful bits?" He smiled, eyes raking her up and down.

Her mouth gaped as she realized she had in fact left Jaxon's in his tee shirt, ran down the main street, and had been interviewed with her thighs barely covered.

"Oh dear," she whispered.

He chuckled. "Yeah, oh dear." He leaned down and brushed a sweet kiss across her lips. "Shower. I'll prepare food for the new arrivals and anyone who decides to help volunteer with the search party."

She could not believe how lucky she was in this moment. How lucky Timmy was.

She opened her mouth but before she could say anything, he kissed her again and whispered, "Please don't thank me."

She nodded as he walked backwards, pointing to the shower. "Get in."

She nodded again, turning her back to him and turned the tap on. Hearing the door close behind him, she pulled the tee shirt over her head and stepped under the spray, praying both Timmy and Liv were going to be all right.

Chapter Twenty-Three
Travis Lockwood

T ravis sat on Hawk's bed, listening to the shower run as he tried to comprehend everything that had recently happened. In the early hours of the morning, he'd gone downstairs to get a glass of water when Steven had tiptoed out of the lounge.

"Hey mate," Steven had whispered, pointing over his shoulder. "Liv's asleep on the couch."

"Cool," Travis had replied.

"I'm just heading home, there's some paperwork I need to go through. Will you be okay?"

"Sure."

Steven nodded, before heading towards the front door, closing it quietly behind him.

Travis stood, looking at Liv fast asleep on the couch. Tasty piece. He contemplated copping a feel of her breast that peeked out of her bra and singlet top sitting like a soft poached egg. He stepped forward, then paused, hearing a scrapping noise at the back door. He headed towards it, unlocking the latch and jerked it open, hardly believing who he was seeing. There, on his hands and knees trying to pick the lock was Phillip Lockwood.

"Dad?" He'd whispered.

"What the hell?" Phillip Lockwood had hissed. "Who are you to me, boy?"

"Dad, it's me, Travis—I'm in this kid's body. I've possessed it."

Phillip had sneered, raising his fist as if to punch him in the face when Travis quickly said, "I know that the first lady you skinned alive was Jaxon William's mother, and she's buried under this house!" He and his father were the only two people privy to that act and information.

Phillip froze, lowering his hand before chuckling, a wicked glint in his eye. "Well fuck me boy, you're alive!" He'd pulled Hawk's body against him and awkwardly patted him on the back.

"You could call it that," he'd mumbled, as mixed emotions swamped him.

"Stranger things have happened around this house, let me tell you. Let's get you out of here then, huh?" Phillip released him.

Travis shook his head. "I'm trapped in this house."

"What?"

"Whenever I try to leave, my spirit leaks out of the boy's body. If I want to inhabit the boy, I cannot leave this house."

Phillip had tilted his head, frowning as if deep in thought. "Right." He'd said finally. "I'll see what I can do about that. In the meantime, I'm getting myself that fine young girl."

"No, dad. Take the little one, that will rattle them more."

"Oh yeah?"

"Trust me, the girl will give you nothing but trouble."

"Righto, lead the way."

He'd taken his dad up the stairs into Timmy's room where the boy was sleeping soundly. As Phillip reached for Timmy, his small body began shaking severely as if he were having a seizure.

"Stop it Sebastian, it's too early." Timmy moaned.

Travis almost laughed at the ghost boys attempt to save Timmy but forced himself to swallow the chuckle. His dad wouldn't approve. Timmy woke then, spotting them both, and screamed, before Travis watched in fascination as Phillip's large, meaty fist clouted Timmy across the head, knocking him unconscious.

"Nice one, Dad." He'd grinned as Phillip threw Timmy over his shoulder.

"Just like old times, hey boy," Phillip turned and headed downstairs.

They crept in the darkened hallway when Liv emerged from the loungeroom rubbing sleep from her eyes.

"What the hell!" Liv had cried. "Hawk, who is this?"

"Um, a friend." Travis snickered.

"Give me the boy, right now!" She'd marched towards Phillip with a look of pure rage on her face; the rage obviously overriding any fear she would have otherwise felt, if she weren't so protective of the boy.

As Phillip turned to face Liv, his eyes widened in awe as Travis had picked up an antique doorstop in the shape of a rabbit and smashed it over the top of Liv's head. She turned slowly to face Travis; a look of utter shock crossed her pretty features before a trail of blood flowed in every direction.

"Hawk?" she'd whispered before passing out cold, making a thump as she hit the floor.

Phillip had looked at him in admiration. "I made a mistake. It isn't just like old times. It's better. You've grown some balls, son."

"Thanks, Dad."

"It's a shame you can't come with me, but I believe you're in the perfect spot to help me make this family's life, hell."

Travis grinned. "I'm already ahead of you there."

Phillip laughed, turning as he headed towards the door. "Be on the lookout for me, son."

Travis had watched him disappear into the darkness before the sun peeked over the horizon. It was the dawn of what would surely be a spectacular day.

He shook his head falling backwards to stare up at the ceiling. How had he gotten so lucky. He laughed, and it felt so good he couldn't stop laughing.

"Hawk?" Ariel said from the doorway, a towel wrapped around her lovely, damp body.

He forced his laughter to turn to tears, rolling onto his belly and sobbed into the blankets.

Shit, that was close.

"Hey," she soothed, stroking a hand along his silky hair. "Come on love, it's okay. Let it out."

He cried harder, not realising how darn good it felt to have a good ole' sook. If only she knew all the ins and outs regarding him and his father. Boy, she'd be the one crying then.

Finally, he rolled over, wiping a hand under his eyes as he looked up into her gorgeous face etched with concern for him. He nearly snickered.

"I'm sorry," he whispered instead, knowing at this moment it would get him close to her. Close to her body.

"Oh Hawk, come here baby." She said, opening her arms to him. He sat up, allowing her to pull him against her as she wrapped her arms around his shoulders, resting her cheek against the top of his head.

His face was pressed to the soft flesh above where the towel was wrapped around her breast. He could hear her heartbeat. She smelt so good. Wrapping his arms around her waist, his sobs quietened, and he slowly inhaled, breathing her in.

"That's better," she whispered, stroking his hair. "We're going to find Timmy, and Phillip Lockwood will go away for the rest of his despicable life."

He stilled against her, feeling a rage slowly build at her lack of respect for his father. He bit his tongue, stopping the foul comment that nearly slipped out. He could feel blood fill his mouth, and swallowed it, liking the way the metallic taste flowed down his throat.

"Okay, I've got to get dressed. Are you going to be okay here for a minute."

He nodded as she released him and stepped towards the door.

"I love you." Were her parting words before she pulled his door shut. The declaration he'd always wanted to hear from her mother's lips.

Chapter Twenty-Four
Jaxon

J axon stood facing the lounge doorway with Steven, waiting to see the man they had rescued all those years ago. The young boy abducted, chained and tormented for months on end, had risen above his childhood trauma. He'd reached out to Jaxon eighteen years ago to reconnect, and to share that he'd been promoted to lead investigator on the National Missing Persons Unit. He'd worked extensively around Australia and was more passionate about his role than any other person Jaxon had ever met. And that was saying a lot. They'd only ever had time to chat via the phone.

"Everyone, this is Stuart Mason," Wren led a tall, balding man in, whose intense expression was made all the more so by his sharp jawline and neatly trimmed five o'clock shadow.

"Please, call me Stuart," he smiled shortly at Wren.

Jaxon reached a hand towards the man who was only a handful of years older than he was. "Stuart, I can't thank you enough for dropping everything to be here."

"Nothing would have kept me away. It's good to see you."

"We're grateful, regardless." Steven said, offering his hand. "It's great seeing you after all these years."

"I wish it were under different circumstances." Stuart nodded, turning to Steven and giving his hand a firm pump.

"So do we all." Jaxon replied.

"I've been informed of the boy's activity before he went missing. Is there anything else you can tell me that you may have forgotten to inform the police?"

"Timothy." Ariel said quietly from behind them. "The missing boy's name is Timothy Harper."

The men turned to see Ariel, standing in the doorway with a tray loaded with a pitcher of iced lemon water and glasses.

Jaxon was relieved to see that her complexion held a hint of colour as eased the tray out of her hands offering her a smile before introducing her.

"Stuart, this is Timothy's sister and legal guardian, Ariel." He placed the tray on the coffee table as Ariel stepped forward to shake Stuart's hand.

"Thank you for coming." She said as Wren poured cold drinks for everyone.

"You're welcome." Stuart said, taking out his phone. "If you don't mind, I'd like to ask you all some questions and record our conversation. It will help with the investigation."

"Of course." Ariel said as she sat on the couch beside Jaxon. Wren sat on the other side of Ariel, leaning against her arm as the questions started. From Timothy's movements during the past week, to everyone's movements the night he went missing. He then proceeded to ask them if they had ever had previous contact with Phillip Lockwood. After forty minutes, Stuart looked around the room.

"I believe there's another member of the family I need to talk with. Hawk?"

"He's upstairs," Ariel answered.

"And he was here last night?"

"Yes."

"Would you ask him to join us please. It will be more helpful when I can account for everyone's movements."

"Sure." Ariel patted Wren's arm as she got up and left the room.

Stuart met Jaxon's gaze and nodded. "We're going to do everything to find him," he assured them.

Jaxon exchanged a knowing look with Steven and saw the first glimmer of a faint smile since they'd heard of Timmy's abduction, and Liv's attack.

When Hawk followed Ariel downstairs, Jaxon noticed that he froze in the doorway as his eyes locked on Stuarts.

"Come on Hawk, it won't take long," Ariel turned to Stuart as if apologizing for Hawk's hesitation. "Hawk hasn't been well lately. Hawk, this is Stuart, and he and his team are going to help us find Timmy."

Hawk nodded and sat next to Steven, who looked as concerned as Jaxon felt himself, the longer he looked at Hawk.

Hawk was no longer the healthy, youthful looking boy. Handsome still, yet he'd grown reed thin, greying flesh pulled taunt across high cheek bones and hollowed eyes. There was also a kind of stench about him; and it wasn't that teenage boy stench who hadn't bothered showering. It was something else. Something wrong.

He looked at Wren and Ariel, trying to catch their attention; but they were both focused on Stuart's questions, and Hawk's answers.

"Okay, that should be all for now," Stuart said after several minutes. Directing his gaze at Ariel, he said, "A few of my unit came with me and are currently collaborating with the local enforcement. They'll have a good understanding of the area shortly and together, I'm confident we can locate Phillip Lockwood, and your Timothy in good time."

"Don't you need our help to form a search party or something?" Ariel asked.

"If it were just a missing persons case, yes. Unfortunately, we are dealing with a dangerous fugitive and that requires a different tactic."

Jaxon watched as she twisted her fingers together, looking thoughtful before she asked, "But what can we do? I can't sit around here and wait for you to find this predator you know nothing about!" she cried.

Jaxon stood, placing a comforting arm around her shoulder as his gazed locked with Stuarts.

A haunted look flashed across Stuart's face before he blinked, clearing his throat. "Actually, Miss Harper I know all too well what Phillip Lockwood is capable of. I was once a victim of his before Jaxon rescued me."

Hawk snickered, before coughing. Wren frowned at him, folding her arms.

Ariel wiped her eyes and looked up at Jaxon, before meeting Stuart's gaze. "I'm sorry," she whispered.

"Don't be. This gives me an advantage when I'm hunting someone like Phillip Lockwood. We will find him, I promise."

Jaxon knew that was something Stuart shouldn't be promising Ariel, but kept that thought completely to himself.

Ariel nodded, looking calmer. "I need you to give me something useful to do or I'm going to go out of my mind," she said softly.

Stuart nodded. "Can you to give me a few items of Timothy's clothing he has worn recently that has not been washed?"

"What for?"

"The canine unit," he returned simply.

She nodded, nestling into Jaxon's side. "Of course, sorry. What else?" She whispered.

"There'll be a meeting at the town hall for the locals and press to gain information and learn the identity of Lockwood. The more eyes we have on him, the better equipped we'll be if he shows his face around town.

I'll have the rest of my unit fly here within the hour."

"That's fast," Jaxon said. "I appreciate it."

"They've been on standby. I'm assuming they can land on the oval, but I'll check with your local man."

"Sergeant Cox." Jaxon supplied.

"Right." Stuart nodded.

"What do you want us to do?" Jaxon asked.

"Rally your troops, friends and neighbours." Stuart said. "I'll see you at the town hall in an hour.

Ariel

Ariel had always been impressed by the town halls exterior, which stood in its former glory since eighteen-hundred and eighty-three. A double story towered and stuccoed building built with local bricks back in the day from Philip's Brick Kiln. She knew this because her Grandfather had spoken about it often, and with pride. The arched doors and windows had classical architraves and the entrance porch proudly took ones gaze upward on a pleasant journey to the clock tower that chimed every hour on the hour since days gone by.

She glanced over her shoulder towards Jaxon's house which sat opposite the town hall and couldn't believe it was only last night that they'd enjoyed each other, and many conversations till the early hours of the morning. And now, here she was about to attend a meeting for the manhunt and an abducted child who happened to be her little brother.

This really can't be happening.

An arm slid round her waist, jolting her. "You doing okay, love?" Jaxon asked as another crowd of people went by them, heading inside the hall.

She nodded, overwhelmed by the town's response. Jaxon and Ray had got on the phones, ringing everyone from school. Steven had contacted every business on Brooke Street, before heading over to the hospital to be with Liv, after Ariel had insisted that it was the best place for him to be.

Wren placed her hand in hers, and together they walked inside.

Leading journalist from the Loddon Herald, Chris Earl, was handing out images of the sketch that Ariel had drawn. Ariel nodded hello to him as Wren took one before they headed toward the front of the hall.

As they sat, Ariel noticed the details printed under the sketch. Lockwood's height, hair and eye colour, and the number to call if sighted, with a statement highlighted in bold lettering that read, "DANGEROUS. DO NOT APPROACH.

Wren turned the paper over and on the other side was a photograph of a smiling Timmy from a few months ago. The caption above read, ABDUCTED: SEVEN-YEAR-OLD TIMOTHY HARPER -along with relative information.

Ariel whimpered quietly and Wren grabbed her hand as Jaxon put his arm around her shoulder, resting his hand against Wren's back.

Stuart and the local reinforcement were at the front of the hall, and he nodded to them as the crowd quietened. The Sergeant and Stuart introduced themselves and thanked everyone for coming. They explained it would be best if the community kept their children close, their doors locked, and homes secured at all times until this manhunt was over.

They asked everyone to keep their eyes open for Phillip Lockwood, and if sighted, to call the number on the printout. Stuart proceeded to explain in brief terms the work he and his men would be doing, and until Timothy was found, advised everyone to stay out of the bush.

All the information became white noise to Ariel, before finally Stuart ended by saying, "Support the Harpers in their time of need. You all need to band together as a community, and from what the Sergeant here has told me about Inglewood, you do that better than anywhere else in Victoria. I thank you all for your time."

Stuart shook the sergeant's hand before stepping off the stage and towards them, as the towns people talked in hushed tones behind them as they began filing out of the hall.

"Thanks so much," Jaxon stood, and shook Stuart's hand.

"Don't thank me till you have Timothy back," he nodded to Ariel, who stood with Wren.

"We have all the faith in the world that that will happen," Reverend Matthews said.

Ariel turned and felt comforted by the older man's presence. "Reverend, would you like to join us for a pot of tea at home?"

"I was hoping you'd ask," he smiled softly and offered her his arm.

"Do you mind if I race to the hospital first? I need to see Liv." She asked Jaxon.

"Of course not, love. Wren and I will take the Reverend home with us, won't we Wren?"

"Yes, of course." Wren slid her arm through the Reverends and smiled up at him.

"Do you want us to drop you off?" Jaxon asked.

Ariel shook her head. "A walk is just what I need."

He dropped a kiss on her cheek. "We'll see you at home."

She nodded, and ducking her head made it past most of the crowd before a high-pitched voice called out.

"Ariel, Ariel wait!"

Ariel turned, folding her arms as Valerie headed towards her, leaving a group of the other mothers standing there gawking after her.

Jesus, just what I don't need.

"Ariel, we're so sorry to hear about Timothy. It truly is just awful."

Ariel nodded, waiting to see if there was anything else. She turned to go after a moment of silence before Valerie reached out and grabbed her arm.

Looking down at Valerie's fingers wrapped around her arm, she met the other woman's gaze. "Was there anything else?" She asked tiredly.

"If you need anything, please don't hesitate to reach out." Valerie seemed sincere and brushed a single tear from her lash. "If it were Aaron, I'd be going out of my mind."

Ariel nodded; grateful Valeria couldn't see that she was close to doing just that herself.

Valerie offered her a sad smile, before releasing her arm, and Ariel quickly walked past the onlookers.

She reached the hospital in under ten minutes and after speaking to a nurse, headed down to Liv's room. She saw her uncle leaning against the wall, hands in his pockets as he stared down at the floor, looking like the world was about to end.

Oh no… please! Not Liv. She felt lightheaded at the thought of losing her friend.

"Uncle Steven?" There was a big question hanging in the air between them.

"Oh, sweetheart, no, no, no," he reached for her, and pulled her into his arms. "She's going to be fine. She woke a little while ago. The doctors with her now."

Ariel sighed against Steven's chest, hugging him back. "Thank goodness," she looked up at him. "Are you okay?"

"I will be, as soon as we find my nephew," he said, sounding as tired as she felt.

She nodded.

"I know this really isn't the time, but we need to talk about Hawk." He said.

Ariel ran a hand over her face and leaned against the wall beside him, remaining silent; waiting.

"There's something not quite right with him, Ariel."

"I know," she replied.

"What is it? Drugs?"

She laughed dryly. "I'd say absolutely not, but unfortunately, he has been acting so out of character I couldn't say for sure."

"Well, despite what we are currently dealing with, I think we need to have a chat with him."

"Do you really think now is a good time?"

He shrugged as he looked down at her. "When is a drug-chat ever a good time, sweetheart?"

She leaned her head back against the wall and closed her eyes. She couldn't remember feeling so tired. And she'd been tired plenty since moving to Inglewood.

Steven angled towards her. "Shit, I'm sorry. You've been bombarded with an avalanche of information in the past few hours." He shook his head. "*Idiot*," he whispered.

"Uncle Steven," Ariel placed her hand on his arm. "You are *not* an idiot. You're a concerned uncle."

"Yeah, maybe so," he offered her a smile. "But our chat with Hawk can wait."

She nodded as a nurse approached. They both straightened off the wall.

"Mr Harper, I just thought you should know that the doctor is going to keep Miss Collins overnight."

"But she *is* going to be okay?" Ariel asked.

"It certainly appears that way, but complete rest is what she needs right now. She took a pretty nasty blow to her head."

"Can I see her?" Ariel asked hopefully.

"I'm sorry, she's just gone off for another scan." The nurse said.

Ariel nodded, disappointed.

"You've got all our numbers?" Steven double checked.

"Yes, if anything changes, we'll call you."

"Okay, I'll be back first thing in the morning."

The nurse nodded before hurrying off.

"Okay, let's go home." Steven slung his arm around her shoulder and led her outside beneath the late afternoon sky. The sun was blocked by silver-lined clouds that were quickly turning black. A cool breeze lifted the damp tendrils off Ariel's neck, chasing away the sweltering heat from earlier.

She sighed. "Finally," she whispered.

"What's that?" he asked, pulling his car keys out of his pocket.

"A cool change."

"Yeah," he agreed, unlocking the car. "Hopefully it will last a few hours."

Thunder rumbled and a flock of corellas squawked raucously overhead as they perched in a tall eucalyptus.

"Oh no…" Ariel cried softly in dismay.

Steven met her concerned gaze. "I know love, the thunder."

They both knew Timmy would be frightened.

She began to cry, quietly at first but then as the numb, surreal fog lifted, she started to feel everything. Then the worst-case scenario of not seeing Timmy ever again played on repeat in her head. She tried desperately to stop the panic attack that was reaching for her, but to no avail.

"Timmy, *Timmy…*" she cried.

"No baby, don't go there." Steven rushed around the car and pulled her into his arms. "Deep breaths," he whispered against her ear. "In and out."

"This can't be happening, she sobbed. "I can't lose Timmy. I can't lose Mama's baby…"

"You won't love. *We* won't." His arms tightened around her. "Come on, let's go home."

She nodded, allowing him to steer her into the passenger seat, as another almighty crack of thunder boomed in the sky. She shivered, hoping Timmy was being as brave as he could be until they found him.

Safe and unharmed, she prayed with everything she had.

Chapter Twenty-Five
Timmy

Timmy pressed his face hard against his drawn knees as lightening cracked like a stock whip against his ear drums. Thunder shortly followed before the sky opened its floodgates and hit the roof above him like horse hooves beating against the road.

His muffled whimper sounded pitiful through his duct taped mouth. His hands and feet tingled painfully where the tape wrapped tightly. From his uncomfortable seat on the dirty floor, he blinked up through the undressed window to see the rain pour down. He sniffed back another sob as he looked around the room he'd been thrown into. Exposed bricks covered in dust made up the walls of his prison. Thick cobwebs danced off a splintered ceiling beam as the wind whistled through the crack in the windowpane. The smell of rotten carpet permeated the air along with stale beer. Two long-necked Vick-Bitter beer bottles sat along the window ledge.

He whimpered again as something moved in the shadows. Narrowing his eyes, he watched a mouse scamper nervously across the worn floorboards and mouldy rug before darting under a stack of musty newspapers. He swallowed the lump of tears burning his throat, wondering if Ariel was looking for him. Maybe she thought he was hiding in the chook pen?

His heart galloped as footsteps approached, before the door was flung open.

"You're awake then," a gruff voice stated.

Timmy stared in fright at the tall, unkempt man dressed in dirty jeans, black boots and khaki jumper. He was the same man who had knocked him out when Sebastian had tried to wake him up. The man reminded Timmy of the freaky people in the movie, *Deliverance*, that Aaron had made him and Paul watch. It had been the only way that they could join his 'popular' group for a day. He shivered, hoping this man wasn't as evil as those people had been, and remained as still as possible.

The man dropped a backpack on the floor as he stalked towards the window. Looking out at the street below, he chuckled darkly. "They'll never think to look this close in town for you. Smartest move I ever made," he turned then, folding thick arms and stared down at Timmy.

"So, you're the youngest whelp of that mother of yours, huh?"

Timmy remained still, wishing he could scream at the disgusting smelling man, but Sebastian had warned him to remain quiet. To not react in anyway, to anything the man did or said. He trusted his friend, so did exactly as he'd instructed.

"Cat got your tongue then?" The man frowned.

Timmy tried not to blink as the man reached down and ripped the duct tape off his mouth. He forced a yelp of pain down as it tugged at his skin and he blinked back tears.

The man knelt close, staring into his eyes. "Got nothing to say? Aren't you going to beg me to let you go?"

Timmy licked his dry lips.

"Thirsty huh?" He reached into the backpack and pulled out a grimy looking coke bottle filled with water. "Here, drink," he ordered as he uncapped the bottle and shoved it towards Timmy's mouth.

Timmy turned his head, refusing, when the man gripped a handful of hair and shoved the bottle to his lips. "You're no good to me dead, kid. Not yet."

Although he didn't want to touch the man's filthy looking water, Sebastian reminded him he needed to drink, so guzzled a few mouthfuls of the lukewarm water, trying not to gag as a foul stench from the man wrapped around him.

After the man recapped the coke bottle, he shoved it into the backpack and pulled out the roll of duct tape.

"Well kid," he said, before stretching out a fresh piece and ripping it off with his teeth. "If you've got nothing to say, I've got some spyin' to do." He firmly pressed the tape across Timmy's mouth, then said, "Goodnight, kid," then before Timmy could react, he raised his hand and struck him hard across the ear, knocking him out cold.

Ariel

Ariel was flooded with gratitude when she stepped into her kitchen. Ray was busy with Jaxon, pouring teas and coffees, while Ena was serving freshly made biscuits and sandwiches. Paul was sitting on one of the kitchen stools playing a card game of snap with Wren, as Reverend Matthews strolled in from the lounge where quiet voices filtered through.

"Ah, Ena, those look wonderful," he smiled as he reached for a platter of sandwiches before turning to go back into the loungeroom. Spotting Ariel in the opposite doorway, he paused. "Hello Ariel, would you like a sandwich?"

Everyone in the kitchen stopped what they were doing and turned to look at Ariel. Steven placed a hand on her shoulder, squeezing gently.

"I don't know about Ariel, but they look delicious, although, I'd like to start with one of those biscuits and a cuppa if you wouldn't mind, Mrs Musgrove."

Ariel watched the older lady's cheeks turn pink with pleasure.

"Of course, my dear, anything for you," her eyes twinkled mischievously as she served two of the largest biscuits onto a small plate and held it out to him.

Ariel moved into the kitchen as Steven crossed to take the plate, dropping a kiss on Mrs Musgrove's cheek. "Thank you, they smell delicious."

Wren slid off the stool and stepped towards Ariel, who put her arms around her. "You doing okay, love?" She asked.

Wren nodded against her shoulder, not answering.

"Who else is here?" Steven asked Jaxon, who handed him a mug of tea.

"Mr Scott, a member of the historical society." Jaxon said.

"Guess I'll say hello," Steven patted Jaxon on the shoulder as Ray crossed towards Ariel.

"How are you? Stupid question, I know. Sorry." Ray shook her head, as Wren slipped away.

"No Ray, please." Ariel rubbed the other lady's arm. "I'm… numb." She shrugged.

Ray nodded. "Understandable. What can I do?"

"What you're doing right now is great. Thank you." Ariel smiled.

"Oh, it's nothing." Ray shrugged off the praise. "I'll just take this tea through, but I'm here if you need me."

"Thanks Ray," she said quietly, watching Ray pick up the tea tray and head in after the Reverend.

"Come on Paul, you can come upstairs and play in Timmy's room." Wren said, offering Paul her hand.

"Okay," Paul said, grabbing her hand as his nana passed him a biscuit.

"There you go my dear. Let me know when you want to go home, and we'll get out of these good people's hair." Ena said to Paul.

"Okay Nana," Paul waved his biscuit in the air as Wren led him towards the stairs.

"Dear girl, when was the last time you ate or drank anything?" Ena asked watching Ariel over the top of her glasses.

"Um," Ariel could feel Jaxon's eyes on her as he wiped the sandwich crumbs off the counter and tidied up the kitchen.

"Obviously too long ago to remember. Jaxon dear, why don't you take Ariel upstairs with a plate of sandwiches and a cup of tea. She needs to rest quietly for a bit. Steven and I will look after the guests."

"Oh, I really should stay down here in case anyone has news…"

"Nonsense," Ena cut her off. "A rest is what you need, and if any news arrives you're only upstairs, not in Bendigo!"

She left no room for arguing, and if Ariel was honest with herself, she was desperate to close her eyes for ten minutes. She nodded. "Thank you."

"Off you go," Ena nodded. "I'm sure Jaxon knows the way."

Jaxon raised an eyebrow as he met Ena's gaze, a small grin played at the corner of his lips. Ariel watched their silent exchange.

My god he is gorgeous.

He nodded. "Right behind you," he said, plating up a sandwich.

She headed upstairs, pausing in the corridor opposite Hawk's room. He'd locked himself up there all day. She knew he was worried sick about Timmy. She stepped towards it when Wren approached.

"Go lay down Ariel, I'll take care of Hawk," she said. "Paul's fallen asleep in Timmy's bed."

"Oh, that's good," Ariel nodded. "Poor boy."

"Yeah, he's doing okay. He's convinced Timmy will be fine because Sebastian is with him."

Ariel smiled, shaking her head. "Kids are so resilient."

"Yeah. So are you. But you need to rest, even for a little while. For all of us."

"Just ten minutes," Ariel whispered, feeling herself fade away as Jaxon reached her, balancing a small tray with a plate of sandwiches and a steaming mug of tea.

"No coffee?" she raised an eyebrow.

"Ena insisted black tea with a spoonful of honey and a shot of whiskey is what you need."

"Thanks, that actually sounds perfect," she said reaching for the tea.

"Come on," he said softly, nodding towards her room. "Are you okay, Wren?" he asked as Ariel headed towards her room.

"Yeah, I'm just checking in on Hawk."

"Okay. Just yell if you need me for anything."

"Thanks Jaxon."

Ariel's heart warmed at their exchange. She was so grateful her siblings genuinely liked Jaxon. She knew Timmy loved him.

She forced the sob down and wandered to her window seat, pushing the window wide open so the storm could blow her tears dry. She tucked her legs under her as she held the hot tea to her chest as thunder rumbled above the house.

"Mama, Grandma... please help us find Timmy," she whispered. "Please bring him home to me." Tears silently fell as she sipped the whiskey laced tea.

Strong arms slid round her as Jaxon sat behind her, holding her gently against his chest. She was grateful in that moment to hear nothing but the wind that howled as the thunderstorm raged. The warmth of his chest against her back comforted her as did the scent of the rain which pelted down furiously like her silent tears, before the sobs she'd been holding back, shook her to her core.

"It's going to be okay," Jaxon whispered against her ear as his arms tightened around her, rocking her gently. "It's all going to be okay."

Ariel cried her heart out, before exhaustion seeped into every nerve.

She dropped her head back against Jaxon's shoulder and closed her eyes as he rocked her to sleep in seconds.

Wren

Wren paused before knocking on Hawk's door. She knew she wasn't 'checking up' on her brother but had to keep up the pretence for Travis. Glancing over her shoulder she made sure Ariel's door was shut, and taking a deep breath knocked on the door.

"Yeah," came Travis's response.

"Hawk, do you want anything to eat? Mrs Musgrove made biscuits and sandwiches."

Silence.

"Hawk?"

Footsteps headed towards the door, and she quickly pulled in another breath, forcing a calm façade as the door opened. She folded her arms, then dropped them by her side as she looked up at him. How could he have grown thinner since this morning?

Hawk's dark blue eyes looked black, yet despite his grey, gaunt skin he appeared to have a sense of energy about him. He looked... *excited?*

What would he have to be excited about?

"Sandwiches and biscuits, huh?"

"Yeah," she said, peeking around him to have a look at his room. Disaster was an understatement. Behind him, the curtain whipped frantically about the smashed window. Rain drenched the mattress and rug. A cricket bat was thrust through in a hole in the plaster beside other holes that had been smashed into the wall. Every draw was open, and clothes spilled out, strewn haphazardly on the floor. The wardrobe had been tipped onto its side, and books were scattered amongst Hawk's posters that'd been ripped off the walls. His mirror was shattered in pieces. Chaos would have been a poetic word to describe the current state of Hawk's room.

"Problem?" He asked staring at her.

She met his dark, wicked gaze and shook her head. "Nope, not my problem. You're the one who's going to get chewed out for trashing your room."

He shrugged, "I look forward to the challenge."

"Well, if you have any love for Ariel, you'll save that battle until after Timmy's found."

"*If* Timmy's found."

Wren gasped as she looked at *Travis*. "How can you even say that?" She hissed. "Of course he'll be found. Jaxon has called in an expert, someone who was taken by that psychotic animal years ago."

"That *psycho* as you say, has eluded the cops for years. That makes him extraordinary, wouldn't you say?"

"No, I would not." Wren snapped, reminding herself who she was *actually* talking to.

"I'll remind myself we all deal with trauma differently, and not punch you in the face right now."

"I don't know little sister; I might enjoy that," he leered at her.

"Agh! Get yourself your own food if you want it."

She turned and ran downstairs, needing to talk to her uncle. This game had gone on for too long. She may have promised Hawk not to drag anyone else in on the *Travis Lockwood* secret, but she didn't know what else to do. She couldn't physically get him out of the house by herself, and she hadn't been able to get her hands on any sleeping pills to drug him. She was at a loss. The only thing she could do, whilst they were in the middle of a crisis was to confide in her uncle who had always been a safe, trusted person in her life.

"Hey Wren," Steven smiled at her as she stood in the doorway. His smile faded the longer he looked at her. "Has something else happened love?" He stood, crossing to her.

She nervously twisted her fingers together as he rubbed her arm.

"Uncle Steven, I need to talk to you outside."

He raised an eyebrow. "There's a storm raging outside. Wouldn't it be better to talk in here?"

She shook her head. "Please?" she whispered.

"Okay," he nodded, before turning to the others and said, "We'll be back soon, I just need a quick chat with my niece."

"Take your time Steven," Ray smiled, refilling the Reverend's cup. A soft snore emitted from Ena's lips from the armchair.

Steven nodded before he led Wren towards the back door and grabbed the umbrella off the hook inside the laundry. He opened it and held it above Wren's head as they stepped outside. The rain slapped at them, and the wind blew the umbrella inside out as they ran towards Ariel's studio.

Steven slid the barn door shut behind them, turning on the lights, he dropped the twisted umbrella in a bucket and headed across to the stack of towels Ariel used to cut up for cleaning rags. Grabbing two, he handed one to Wren as he rubbed the other through his saturated hair.

"Thanks," Wren said, making no move to dry herself.

Steven slung his towel around his neck, before placing his hands on his hips as he waited for his niece to say something.

Wren looked at Steven, not knowing where to start. Would he even believe her? She blinked the water droplets out of her eyes and swallowed as he stepped towards her.

Taking the towel from her, he gently wiped her face dry and swept wet strands of hair from her face, before cupping her chin.

"Start at the beginning," he said quietly, before sitting on a stool, waiting.

She sat beside him, holding his gaze as she began. "I don't know if you're going to believe me."

"Sweetheart. You've never been a liar. I trust you."

She waited a beat, then said, "Hawk isn't Hawk anymore."

Steven nodded. "Is he on drugs?"

"No, it's nothing like that." She shook her head. "Hawk isn't Hawk because Travis Lockwood has *possessed* him. He's making Hawk do and say awful things. Hawk has literally no control over his body, and the only way we can get Travis out of Hawk, is to physically remove him from the house. Hawk warned me not to tell anyone because he said Travis would hurt me or Ariel. And on top of that Travis has physically been hurting Hawk's body." She didn't blink, watching her uncle digest every word.

Finally, after what felt like minutes, Steven reacted, sighing loudly and joining his fingers around the back of his neck.

"Right."

Wren waited for something more, knowing he needed time to process, but not knowing how much time Hawk had, the longer Travis Lockwood remained in his body.

"Do you believe me?" She asked in a small voice. "I really need you to believe me..."

"Just tell me how you know all of this?"

"Because Hawk astral projected, or something like that, into my room one night and told me, and because Hawk would never act the way Travis has been making him act."

Silence ensued. Wren's heart sank. Of course Uncle Steven wouldn't believe this story. She wouldn't have believed it herself if someone had told her out of the blue.

"Makes sense," Steven finally whispered, dropping his hands onto his lap.

"Astral projection?"

"No," he shook his head. "When Liv woke, the doctor asked her if she'd seen her attacker. She kept repeating Hawk's name. We assumed Phillip Lockwood had hit her, but if Travis was controlling Hawk... Jesus." He ran his hands over his face. "This cannot be happening. Phillip Lockwood's back in town and has kidnapped Timmy, and his depraved son is in possession of Hawk's body. After everything they've done. To my sister, to all those innocent people…" He closed his eyes briefly.

"I know what they did to Mum," Wren said quietly. "I saw the newspaper articles in the garage."

Steven met her gaze and placed a hand on her shoulder. "That's not all baby girl, but now is not the time."

"When is the right time for bad news?"

Steven laughed softly. "You and your sister have such an ability to manage the worst kind of news," he shook his head.

"Yet, you're not going to tell me, are you?"

"No baby, that's a discussion you need to have with Ariel."

Wren nodded, accepting his decision.

"And to think I thought Hawk was on drugs, and here he is, possessed and needing our help. *Damit*."

"It's all right Uncle Steven, we can help him now."

"We need to talk to Ariel and Jaxon, right away."

Wren nodded.

"Stay here, I'll get them. I think it's best if we don't talk where… *Travis*, Jesus, might overhear us." Steven headed towards the door and slid it open.

"Uncle Steven," Wren called. He turned, the rain whipping at his face. "Thank you."

"Sit tight." He offered her a quick smile before sliding the door shut and vanishing into the darkness.

Sighing, she wrapped her arms around herself, feeling somewhat relieved that her secret was now in the hands of an adult.

"Sorry Hawk," she whispered. "But we are going to save you. Just hang on a little longer, and you too Timmy."

She brushed a tear away as the wind howled and the rain pelted the tin roof. They *were* going to get through this with *all* her family intact. She closed her eyes and prayed fiercely to Arch Angel Michael, the one angel she had always found comfort in talking to.

Chapter Twenty-Six
Ariel

"Thank God that's what it is!" Ariel said once Wren and Steven had relayed the information regarding Hawk and Travis Lockwood.

"Come again?" Steven raised an eyebrow.

"Oh Uncle Steven, if you'd heard some of the vile things that have come out of Hawk's usually sweet mouth… let's just say, him being possessed is a relief knowing it wasn't my baby brother acting so despicably."

"Fair point," he said, and began pacing.

"But we still have a huge problem on our hands." Jaxon said, folding his arms.

Ariel turned to him. "True." Her elated feelings ebbed slightly. "Will Reverend Matthews know what to do?"

"I'm sure he will, yet if it's as simple as getting Hawk's body outside, I feel we can do that ourselves, without involving the Reverend." He said, his handsome features pinched slightly as he considered their options.

"We have to be careful though." Wren advised. "If Travis suspects that we know that he is in Hawk, he'll hurt Hawk... maybe even kill him." She ended on a whisper.

"Over my dead body," Ariel said furiously.

"Easy now," Steven said, his voice filled with admiration. "No one's dying. Not on my watch."

Ariel nodded, relieved to have such loyal men by her side. She looked over to see Jaxon place his hands on his hips as he stared at the floor.

"What is it?" She was learning his tell-tale signs, and by the looks of things he was concocting a plan.

Steven stopped pacing. "Jaxon?"

"This could be a really bad idea..." Jaxon met Steven's curious gaze, before turning to Ariel.

Her heartbeat quickened at the intensity behind his eyes. "Just say it."

He nodded. "So, Travis can't leave this house in Hawk's body?"

"That's right." Wren said.

"And we'll assume Phillip Lockwood won't try to get in if we are all here?"

"He's as big a coward as he is cunning, so I'd say not," Steven agreed.

"Then maybe we clear out and give the Lockwood's a chance for another family reunion? Then we follow Phillip back to where he is holding Timmy, and then work on getting Travis out of Hawk?"

Everyone remained silent for a moment, digesting this plan.

"That could work?"

"Do you think you should make a call and update Stuart first?" Ariel asked.

"We'll clear out and head straight to the station and update him then. If Lockwood is watching, nothing will seem odd. After all, our boy is missing and it would seem plausible that we'd head to the station for updates or to help."

The plan altogether wasn't a bad one, *if* they were teenagers and they *weren't* dealing with a murdering psychopath. But the only thing Ariel could focus on in that moment was that Jaxon had referred to Timmy as, *our* boy.

"Ariel?" Steven tapped her shoulder.

"Sorry, what?"

Steven frowned. "You okay?"

She sighed. "None of us are okay right now, Uncle Steven."

"Yeah, right. It's just you didn't comment on Jaxon's other idea."

She turned to find Jaxon watching her with a concerned frown. "I'm sorry, what was your idea?"

"I'm going to stay while the rest of you head to the station."

"Um, no you are not." She folded her arms.

"Ariel, I've got combat training, and he won't be looking for me when you all leave. We can't leave Hawk's body in the hands of Travis and Phillip Lockwood."

"Please Ariel," Wren whispered. "We can't leave Hawk alone."

She turned to see the desperate plea in Wren's eyes.

"I'll stay too," Steven nodded.

"No, you won't." Jaxon said in a voice that held no room for argument. "You need to be with your nieces."

Ariel nodded, turning to Steven. "Please, Uncle Steven?"

"Yeah, okay sweetheart." Steven turned to Jaxon. "This entire plan is making me nervous."

"Look, by the time you reach the police station it won't even be five minutes. Lockwood may not even show his face." Jaxon reasoned.

Ariel rubbed her eyes, sighing. "I don't know."

Strong arms slid round her, pulling her into a warm embrace. "Look, it's going to work out. I promise." Jaxon said.

She wanted to say something about making promises you couldn't keep when a warm presence surrounded her. She could have sworn she smelt her mother's perfume. It comforted her immediately. "Okay," she agreed.

"Good. Let's go in and tell everyone that we're heading to the police station." Steven said. "We'll drop Ena and Paul home on the way. Wren, can you wake Paul and bring him downstairs?"

"Of course." Wren nodded.

"Steven, tell Stuart our plan. He'll be pissed, but no doubt he'll set up surveillance."

"If he hasn't done it already," Steven said.

"True. If that's the case, we've nothing to worry about." Jaxon turned to Ariel. "Are you ready?"

She nodded, before wrapping her arms around his neck, holding him close to her, breathing in his comforting scent.

"Let's do this," Steven said. "Ariel, it will be up to you to let Travis know we're heading off. Tell him everyone is leaving."

"Okay."

"Come on Wren." The wind blew into the studio as Steven slid the door open. Tucking Wren under his arm they vanished into the raging darkness.

Ariel met Jaxon's caramel gaze. "You'll be careful, won't you?"

"You know I will, beautiful. Everything's going to work out."

She nodded.

He brushed a sweet kiss across her lips. "Let's go."

Taking her hand, he led her out into the storm and towards the house to begin phase one of their plan.

As they rushed through the back door, Ariel shook the water droplets from her hair and followed Jaxon towards the stairs. She heard Steven's hushed voice from the loungeroom, no doubt informing the others it was time to go. They passed Wren on the stairs holding a sleepy looking Paul's hand.

"Good job," Ariel whispered, giving her a warm smile before they continued to the top stair. Jaxon gently took her chin, holding her gaze for a moment before going into her room, closing the door halfway.

"We've got this," she whispered and went towards Hawk's door and knocked softly.

"Hawk," she called. "We're going down to the police station. Do you want to come?" She asked, knowing full well that he wouldn't because he couldn't.

The door jerked open and she swallowed the snarl that wanted to escape. How *dare* this *thing* hurt her brother. She could clearly see him rotting from the inside out. He looked ghastly. Poor Hawk! And his bedroom looked as if a tornado had torn through it.

He stared at her blankly.

"Guess that's a no then." She answered for him and turned to head downstairs.

Before she could take another step he reached around her throat and squeezing her windpipe, dragged her back against his body.

She gasped, thrusting her elbow into his ribs, not wanting to injure Hawk's body, but hoped to get Travis off her without needing Jaxon's help.

Travis grunted in pain and wrapped his other arm around her waist in a python like grip. How could someone so wretchedly thin be so strong? She dug her fingernails into his arm as she struggled to get free. Feeling his warm breath close to her neck made her freeze uncomfortably. Then, his lips caressed her flesh in a spine-tingling kiss as his tongue lapped at her flesh.

"What the hell…" she whispered before the kiss turned into a bite as he sunk his teeth into her flesh.

She screamed in pain as teeth tore at her skin and she could feel blood seep from the wound. Using all her strength she slammed her heeled boot down on top of his bare foot, and cringed, hearing bones crunch before he screamed in her ear, thrusting her away from him.

She spun around to see Jaxon behind Travis, wearing a look of murder across his gorgeous face. She shook her head, placing her hand over the bite where blood seeped between her fingers.

She stared into her brother's furious black eyes as Jaxon silently disappeared back into her bedroom.

"You bitch!" Travis yelled, hoping on his other foot and leaning against the wall for support. No doubt she'd broken some bones in Hawk's foot. *Sorry Hawk…*

"I see you," she whispered.

His head snapped up and their eyes locked.

"You see what?"

Shit, cover up, quick!

"I see that it's obvious you've been taking drugs. It's the only answer as to why you've been acting like such a jerk lately."

"Is that what you think?" He laughed. "Drugs?"

"I don't have time for this, we're going to the station for an update. When this is all over, we're going to deal with you."

"Good luck with that," he snarled before spitting at her, spraying her face with his saliva and her blood.

She clenched her jaw, wanting to punch him in the face, but reminded herself that it was poor Hawk's face that would hurt, not Travis himself.

She glared at him before storming downstairs, hearing his bedroom door slam. She dashed into the guest bathroom to clean herself up, cringing when she gingerly dabbed at her neck with a damp face washer, before washing her face free from spit and blood.

"Bastard," she whispered.

A shadow filled the doorway, making her jump. "What happened?" Steven asked quietly, eyebrow raised.

"Travis Lockwood," she let out a breath.

"I'll kill him!"

"Shh, Uncle Steven. It's okay, we need to go."

"Yeah, okay. Everyone else has left. Wren, Ena and Paul are waiting in the car."

She nodded, turning towards him, trying to hold herself together.

Questions tumbled around her mind like an overloaded washing machine. Who was her father? Was it Phillip? The psycho who had kidnapped Timmy and murdered her mum? Or was it Travis? The evil entity who possessed her brother. Either alternative filled her with disgust that she shared DNA with both of them, regardless of who it was.

"Ariel?"

She met Steven's concerned gaze.

"It's just a lot," she whispered.

"I know sweetheart, but you're not alone," he said tenderly. "Come on."

They headed towards the front door as another crack of thunder broke the eerie silence that filled the house, and the grandfather clock began to chime out of time.

Ariel shivered as she reached to pull the front door shut and froze as a dark shadow loomed towards her from the other end of the corridor. The lights popped and sizzled with such force that the bulbs exploded, leaving a trail of darkness as the shadow edged closer. A gale force of foul wind whipped her hair around her as she stood frozen, watching the shadow take human form of a woman, then flicker like a black and white TV losing reception. Eyeless sockets and a gapping mouth hung wide and emitted a high-pitched wail that made her eardrums throb painfully.

"Ariel! Come on," Steven yelled.

She slammed the door shut and stepped back hastily, breathing heavily. The eerie cries and sound of bones scratching at wood sent chills down her spine.

Could things get any worse?

"*Ariel.*" Steven cried out again.

She staggered back then turned and ran through the rain towards the car door that Wren was holding open for her.

"What did you see?" Wren asked when she slammed the door shut.

"I don't know," she whispered, shivering. Wren leaned against her side, and she wrapped her arms around her as Steven pulled out and headed towards Ena's house.

"It will be all rights, dears." Ena said, gently patting Steven's knee as they pulled up under her carport.

"Thank you, Mrs Musgrove." Steven said, before getting out and scooping up Paul, then went around to help Ena out of the car.

Once Paul and Ena were safely inside, Steven got back in the car and drove to the police station. They were wet, anxious, and exhausted when they stepped into the warm station. Despite the late hour there was a flurry of activity. Phones were ringing and voices exchanging ideas and scenarios drifted from behind a closed door.

Standing in the waiting area, Ariel noticed Wren wringing her fingers together, and Steven rubbing at the back of his neck. She instantly relaxed her arms and gently patted them both on the back as she walked forward to ring the bell on the counter. She glanced at a large map of their town and surrounding areas, before footsteps approached.

"Can I help you?" A freckle faced woman asked, tired lines mapped her eyes. Her name tag read 'Constable Beck.'

"Is lead investigator, Mason around?" Steven asked.

The constable looked from Ariel to Steven. "He's in a meeting."

"No worries, we'll wait here."

Sergeant Cox walked through from an adjoining room and spotting them, crossed towards them. "Thanks Janeen," he addressed the constable, before asking, "How are you all holding up?"

Ariel bit her tongue, halting the negative reply in her head as Steven answered. "We're okay. Just wanting to see how everything's going."

Sergeant Cox nodded. "We've got the entire town cut off. Roadblocks were put in place as soon as we got your call, and Mason has surveillance in place. Apart from a handful of do-gooders claiming they've spotted Lockwood, and some kids prank calling, everything is going smoothly."

"Great. What can we do?"

"Just sit tight and trust that we're all doing our jobs to the best of our ability."

"That's fine and good Sergeant, and we're grateful for all that you're doing. But my seven-year-old nephew is out there somewhere, and I'd really appreciate it if you'd give me a useful task to assist in finding him as soon as possible."

Ariel glanced at her uncle and knew that despite his polite tone he was close to exploding. She placed a comforting hand on his harm and waited the ten seconds it took for him to look away from the sergeant, and directly at her.

"Uncle Steven." She held his gaze, hoping he'd hold it together. If he lost it, she honestly didn't know how she'd cope.

"There's Reverend Matthews and Mr Scott," Wren said, pointing to a door that opened behind the sergeant.

The sergeant glanced over his shoulder. "The Reverend has always been a great support to locals during difficult circumstances such as these. You are welcome to go on through and join him. Coffee's not great but help yourselves." He pointed to the left where a corridor led towards the room.

"Thank you," Ariel said as Wren hurried towards the Reverend.

"No problem. When the detective has finished with the meeting I'll let him know you're here." Sergeant Cox nodded, before reaching towards the shrilling telephone. "Inglewood police department, Sergeant Cox speaking."

Ariel allowed Steven to steer her away from the sergeant and behind Wren as he said to her, "One thing at a time. Let's see what the Reverend thinks of our Travis and Hawk situation while we wait for Stuart."

She nodded as the Reverend turned to greet them.

"Let's sit down," he suggested, sitting himself. "Wren has told me there is another troubling situation that may require my attention."

"Well, at least your opinion, Reverend." Ariel said, sitting beside Wren as Steven and Mr Scott joined them.

"Where's Jaxon?" the Reverend asked, looking towards the door as if expecting Jaxon to stroll in.

"That's part of our story," Wren sighed.

"Well, please, begin."

As Wren began, Ariel silently sent a prayer out into the universe, that Timmy, Hawk and Jaxon be kept safe.

Chapter Twenty-Seven
Travis Lockwood

Travis lined the cricket bat up towards Wren's perfume bottles standing in a neat row along her dressing table, before swinging the bat and smashing them to pieces. Over-sweet perfume filled the air as he turned to smash her mirror and kick a few holes in the wall. He laughed as he looked about the girl's room, wishing he could see her face right now. He'd already ruined the brat's room, along with his toys and books. After taking a piss on the kid's bed, he'd taken great pleasure in masturbating over Wren's pillow whilst breathing in the sweet, musky scent from her undies that he'd grabbed out of her wash basket.

"Next," he said, turning to wreak havoc on Ariel's room.

"We alone, son?" Phillip's voice startled him briefly from downstairs.

He placed the cricket bat behind his neck, resting his wrists over each end as he strolled towards the top of the stairs. "Yeah, we are," he looked down to see Phillip standing with a can of petrol in his hands.

"What are you doing with that?"

"What does it look like?"

"You can't burn the place down."

"Why not?"

"I can't leave, remember?"

"You can't leave when there's four walls that hold you here." Phillip said.

"That's your assumption.

Phillip shrugged, "Maybe if the walls are gone you'll be free?"

"And what if you're wrong?"

Phillip laughed. "Then not much will change, will it? You're already dead, son."

Travis frowned as he looked away, remembering what a prick his father had always been. Travis had only ever been useful to Phillip as a sidekick or scapegoat.

Meeting his father's amused gaze he asked, "So you expect me to be happy about burning to death in this body, and then be trapped to a patch of dirt?"

"There ain't much I can do about that now, is there?"

Travis remained silent.

"Anyway, it will be a real hoot to watch this house burn to the ground." Phillip laughed. "Man, those do-gooders would be turning in their graves if they knew how many bodies we minced and buried underneath this house, hey, wouldn't they?" Phillip spat on the carpet.

Travis didn't reply as he watched Phillip pour petrol along the floor towards the front door, tossing it into the rooms before splashing it over the walls.

It would be a real shame for this house to burn.

After the old Harper's had died, Steven had come and gone as he'd begun the renovations, and Travis had been entertained for months on end moving stuff around and causing mischief.

He'd always managed to avoid the darker entities that resided here. They gave him the creeps, even *before* he'd joined them in the afterlife. Sebastian had been harmless, probably because he'd been terrified of Travis. He'd earned the nickname, *the butcher,* for good reason. The ghost kid had seen a lot in his days, including watching himself and Phillip flay Jaxon's old lady before her death. He could remember each and every horrific act he'd ever done. Some he'd been proud of; others even gave him nightmares.

He'd practically spent his whole life here, in this house. And that had been okay for the most part. It was home.

Home.

As he admitted it to himself for the first time, the scent of Channel No 5 drifted around him as fond memories resurfaced. Memories of how kind Mrs Harper had always been to him. How she'd snuck him hard boiled lollies when she'd seen that he'd been crying. How she had always made him a chocolate cake for his birthday, and whenever she'd return home with treats or gifts for Steven and Sparrow, she had always made sure that Travis had never missed out.

Mr Harper had instructed him in how to use woodwork tools to make repairs around the house, and build fun projects with Steven, before Phillip had put a stop to him spending time alone with any of the Harpers. He could have made them his real family… maybe he could make them his real family now? Had he left it too late? Why hadn't he thought of this before now? Before he'd ruined everything? Well… the house was still standing, so everything wasn't *entirely* ruined.

"Those Harpers were lucky we needed them alive, otherwise I'd have killed them in their sleep. I've got plans for those girls too, it will put what I did to their old lady to shame." Phillip cackled. "It'll be my best kill yet. Are you listening, son?" Phillip's question pulled him out of his trip down memory lane.

"Yeah," he wasn't really. And the fact was, the longer Phillip rambled on, the more Travis realised how much he'd always *hated* his father. He despised him more than words could say. The way Phillip had treated him as a child. Tortured him when the Harpers weren't looking. Interfered with his relationship with Steven, Sparrow and Jaxon. He'd been a lonely kid. An angry kid. A conditioned kid for the worst, most horrific future surrounded by death and therefore what choice had he had but to become a dangerous adult?

"It was a bonus we got to kill Jaxon's old lady though," Phillip laughed again. 'Man, she was a spitfire that one."

"Yeah, she sure had some fight in her," he muttered, distracted.

"It's the wild ones who make the killing fun," Phillip said with a note of admiration.

Travis thought of Wren and Ariel, and the fight they would both put up if it came down to protecting their loved ones. Their home. The thought of them struggling against him as they fought for their lives ignited a ball of lust in his groin. But it did something else too. An unfamiliar feeling grew inside of him, one he hardly recognised. Protectiveness. Were these his feelings, or Hawk's? He could feel the boy growing stronger within him as his hateful heart became remorseful.

"You're not burning this house down," he said quietly.

"What?"

"I don't want you to burn this house down."

"And you think you're gonna stop me? Over your dead body." Phillip threw his head back and roared with laughter.

Travis rolled his eyes. "Yeah, funny pun, *Dad*. But I'm dead serious."

Phillip straightened and sneered at Travis. "Son. It's been a great family reunion and all, but you've been dead to me for years. Burning this house to the ground along with killing every member of this family has been on my to-do list for close to two decades. So shut up and enjoy your second death."

"I'm not alone, and I know the other person in this house isn't going to let you burn it down either."

"You said we were alone."

"I lied."

Jaxon

Jaxon froze. How had Travis known he was there? He crept along the corridor as he listened to the Lockwoods conversation, shocked and furious with all that he'd heard so far. He was reeling with the information that the Lockwoods had murdered, then buried people under this house, including his own mother. Had skinned her alive? He couldn't think on it, not now.

Phillip's comment regarding what he wanted to do to Ariel and Wren, further made him want to get his hands around Lockwood's throat and watch his eyes become lifeless as he strangled him.

If he could just get the cricket bat off Travis, he could knock him out and drag him outside and get him out of Hawk's body. Then he hoped Phillip would take off to his hideout and lead Stuart straight to Timmy. It wasn't a tight plan, but it was a start.

Surely the house was under surveillance by now?

"Who else is here?" Phillip roared. "Answer me now or I'm dropping this lighter."

Jaxon stood at the top of the stairs glaring down at them. "I wouldn't suggest it," he said coldly.

"Well, if it ain't our old friend, little Jaxon Williams," Phillip sneered. "Grew up to be a handsome devil, didn't ya?"

Jaxon didn't bother replying, but kept his gaze fixed on Phillip's hand that held the lighter.

"What do you expect to gain from this?" he asked.

"The satisfaction knowing it was me that done it." Phillip leered.

"Who did it," the teacher in Jaxon couldn't help himself.

"What?"

"The correct phrase is *who did* it, not *that done* it."

Phillip's eyes narrowed. "Always the smartarse, weren't ya, kid? Do you want me to tell ya 'bout ya old lady's final hours? How we drugged her out of her mind, then skinned her alive." Phillip chuckled darkly. "We scored her like a roast pig, didn't we son?"

Phillip didn't bother waiting for Travis's reply. "Then, after the drugs wore off, we really had some fun poking around her exposed nerves. She lasted five hours before the shock killed her. Then we cut her up in the old man's shed and buried her under the house."

Jaxon felt a rage he hadn't felt since Henry Lee had died.

"Got nuthin to say now, hey smartarse?" Phillip shook his head.

Jaxon glanced across at Travis. "You can stop this, Travis."

Travis gasped. "How'd you know?"

"Wren's a clever young lady. You've had your fun but it's time for you to step outside, and out of Hawk."

Travis shook his head. "I don't want to… it's been so good to feel alive again."

"I'm sorry about that. You are where you are because of your own actions." Jaxon kept Phillip in his line of vision as he addressed Travis.

Travis was silent, and Hawk's features took on the first look of remorse that Jaxon had seen in a long time.

A good sign.

"Enough chit-chat ya sops!" Phillip snapped as he clicked the lighter and tossed it ten feet in front of him. The hallway lit up and flames crackled as they swept towards the front door and into the rooms, roaring as it ate up the petrol and all flammable material in its path.

Jaxon paused halfway down the stairs as the flames licked along the hallway rug and up the walls.

"Guess you'll see ya old lady soon enough. Say hi to her for me." Phillip hooted as he ran out the back door, with a, "See ya later, kid," before disappearing.

As the flames danced along the ceiling, Jaxon snapped into action and raced downstairs, meeting Travis's eyes that were wide with fear.

"Get the fire extinguisher," he ordered, pointing towards the kitchen.

Travis remained frozen, staring as the flames rose higher sweeping above his head.

"Now, Travis!" Jaxon yelled as he jumped over the flames licking along the carpet and raced into the lounge to grab the woollen throw blanket off the back of the couch.

The smoke from the carpet filled the air with an acidic campfire smell, before melting plastic singed the air with toxic fumes. Jaxon's heart galloped uncomfortably as he navigated his way towards the laundry as the smoke rose higher.

Dropping the blanket into the cement trough he ran the tap, saturating the blanket as he searched for the plug. Finding it under the sink in an ice-cream container, he stuffed it into the sinkhole and left the water running as he dragged the sodden blanket out and raced towards the flames that were blazing a trail up the stairs.

The grandfather clock began chiming out of time before it too was consumed with flames filled with heat and destruction; the hairs on Jaxon's neck rose as the chiming turned to human screams filled with terror.

Using the sodden blanket, he beat at the flames in front of the stairs as he yelled, "Travis, where the hell is the fire extinguisher?"

"I can't find it."

The creak and groan of timbers contracting sounded as the flames greedily consumed all in its path. Jaxon's heart thumped in his chest.

How can this be happening? Ariel and the kids had already lost so much.

He slapped at the flames as he edged backwards towards the kitchen, crouching low as the smoke flumes permeated his lungs and hung in the air like thick toxic clouds.

"It's beside the oven," he yelled, turning to see Travis bending with his hands on his knees, gasping for clean air as the kitchen steadily filled with black smoke.

"You have to get out of here," Travis cried.

"I'm not giving up," Jaxon replied, edging towards the fire extinguisher. "Damit," he cursed, finding the space empty where he knew the fire extinguisher normally lived.

"Yeah, I think our pal, Phil, removed it." Travis coughed again; the sound of phlegm rattled in his chest as he wheezed.

"Travis, get outside."

"I can't," he cried, shaking his head. "I'm not ready to give this body up."

"You have to! It's the only way. You're only going to burn to death if you stay, and Hawk deserves better than that."

"What about me!" Travis screamed as flames rolled along the kitchen ceiling. They both dropped lower.

"What about you, Travis? You raped and murdered innocent people, including Ariel's mother! So, tell me… what about you!" Jaxon yelled, fury lacing each word.

"You know the childhood I had," Travis returned as vehemently.

Jaxon wacked at the flames licking along the kitchen floor. "We don't have to become the products of our childhood," he returned.

"I was conditioned to become what I am, from day one and you know it! You saw it!" Travis cried.

"You could have risen above it! Chosen different! You could have come to us for help!" Jaxon said.

"It was too late by then! I didn't have a choice."

"Everyone has a choice!"

"You'll never understand!"

"Maybe not. But you've got a choice right now Travis, and that is to get out of this house, and give Hawk back to us!"

Travis was silent, and Jaxon feared the worst as smoke filled his lungs, making him not want to breathe at all. He doubled over as tears streamed down his face; his vision almost lost in the flume of smoke.

"Travis, this is your last chance to do the right thing…" he wheezed as the staircase shifted, groaning timbers ready to give way. A roaring furnace sounded upstairs, and Jaxon was terrified the ceiling was going to cave in. He had to get Hawk's body outside; right now.

"I wanted a family," Travis cried. "I wanted to belong so bad, and I almost did. Until my bastard father made me befriend all those kids. He used me as bait!" he cried.

"He used you for a lot of things, Travis, and I'm sorry for that. But Hawk doesn't deserve this either. This is *his* life. You have to give it back to him."

"I can't."

"I'm not letting you burn in this house. Willing, or unwilling, you're coming with me." Jaxon coughed, dragging the neck of his tee shirt up to cover his nose, trying to prevent as much smoke intake as he could. He heard a body thump in the corner of the kitchen.

"Travis?" he yelled.

Nothing.

"Travis?" he dropped to his hands and knees, dragging the throw rug with him as he patted the floor in front of him, making his way to where Travis's voice had been.

Sparks sprinkled down and a bright flicker of flame lit up the room as the lace curtains ignited. He saw Travis slumped over in front of the fridge. Light bulbs popped and shattered as the flames tore through the house.

Dropping the rug, he fought against a violent cough and lost, as he rolled Hawk's dead weight into the centre. Finding the sides of the rug, he threw them over Hawk and rolled him up in it. Wheezing as smoke-fingers squeezed his lungs, he crawled towards the doorway, dragging Hawk behind him. It was impossible to see, and every breath was torture. He reached the door and heard the crash of the dining table fall and glass shatter.

Burnt greenery, he assumed were Ariel's house plants, which had filled every space, now victims to the flames. He grit his teeth, knowing he was close to the back door, yet didn't know if he had the strength to make it. Every breath ripped through his raw throat and nose; fatigue weighed heavily. Melted plastic dripped into hissing puddles and the toxic fumes burned his nostrils.

The heat was unlike anything he'd ever experienced, but he drew on everything he had and stood, lifting Hawk onto his shoulder as he prepared to run towards the back door.

Taking a deep breath, he sized up the flames that swept along the floor and was filled with relief when the laundry sink overflowed and water ran under his boots, and into the flames. Unfortunately, the water did nothing to diminish the flames which licked along the walls and rolled over the ceiling like an orange tsunami.

"We can do this," he muttered, before pulling in a shallow breath and strode towards the back door that the flames hadn't yet reached. Grabbing the doorknob he pulled the door open and almost wept in relief as cool air rushed towards him, gifting his lungs with crisp, clean air. As he pushed the screen door open, a groaning, splintered sound exploded above him. Jaxon lunged for the doorway and was halfway out when the ceiling beam gave way, scattering bright sparks and ash before catching his shoulder and pinning him to the ground.

The storm raged and sheets of rain fell over him and into the house as the flames crackled behind him, devouring everything in its path.

"Hawk," he moaned, hoping to God that the burning beam was not crushing the boy. "I'm sorry mate." He tried to move, but a heavy fog crept into his brain, making the world around him fade away.

Images of when he had first visited Steven as a kindergarten mate, eating ice-cream in the wade pool under the peppercorn tree. Primary school years playing in the sandpit and making the train tracks up in the playroom. School holidays where they spent time in the barn, spying on Sparrow making out with a boyfriend. High school years where any bully that looked at them, or anyone else the wrong way received their wraith, in the kindest, most diplomatic way a fifteen-year-old knew how to deliver. Years in this house, where love knew no boundaries. Where family, loyalty and a safe haven meant everything.

Chapter Twenty-Eight
Ariel

"Where's Jaxon?" Stuart asked once he'd joined their group.

"He didn't want to leave Hawk on his own." Steven began.

"Why didn't the boy come with you?" Stuart looked confused.

"It's complicated." Ariel said, placing her untouched coffee on the table.

Stuart met her gaze as his mobile rang and reached for it, quickly exiting the room to answer it.

"Jaxon will be all right at the house." Reverend Matthews said. "He has protection."

Ariel nodded as if the Reverend's comment made complete sense. She ran her hands over her face, itching to wrap her arms around Timmy. To have a conversation with *Hawk*, and to tuck herself onto Jaxon's lap and sleep for a week.

Stuart returned moments later followed by Sergeant Cox. "We've had a sighting." Stuart said.

"Stay here and we'll get updates to you as soon as possible." Sergeant Cox said.

"I'm coming with…" Steven was cut off when a flustered constable rushed into the room.

"Sergeant, there's a housefire on Grant Street," he reported breathlessly as a fire siren wailed in the night.

Ariel froze as she met Steven's, then Wren's widened gazes. "It can't be," she whispered, feeling the blood drain from her face.

"What number?" Steven demanded.

When the constable answered, Steven, Wren, and Ariel went to run out of the station when Sergeant Cox stood in the doorway. "Stop! It won't be safe."

"No offence, Sergeant, but if you don't get out of my way I'm going to throw myself out of the window!" Ariel shouted.

Stuart raised an eyebrow before saying, "Sergeant, surely you can take the family and keep them safe. I've got to follow this lead."

Sergeant Cox nodded, "Very well, let's go." He said leading the way to his cruiser as Stuart jogged towards his vehicle.

Ariel's blood pumped like a wave crashing against her eardrums as she prayed. *Please let Jaxon and Hawk be safe.*

Piling in the car, the sergeant took off towards the sound of the wailing siren as rain pelted at the windscreen.

"Surely the rain has helped?" Wren whispered.

"I'm sure it has love," Ariel reached across and took her sister's hand. How much more could these kids endure?

Within a minute they pulled up across the street, opposite the fire truck where equipment was hastily being unloaded, and neighbours lined the street. Ariel stepped out of the car, followed by Wren and Steven as they looked on with horror.

"Stay here," The sergeant ordered before he jogged across the road to speak to the fire captain.

"This can't be happening," Ariel cried as the rain slapped at her face.

Steven put his arms around her and Wren's shoulders as they watched their beloved family home put on a spectacular light show as sparks flew high into the night sky like fireworks before being consumed by the rain.

"I can't just stand here," Ariel shook her head and stepped away from Steven before he caught her arm.

"Where do you think you're going?"

She turned on him, "I need to get in there! I need to know Hawk and Jaxon are alive!" She cried.

"Let the firefighters do their job, love. If we get in their way or get hurt, it could jeopardize them getting to Jaxon and Hawk."

Ariel shook her head. "I won't go inside, I'll stay as far away from the fire as possible. Please Uncle Steven, stay here with Wren."

Steven rubbed his face briefly as he stared down at her. "Do *not* go inside that house, Ariel." He said sternly. "I mean it!"

She hugged Wren, and quickly brushed a kiss across her uncle's cheek.

"I promise." With that, she raced down the street, and towards the back alley and entered the yard through the back gate. Smoke filled the air and burnt the back of her throat as she drew closer. The heat was intense.

"Lady," a fireman yelled. "You need to get back!"

"This is my house," she screamed as she raced by him, and down the back yard towards the chook pen, ready to release them over the fence if the fire came any closer.

Facing the house, her heart sank as the roof collapse; timber and iron clashing like an out of tune orchestra. She covered her mouth with shaking hands as the flames leapt across the space, consuming the barn and all her precious art.

An ambulance siren sounded in the distance, drawing closer with every ragged breath she pulled in, as the firefighters saturated everything consumed by flame.

Sobbing quietly, her eyes adjusted to the shapes and shadows of the house and yard. She froze when she spotted two figures laying underneath the peppercorn tree. Gasping in fear, she ran across the yard and fell to her knees beside the still figures of Hawk and Jaxon.

"Over here!" she cried, waving across to the firefighter, who grabbed his radio and started talking into it as he rushed towards them.

"Hawk, Jaxon," she cried, being careful not to move them. Hawk was laying on his back, and Jaxon was on his stomach. She was desperate to roll him over and look at his face. Leaning closer, she placed her ear near Hawk's nose and sobbed in relief when a soft breath hit her face.

"Thank god Hawk," she whispered. "Thank god." She gently placed her hand on his chest, as she wiped tears away. The rain suddenly ceased allowing her to look up at the night sky as she pulled in a deep breath, thinking of her mother and Grandparents looking down at this scene.

"I'm sorry," she whispered as guilt consumed her. Somehow, she felt responsible for this mess. For the loss of their home.

"Excuse me, miss." A paramedic said from behind her. She nodded, getting to her feet and moving out of the way as Steven and Wren raced in the back yard. The fire was under control and slowly dying out.

"Hawk!" Wren cried, running into Ariel's arms.

"He's breathing love, he's okay." Ariel hugged her as Steven ran a hand over the back of his neck.

"Jaxon?" He asked. She shrugged, swallowing her tears.

They were joined by two more paramedics and a firefighter who did a quick assessment, before efficiently lifting Hawk and Jaxon onto stretchers.

"Is he…" Ariel couldn't ask as she pointed to Jaxon.

"They're both alive, vitals are steady, and they appear to have minor injuries." One of the paramedics answered as they carried the men towards the back gate where the ambulance had pulled up to.

"Oh thank you," tears of relief filled her eyes as she leaned down, resting her palms onto her knees. One thing down. Now, to find Timmy.

"Wren, do you want to go with Hawk?" she asked, straightening.

"Yes," Wren nodded, wiping her tears.

"Okay. I'm going to find the Sergeant and ask if he's heard from Stuart."

"What do you want me to do?" Steven asked.

"Do you want to go to the hospital? Check on Liv and keep your eye on Hawk and Jaxon?"

"Yep. I'll ring you with any updates."

"Okay."

"Come on, love," he took Wren's hand and putting his arm around Ariel, led them towards the ambulance. "Can we grab a lift with you?" He asked the younger paramedic.

"Sure, no problem, it's a quick trip, jump in the front," he said, eyeing off Wren as he closed the back door and headed towards the driver's side.

"I'll stay in touch." Steven said to Ariel.

She nodded, wrapping her arms around herself and watched them get into the ambulance before it pulled out and bumped along the gravelled back lane.

Sighing, she looked back at the ruins that was their home and shook her head. Dampened smoke filled the air and would for some time. Searching for the sergeant, she found him interviewing the neighbours with one of his constables.

He frowned when he saw her. "I told you all to stay with the vehicle." She shrugged.

"I'm sorry about your home," he said.

"Me too. Any news about Timmy."

He nodded. "Someone believes they've seen Lockwood. Stuart has his team on it. Would you like to come back to the station with me?"

"No. I need to walk."

"I don't know if that's such a good idea with Lockwood on the lose."

"I don't think he'd be stupid enough to show his face when there's all this law enforcement around, do you?"

"Still, be careful," he said.

"I will."

"Constable," he yelled, waving to the police car. "Let's go."

Ariel turned and walked down the street, leaving the bustle of firefighters and curios neighbours behind. She was forcing a calm she didn't feel, knowing she could not lose it. Not yet, anyway. She had to keep it together until they found Timmy. As she crossed the road, she glanced down Brooke's Lane where one of Stuart's men stood. Others were jogging down the alley. Recognising her, he nodded.

"Miss Harper, you really shouldn't be out here."

"Would you be out here if your loved one was missing?"

"I would," he replied.

"There you go," she said continuing on, turning onto the main street, grateful at least that the rain had stopped. She listened as thunder rumbled off in the distance. "It's okay Timmy," she whispered. "We're going to find you."

Timmy

A streetlight filtered in through the window. Sticky heat slid into Timmy's eyes as he blinked rapidly, trying to clear the red haze of blood from his vision. Sebastian squatted in front of him.

"Keep still," he said, before wiping his finger along the trail of blood.

Timmy wanted to ask Sebastian what he was doing, but the tape over his mouth prevented him from asking.

Sebastian stood, and Timmy watched in awe as he floated up to the top of the window and started to wipe his fingers across the dusty glass before returning to wipe at some more blood. Timmy couldn't make out what Sebastian was writing on the glass. It looked like *9I3H*.

"Mmm," he mumbled around the tape. "Mmm."

Sebastian frowned, then laughed before ripping the tape off Timmy's mouth.

"Why didn't I think of that before," he giggled.

Timmy licked his lips, wishing Sebastian could release his hands and feet, but he'd tried that earlier with no luck. The tape was on good and tight.

"Thanks," he said, before asking. "What did you write?"

"Why, *help*, of course."

"Genius," Timmy whispered.

"I know," Sebastian grinned.

"Who's going to see it though?"

"What do you mean?"

"It's dark out, and in here."

"Yeah." Sebastian folded his arms.

Timmy looked around, wondering what he could use to cut his bindings when he spotted the beer bottles.

"Sebastian, could you knock a bottle hard enough to make it break?" He asked.

"Sure I can. Good idea!" Sebastian focused on a bottle, then slapped his hand towards it. They watched it fly forward to hit the floor and roll unbroken to a standstill.

"Not hard enough. Give me a second," Sebastian said.

"You've got this, mate." Timmy assured him.

Sebastian closed his eyes, before flying around the room in a circle, and straight towards the window, his palm open and slapped at the beer bottle with all his energy, sending it towards the brick wall smashing into jagged pieces.

"You did it, Sebastian!" Timmy cried, as Sebastian looked on with pride.

Timmy used his legs to scuttle towards the broken bottle, his backside sliding across the dusty floor. Careful of the broken pieces, he grabbed the bottle and pushed it between his thighs, and used the jagged neck to cut through his bindings. Finally, the glass tore through the duct tape.

"Finally," Timmy said, hugging his arms painfully as pins and needles danced along his nerves. "Ouch," he cried, trying to pull the tape off his ankles. Finally, he threw the tape aside and tried to stand, but his legs were too numb. He sat there, using his numb hands to rub the life back into his legs.

"You need a drink." Sebastian said.

"No way. I'd rather die of thirst then drink his water," he said, screwing up his nose. After several minutes, Timmy sighed as the pins and needles began to fade. Creeping towards the door on his hands and knees, he turned the handle, only to find it locked.

"Damn it," he bit his lip, turning towards Sebastian. "What are we going to do? We have to get out of here before he gets back."

"Maybe we can break the window and climb out?"

"Is there a ledge underneath the window?"

"I'll have a look." With that, Sebastian disappeared through the bricks. Retuning seconds later wearing a worried expression.

"What?"

"There's a tiny ledge, but the fall is a big one if you slip."

"How high up are we?" Timmy asked.

"Two stories."

Sebastian drifted down towards the man's bag, and popped his head inside, coming out with a grin. "He's got matches in here. We could set the curtain on fire?"

Timmy frowned, as he eyed off the lace curtains. "Yeah, they won't burn much but should burn bright enough for someone to see?"

"Then you could burn those newspapers and chuck 'em out the window?" Sebastain suggested.

Timmy grinned. "That's a great idea."

Timmy used the door to help him stand on shaky legs, wincing in discomfort. Reaching into the man's bag, he grabbed the matches and walked over to the pile of newspapers. Rolling several up he turned to the window and used them to smash out the thin old glass.

Fresh air rushed into the room, and Timmy sighed as the familiar scent of eucalyptus filled the room. "Home," he said quietly.

"Your home?" Sebastian asked.

"Inglewood." Timmy replied, striking a match and watching it light up the room before it fizzled out. He struck another match, holding it to the bottom of the curtain. It flared instantly, the bright flame licking upwards eating the thin lace.

"Light the other one," Sebastian said. Timmy set the other curtain up in a blaze.

Timmy held the newspaper to the burning curtain, but it only smouldered. "The newspaper's too damp!" He threw it out of the window before running towards the pile of papers and grabbing more, ran back and threw them out the window. The curtains were burning brightly, but quickly. Timmy tried not to breathe in the smoke as he threw more newspapers outside. When he'd thrown all the newspapers out, he hefted the backpack out the window too.

Sebastian turned towards the door. "Timmy! Someone's coming!"

Timmy involuntarily whimpered as he spun towards the door along with his friend, trembling at the thought of the disgusting man returning. Holding up his fists, he cried aloud as Sebastian vanished though the door leaving him all alone to face the man.

Chapter Twenty-Nine
Wren

W ren hadn't slept and had only showered after Steven had threatened to drag her in the shower himself if she didn't. Sitting by Hawk's side, she prayed he'd return to her as himself. Holding his hand, she leaned over and whispered, "Hawk, please tell me it's you. Please come back to us. Timmy needs his big brother," she squeezed his fingers, wiping a tear away.

"Hey Wren," a calm, soothing voice said from behind her.

Turning, she was surprised to see Lance Meek standing in the doorway holding a giant Snickers, and a bunch of lavender.

"Lance, what are you doing here?"

"My dad's a fiery, he told me what had happened to your house, I'm sorry."

She nodded her thanks, wiping at her eyes. "It's two o'clock in the morning."

He grinned. "Yeah, it is. My mum dropped me off." His green eyes sparkled tiredly.

He is so cute.

"These are for you," he said clearing his throat as he offered her the flowers.

"Thank you," she tried to look as if boys gave her flowers every other day, but felt her face grow warmer.

His smile widened as he placed the Snickers on the hospital trolley. "You're welcome."

"Do you want a coffee?"

"Nah, thanks."

She didn't know what else to say as they silently looked each other over.

"So, how's the big guy?" he said, smile fading as he looked down at Hawk.

She turned back to her twin and said. "He hasn't woken up yet."

"Any news of Timmy?"

She shook her head as another tear betrayed her and rolled down her cheek.

"I'm really sorry for everything you're going through," he said, sitting on the bed near Hawk's legs, facing her in the chair. He took her hand that was holding the flowers, and gently rubbed his thumb over the back of her hand.

She watched as he reached across and took Hawk's other hand gently, being mindful of the IV.

They sat silently, the three holding hands as the hospital clock ticked the minutes away.

Wren occasionally glanced at Lance under her lashes, and promised she wouldn't do it again every time she found his gaze pinned on her. But she couldn't help herself. He was being so tender with Hawk, and very considerate coming to visit at this hour.

A movement at the door caught her eye, and she cried in relief seeing Jaxon standing there. His hair was wet as if he'd recently showered.

"Look who's up!" Steven said from behind Jaxon.

"Jaxon, are you alright?" She asked softly, getting up to hug him. "Thank you for getting Hawk out of the house."

He wrapped his arms around her, and she forced back the sob that almost escaped.

"You're welcome. He hasn't woken up yet?"

She shook her head. "Do you think Travis has gone?" She whispered.

Jaxon nodded. "I truly hope so."

"G'day Lance." Steven said. "Thanks for coming at this ungodly hour."

"Couldn't keep me away, Mr Harper."

"Steven, please."

Jaxon dropped his arms and turned to Steven. "I'm heading out."

"Where?"

"To the station for a start. I'm presuming Ariel will be there?"

"I believe so."

Jaxon nodded.

"Mate, you were out cold."

"And now I'm not."

"You really shouldn't leave the hospital." Steven said.

"I'm fine, stay here with the kids and Liv," Jaxon said heading out.

Steven looked at Wren and raised an eyebrow. "Can't tell these kids anything these days."

Wren smiled as a nurse called out, "Mr Williams, Mr Williams, you really shouldn't be out of bed!"

Steven chuckled. "If I can't stop that man from doing what he wants, no one can."

He ran a hand along Wren's tear-stained cheek. "You doing okay sweetheart?"

"Yes. It's nice having Lance here."

Steven looked across at Lance and said, "Hopefully between the two of you, you can talk Hawk into joining the land of the conscious."

"We'll certainly try our best." Lance said.

"How's Liv, Uncle Steven?" Wren asked.

Steven smiled, "She's eating all the hospital jelly and threatening to join the search for Timmy, so I'll get back to her and make sure she stays put."

Wren chuckled. "I love Liv."

"Yeah," Steven returned as he turned to head out. "Me too."

Wren smiled after her uncle as he called over his shoulder. "Lance, please come get me as soon as Hawk wakes."

"I will," Lance said as Wren sat back down and took Hawk's hand, as Lance gently took hers.

"Your family is pretty great," he said.

"Yeah," she whispered, her smile fading as she thought of Timmy, and looked upon Hawk's pale face. "They're the best."

Ariel

Ariel walked past the Fat Butcher when a bright light ahead caught her attention. Frowning, she peered at the orange glow, startled to see newspapers flutter down from the double story building on the corner of Chancery Lane. Boots pounding the pavement, and she turned to see three men hightail it behind the Royal, heading down Brooke's Lane, as another man yelled into his radio from across the street, before he ran towards the building where the newspapers littered the street.

Her heart skipped a beat. "Timmy..." she whispered, before a blinding pain exploded behind her eyes as someone struck her on the back of her head.

Stunned, she tried to keep her balance, but fell forward and was caught in rough arms, before being hauled against wet wool that stunk so bad it made her gag.

"Shut up, bitch," a rough voice grated as he turned, slamming the side of her head against the sidewalk pole as he marched in the opposite direction of the commotion.

"Timmy," she groaned.

"He's already dead," he spat. "Gutted like the trouble making little shit he was, just like his mother. And you're next."

Tears fell as bright white stars danced in a sea of black before she stumbled in the arms of none other than her mother's murderer. Ariel struggled to clear her vision, but another cuff to her head had more stars bursting behind her lids.

He tugged her towards a rusty Ute, and she squinted, trying to focus on the number plate, only to see there was none. He threw her in the back and she groaned as something sharp poked in her ribs, stealing the air from her lungs. He slammed the tray closed, tossing a heavy tarp over her head.

Footsteps sounded, then the Utes door slammed, moving Ariel into action. She pushed at the tarp planning on throwing herself over the side, before the Ute accelerated at a speed that sent her crashing backwards. They sped along the road before turning sharply, and not long after they made another turn before crossing the railway line. Further along, they turned down a gravel road that had potholes bouncing her beaten body like bones in a game of knucklebones. She had a creeping suspicion that they were headed deep into the bush. A place where people got lost, and some never found. She thought of Timmy then, and fell into a void of darkness.

Ariel woke to a pounding head and carefully took a breath. Stale, dry air filled her lungs along with a trace of something dead; its rotten stench danced across her taste buds. She coughed, opening her eyes to find herself in an abandoned mine shaft. The early morning sun shone through the leaves of the Blue Mallee trees that she could see through the entrance of the shaft. It was wide enough for a small man to walk through and was braced with support beams trailing along the walls and roof.

Dry leaves rustled in the breeze, and twigs lay scattered along the dirt floor. She shifted uncomfortably as rocks scraped beneath her tied hands.

Corellas screeched in the trees above, breaking the eerie silence of the bush.

How far off the main road am I? And where is…? She didn't want to think about *him*.

Timmy… Oh no… Everything *he'd* said came rushing back to her.

He's already dead. Gutted like the trouble making little shit he was, just like his mother. And you're next.

Bile clawed its way up her throat and she turned to her side, retching on the dirt floor as tears clogged her throat.

"No, it can't be true… *Timmy*," she whimpered. "I'm sorry Timmy… Mama, I'm so sorry…" her tears poured as she sobbed.

Closing her eyes, she fell against the dry, rough rock wall as a wave of despair crushed her. Her *baby* brother. She moaned in anguish, thinking about his final hours. He must have been so frightened, terrified. And she hadn't been there to protect him. And now, he was dead. Murdered by the same man who had caused so many, such grief – including the murder of their mother. She tried to cling to the devastating reality before her, but it was all too much. She didn't remember passing out.

Jaxon

The commotion at the station indicated that there was either good news, or bad news. He marched up to the counter, tapping his fingers along the shiny surface as another constable rushed by, and four of Stuart's uniformed men walked out of a room blowing on coffees. The waiting room clock read two-thirty a.m. He tapped on the golden bell sitting near a sign in book.

"Can I help you?" A constable asked.

"I've got this," Stuart called from behind Jaxon. "It's good to see you're okay. I was informed about the fire."

"There was nothing I could do to put it out." Jaxon rubbed his face, feeling slightly exhausted.

"You saved the young man's life." Stuart said.

"Yeah, apparently I did."

Stuart raised an eyebrow at Jaxon's odd statement. The fact was, Jaxon couldn't remember a thing after the ceiling beam had knocked him out. He had no idea how they'd gotten outside.

"Should you even be here?" Stuart asked.

"Have we got news on Timmy?" Was Jaxon's only response.

"Follow me." Stuart led Jaxon out of the waiting room and through a small corridor to a first aid room.

Sitting on a stretcher, sucking on a hydra light icy pole, was Timmy. Jaxon nearly staggered towards the dark-haired boy; his relief seeing that he was safe was overwhelming him. "Timmy," he managed to whisper.

Timmy looked up as the nurse finished cleaning the blood from his forehead.

"Mr Williams!" Timmy cried and dropped his icy pole, climbed down from the stretcher and ran into Jaxon's arms.

Jaxon scooped his little body up, holding him close as he rocked him gently. "It's so good to see you." His voice broke, and he took a deep breath, trying to get his emotions under control. "We were so worried about you."

"Some smelly deliverance man took me. Sebastian said it was a Lockwood." Timmy's arms tightened around Jaxon's neck.

"Deliverance man, huh?"

"Yeah," Timmy yawned.

Jaxon turned, meeting Stuart's gaze. "Did we catch the smelly man?" Stuart shook his head.

"Excuse me?" The nurse behind Jaxon interrupted.

"Oh, I'm sorry," Jaxon apologised. "You weren't finished?"

"I was, but he needs to go to the hospital for an X-ray. Are you his next of kin?"

"I'm his teacher, and soon to be his father." He replied, shocked that the statement slipped so smoothly from his lips. Timmy didn't react. Jaxon assumed he was exhausted as he was snuggled into his neck breathing deeply.

"That'll do," Stuart nodded to the nurse. "I'll drive you."

"Thanks."

The nurse gave instructions on where to take Timmy at the hospital and said she'd already rung ahead and booked him in.

"Where's Ariel?" Jaxon asked Stuart. "I thought she'd be here."

"Isn't she at the hospital?" Stuart asked as they headed out of the station, getting into Stuart's jeep.

"No," Jaxon frowned, strapping Timmy into the back seat and sitting beside him as they took off.

"She won't be too far, I'm sure."

A knot of worry formed in the pit of Jaxon's gut as they pulled up at the hospital. Scooping Timmy up, he headed to the desk where a young nurse was waiting.

"Timothy Harper?" She asked.

"Right here," Jaxon nodded.

"Follow me please," she turned with her clip board and headed down the corridor.

"Can you find Steven?" he asked Stuart. "He'll want to see Timmy. And can you ring Ariel's mobile? I lost mine in the fire."

"Sure thing."

"Steven should be in room twenty-one."

Stuart nodded, before Jaxon followed the nurse.

"Where's Ariel?" Timmy asked.

Jaxon met Timmy's exhausted gaze as he carried him behind the nurse. "She went looking for you. I'll find her for you."

"I know you will. Thanks Mr William's." His little arms tightened around Jaxon's neck.

"So, Sebastian was with you, huh?"

"Yeah, but he left when the men with the guns charged in. He said he had something else to do."

"Busy boy."

Timmy laughed. "He's so much fun. He helped save me."

"Did he? Well, I look forward to thanking him." Jaxon dropped a kiss on the top of Timmy's head before placing him onto the bed where a small gown was placed.

"If you could take of your top, Timothy and put on this gown, we can do your X-ray and then you can get into a comfortable bed." The nurse smiled kindly.

Timmy yawned loudly. "Yeah, I am tired."

Footsteps approached as Steven stepped through the door. Jaxon turned, to watch his lifelong friend smile from ear to ear as tears spilled down his face.

"Timmy," he said softly, before rushing forward and scooping the little boy up, crushing him in his arms.

"Uncle Steven, I can't breathe," Timmy giggled.

Steven relaxed his hold to gaze upon his nephew's face. "How are you, mate?"

"I'm tired, and I stink. I need a shower and some jelly."

Steven took a big breath, then gasped, staggering back playfully. "It's true mate, you really do stink!"

"Uncle Steven!" Timmy laughed.

"Righto, X-ray, shower, jelly and bed. Deal?"

"Deal," Timmy nodded.

Steven dropped a noisy kiss on Timmy's cheek, before placing him back down. "I'll call Ariel," he said, pulling out his mobile.

After the nurse had finished with Timmy, it was decided that he would share the room with Hawk, as there was a small cot in there.

Steven piggy-backed Timmy to the room as Jaxon opened the door, asking quietly, "Would you like a visitor?"

Wren turned towards him, and when Steven stepped into the room with Timmy clinging to his back like a monkey, Wren burst into tears.

"Timmy," she cried, releasing Hawk's hand, before rushing past Lance and reaching for her brother.

Jaxon felt his throat constrict and met Steven's gaze. His friend looked as exhausted as he'd been the day he'd been told his sister had been murdered. He placed his arm around his shoulder.

Steven threw his around Jaxon's shoulder as the men looked on as the siblings reunited.

"I was so worried about you, Timmy." Wren said.

"It was scary."

"I'm sorry about that. Are you all right now?" She kissed his cheek.

"Yeah." He hugged her before asking. What's wrong with Hawk?"

"He's just sleeping," Wren said quickly. "You were so brave, weren't you?"

Timmy looked proud. "I was, only because Sebastian was with me. He helped me escape from the deliverance man."

Wren raised an eyebrow as she looked between Jaxon and Steven.

"Let's save that story," Steven said. "Timmy, you need a shower."

Light footsteps approached, and Ray stepped into the room carrying a large duffel bag. "Hello," she smiled. "I hope you don't mind, but I've collected a few items of clothing in all the kids sizes."

"That was so thoughtful of you, Ray." Jaxon said as Steven reached to take the bag from her.

"Not at all," she said, kneeling down to look at Timmy. "How are you, Timothy?" She asked softly.

"I'm okay Mrs Sommers."

"I think you'll really like some of the clothes I got for you. Would you like to see?"

He nodded, before asking. "Why do I need your clothes? Where's mine?" He looked up at his uncle.

Wren quickly reached into the bag and pulled out a colourful Sponge-Bob SquarePants dressing gown and pyjamas. "Because this is so cool Timmy." She took his hand, distracting him from his question. "And you need a shower before you can sit with Hawk."

"Okay," he allowed Wren to steer him towards the bathroom.

Lance stood, "I'll just go grab a cuppa. Can I get anyone anything?"

"No thanks," Steven smiled warmly as Lance headed out.

Finally, the adults were left to talk freely.

"I'm so sorry to hear about the fire," Ray shook her head. "It seemed to happen shortly after we'd all left?"

"Yeah," Steven said. "It was one hell of a night, all right."

"Jaxon, I was told you were there." Ray said.

He nodded, running a hand through his hair before folding his arms. "It was pretty grim."

"I can imagine. Ariel must be so relieved all the kids are safe." Ray looked around. "Where is she?"

"That is a question I want answered too," Jaxon said quietly as another set of footsteps approached.

Stuart stepped in, nodding to Ray and addressed Steven and Jaxon, "Can I have a private word with you both?"

"Sure," Jaxon said.

"I'll go," Ray said.

"No, Ray, please, would you mind sitting with the kids for a bit?" Jaxon asked. "We've got to sort a few things out."

"Of course I can," she sat in the chair under the window as the men left, closing the door behind them.

"Has anyone sighted Ariel?" Jaxon asked.

"Should I be worried?" Steven raised an eyebrow, turning to face Stuart.

"I can't be sure. One of my men sighted her not long before we located Timothy. She was walking by Brooke Lane when he spoke to her."

"Well, she can't have just disappeared. Maybe she went back to the house." Steven suggested.

"I'm going to look for her. I promised Timmy I'd find her." Jaxon said.

"We'll all go." Steven nodded. "Hang on a sec," he opened the door and went into the room. Returning a minute later, he said to Jaxon. "I've just told Wren what we're doing. Ray is happy to sit tight until we get back."

"I'll drive," Stuart said, and within twenty minutes they'd driven down every street in town, excluding the roadblocks that were still in place as the manhunt for Lockwood was still on.

Pulling up in Ariel's driveway, they sat silently looking on at the smouldering debris of the burnt house. The fire crew were still racking through the ruins, piling the galvanised sheeting to one side making sure all hot spots were extinguished.

"I'm sorry mate," Jaxon said quietly, feeling the loss of Steven's family home too, having spent a great deal of his life within those walls.

"Me too," Steven replied.

"Well, she's not here." Stuart stated the obvious.

"Her mobile goes straight to voicemail," Steven said.

"Yes, I noticed that." Stuart said, tapping his fingers against the steering wheel.

"Where would she go…" Jaxon whispered to himself.

"Yours?" Stuart asked.

"No, why would she? She can't get in."

"She wouldn't leave the kids." Steven said.

"Especially thinking Timmy is still missing." Jaxon agreed.

"She said she was going to the station. *Jesus*, where is she?" Steven sounded frustrated.

"I've got a really bad feeling about this," Jaxon turned in the front seat to meet Steven's worried gaze.

"Yeah," Steven nodded.

"Let's get to the station and I'll put out a BOLA alert." Stuart said.

"Shit," Steven sounded like the wind had been punched from him.

"It's going to be okay, mate." Jaxon tried to reassure his friend whilst he himself, was feeling sick inside. He couldn't lose her. Not now, not ever.

Stuart pulled out from the curb and accelerated towards the police station. "I'm going to do everything in my power to find her," he assured the two men, who many years ago had saved his life.

Chapter Thirty
Ariel

"Oh *god*..." Ariel groaned, licking her dry lips. Taking a deep breath to help clear her thumping head, she screwed her nose up.

"Yuck," she referred to both the taste in her mouth after vomiting, and the rotten smell she'd caught earlier. The heat of the morning wasn't helping whatever it was that was dead. And she had a *really* bad feeling it wasn't an animal. The stench now permeated the entire mineshaft. Shifting her legs, she turned to take a good look around; goosebumps spread across her flesh.

A filthy mattress propped against the wall ten feet away was covered in rust patches along with a brighter stain that looked like fresh blood. Rusty springs protruded through the frayed blue and yellow striped material.

"That doesn't bode well..." she whispered, as she tugged at the restraints binding her wrists.

She grit her teeth as her fingers slid over the slippery knot of rope that was binding her wrists, as she inspected the rope around her ankles.

She didn't know how long she had till *he* came back, and she was *not* going to be here waiting for him. She fingered the knot behind her back, her fingers sliding off the slick rope. Squinting her eyes, she focused on the rope around her ankles, and leaning closer, moaned as she realised the rope was drenched in blood.

"Shit," she hissed. "This guy is seriously *fucked* up!" She shook furious tears from her eyes and desperately tackled at the knots binding her wrists. How the *hell* was she going to get out of here? She angled her back towards the wall and rubbed the rope against the sharp rocks jutting from the cervices. Several minutes after getting nowhere fast, she pulled her ankles towards her backside, and using her hands to steady herself against the wall, pushed her legs straight and finally stood upright.

"Should have thought of that earlier!" With her ankles bound, she hopped towards the entrance as carefully and quickly as she could, keeping her balance. She didn't need to bend as she cleared the roof of the entrance easily. Pausing, she listened for footsteps in the bush.

The Corella's screeched cheerfully before taking off in a cloud of white as the entire flock headed sky high. The breeze playfully fingered her locks, as the sun kissed her face good morning. Nature was giving her a positive sign that all would be well.

She shuffled out of the mine shaft and hopped a few feet forward as she contemplated which way to go. There was no sound of traffic. Not even a distant grinding of air-breaks as they travelled through town.

"One way is as good as any other," she guessed. "As long as I get the hell away from here." With that decision made she started hopping through the bush, around small brush and over fallen branches. Sitting on a large log, she threw her legs over it, balancing with her hands before sliding off and continued her jaunty escape.

She almost laughed thinking this was too easy, when she remembered Timmy was no longer breathing in this world.

Don't, she begged herself when she felt like giving into the grief and giving up. She'd cry her heart out when she was safe. Hawk and Wren still needed her. As she continued to hop, she recalled the sports day when Timmy was in four-year-old kindergarten participating in the potato-sack race. His tiny body almost consumed by the hessian bag, as his little legs bounced up and down, just as she was doing now to escape a killer.

Her next hop was met with a twisted root, and she lost her balance, falling hard. Closing her eyes to prevent any twigs poking into them; receiving a sharp stab to her ribs. Stars danced behind her closed lids as pain stole her breath.

She grit her teeth, halting the swear words and rolled off the pointy stick. The pain was excruciating. Looking down, she saw blood seeping through her tee shirt; could feel it pooling on her flesh. Dropping her head back, she stared at the blue sky framed by the network of leaves and branches as they danced in the breeze. Surely, she could just lay here till someone found her.

"Hey girlie, where do ya think you're going?" *His* gravelly voice called.

She froze. He wasn't the *someone* she'd been referring to.

Rolling towards a tree she quickly propped her back against its trunk, and using her legs to push herself upright, she hastily resuming her escape. Glancing over her shoulder she saw no sign of him. She could do this. *Would* do this.

The bush was moist after the storm and the eucalyptus scented the air, filling her burning lungs with the fuel it needed. She forced herself to bounce quickly, and grit her teeth, heart galloping as snapping twigs and steady footsteps sounded behind her.

Seeing a large ghost gum with a thick trunk, she hopped towards it and hid behind it, trying to steady her breath as he began whistling an odd tune. *Damn, he was creepy!*

Closing her eyes, she silently prayed to the Angels above for protection, along with her Grandmother and Mother. Surely someone would hear her and think she was worth saving?

The whistling stopped and a twig snapped close to her. Opening her eyes slowly, she saw him standing five feet in front of her, hands on hips, his back to her. She dared not breathe as he started whistling again yet made no move to continue his search. She studied the man who had raised a killer. Tortured and murdered the innocent.

Her rage boiled silently, as she willed him to walk on. Checking for twigs or branches, she wondered if she could move to the other side of the trunk undetected.

He walked forward, slow, and steady as if he had all the time in the world as he resumed whistling his irritating tune.

She made the move to hide on the other side of the tree, sighing in relief when he continued moving away. Dropping her head back against the trunk she bit her lip, wondering where to go from here.

The whistling stopped as twigs snapped, before silence ensued. Opening her eyes she screamed, startled to find him standing directly in front of her wearing a wicked grin across his grubby face.

He laughed. "Fun game, ain't it? I wonder how fast you can hop back?" He reached into his jacket and her eyes widened when he pulled out a stock whip.

"Guess we'll see now, won't we? I'll give ya twenty seconds head start. Go." He stepped back, allowing the whip to uncoil as he gripped the handle.

Ariel didn't hesitate, and hopped past him, going as fast as she could, hoping to keep a good distance in front of him so he would not whip her. Her heart galloped frantically as she hopped over dry sticks and small shrubs, thankfully keeping her balance as his ridiculous whistling resumed. She held the frightened sob at bay as she continued in the direction she'd come and heard the crack of the stock whip behind her. He was taunting her, cracking the whip repeatedly as she hopped away as quickly as she could. She would not give him the satisfaction of crying out in fright.

"Hop along, little rabbit," he laughed, as she hopped faster, hearing the stock whip crack once more. Only this time, he didn't miss.

The whip whistled near her head, before slashing her flesh. Her scream escaped of its own accord as pain exploded in her shoulder. She stumbled, falling hard against sticks, rocks, and brush. Panting as she went to roll over to keep her eye on the murdering bastard, before he stepped on the small of her back applying pressure and pinning her in place.

Her eyes widened in fear when he wound the whip around her neck to the point of cutting off her airway, when she felt him stick something between her ankles. Then he dragged her onto her knees before he took hold of her elbows and jerked her to her feet.

"Move," he commanded, and shoved her in the back. She realised he'd cut her ankle bindings and wished that her hands had been bound in the front. At least then she could try to grapple the whip away from him, maybe fight and escape.

"Ya know, I've given this some great thought, and I think I'm gonna end ya just like I did that mother of yours," he laughed, interrupting her internal plan to escape. "What do ya think about that, huh?"

"I'm thinking it's incredible that someone as stupid as yourself, has actually gotten away with your crimes for so long." She snapped without thinking of the consequences.

He surprised her by laughing louder, not seeming bothered by her insult whatsoever.

"Ah, a fighter just like she was. I sure am gonna have fun with you. You're gonna experience pain unlike anything you ever have before," he laughed again, jerking on the whip.

She cursed as the whip pressed against her windpipe. Spotting the mine shaft entrance, she silently prayed once more, for some kind of miracle to help her out of this situation.

Wren

"Wren, where's Uncle Steven and Jaxon?" Timmy demanded after finishing his seventh tub of jelly for breakfast.

"Looking for Ariel." She pushed his fringe out of his eyes as he snuggled against her. He hadn't wanted to sleep on the cot and hadn't left her lap since his shower. He'd slept in her arms till they'd gone numb from holding him throughout the early hours of the morning. Lance had kindly offered to hold him whilst she'd gone to the toilet and had an hour sleep beside Hawk. He'd been so thoughtful. Mrs Sommers had been lovely too and had only just left to make a few phone calls.

"Why hasn't Hawk woken up yet?" Timmy grumbled.

"He must need a really big sleep to heal, I guess." Wren sighed.

"Here we go," Lance said walking in the room, holding a drinks tray. "Hot chocolate with marshmallows, a herbal tea and a cappuccino."

"Yum, thanks Lance." Timmy wiggled off Wren's lap to climb up on the bed to sit beside Hawk.

"Thank you," Wren smiled shyly at Lance as he stood next to her, passing Timmy his drink, his gaze steady on her.

"You're welcome," his fingers grazed hers as he passed her a cup. A warm flutter grew in her belly.

Don't blush, she begged herself, but could feel her cheeks grow warm. Glancing at him, she saw the corner of his lip turn upward. *Damnit, oh well...*

"Hey Sebastian," Timmy laughed. "Where have you been?"

Lance raised an eyebrow. "This the friendly ghost?"

Wren had caught him up on most of their experiences since moving into their ancestral home. She nodded, startled when Timmy yelled, "What? Oh *no!*"

"Timmy?" her heart raced as the blood drained from his little face and his eyes filled with tears. *What now?*

"Wren, the bad, dirty man has Ariel! We have to save her!"

Wren stood quickly and would have dropped her hot drink if Lance hadn't reached over and quickly taken it from her.

"What's going on?" he asked.

"Lockwood has Ariel. Timmy," she turned to him. "Ask Sebastian exactly where he has taken her?"

Timmy nodded and tilted his head, listening. Wren anxiously wrung her fingers together, wondering how much more her family had to suffer at the Lockwood's hands.

"Timmy?"

"Stuart's place."

"What?" she was confused. She hadn't known Stuart had lived in Inglewood.

"Sebastian said she's at Stuarts," Timmy shrugged. "Sebastian, wait!" Timmy cried, sliding off the bed and ran out of the room.

"Timmy!" Wren ran after him, and almost cried in relief when she spotted their uncle walking towards her, carrying Timmy in his arms. Jaxon and Stuart right behind him.

"What's going on?" Steven asked as Timmy kept yelling after Sebastian. "Timmy, it's alright. Calm down." Steven rubbed a hand up and down his nephew's back as he looked at Wren.

"Uncle Steven, Jaxon. Sebastian has told Timmy, that Lockwood has Ariel at Stuart's place!" she cried as the three men exchanged a worrying look.

"Do you remember the way?" Stuart asked Jaxon.

"I do."

"Jaxon, Steven, you're back." Ray said, carrying an aromatherapy diffuser. "Any news of Ariel?"

"Yes Ray, and we are leaving right now." Wren heard the urgency in

Jaxon's voice.

Steven hugged Timmy, before passing him towards Wren. "We're going to get your sister back. Just stay here with Hawk, no one leaves this hospital."

Wren nodded as Steven turned to Ray. "Can you please watch over the kids?"

"I'm not going anywhere," she said as the men had already turned away and marched down the corridor.

Wren turned to Lance who had placed his arm around her shoulder, looking down at her with an intense expression. "It's going to be okay."

"Is it?" She whispered, quickly wiping a tear on the top of Timmy's head.

"Come here, mate." Lance reached for Timmy and hefted him on his shoulders. "How about we go and find something delicious from the canteen, which doesn't involve gelatine?"

"How about an egg and bacon roll?" Timmy suggested.

"Perfect. Wren?"

"I don't think I could eat anything."

"Which is why you should, darling." Ray said kindly. "What about a smoothie?" Ray suggested.

"Coming right up," Lance said, before turning and bouncing Timmy up and down as they headed down towards the cafeteria.

"I thought some aromatherapy might help Hawk," Ray said kindly, placing her hand gently on Wren's arm. "And I think it will help you too."

"Thank you." Wren said quietly as the older lady steered her into the room and began setting up the diffuser.

Wren crossed to Hawk's side, and leaned down, dropping her face against his chest. "Wake up, Hawk, I need you." she mumbled into the hospital blanket. "Please wake up." Her tears flowed silently as she hugged her brother hard. When was this nightmare going to be over?

She had all the faith in the world that her uncle and Jaxon would find Ariel, but prayed they would find her in time, before that psycho hurt her. Or worse.

Jaxon

Jaxon dove into the back of the land cruiser, as Steven and Stuart slammed the front doors. Gravel crunched and sprayed under the tyres as Stuart spun the car around and accelerated at a high speed towards the reservoir.

"Jaxon, are you sure you know the exact location?" Stuart asked.

"I do. Drive straight till you hit the next right. We'll have about eight minutes of dirt track, then we'll be on foot for about a kilometre. The bush is dense, but then it opens up. We'll have a clear line straight into the mine."

Steven turned in his seat to meet Jaxon's gaze. "How do you know the timing of how to get there?"

"I've come up here every year that I could, since the day we rescued Stuart," he replied simply.

"Since the day *you* rescued Stuart," Steven said, before Stuart cut them off, relaying the information to his team via the police scanner, then turned the cruiser down the dirt track.

Jaxon held his curse in as Stuart marginally slowed down as he navigated the twisting, narrow road filled with ditches and potholes.

As soon as Stuart reached the end of the road, Jaxon's door was opened, and he was running before the vehicle had completely stopped.

"Jaxon, wait!" Stuart called, as Jaxon jumped over a fallen log and ran at full speed up the steep incline, occasionally slipping on rocks and using his hands to push himself upwards and onwards. Once he reached the top, he steadied himself on strong legs and allowed himself to slide down the hill leaving a trail of dust in his wake. Hitting the bottom, he did not pause, and ran like the devil himself was on his heels.

He would *not* lose Ariel today, come hell or high water!

Ariel

Once they returned to the mine shaft, Lockwood charged ahead and tossed the mattress on the ground before throwing Ariel onto it. Stars burst behind her eyelids as a spring viciously poked into her spine.

He tugged the whip from her throat, as he pulled his filthy woollen jumper over his head.

Her stomach roiled as he reached for his belt buckle, undoing it before drawing down his jeans zipper.

"If you touch me, I'm going to kill you!" she spat.

"Wrong, girlie," he said, before sitting on her stomach. "First, I'm going to gut you like a fish, then I'm going to have my way with your dead corpse. More enjoyable that way." He laughed when he saw the horrified expression on her face.

"You belong in *hell*," she hissed.

"Is that so, huh? Well, before I get there, I'm gonna enjoy myself some more." He reached for something in his back pocket before holding up a rusty pocketknife.

"I would have used the nice sharp one I used on ya brother, but I couldn't get to it in time. So, this will have to do. Mind you, it's gonna hurt more but the bitch's daughter deserves that, don't ya?" he leered down at her.

"I hope she gave you hell in the end," Ariel whispered.

"Oh yeah, she did." He nodded, wearing a serious expression. "The bitch broke me ankle," he sneered, before shaking his head. "And do ya wanna know what the last thing she said to me was?"

She stared hatefully at him, gritting her teeth. She wouldn't ask him a *damn* thing.

"She kept screaming out her babies' names." He leaned closer, tapping the knife against her breast with each word he uttered. "*Ariel, Hawk,*

Wren, Timmy…I love you my babies…Mama loves you…" His lip curled. "She kept yelling your names over and over again, like some kinda mantra was gonna save her. Funny thing was, even after I gutted her, when she was bleedin out, she didn't stop saying your names till her eyes went all dead. That must be true love, huh?"

"You'll never know," she said, before whispering, "Hawk, Wren, Timmy, Steven, Liv, Jaxon… Hawk, Wren, Timmy, Steven, Liv, Jaxon."

"Shut up, bitch!" he yelled in her face, running the blade along her tee shirt, before ripping it open.

"Hawk, Wren, Timmy, Steven, Liv, Jaxon," she raised her voice as he slapped her hard. She only yelled louder, tears filling her eyes as she thought of her loved ones.

"Hawk, Wren, Timmy, Steven, Liv, Jaxon," she screamed, closing her eyes. "Hawk, Wren, Timmy, Steven, Liv, Jaxon," she continued, visualising their sweet faces and the love she felt for each of them; desperately trying to block out the demented man on top of her.

The knife pressing against her windpipe had her eyes flashing open, but she continued calling out her loved one's names.

Lockwood leaned down, the knife painfully cutting into her skin, only allowing her to whisper their names, and she continued to do so, watching as he gripped the knife in both hands, raising it above his head.

Mama, Grandma, Timmy… I'll see you soon…

She watched wide eyed, as he slammed the knife towards her chest as she continued repeating the names that would carry her into the next life, wishing his wasn't the last face she'd ever see.

Waiting for the pain to strike her – for the end to come… she was struck speechless as the knife froze an inch above her chest.

"What in blazers?" Lockwood frowned, trying to pull the knife back to stab at her again.

Ariel watched as he appeared to be struggling with an unseen force. The knife swept left, then right, then flew out of Lockwood's hands and across the mine, hitting the stoned wall and dropping to the ground.

"Who needs a knife to finish what needs to be done!" he yelled before wrapping his hands around Ariel's neck and tightened his fingers, squeezing the life out of her.

Ariel's vision blurred as she kicked her legs, desperately trying to dislodge him.

I must be dying… she had to be, because she could clearly see a small figure of a little boy in a torn shirt, wearing braces and a tattered miners cap, standing beside the mattress. If she could see the dead, then surely, she must be joining them?

Screen shot images flashed before her eyes as her legs lost all mobility, and the air left her lungs. Lockwood released his fingers and her head lolled towards the entrance of the mine shaft; the light beckoned her forward before the shadowed figure filled the mine's mouth, blocking her departure.

Has the devil come for me? Or an Angel?

"Get away from her you *filthy* bastard!" Devil or Angel, his voice had her convinced she'd follow him anywhere.

"William's, you snivelling git," Lockwood stood, leaving her dead body as he faced the newcomer.

William's?… that sounded familiar…

"It's clear to see you've never evolved from the foul thing you are." The Devil-Angel sneered."

"Like your opinion matters," Lockwood scoffed.

"It should. I'm about to take you down once and for all."

Lockwood laughed. "I'd like to see you try."

The Devil-Angel walked forward, casually rolling up the sleeves of his shirt as if he had all the time in the world. She wanted to shout a warning as Lockwood reached for the whip and cracked it towards the most handsome face she'd ever seen in her life, but she didn't need to be concerned. As the whip reached the Devil-Angel, he allowed it to coil around his muscled bicep, before dragging Lockwood towards him, then punched him in the face. The sickening crack of bone was a fair indication that Lockwood's nose was broken. He stumbled back, blood pouring into his mouth before he turned and lunged for the knife.

Ariel floated above her body, seeing everything that was happening around her, and watched the Devil-Angel flex his fingers after punching Lockwood with such ferocity. She wanted to cheer, but could feel the blood leave her face; if that were even possible. Lockwood ran straight towards the Devil-Angel as he screamed in rage, knife raised.

The Devil-Angel danced out of the madman's way, but the madman was cunning, and anticipated the move, thrusting the knife behind him as he twisted to catch the Devil-Angel in the back, under the rib cage.

No! Ariel screamed, only she couldn't hear herself. No one could. Her heart ached as she watched him crumble to the ground, close to her lifeless body. It wasn't fair!

Two more men ran into the mine shaft, both ducking through the entrance before standing tall, one had a gun aimed at Lockwood.

"Freeze, but trust me, I won't mind if you don't."

A familiar chuckle reached her ears, and her heart lightened. *Uncle Steven...*

"Welcome home, kid," Lockwood sneered at Stuart. "Remember how much fun you had when you lived here? I still dream about all the joy you used to give me."

Stuart's featured tightened, as he manoeuvred the safety switch off. "Yeah, I bet."

"Is that all you've got? I'm sure after all these years you'd want some revenge?"

"I'm getting it right now, taking you in alive so you can spend the rest of your *miserable* life in prison, where I know the worst of the worst are kept. But in this case, they'll be my allies, because they *detest* the likes of you. You won't be killed, but you *will* suffer every day for the rest of your useless life." He aimed the gun right at Lockwood's chest, when Steven's voice rang true.

"Stuart, no… you'll bring the mine down."

"Do you trust me, Harper?" Stuart asked, hand steady.

"Technically… sure…" Steven held his hands up as if to calm everyone in the mine. His eyes locked on the Devil-Angel. "Jaxon?"

"I'm okay."

Her heart stuttered. She'd been so focused on the other men she hadn't noticed that the Devil-Angel had made his way across to her body, and was holding her in his arms, his cheek resting on the top of her head, tears falling silently down his face.

This *really* wasn't fair!

"Is she?" Steven's voice caught.

Jaxon didn't answer as Lockwood stepped back, deeper towards the dark shaft of the mine.

"One more step Lockwood, and you're done." Stuart spat.

"And so too, will you be," Lockwood laughed as he bolted towards the black hole that disappeared into nothingness.

"Stuart, *no!*" Steven yelled, as Jaxon tucked Ariel under his body, as if to protect her if the mine collapsed. The click of the gun exploded around them as a bullet flew in the air, sailing into the darkness towards the space where Lockwood had disappeared. Only Ariel noticed it wasn't a bullet but looked more like a dart.

That's weird…

It sure is. The little boy agreed, floating with her.

Sebastian?

Yeah, it's me.

She didn't know why she felt like crying.

It's okay, he said as if he could read her mind. *We've all been through so much together.*

We have, she smiled. *Thank you for taking care of Timmy for me…*

Timmy is my best friend.

Do you know where he is?

The little boy nodded.

Can you tell me?

He shook his head. *Not yet, it's not your time.*

What do you mean?

It's time for you to go.

But I need to find Timmy first, please. Tell me where to find him! She cried.

He simply smiled at her, then floated towards her and touched her cheek gently as he whispered, *I'll always be his friend. I'll always look out for him, no matter what. Goodbye Ariel.*

Sebastian, wait! I need Timmy. Timmy! she cried in the dark void. She sobbed as everything disappeared around her, and she could feel herself fading. This could *not* be the end. Surely?

Timmy, she cried… "Timmy, please don't leave me." She cried again, crying as if the world was ending. She could feel wet tears trail down her cheeks, and a calm voice whisper against her ear.

"Ariel, Ariel, wake up… wake up, love. Timmy is okay. He's all right. He's waiting for you at the hospital with Hawk and Wren." Smooth fingers wiped her tears as sweet lips brushed across her cheek. A delicious scent wrapped around her.

"Shh, everything's going to be all right." That voice broke, desperate to reassure her.

She frowned, releasing one more sob as her eyes fluttered open, to gaze upon the most beautiful face she'd ever seen in her life. She felt so discombobulated.

"Jaxon is it really you?" she whispered, grateful that her hands had been released from their bindings so that she could reach for him.

"It is love."

She cried then, harder than before as he pulled her into his arms, holding her closer than she'd ever been held. She remembered he'd been injured. Reaching behind him, her fingers swept along where she'd seen Lockwood stab him in the back, only to feel a hard vest. There was no blood. She looked up at him. "You're okay?"

"I am," he dropped a kiss upon her lips before he stood, pulling her up. He removed his shirt and placed it around her shoulder, buttoning it up to cover her exposed bra under her ripped tee shirt.

"Thank you," she said, as a whirling sound filled the shaft, scattering leaves.

"That'll be the helicopter," Stuart said, walking forward before disappearing into the darkness, returning moments later, dragging Lockwood out by his leg.

"I'm impressed, and grateful it was just a tranquiliser gun," Steven chuckled.

Stuart dropped Lockwood near the mouth of the shaft and pulled out his radio, giving a few commands as Steven walked across to Ariel.

"Excuse me, mate," he said to Jaxon, before reaching for his niece, crushing her to him. "I think we've had enough excitement to last a lifetime."

Ariel sighed against her uncle's chest, wishing she could sleep for a week. "I need to see Timmy and the twins."

"Of course love."

Turning to leave, three uniformed men filled the entrance, nodding to Stuart before they grabbed and bound Lockwood, then dragged him out of their sight.

Stuart turned to Ariel. "You're a brave young woman."

"Not really," Ariel shrugged, before addressing them all. "How did you know where I was?"

"Timmy, with the help of his pal, Sebastian." Stuart answered.

Ariel smiled. "Of course."

"You don't seem surprised." Jaxon raised an eyebrow.

She shook her head, before saying, "Lockwood told me he'd killed Timmy.

"Bastard," Steven cursed.

"Coward," Jaxon added.

"He always was," Stuart said softly. "Timmy is one of the lucky ones."

They turned towards him. None of them could surmise the hell he'd endured in the Lockwood's clutches as a young boy. Ariel was grateful that he'd had some kind of vengeance. "Thanks for coming," she said to him.

"You're welcome," he offered her a small smile.

"Let's get out of here." Jaxon said, reaching for her hand and tucking her under his arm as they exited the mine.

The early afternoon sun shone as it had when she'd been trying to escape Lockwood, yet now it held a sweet note of peaceful days to come. She was a true believer in manifesting a good outcome, and right now was the perfect time to manifest some peace for all of her babies.

The helicopter sent a tornado of wind as it rose higher, scattering leaves and dust bunnies before it ascended then departed. Watching it disappear from view, taking the evil killer with it, she started to relax. All her siblings were together and waiting for her, and this moment moving forward, was the start of the rest of their lives. She was going to do everything in her power to make sure theirs was the best it could be.

Chapter Thirty-One
Ariel

A fter Steven had phoned Ray to check on the kids, he had convinced Ariel to get cleaned up before seeing them. She agreed after a closer inspection of herself and felt much better after a hot shower. Quickly searching through her uncle's draws, she found one of Liv's cotton sundresses and pulled it over her head before running downstairs, raking her fingers through her hair, pulling it up into a high ponytail.

Jaxon was waiting for her in the café and held out his hand.

"You look beautiful as always," he said gently as he led her out to the running car where Steven was waiting for them. He opened the car door, and slid in the back seat after her, putting his arm around her shoulder.

"Better?" Steven asked as he pulled off from the kerb.

"Everything will be better as soon as I see my kids," she said, leaning into Jaxon, grateful for the short trip to the hospital. "Here we go," Steven said, parking the car.

Ariel's heart pounded as they made their way inside, and she followed Steven along the corridor and into the room where her siblings were.

Tears automatically filled her eyes seeing Timmy laying next to Hawk, reading him a story. Wren's head was resting against Lance's chest, his arm around her shoulders. Ray was asleep in the chair opposite them.

"Hello Timmy, love," she whispered.

His precious dark gaze lifted to hers. He threw the book down and bolted upright yelling, "Ariel! You're back." He scampered along the bed, and stood at the end, launching himself into her waiting arms.

They were both laughing, but Ariel's laughter soon turned to tears.

"Why are you crying Ariel?" Timmy frowned.

"Because I'm so happy to see you, to see you all," she hugged his little body tight and took a deep breath, before leaning back to smile at him. "How are you my darling boy?"

"I'm fine. But a nurse told Wren I've got to see a trauma Budapest or something."

"Trauma therapist," Wren said, standing and reached for Ariel. "Are you okay?"

"Of course sweetie. How are you?" she juggled Timmy on her hip so she could cup Wren's pretty face, checking she was in fact, okay.

"I think we could all benefit from some post trauma therapy." She smiled, shrugging.

"We'll do whatever it takes, love. Whatever you all need." Ariel nodded, pulling Wren against her.

Ray stood, and said softly, "It's good to see you, Ariel."

"You too Ray, thank you so much for staying with the kids."

"Of course. Now that you're here, I'll pop off home."

Ariel smiled. "I hope you get some decent sleep."

"No doubt. Let me know if you need anything,"

"Thanks Ray." Jaxon said.

As Ray headed out, Ariel's gaze fell on Hawk. Her sweet, handsome brother. His features paler than ever in the stark hospital room; his black hair a contrasting slash across his face and pillow.

Kissing both Wren, then Timmy, she smiled as Jaxon scooped Timmy

370

from her, and Lance took Wren's hand. She placed her hand on Hawk's foot and lightly massaged her way up his body, before taking his hand in hers. Sitting beside him, she pushed his silky fringe away from his eyes, before dropping a kiss against his forehead.

"Hey beautiful boy, it's time to wake up, don't you think?" she whispered, noticing his eyes moving under his lids. "We've got another adventure ahead of us, and we need your help to make it happen."

"What adventure," Timmy chirped.

"Well, we need to find a new home, of course." Ariel answered keeping her eyes on Hawk's face.

"You can stay at mine as long as you like," Steven said.

"How's Liv?" Ariel asked.

"Turn around and see for yourself," her friends sweet voice retorted.

Ariel slipped off the bed and quickly walked towards her friend who had nice colouring and was looking healthy. "Thank god you're alright, Liv." She hugged her lifelong friend hard, which Liv returned in earnest.

"Thank god we *all* are," Liv said.

"Truer words were never spoken," Steven said.

"I've been discharged," Liv said, keeping her arm around Ariel's waist as she met Steven's gaze. "I'd really like to go home."

"Me too," Timmy said.

"I tell you what," Steven said, nodding to Wren and Lance. "Let's head out and leave Ariel with Hawk. I'll fix my famous lasagne and garlic bread, and we can snuggle in and watch movies for the rest of the afternoon. Sound good?"

Wren met Lance's gaze. "You don't have to if you…"

"Oh, I want to," he cut her off. "Thanks," he smiled at Steven.

"Sorted." Steven said, before asking Ariel. "Is that fine with you, love?"

Ariel nodded. "Thank you, Uncle Steven." She felt relieved that Timmy and Wren would have a familiar roof over their head.

After everyone kissed and hugged her goodbye, Ariel listened to

Timmy's excited voice trail down the corridor before disappearing completely. She sighed, turning back to Hawk, and jumped, before laughing, when Jaxon's hand on her back startled her.

"Sorry," he dropped a kiss on top of her head, before pouring her a glass of water from the bedside table. "Here, I'm going to get us some food. Do you want a hot drink?"

"No, thanks. Sandwiches would be great though."

"Coming up," he smiled, before turning towards the door.

"Jaxon?"

His gaze met hers. "Yes?"

"I… I."

He smiled. "Take your time."

She blew out a breath, pushing a silky strand off her neck. "Thank you." she managed, thinking now wasn't the time to declare how much she loved him.

"You're welcome," he smiled. "I'll be back in a jiff." She watched the door close behind him, then sat beside Hawk again, and picked up his hand.

"Hawk Harper, my darling brother. I can't do any of this without you. I need you to wake up, honey." Feeling exhausted after seeing that all her loved ones were indeed okay, she lay beside Hawk, placing her arm around his waist, and allowed herself to close her eyes and relax. "Please, just wake up," she whispered, like a wish, then fell asleep almost instantly.

Hawk

Hawk knew the exact moment that Travis had left his body. He'd felt the painful exit as the female entity had manipulated Travis out of him. She wasn't gentle, and no matter how much Travis had begged and pleaded, she only made his exit back to the darkness all the more painful. She had told Hawk that Travis didn't deserve to go into any shade of light. That his destiny was everything he deserved, and more. Although Hawk was grateful for the entity's help, he was terrified too. There was something malignant about her.

He looked upon the form of Travis Lockwood, the bastard who had stolen *him* from his family, *hurt* his family. Travis was struggling to get back into Hawk's body, but he was trapped in the woman's grip as if he were nothing more than a moth.

"Who are you?" Hawk asked the woman, not really expecting a reply.

"*I'm not sure who I am now… but once, I was Helen Williams,*" she'd answered. "*And I'm here to help you and my son.*" She nodded toward Jaxon who hadn't moved since the beam had knocked him out.

Hawk was fearful that they'd burn to death, after everything else he'd endured, and couldn't imagine how a *ghost* could help them. She had stepped towards Jaxon, and leaned down to effortlessly move the beam that was pinning them down. She looked past him, towards the doorway and nodded.

He turned his head, and gasped when a white light floated towards them. As much as he wanted to see who, or what the light was, it became so blinding he had to squeeze his eyes shut. He felt the light surround them, cocooning them in its orbit.

"*Be well, Hawk, all will be well,*" a soft voice echoed around him.

He risked a peek through the tiny slit in his eyelids but had to slam them shut again.

"*You are cleansed, you are whole. Sleep now, and wake when you've rested.*"

"Who are you?" he whispered.

The only other voice he heard, before blackness swallowed him whole, was Travis Lockwood screaming, "I'm sorry Hawk! I'm really sorry!"

Hawk didn't move when he fully woke. He wanted to bask in the feeling, of *feeling*. To *feel* refreshed and rested. To *feel* the air going in and out of *his* lungs. The sheets beneath his rested body. The warm, solid body beside him. Tears slipped from his closed lids, and he could *feel* them trailing down his flesh. He couldn't help the laugh that slipped from his lips. That *felt* amazing too! Soon his laughter turned to anguished sobbing, as everything that Travis Lockwood had made him do to his family, and to himself, flashed like a movie beneath his closed lids.

"Hawk, it's okay baby, shh, it's okay…" Ariel soothed, sliding her hands up his chest, along his neck to cup his face, wiping his tears gently. "Everything is going to be okay sweetheart, let it out. Let it all out," she whispered lovingly, kissing his brow and allowing him to cry himself dry.

"Ariel," he whispered, after what seemed like a lifetime saying his sister's name, putting his arms around her. "It wasn't me, none of it. It wasn't me. I'm sorry…"

"Shh, Hawk. It's okay. You don't have apologize for a single thing. We know it wasn't you. We know what happened."

"I don't ever want to say his name again," Hawk whispered.

"And we never shall," she declared, wrapping her arms tighter around him. "I've got you. I've got you baby."

"Jaxon saved me," Hawk whispered.

"I know baby."

"Jaxon's mum, and something else, saved us." He watched her eyes widen, before she nodded slowly.

"What about Timmy?"

"He's safe and sound, love. We all are." Ariel assured him.

Hawk cried in relief, then sobbed himself to sleep.

Chapter Thirty-Two

Jaxon

J axon stood on the back deck watching Ariel and Timmy walk
around his back yard. The chickens clucked in the old coop, which
Hawk had patched up and Wren had decorated with metal sunflowers and windmills from the co-op. It was a perfect day for a barbeque,
and today he'd invited all their friends to join them in thanks for their
help during the crisis.

He was relieved that the interviews and conversations regarding
the 'Lockwood' name was behind them. He'd spent the last fortnight
corresponding with Stuart, keeping Steven updated on Lockwood's
imprisonment. They discussed him only when Ariel and the kids weren't
around.

He grinned, hearing Timmy laugh and watched him chasing a butterfly. Man, the kid was *so* resilient.

"Hey Jaxon, is Paul here yet?" Timmy asked.

"No mate, but any minute now." His gaze swept towards Ariel, and smiled as she headed towards him, past the rows of lavender bushes and up the stairs of the deck. She'd caught up on sleep; the dark grooves beneath her eyes had completely disappeared. He'd never seen her looking more beautiful. The off the shoulder black sundress covered in large, red poppies made her look like a sultry gypsy.

"Hello," he smiled down at her as she stood a foot away, looking up at him. Her fiery locks dancing the breeze.

"Hello yourself," she grinned. "Something smells good."

"All the meat is just about done, and Wren and Hawk have finished up the salads and desserts with Liv." He reached out, slipping his arms around her waist, drawing her against him. "Although, I think I've got the most morish dessert right in front of me."

"I was thinking the same thing," she returned, tilting her head back as she offered him her lips.

"Mm, I don't mind an appetiser, thank you," he said huskily as her arms wound round his neck. His hands slid to her hips pulling her flush against him. He tried not to chuckle in satisfaction as her eyes darkened the closer his lips drew towards hers. He kissed the corner of her pretty mouth, then the other, before collecting her lips in a smooth, sensual kiss. Consumed instantly by her sweet, floral scent as it drifted around him. He knew he'd never get enough of her, even if he was with her for the rest of his life.

Her soft lips parted beneath his as she moaned in pleasure, granting him deeper access, as his tongue swept inside her mouth, teasing her gently, showing her with his tongue, what he wanted to do to her all over.

"My god," she panted. "Stop." But continued kissing him.

He did chuckle then, pulling back to gaze upon her gorgeous face. "I love you," he said simply, watching for her reaction.

She stared up into his eyes, before smiling slowly. "I know."

"Do you now?" he raised an eyebrow, watching her cheeks pinken.

She bit her lip, looking almost shy for a moment, before her bright smile resumed.

"I've loved you for a while now, myself," she returned.

"Have you?"

"I have."

"Well, isn't this cosy," Steven said from behind them.

Jaxon turned with Ariel in his arms, glad to see a wide smile brightening Steven's face.

"Guess I'll be the authority figure around here after all, *nephew-in-law*," he chuckled, lightly punching Jaxon's arm.

Ariel laughed. "Uncle Steven, you've always had the best sense of humour."

"True." Steven smiled at Ariel. "I just came out to tell you that the guests are arriving."

"Thanks mate," Jaxon nodded, before calling, "Timmy, Paul's here."

"Yeah!" Timmy yelled, racing through the orchard, past the lavish gardens and up the lavender path and past them to get to his mate.

Jaxon returned his gaze to Ariel's and was shocked to see her eyes filled with tears. "Ariel?" he whispered, cupping her cheek.

She shook her head. "It's okay, I'm just, so happy, despite it all." She leaned her cheek into his palm.

"Because of it all," he whispered, wrapping his arms around her and holding her close. He dropped his face into her neck, breathing her in.

"Yeah, because we're all okay. For that I'll be eternally grateful to whoever it was, watching over us."

He rocked her gently as the sound of laughter and excited conversations flowed behind them, drawing closer. Kissing the top of her head he offered his hand which she took, gripping tightly wearing a breathtaking smile.

"Let's greet our guests," he said.

"Yes sir, Mr Williams," she grinned up at him before they turned, and were surrounded by a sea of friendly faces filled with love and kindness.

Wren

A few hours later as some of the guests were leaving, Wren trailed up the stairs of Jaxon's house, impressed and relaxed at every turn. His house was filled with a calm she hadn't felt at her Grandparent's house. Light filtered in through every window where gardens brightly framed the view to the yard. It felt safe. Sitting on the top step, she sighed, sipping her raspberry lemonade as she heard Hawk and Lance's laughter floating down from above her.

She smiled, loving that her twin was fully himself again. She'd been watching him like a, well, like a Hawk the past fortnight since he'd woken, worried whenever she saw him wearing a serious expression or looking guilt-ridden. It broke her heart thinking about everything he must have endured, being a prisoner of his own mind in his own body.

He'd been attending sessions with a therapist but seemed to enjoy his daily chats with Reverend Matthews more. The kind man had left earlier, after sharing a few laughs with Ariel and Jaxon, before having a private conversation with Hawk in Jaxon's study. Hawk always seemed so relaxed after his chats with the Reverend.

"Hey, you," Lance whispered against her ear, making her squeal in fright, before she laughed, shaking her head.

"Hey yourself," she smirked as he sat beside her.

"What are you doing all alone?"

"Just having some quiet time. Wondering where we're going to live."

"I'm sorry you lost all your things," his dark features turned down.

"Please, don't be. They're just things. My family is all that really matters to me. Most things can be replaced at the Op shop, or Kmart." She shrugged.

He laughed, shaking his head.

"What?"

"You. You'd have to be the coolest girl I've ever met."

"Well, this town is small."

"Huh, funny. You know our high school is pretty big, don't you."

"Well, sure, but compared to Melbourne high schools…"

"Don't try to diminish the compliment, Wren." He bumped his broad shoulder gently against hers.

She smiled, "Thank you. I think you're the sweetest guy I've ever met."

He grinned. "Now *that* is a compliment!"

She leaned against him, enjoying being close to him.

"Do you want to go horse riding with my cousin, Hannah, and me tomorrow?" he asked.

"Sure," she nodded, as footsteps sounded behind them.

Lance stood, and Hawk sat beside her, placing his arm around her shoulder. She looked up at Lance as he started down the stairs.

"I'll see you both tomorrow, nine a.m."

"You've got it." Hawk agreed. "Thanks mate."

"No worries. Bye Wren."

"Goodbye Lance," she smiled, as he raced the rest of the way down the stairs and disappeared from their view.

They sat for a few minutes in comfortable silence as Hawk dropped his cheek down to rest upon Wren's head.

"You okay?" she asked.

"Yep."

She sighed loudly, feeling tears well.

He raised his head looking directly into her eyes. "What is it?"

She shrugged, wiping a fingertip under her eye, collecting the tear that almost fell.

"Wren, tell me." he begged quietly.

"I'm worried about you. About Timmy and Ariel! We've got no place to live. We've lost all of Ariel's art in the fire, and I know she's being brave because of us! But she had so many commissioned works finished

Hawk… and she's lost them all."

"She was insured Wren, which has to be some consolation?"

"It's not," Wren whispered. "I know how hard she's worked. How tired she was before all of this started, and I don't know how to look after her!" Wren cried, before actually breaking down, covering her face with her hands, crying in earnest.

"I might be able to help out with that," a calm voice said from below.

Wren looked through her fingers to see Jaxon standing a few steps below them, with Timmy on his back.

"Do you mind if we have a quick chat in the upstairs library?" He asked.

Hawk stood, reaching for her hand, which she gave him, allowing him to pull her up.

"Sure," Hawk answered for them both.

Jaxon nodded towards the left. "Fourth door down the hall."

How big is this house? She allowed Hawk to pull her in that direction as Jaxon and Timmy followed behind.

As Hawk opened the door, Wren gasped in surprise at the room before her. Letting go of Hawk's hand, she ran into the middle of the room, turning in a circle to take the majestic views of the room in. Floor to ceiling bookshelves lined the walls and a massive round window faced the back of the house and its glorious garden views. Comfortable seating was positioned in appropriate spaces with small coffee tables filled with books and candles. An impressive telescope was on a platform leading to the domes glass ceiling for star gazing.

"Oh, my stars," Wren whispered.

"I'd say," Hawk agreed as Timmy ran up the winding stairs to reach the telescope.

"Exactly," Jaxon smiled as he pushed his hands into his pockets and strolled to the far wall, leaning casually against a narrow desk as he watched Timmy squint through the large, golden telescope.

Wren looked across at Jaxon as he watched Timmy. He was an extremely handsome man, who seemed to have such a sweet, sensitive side. He turned his gaze to her in that moment, and she forced herself not to look away.

He smiled and pushed himself away from the desk and asked gently, "Timmy, would you mind coming down here for a moment?" He sat on a three-seater, brown leather Chesterfield.

"Sure," Timmy yelled, racing back down the staircase before launching himself on Jaxon's lap. Wren sat opposite Jaxon, and Hawk joined her. She loved this room, and wished she could stay here forever.

"What's up?" Hawk asked.

Jaxon grinned, obviously appreciating Hawk's forth righteousness.

"I know you've all been through a great deal, and I want you to know how incredibly brave and strong I think you all are." He said, meeting Timmy, then Hawk's and Wren's gazes. "I think you're amazing young people, and I'm always going to be here for you, no matter what." He paused, allowing them time for his words to infiltrate, before continuing. "I also want you to know, it's not just your sister whom I love."

Silence ensued as Wren felt the impact of his words. She met Hawks gaze, who raised an eyebrow, grinning slightly.

Timmy tapped Jaxon's knee. "Mr Williams, are you saying that you love us?"

"I am, Timmy. That is exactly what I'm saying. And I'm also asking you all if you would like to live here with me? I thought I'd ask you all first before I ask Ariel. I don't want you to feel forced to live anywhere you don't want to."

Wren felt tears threaten again. The town hall clock across the road chimed, but this time the chime didn't send uneasy goosebumps across her flesh. It soothed her, or was it the comfort of Jaxon's house? To live here where the air felt light, where the man who lived here had been nothing but kind, patient and supportive to them all. A man who made her beautiful sister sparkle all the more brightly.

"Yes, please," she whispered through her tears.

"Hell yes," Hawk answered, standing.

"Oh Yippee!" Timmy yelled, as Jaxon swooped him up and walked towards Wren and Hawk. Hawk stood, wrapping his arms around Jaxon and Timmy, and Wren finally stood, meeting Jaxon's gaze as tears streamed down her face. He placed his arm around her shoulders as she sobbed in relief, and happiness.

Chapter Thirty-Three
Ariel

"Ray, I can't thank you enough for everything you've done for us."

"Oh please, Ariel. It's nothing."

"No, it's not nothing, trust me. I feel as if I've made another friend."

"As do I," Ray smiled warmly.

Ariel hugged Ray as she went to leave and was thrilled when the Ray hugged her warmly in return.

"Bye," she smiled.

"I'll see you in your next art class." Ray grinned, before heading out to her car.

"Wow, you are one popular girl today," Liv said, sliding her arm around Ariel's waist, holding a vodka in her other hand.

"Yeah well, I missed my chance in high school, so I guess I'm making up for it now."

"Huh, funny too."

"No doubt," Ariel winked, taking Liv's drink and sipping it.

"Sweetheart," Steven called from behind them.

"Yes," they both answered as they turned around, laughing.

"Sorry, my mistake," Steven grinned, "I meant, *sweethearts*, has anyone seen Jaxon?"

"He went upstairs with Timmy." Liv answered.

"Okay, I was just wondering if you wanted to call it an afternoon, or if you wanted us to hang around a bit?"

"Oh I'd love a dip in the pool," Liv begged.

Ariel chuckled. "Please, dive in. I'll check on Jaxon, but I'm sure he wouldn't mind us hanging around for a bit?"

"Of course not," Steven said, as Liv laughed, running in the direction of the pool.

"I'll start the clean-up." He fiddled with his phone before a stream of classics from the eighties burst through the blue tooth speaker. He grinned at Ariel. "Can't start cleaning without the right gear."

"Uncle Steven, I love you so much." Ariel grinned, hugging him.

"And I love you more than you can even imagine," he said softly, wrapping his arms around her. "I'm so proud of you." He kissed the top of her head.

She smiled up at him. "Would you still be proud if I asked you to make me a double vodka?"

He laughed, shaking his head. "After what you've been through, I'm proud that you haven't touched ice yet."

"Uncle Steven!" She laughed, shoving him. "Extra ice, thanks."

He saluted as she started walking upstairs. "Yes Ma'am."

She shook her head, feeling happier in that moment than she could remember. "Don't you ever leave me," she called.

"Not for a long time, baby-girl," he returned just as smoothly. "I made a promise to your mother."

She paused, eight steps up the staircase. "What did you promise her?"

He smiled up at her. "To always remind you that you are loved always,

beyond your comprehension." He grinned, pointing to the music…
"*Don't you, forget about me….*"

Ariel grabbed her chest, beaming at him as tears filled her eyes, as the
Breakfast Club movie soundtrack belted out one of her favourites.

"Good one, Uncle Steven."

"Sparrow loved this one too," he grinned.

"No doubt," she smiled, before turning to head upstairs as the lyrics
followed her, comforting her as she imagined her mother singing.

'*Tell me your troubles and doubts.*

Giving me everything inside and out and

Love's strange, so real in the dark

Think of the tender things that we were working on.

Slow change may pull us apart.

When the light gets into your heart, baby…'

The lyrics faded as she opened the library door, closing it quietly
behind her as she looked upon the scene before her. All her babies were
in Jaxon's arms. Wren was sobbing as she clutched at the handsome man,
that she felt she couldn't live without. No. Did *not* want to live without.

Hawk's head was dropped forward onto Jaxon's chest, and Timmy
had his face buried in Jaxon's neck, as their arms were all bound around
each other. What was going on?

"Hello, my loves," she said quietly, hoping not to startle them.

Jaxon raised his head, his deep caramel gaze penetrating hers. She
was startled to see tears glistening in the depths of his beautiful eyes. His
gentle smile relieved her as he nodded, letting her know all was well.

"Hey, beautiful, want to join us?" he asked.

Wren and Hawk looked towards her then, and her heart hurt seeing
the twin's tears.

"Is everything okay?" she asked hesitantly.

"It will be, if you'll just say yes," Wren smiled through her tears.

She wanted to say yes, to anything that would stop Wren's tears.

"Yes to what?" She asked as she reached them, placing her hand on Hawk's and Wren's backs, feeling their warmth through their thin summer layers.

"Yes to all of us living here with Jaxon, as a family," Hawk said.

Ariel raised her eyebrow as she met Jaxon's dreamy caramel eyes. "Is that so?"

"It is, beautiful girl of mine," he replied simply.

"Ariel, I can look at the stars at night, and wish Mama happy dreams every time I see her star!" Timmy beamed.

Ariel's heart lurched, and she felt the overwhelming urge to cry. *Again.*

"This has to stop," she stated firmly, watching their four faces frown as one.

She shook her head, laughing. "Sorry, that came out wrong. I mean, me wanting to cry every time I see anyone of you looking remotely sad." She shrugged.

"We're not sad," Wren said. "Just say yes, please Ariel."

"My heart can't take it anymore. Yes, to anything you all want. Yes, to us all living together." She laughed.

Hawk sighed in relief and Jaxon beamed at her. "Good decision, sweetheart," he said.

"Jaxon, you are pure kindness," she said. "I'll never be able to thank you enough for sharing your gorgeous home with us all."

"Trust me, sweetheart, the pleasure is all mine."

"Yay!" Timmy cried, clapping his hands in excitement. "We're going to live with Mr Williams! Paul's gonna love it!" He laughed.

Ariel met Jaxon's gaze as they shared a knowing smile, as Wren threw her arms around Ariel.

"Thank you, Ariel."

"No. Thank you." She squeezed Wren, before cupping Hawk's chin. "I'm so proud of you. All of you." She ruffled Timmy's hair. "Now, who wants to join Liv in the pool?"

"I'm in!" Hawk laughed, high fiving Jaxon, grabbing Timmy then kissing Ariel, "Come on Wren, let's go!"

Wren laughed as she ran out of the room with her brothers, leaving Ariel and Jaxon alone.

"Living together, huh?" she said, turning to face him.

"Mhm." He watched her, unblinkingly.

In this room, filled with books, shadows and ambience, she could imagine them curling up having many detailed and deep conversations. This home was filled with endless possibilities.

"Jaxon, are you sure?"

"I would never have asked the children first, if I wasn't," he replied smoothly, watching her in that very sexy teacher's stance that he effortlessly held.

Her heartbeat quickened as he studied her silently, as if she were something tasty to eat. She watched the way the sun filtered through the skylight, warming the dark honey tones in his hair. His dark caramel gaze tracing her every move.

"What is it that you want?" he asked quietly. "Really want?"

She bit her lip, considering her reply, before answering. "I want my kids to be happy, to be safe, to *feel* safe. I want them to know that no matter what, I will always be here for them."

"I want that too," he said.

She smiled softly. "And that's partly why I love you, because you want that for them, no matter what's between us."

"That's true," he said. "But I want you to be happy too. I need you to be happy."

She stepped closer to him. "Jaxon Williams, I don't think I've ever met such a caring, deep, selfless man in all my life…"

"Don't let Steven hear you say that." he smiled.

She laughed softly as she took his hands, lifting them to her lips. "Are you certain? I mean, things are bound to get complicated as we dive a bit deeper with the kids' therapy after all that's happened?"

"Have you not been paying attention Miss Harper?" He slid his hand around her waist, gently pulling her against him. "Deep, is right up my alley."

"Is it?" She smiled, butterflies scattering in her stomach.

"You know it is. Just be grateful I'm not asking you to marry me this week."

"What?" She paled.

He laughed. "Don't worry, I'll give you another month to think about it," he said, sliding his other hand along her waist, before pressing the small of her back, bringing her closer to him.

She bit her lip to try to stop herself smiling. *My god he is cute!*

"What?" He asked, before brushing his lips across hers.

"Can I hand in my permission slip early?" She whispered, before running her tongue along his bottom lip.

"Permission slip?" He sounded confused, as if it were hard to focus on their conversation as she kissed him.

"Mhm," she said, running her fingers through his hair, loving the sigh that escaped his lips.

"My permission slip to attend our wedding?"

He pulled back, eyes seeming unfocused as he watched her tongue trace her bottom lip. "I beg your pardon?"

"You heard me," she grinned.

"Please repeat what you said, Miss Harper."

She laughed. "Would you like my permission slip earlier, to attend *our* wedding, Mr Williams?"

He stilled, gazing into her eyes, before asking, "Do you really mean that?"

"Would I lie to you?" She laughed, loving the way his gorgeous lips curved upwards.

"Well, well, well Miss Harper. I believe you're about to receive a distinction."

She returned his laughter as she leapt up, wrapping her legs around his waist. "I can hardly wait!"

He gripped her hips, holding her steady as he claimed her lips, devouring her as if she were the last tasty morsel on this green earth.

"Hey!" Timmy yelled from the doorway. "Uncle Steven says you two are to get downstairs right now," he giggled, as they jumped at his intrusion.

Ariel laughed, slipping down from Jaxon's waist.

"Thanks Timmy," Jaxon said. "We are right behind you."

"Good." Timmy raced off as Jaxon reached for Ariel's hand. "Here's to the rest of our lives, beautiful." He said lovingly.

She beamed up at him as they walked out of the room, and down towards their loved ones. "I can hardly wait." She kissed the back of his hand as she heard Hawk laughing and splashing from the pool area. Wren and Liv's laughter filled the air as Steven yelled out, "Bombs away!"

Hitting the bottom stair and heading towards the pool, Ariel saw Timmy leaning against the wall. "You wanna swim Sebastian?" He asked the space beside him. "No? That's okay. You can swim later in the bath if you wanna." He said before laughing and running towards the pool, yelling out, "Catch me," before throwing himself into the water in front of Steven.

Ariel smiled towards the wall, and whispered, "You are welcome, Sebastian."

"What's that?" Jaxon asked as he pulled his tee shirt over his head then stepped out onto the deck. Seeing his sculptured muscles and gorgeously defined torso, she was suddenly lost for words as she stepped beside him.

"Never mind," she mumbled. "I'll tell you later."

He cupped her chin and brushed the sweetest kiss across her lips. "I'll be right here."

She smiled as he dove into the pool, looking like a pro. She couldn't imagine she'd ever get enough of him. Stripping off her sundress, and diving into the pool to float amongst her loved ones, where laughter and banter flowed, she smiled up at the afternoon sky, silently thanking the angels above, along with her Mother and Grandmother, for everything that was before them.

To say it had been a chilling summer in Inglewood was an understatement, but she knew in her heart of hearts, that every summer from here on out with Jaxon and her family, would be filled with nothing but heat, laughter, love and light for them all.

The End

Aknowledgement of Country

I respectfully acknowledge the traditional owners of the Goldfields, including Inglewood; the Dja Dja Wurrung people and Loddon River tribe people as the custodians of the land where this novel is based. I pay my respect to all Aboriginal community Elders, past and present, who have resided in the area and have been an integral part of the history of this spectacular region.

Acknowledgements

I've been in love with the town of Inglewood for as long as I can remember. My family have called this place home for five generations. My Great-Grandparents settled in the tiny cottage with its ornate metal framework which sits right alongside the closed railway track that passes through to Robinvale. My Mum was married at St Augustine's church on Sullivan Street, and my twin and I were Christened there when we were eighteen-months old. My Nana, Aunts, Great Aunts, Uncles, cousins, sister and niece, have always made visits to Inglewood beyond remarkable. Funerals, Weddings, 21st's, Easters and Christmas parties have always been more than just a celebration when it comes to our family getting together in Inglewood, and celebrating life as we know it.

I'd like to thank all my wonderful family who have supported me in writing the Victoria Collection, and your excitement in the inclusion of Inglewood in this series. Along with all the store owners who have shared in my desire to celebrate this gorgeous town this way. Catherine and Barry Norman from Fusspots. Alan from the Inglewood Takeaway.

An Aunt I didn't know I had till I was in my late Thirties, Gaylia Bell from Loddon Larder. Chris Earl from the Loddon Herald Sun, and all the Inglewood folk!

To my Editor and dear writing friend, Sue Croft. Thank you for your support and dedication in wanting to collaborate with me on this novel; my first attempt at paranormal-horror. Working on this project with you has been too much fun, and I thank you dearly for your insight, passion, knowledge and lively conversations regarding the written word, and the joy of fiction/fantasy writing. Thank goodness for you and Stephan King!

To my cover artist, Lorena Carrington. It has been a dream come true and such an honor having a cover designed by you. It is an absolutely stunning cover and I thank you for agreeing to be part of this project and allowing me to mark off another tick on my creative bucket list.

My darling publisher and friend, Karen Weaver – This journey with you gets better with every story shared with our beautiful readers. I'll never be able to thank you for your care, kindness and constant energy in celebrating all the little things, and marvellous things with me in my writing adventure thus far. Thanks for all the laughs and making this journey such fun.

To the MMH Press team – As always, I appreciate all that you do and for the magic you weave behind the scenes.

Sonee Sing – words cannot express the sheer joy you have gifted me this past year, plus many months. The time we spent together in Rockingham and Ireland have meant the absolute world to me. The belly aching laughter, D & M's and sharing our love for the written word, fantasy, Poetry & Writing and Such, along with a deep respect for our friendship has truly been a gift from above. I've found a true soul-sister in you. Thank you.

To my soul sisters – Louise Manna, Leah Martin, Sally Taylor, Kym Stante and Jess Fowler – what can I say that hasn't been said. I love you all dearly for the individual, quirky, loveable, successful powerhouse individuals that you all are. Your roles in supporting the vulnerable in this world, makes me proud to call you friends that have become my sisters.

To my gorgeous PWC clan, I miss you when I'm not with you. Liz Hicklin, Kelly Clarke, Sue Croft, Rebecca Frazer, Muriel Cooper, Danielle Blythe, and so many others. You are incredibly talented in every way and I love watching you all create such magic with your beautiful books.

To each and every reader – Your joy in the written word including mine, makes the sun shine endlessly in my world. Thank you Patricia Lovell, Siobhan Collins, Nozi Khanda, Zane Weitering, Thomas Martin-Angus, Ella Whitford and Ireland Turner, just to start! Your excitement and appreciation for the worlds I create spur me on every time. To all those magnificent Beta and ARC readers, thank you for your time, feedback and passion for this novel. Sonee Singh, Sue Croft, Danielle Blythe, Kelly Clark, Sally Taylor, Nazi Kanda, I loved having you along for the ride.

To my L'Arche family; from Mentone to Blackrock and Cheltenham – our Core-members & their families, especially Jo E. and Cameron S.

Katelyn Finlay, Louise Manna, Cate Nygen, Dave Scott, Brian Judge, Cam Cutts, Debbie Finlay, Vicki Abbatangelo, Betzabe Sobarzo and Irene Pantalone. Thank you for all the laughs, support and conversations that have always helped me improve in my role. What a ride I've had since I've joined you all.

Last but never least, the men who make my world spin in such a glorious way and keep the earth grounded beneath my feet. Jade Robert, Jesse Liam and Zane Bowie Weitering. Words will never be enough to express the deep love I have for each of you. Thank you for loving and supporting me. This ride that I'm on is so much more fun because of each of you and what you bring to our clan. Thank you for keeping it real. Xx)

And as always, Lynette Martin – Mummy Bear, Great Grandma &

Grandpa Radnell, Nana Meek, Aunt Dorothy and Great Aunt Ena Musgrove, along with all my beloved departed. This ones for you all. Hope I've made you proud. xx) Mickey.

Noorat

Inglewood

Glenormiston South

Frankston

Sweet
Water
Creek

ABOUT THE AUTHOR

Mickey Martin is a romantic writer at heart who feels it is important to leave the reader with messages of hope and healing. Mickey is also a non-fiction writer under her married name, Michelle Weitering. Here she seeks to write and make a difference inviting the reader to question what more they can do to make our world a better place through deeper acts of consideration, selflessness and kindness.

As a Mental Health and Disability support worker for International L'Arche Melbourne – Mickey uses her writing to become a voice for those living and dealing with issues such as anxiety, depression and other important social issues surrounding mental illness in order to raise awareness for mental health.

Mickey is celebrating her love for her home state, Victoria - stretching from the Western District, The Golden Triangle and The Mornington Peninsula with her current series – **The Victoria Collection.** *Soul Keepers of Glenormiston. Obsidian Souls. A Chilling Summer in Inglewood*

and Sweet Water Creek. Mickey is hoping to do for Victoria Tourism what *Outlander* did for Scotland. This collection explores multiple genres from urban fantasy, supernatural, haunting paranormal-horror and fated-mate-shapeshifters.

Like all Martin's novels, this series weaves plenty of unrelenting surprises mingled with romance and unrelenting plot-hangers which allows her charismatic characters to create gripping friction on every level, keeping readers on the edge of their seats.

Mickey is currently working on the fourth novel in the *Victoria Collection, Sweet Water Creek,* as well as a poetry collection titled, *Poetry and Such* with her dear friend – award winning poet, Sonee Sing.

Mickey is a multi-award-winning author and shareholder with MMH PRESS, and is a member of the Peninsula Writers' Club where she adores connecting with and supporting like-minded souls on their writing journey. Mickey loves hearing from her readers and you can connect with her on the following links.

www.instagram.com/mickeymartinbooks
www.facebok.com/michelle.weitering